The Tree Wizard
of Ialana

Book Four of the Ialana Series

KATLYNN BROOKE

To my husband, Charles, without whom this book would not have been possible, and my mother, who always encouraged me to write—Katlynn Brooke

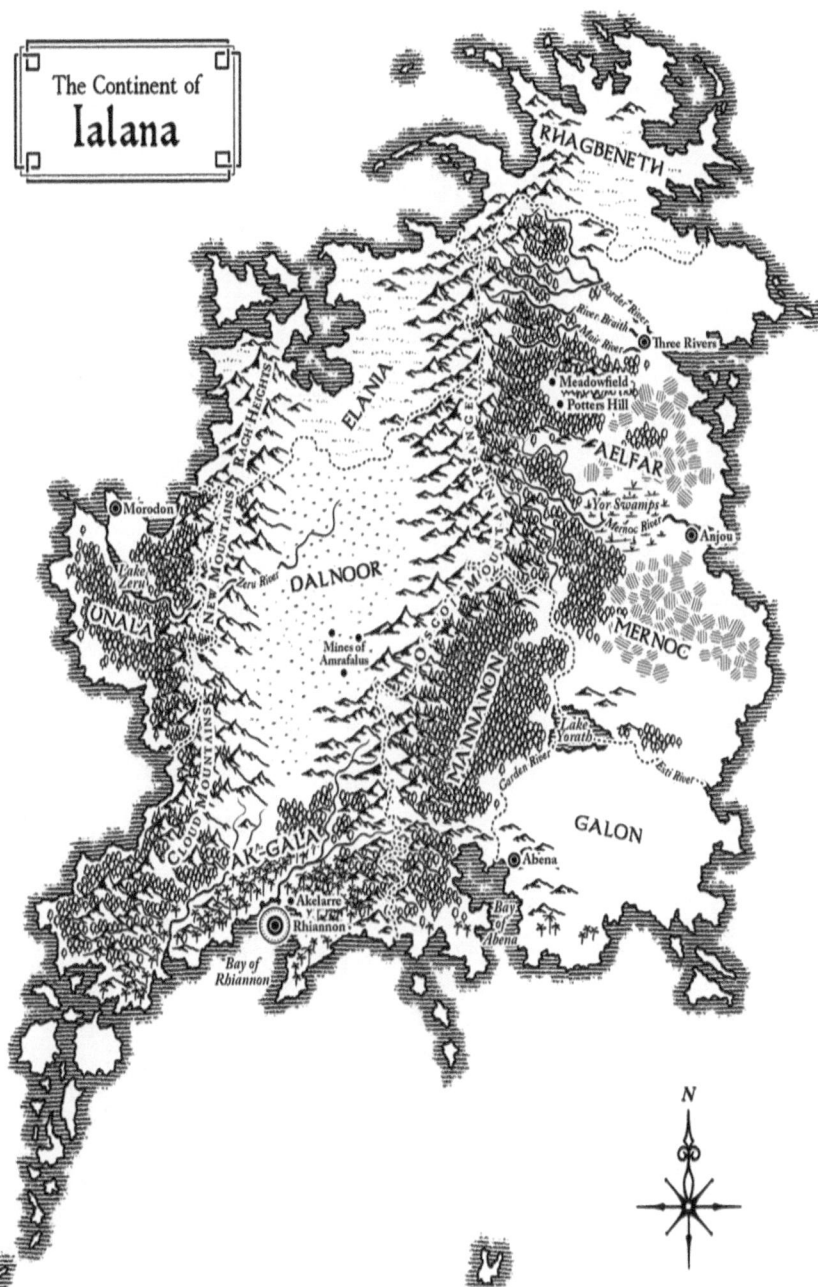

The Continent of **Ialana**

RHAGBENETH

ELANIA

Border River
River Braith
Mac River
Three Rivers

Meadowfield
Potters Hill

AELFAR

Morodon

Lake Zeru

Zeru River

UNALA

DALNOOR

Mines of Amrafalus

Yor Swamps
Mernoc River

Anjou

MERNOC

NEW MOUNTAINS

RAGE HEIGHTS

STONE MOUNTAINS

MANNANON

Lake Yorath

Garden River

Eiti River

GALON

CLOUD MOUNTAINS

AR-GALA

Abena

Akelarre
Rhiannon

Bay of Rhiannon

Bay of Abena

N

BELE
2016

Contents

1. Unala, Day One   1
2. The Sorcerer   6
3. The Girl   8
4. Ulovia   14
5. Galon   20
6. Askoroth   28
7. The Tree   31
8. The Problem in Mu'A   37
9. Hag-wraiths   43
10. Who Am I?   45
11. The Farm, Aelfar, Day One   48
12. The Stone of Creation   53
13. Evacuation   58
14. The Locator Stone   65
15. The Eldred   69
16. Bean   73
17. King Sinhail, Ulovia   76
18. Peatatoo   86
19. Yorli   94
20. Peatatoo's Tale   100
21. The Pendant   103
22. Shadow Goblins   107
23. Deception   110
24. The Halls of the Elluin   114
25. Anwyn: The Hall of Records   116

26. The Djinn Stone 121
27. Thief! 126
28. Spherical Coins 128
29. Despair 134
30. The Battle Begins 140
31. The Six Healers, Mu'A 144
32. The Dwellers 146
33. Negu 152
34. Lost 156
35. The Screamers 159
36. Ardvale 163
37. The Dragon 169
38. Elemental Command 174
39. The Golden Tip 180
40. Goren's Plot 190
41. Glaciers and Gravity Wells 193
42. The Fourteenth Magus 200
43. The Girl 206
44. Journey's End 212
45. Return to Golden Tip 218
46. The Portal Key 221
47. The Tree Wizard 227
48. The Secret of the Golden Tip 232
49. The Hall of the Elluin 237
50. The *Dawn Star* 246
51. Anwyn 256
52. Mu'A 259
53. Capture 262
54. Lhathron and Anwyn 272
Acknowledgements 275
About The Ialana Series 277
About the Author 279

The Tree Wizard of Ialana

Book Four of the Ialana Series

1.

Unala, Day One

Silver eyes glinting in the moonlight, he scanned the vast swath of star-studded sky, his flute resting in his lap. It was a rare, cloudless night for these usually mist-shrouded hills, and around him nothing stirred. The shrill wail that had made his neck hairs rise still echoed in his ears.

The broad ribbon of the Zeru River that cleaved the land of Unala in two, from the mountains to the sea, wound silently through the valley below. Tall conifer spires, dwarfed by the magnificent uakus trees that covered the valley floor between river and foothills, reached like fingers to the starry sky. All quiet there, too, he thought.

His gaze swept over the verdant forest sprawling thickly to the western coast, and he shook his head as he lifted the flute again to his lips and blew a quick succession of musical notes. Their forest-green sparkles eddied and scintillated in the air. He smiled, but then paused, delicate fingers hovering uncertainly over the flute's stem as the shimmering glow around him faded into darkness.

He waited, pointed ears twitching. *There!* He'd heard it again. His head jerked around to the majestic, snow-shrouded peaks of the Cloud Mountains behind him. He looked up. The wails had come from the sky, he thought, not the valley. The intensity rose to a crescendo, as if a battle waged above him, but still he saw nothing.

It was then that a bolt, like a spear launched from an invisible weapon, tumbled toward him. He ducked, and it screeched over his head a mere hand's breadth away. With a loud crack, it slammed into the rock where he sat, and a white-hot fountain of hate surged like fast moving lava over the surface toward him.

Quick as a tree squirrel, as the once-solid platform beneath him cracked and fragmented, he threw himself backward, his body rolling onto firmer ground. Chunk by chunk, the overhang dropped soundlessly into the void below.

Breathing heavily but still holding onto his flute, he crawled under the cover of a sparse bush that clung to the hillside slope. His hand shook as he stowed his flute in an inside pocket of his cloak and cautiously peered out from beneath the scraggly twigs. Shrieks and splinters of fire blazed across the valley, jagged spikes of fury that had been powerful enough to shatter his ledge like a knuckle-knocker hitting a crait-hen egg. Far above the hill and over the river a tiny blue orb zigged and zagged as it blinked on and off like a firefly.

Open-mouthed, his hands balling into fists, he tracked it as it moved across the valley. A bolt struck the bright orb, sparking and crackling over its surface, causing it to falter and dim. The cry of a woman in pain drifted down to where he crouched.

The clamor grew louder. Triumphant cackles and whoops of laughter rolled toward him in waves, shadows swirling and dancing, and from their epicenter the spark began to drop. It drifted slowly downward, followed by a thin thread of smoke. The dark shapes coagulated into a single, swirling red orb, and then disappeared into the blackness below.

A silence descended once more on the valley. Heart pounding, he staggered to his feet. Something down there was in trouble. He approached the crumbling cliff where his ledge had been and stared down into the void. He wasn't the target of this battle, he thought. He could just go home and pretend he hadn't seen anything. No one would ever know. He shook his head.

I would know.

He spun around, willing his reluctant feet to follow the stony track leading down the hill and into the forest by the river. He had seen exactly where the spark had fallen. He hoped he could get there in time, before—before what, though? It could be too late already.

His breath came in ragged gasps as he slid and stumbled down the steep, narrow trail. He needed only one slip, and it would be the quicker way down for him. *And then I'd be no good to anyone.* He sped down the twisting trail, each moment flying by quicker than the last, but finally he reached the valley floor. He bent over with his hands on his knees to catch his breath, briefly scanning the trail ahead.

Don't be careless now, Bean. No idea what to expect, do we?

He straightened up, and took a deep breath. Using every sense available to him, he crept softly, deeper into the forest.

He stopped again and turned his head. A strong odor of burning, like that of hair or cloth, assailed his nostrils from the right. His other senses told him the things were still there. Their presence intruded into his mind like shards of dark glass. He moved closer. They stood around a body on the forest floor and talked among themselves in a guttural murmuring. There were six or seven of them; he could tell by the eyes, glowing like red-hot coals.

Their words became clearer as one of them launched a kick at the prone form on the ground.

"Why blame me, Goldark? I didn't deliver the killing blow," he heard it say, its voice thin and piercing. "We need to —" His voice cut off as the one that must have been Goldark growled.

"Silence! Who do you think you are? I'm in charge, and I give the orders, not you."

"I don't think she's dead," another one said. "Her merkaba remained stable until she was closer to the ground."

"Well then, we must take her back with us," said the one that was Goldark. It moved closer to the figure on the ground. "Mistress says Astrabal wants the girl alive. Maybe he can still get it out of her."

The watcher crouched down and pulled his cloak tighter around his shivering body. What were these creatures? Gathering together every scrap of courage he could muster, he fumbled under his cloak, lifted his flute to his lips and blew.

The creature closest to him spun around, red eyes pinning him with a gaze that took his breath away. With each note, his arms grew heavier, until it took all his strength just to keep the flute to his lips. He tried to draw in a breath, but the muscles in his diaphragm refused to obey his command. He choked as his vision clouded, and the world around him dimmed. Muffled words reached his ears, murmurings that he could not identify drew closer. He could only watch as the creature, its tentacle-like arms outstretched, moved toward him. He wanted more than anything to drop the flute, to lie down on the forest floor and sleep forever. He tried looking away, but he couldn't move his head.

Don't look at them, Bean. He squeezed his eyes shut, and with one last effort succeeded in drawing in a tiny breath. With a sharp exhalation, he blew again into the flute. Sweat beaded his face, and he fell to his knees, gasping.

It was enough. The creature screamed.

Emboldened, but with his eyes still closed, he took another breath, stronger this time and blew again. The notes tumbled out as waves of color, clear and brilliant of hue. The shadows hissed and wailed as the colors radiated, spiraling around the flute. His fingers danced, faster and faster as his fear began to dissipate. Discordant screeches from the cringing shadows mingled with the pristine notes from his flute.

A column of glowing light, a standing pillar of sound, coiled around his body. He opened his eyes now and strode toward the creatures. The column moved with him, expanding in size with every breath he piped. A brilliant tendril emerged, enveloping an approaching dark form. The howl that came out of the hole in the creature's face made his blood run cold, but he continued to pipe.

The shadow shuddered—gave a small hop and a leap as if to fly away—only to encounter more of the incandescent glow. With a pop and a flash, it vanished. The other shadows moaned and shrank back, uncertain as to what it was they faced. One of them lifted a claw and a fiery bolt shot from it in his direction, but as soon as it struck the column, it dissolved into nothingness. Two more shadows disappeared into the brilliant light. With earsplitting shrieks, the remaining three fiery sparks fled into the night sky.

He hurried over to the prone figure on the forest floor and knelt beside her. Just as he thought, it was a young female. His long fingers gently probed her wrist, feeling for a pulse, but there was no sign of life. He tried her neck. Was that her pulse, he wondered, or was it just the flutter of dying muscles? Maybe the shadows were right, maybe she *was* dead. But he wasn't going to give up.

He lifted his flute again and blew, the notes softer this time, the air more lilting. The colors spread out in a gentle, pink wave toward the body. He piped for a while, then stopped and listened, feeling again for a pulse. He changed the notes and the colors flashed a fiery green. They swirled around the body before entering the visibly bruised and bloodied areas on her head. Sweat glistened on his face, but he did not let up, not even for a moment. Still, the girl did not move.

Once again, he felt for a pulse. He wiped his brow with his robe, then began again from the beginning. He did not know how long he'd piped, but it was only after he put his flute away and sighed, shaking his head, that he heard it: a gasp. He froze, and waited. There it was, again! He placed his hand to her neck, and—yes! A strong pulse. He removed his cloak, and wrapping it around the woman he lifted her up in his arms. He turned, and like a shadow, disappeared into the forest.

2.

The Sorcerer

They found him in his lair in the upper reaches of the keep, his thick body a dead weight on the cold stone floor. A soldier slapped the sorcerer's face—a face as broad and flat as a spade—as another emptied a water skin over the man's head.

"Is he dead?" one of the soldiers asked with a gap-mouthed stare.

"Naw, he's probably drunk," the captain responded.

"I've never seen him drunk," the third said, "but he does spend a lot of time in the tavern."

"Drunk or not," said the captain, "Ortzi still wants to see him. We'll carry him down."

Two soldiers, one on each side, grasped him under the arms and started to lift his body. Hora's eyes flicked open, shut, then opened again wider. The soldiers jerked away in disgust, releasing him, and he slumped back to the floor. Eyes wide, their foreheads puckering, the soldiers looked at each other as if they could not believe what they had seen: an orange flame that flickered behind the coal black, shark eyes of Ortzi's sorcerer.

Hora sat up, this time on his own. He blinked again, but now his eyes were their normal brown, and the soldiers glanced uneasily at each other again.

The captain was the first to recover. "Sir, Ortzi has requested your presence. Immediately." His eyes swiveled around the room, suspicion written all over his rough features. He hated coming up here. *It wasn't natural*, he thought. Sooty candles still smoldered on the window sill, dusty bottles and jars, containing only Idris knew what, sat untidily on shelves, a clutter of scrolls and books on the floor, but what was most discomfiting to the captain sat on a nearby table: a ceramic bowl filled with water. It was what was in the water, though, that gave him the chills. It looked like blood. As the captain gazed, mesmerized, into the bowl, Hora stood up and with a quick movement, picked up a cloth and threw it over the bowl.

"You can go," he said to the captain, "I'll get to Ortzi without your help. Now leave me alone."

The captain nodded with relief, and he and his soldiers peeled out of the door as if all the shades of Iochodran, the dark kingdom of the dead, pursued them.

Hora sank down onto a small stool and cradled his hurting head in his hands. *What have I done?* he wondered. *Did it all really happen?* He picked up a corner of the cloth and cautiously peeked into the bowl. The blood-tinged water was gone. It was just ordinary water. Obviously, the soldiers had seen it, but he wasn't bothered by that. It would only add to his mystique. They would show him the proper respect from now on. The thought made him smile, but it was a smile that did not reach his eyes. It had worked, though. His magic had, for the first time in his lackluster career, worked! Ortzi, the warlord ruler of Galon, would be pleased. He took a deep breath, closed his eyes, then taking another deep breath, he vanished.

3.

The Girl

She floated up from a bottomless, black pool of water. Music, talking, and then more darkness and silence. She sank down again into the depths. She wanted to stay there. It was peaceful, warm, and quiet, but something tugged at her again. *Why won't it leave me alone?*

She fought against a rising cacophony in her head, and the pain—it was unbearable. *Why do I hurt so much?* She blinked her eyes as stabbing knives of light flooded into her brain. She moaned and tried to move, but another wave of torment swept through her.

"Yes, yes, it will hurt, but you'll be all right." It was a male voice, and a gentle hand on her cheek.

She could hear the musical notes again. *Is that a flute? Please, just let me go . . .*" She drifted down, back into the darkness.

She opened her eyes. Her body no longer throbbed with pain. She touched her face, felt all over for wounds, but there were none. She sat up. She was in a bed with clean linen covers, and the morning light pierced the narrow slits of a shuttered window, falling obliquely onto a wooden floor. She blinked and rubbed her eyes: there was something strange about the walls; they were wood, too, but they didn't look like logs. It was as if they'd been carved out of a solid block of timber. She sniffed. A woodsy aroma, like freshly cut greenwood, and was that mushroom gravy she smelled, too? Her stomach grumbled.

"Oh, you're awake!"

Startled, she turned her head. An extraordinary man sat on a chair next to the door, long legs sprawled out from under a dark cloak, with baggy, drawstring pants tucked into heavy boots. His ice-blue eyes had a silver sheen, and his wavy hair was midnight black. It wasn't only his eyes that seemed so strange to her, but also his pointed ears.

She gaped.

"Looks like you've never seen an Eldred before, but never mind. We don't bite." He chuckled. His voice calmed her, and she relaxed.

An Eldred?

"What is your name, girl?" His tone was frosty now, with none of its previous joviality. "And perhaps you're well enough to tell us how you came to be attacked by those things, and what exactly they were."

"What things?" She blinked her eyes. "Where am I? Who are you?" Her hand moved upward, toward her neck. A look of alarm crossed her face momentarily, but then it disappeared, replaced by bewilderment.

The Eldred's eyes sharpened, and he stared with a small frown at her hand as it fell away from her neck. "Well, if that's the way you want it, I'll go first." He smiled, his eyes friendlier. Rising from the straight-backed chair, he moved to sit on the side of the bed, facing her. "Bean saved you."

Bean?

"Bean Ironweed. He'll be back soon. He's downstairs getting food for you. My name is Grayfell. Grayfell Ironweed." He touched two fingers to his forehead. She assumed it must be some type of greeting. "You look human to me. I don't think you're one of those infernal shape-shifters, or you would have shifted by now, but I do wonder what a human was doing falling out of the sky."

He looked at her expectantly, but she only stared back.

"Well then . . ." His voice ended on a sigh, but he continued to question her. "What do you know about us—the Eldred?"

She shook her head.

His face hardened. "I hope you're not lying. We don't take kindly to spies. Our kind have claimed the Cloud Mountains for eons, and so far, we've been unmolested by humans. We've had enough trouble as it is with Shadow Goblins and Screamers, but we've never seen your kind around here."

My kind? She wondered what he meant.

As Grayfell spoke, he studied her face intently, so much so that her cheeks flushed.

"You look human, although I doubt that you are. We understand, despite our isolation, that humans and other life-forms inhabit Ialana, the land in which we reside, but we'd hoped to keep them unaware of us for as long as possible." Taking a deep breath, he continued, "But if humans have discovered the power of flight, we may be looking at a problem for Unala."

Flight? A cold wave of fear passed through her. What had she been doing? Why was she here? She didn't belong here. This *Unala* was obviously not her home. This man had never seen her before. "I don't know what I'm doing here," she finally responded.

"Do you remember your name?"

She thought for a while. "No."

Grayfell sighed again. "Either you won't tell me, or you truly don't remember. It's not so uncommon for a knock on the head such as you suffered to cause a catastrophic memory loss. Let's hope it's only temporary. We'll have Bean work on you and see if we can recover it."

"Bean?"

"Yes, yes—I told you, the Eldred who saved your life. Pay attention. Ah, here he is!" Grayfell turned to look at the door as a younger man stepped through. He was tall, too, and he had to duck his head to get in.

10

The girl's hand went to her neck, again. This Bean was even stranger looking than Grayfell. He wore a green tunic under a green cloak. His leggings were tucked into tall boots, and his dark hair hung in a braid down his back. Of course, he, too, had the pointy ears. He glanced at her just long enough for her to notice his silver sheened eyes before he glanced away.

He held a wooden platter with an unidentifiable, steaming brown mass in its center, and in his other hand a birch tree bark mug filled with water. He gently placed the mug and plate on a small table next to her bed.

She squinted at the mysterious, spongy mass in the plate, then reached eagerly for the water and swallowed it in a few gulps. She was so thirsty! Wiping her mouth with her hand, she blurted out, "I can see why you're called Bean. You're skinny, and green, like a string bean." Covering her mouth with her hand, she felt the rising heat of embarrassment. She was not normally so outspoken, was she?

Grayfell laughed, but Bean did not react. His silver-gray eyes were unreadable.

"Sit down, Bean." Grayfell nodded to the chair. "I'm trying to determine just who this young lady is. It seems she's suffered a memory loss, but I'm not sure if she's play-acting or if it's real. You will know." He nodded sagely and gave the girl a look that told her he meant every word. "Bean's *flute* will know," he amended. He looked at Bean. "Play."

Bean took out his flute from beneath his cloak, put it to his lips, and softly began to play a haunting melody. Flinty eyed, Grayfell glared at the girl again.

"Now," he barked, "who are you? What's your name?"

She closed her eyes. She wasn't sure, though, if she could—or even if she should—remember. Something had happened. Something bad, something that she would be much better off not remembering. She covered her ears with her hands, but the music didn't stop. Inexplicably, a wave of intense sadness, a longing for something she couldn't name flowed into her, but still she couldn't remember who she was. Tears of frustration welled up, and Grayfell handed her a linen handkerchief to wipe her eyes.

11

At last the music stopped, and Grayfell's unrelenting gaze softened.

"Well, Bean says you're telling the truth. You really don't remember who you are." He patted her shoulder. "There, there. Bean, you wait here with her. I must return to the city." He glanced back at the girl. "We call it Ulovia."

Bean blew a sharp toot on his flute.

"No, don't worry. I won't tell anyone about her, at least not just yet. I, too, want to find out more, before Yuki gets her hands on her. The king's daughter never means well. You make sure she eats." He nodded at the untouched plate. "I have other matters to attend to. I'll be back by this evening." He gathered his cloak around him, placed the hood over his head, and then he was gone. A shimmer moved toward the door, and the girl's mouth fell open.

This man could make himself invisible!

She looked at Bean. He pointed to her plate and made eating motions with his hand.

"Don't you talk?" she asked.

His lips parted, but then snapped shut again, his silver-gray eyes still unreadable. He, too, stood and left. She picked up the plate and poked the spongy mass with a finger. She lifted the plate to her nose and sniffed. Mushroom gravy! That's what she'd smelled earlier. She broke off a small piece and nibbled at it. It tasted like mushrooms. She broke off another piece, then another, and it wasn't long before the last morsel had disappeared. She'd been hungry, and she wondered how long she'd been unconscious. She tried as hard as she could to remember something, anything—her name, her family—but nothing came to mind. She wore a soft linen garment that she knew somehow was a night robe. It had been charred in spots, as if she'd run through a fire.

Wondering what she looked like, she looked around the room, but there was no mirror. She pulled a strand of her long, singed hair in front of her face. She was—how, she didn't know—a strawberry blonde. Were her eyes silver, too? She didn't think so. They were hazel, just like her mother's.

She caught her breath. She had remembered her mother's eyes! She did seem to recall some things about herself and her world, but just not who she was or where she came from. She remembered Ialana, that was where she—no. She did not live there. But she had at one time. Only she couldn't remember when or where exactly.

How old was she? She was eighteen. She wondered how old Grayfell was. He was older than she—that was obvious—but Bean looked to be more around her age. What a strange person he was! She laughed. She tried to get off the bed, but her legs felt wobbly as her bare feet touched the cool floor. She wanted to look out the window. This was an odd place. Made of wood. All wood. She shook her head. She would wait until she felt a little stronger.

Puffing out her cheeks as she exhaled, she leaned back on the pillow and stared at the ceiling. *How on earth did I get here?* She closed her eyes and slept.

4.

Ulovia

Grayfell, deep in thought, took the path that wound through the forest and away from Bean's uakus trees, the path that curved down toward the river Zeru. The only sign of his passing was a shimmer of air as it was displaced by his body.

That trick had startled the girl. He scarcely noticed the rare, summer sun that fell warm on his face. Its golden light filtered through the trees, sparkling and shimmering on the path in front of him.

I could have done that disappearing trick outside the room, but I needed to observe her reaction. According to Bean, she is no ordinary girl. He has seen her fly. I wonder what other skills she possesses?

He sniffed, his musings cut short by a startled deer that had not seen him coming. He quickly stepped off the path as the deer hurtled through the spot where he had just been and disappeared into the thick undergrowth.

I must be more aware. If those creatures are still around, they might sense me as the deer did. While I feel they're more shadows of the night, it is not unheard of for the vilest creations of Iochodran to manifest in broad daylight.

Bean's description had sent chills down his spine. Dark stuff, for sure. Was the girl a sorcerer run afoul of her masters in the underworld of Iochodran?

With one part of his senses more in tune with his surroundings, he allowed his ponderings to continue, only with less intensity.

He must protect Bean, but at some point, he wondered, would he feel compelled by his loyalty to his king to tell him how Bean had healed the girl? If the king knew, then so would his daughter, and then by extension, Goren.

Goren and Yuki—he snorted. The king's advisor and his daughter. Eblenor had warned him to be watchful of those two. He pounded his staff on the ground for emphasis as he walked. He wished his old mentor was still alive; Eblenor would have known what to do.

What would he have done had he been in Bean's place last night? Would he have left the girl to die? But then he didn't have Bean's abilities. Only last night, for the first time, he had witnessed a new and unexpected facet to Bean's talents when he had miraculously healed the girl of her severe injuries.

No one must know about it, especially not Yuki and Goren, he thought. All his life Bean had been regarded as a simpleton—a mute simpleton at that. Grayfell pressed his lips together in a hard line. He would keep it that way for as long as he could.

The dazzling sunlight reflecting off the river made him squinch up his eyes. He didn't like traveling by day; it hurt his vision. The suspension bridge swayed perilously under his feet, but he paid it no mind. According to Bean, the girl had literally fallen from the sky. Bean could not lie. She had appeared as a spark of light, he'd said.

He'd heard of these things from Eblenor, the ancient legends of the Elluin that had carried down from generation to generation. They, the elders, had once had these abilities, the ability to create spirit vehicles, orbs that could enable one to bilocate or transport a physical body from place to place instantaneously and invisibly. Was this what Bean had seen?

By the time he reached the entrance to the tunnels carved under the mountain, the Halls of Ulovia, he had arrived at a conclusion. The girl was a sorcerer, a craft-practicing witch at the very least. He was sure of that. She must be closely watched, and as soon as she regained her memory, he and Bean would extract everything she knew. Only then could he come to a decision about what to do with her, and what to tell the king. He hoped her fate would not be a bad one. He liked her. She hadn't complained, not even once. She was brave.

He slipped unseen past the entrance guards and strode down smoky tunnels lit by flaming torches until he reached the imposing doors to the king's chambers. Unwrapping his cloak, he pulled down his hood, startling a young Eldred guard stationed at the entrance. He grinned. This one must be new to guard duty and had probably never witnessed his sudden appearances.

"I need to see the king."

The guard, collecting himself, nodded and allowed Grayfell to pass. He must do this quickly. He had other matters to attend to, matters that were even more disturbing to him than the appearance of the girl. He hadn't had time to consult with the king over those concerns yet. Bean had sent out an urgent call for him last night, right after he had witnessed the other terrifying events in his scrying bowl. Instead of going to the king right away, he'd hastened down to the forest to see what was frightening Bean. The other matter could wait, he'd thought.

More guards stepped aside as he nodded to them. Enormous granite pillars loomed on either side, their gilt crowns and embedded jewels glittering in the light of the torches. He hoped Yuki wouldn't be there.

But she was. Goren, the King's advisor, stood by her side, his wolfish face darkening with annoyance as Grayfell strode in.

Princess Yuki, her silver-white hair pulled back in a severe knot on top of her head, her almost-white skin covered by a glittering, gem-encrusted cloak that nearly blinded him, rolled her eyes as he approached. King Sinhail, on the other hand, crinkled his nose in delight. He wore the same food-stained robe and tunic he'd worn yesterday, his gray-flecked beard greasy from his last meal.

"Grayfell!" he chuckled as he slapped his thigh. His fleshy body seemed to vibrate with joy. "I've been looking all over for you. We're planning the Festival of Elluin, and we need our wizard's expertise."

Yuki gave her father a withering glance and turned to face Grayfell. "We don't need you. It's all in hand. We know what we're doing."

The king's smile vanished. "Yuki! Grayfell has always—"

"Your Majesty, I must interrupt. I have an urgent matter to discuss with you." Grayfell shot a meaningful glance at Yuki and Goren, but they stood like uakus trees at King Sinhail's side as if they had not heard him. He shrugged. He hadn't thought he'd get rid of them that easily.

"Well, what is it, then?" King Sinhail's smile faded. "I'm hungry. It's way past my lunchtime." He looked longingly toward the dining hall where tempting smells wafted through a large, arched doorway.

"I've just consulted my scrying bowl," Grayfell lied—he had consulted it last night, "and I've witnessed something disturbing." He had their attention. Yuki's head whipped around, her blue eyes narrowing. Goren's spine straightened, but Grayfell did not miss the sneer that flashed briefly across his face. "There are eyes upon us. Dark forces. The Lords of Iochodran have sent their scouts into Unala, for what purpose, I cannot divine."

"This is terrible news!" Sinhail's silver-blue eyes brimmed redly.

"Are you sure?" This from Goren.

Yuki simultaneously asked, "How many?"

Grayfell glanced at Yuki, lifting his chin. "I have no idea how many. Astrabal, the Demon Lord, has uncountable legions at his disposal. But that's not all." He turned back to the king. "We may be looking at settlers as well, human colonizers, approaching Unala at some unspecified point in the future. We need to prepare."

"Yes, we do," said Goren. "Do you think that Iochodran sending their scouts here and these invaders must be connected?"

"That I could not see, but I would think so," Grayfell responded.

King Sinhail rubbed his chin. He seemed to have recovered from his initial shock. He turned to his advisor. "Goren, what do you suggest we do?"

Goren leaned forward. "We fight, of course. We prepare our army, our soldiers. We'll need to forge more swords and weapons. We'll put our miners, the Inaka, on notice. We need as much metal ore as they can dig out with their ugly little claws, and our forges will resound again. Our metal workers have had it easy over the past hundred years."

"We haven't even had to fight the Shadow Goblins in a while," Yuki said. "We've gotten soft." She threw another disgusted glance at her father.

"I don't want to fight," he said. "I don't want us to fight. We'll leave Unala before they get here. We'll take what we can. I've always wanted to return to the Golden Tip in the New Mountains. That was our first home, the home of our ancestors. We can make it our home again, and—"

"—humans or other beasts could not survive long there," finished Yuki. "We've heard all that before. I'm tired of hearing it, Father. You have said it yourself"—she mimicked her father's voice, "'there's nothing there but snow and tapped out mines.' That's why our ancestors came here in the first place."

"It would be foolish to abandon our mines and settlements here," Goren agreed. Yuki directed a grateful glance toward him. "Sometimes we have no choice but to fight, to the death if necessary. No, the Golden Tip is not an option."

"Did someone crown you king? We will discuss this later, Goren." Sinhail looked at Yuki. "And no, we are not tapped out in the New Mountains. I just say that because it sounds better than—"

"—because they ran out of food," she finished, glancing meaningfully at her father's stained robe. "Eldred like you, the descendants of Elluin, who no longer thought breathing the sun was nutrition enough—instead, they began to eat plants for sustenance, and lately, we're consuming animal life, too. Do you think our present-day Eldred will survive the New Mountains?" She looked pointedly at her father's belly again, and he blushed.

"I could do it," he mumbled.

Grayfell intervened. "There must be a solution. War cannot stop the forces of Iochodran, and if Astrabal is supporting the invasion, we must be prepared in more ways than simply fighting. Allow me to give this matter some thought. I have some ideas, but nothing definite yet. I need time."

"Don't take too long," growled Goren. "We don't want to be caught sleeping."

Grayfell nodded. "Then I request a stay of questions for a while until I can find out what, exactly, is occurring."

Goren opened his mouth as if to object, but King Sinhail lifted his scepter with the golden eagle on top and slashed it downwards. "Granted! No questions. Grayfell, get on it, but as soon as you find out anything, I want to know."

Grayfell nodded again.

Sinhail pointed his scepter at Goren. "You put the Inaka back to work. Fire up the forges, put the army on alert, and make sure we have enough weapons."

Grayfell turned to leave quickly before Yuki or Goren could pull him into their plans. Goren's washed out eyes had sparked with interest when he'd mentioned "dark forces." He must make his own plans. He could hear Sinhail's stomach rumbling as he walked away. Goren was right, though; he must find a solution, and quickly.

He hoped that the girl would tell him something. She had to know. He would get it out of her. He and Bean.

5.

Galon

Ortzi jumped as Hora appeared suddenly in front of him.

"What…don't do that! I didn't see you come in!" His thick brows beetled in consternation. His magician had not just appeared out of thin air, had he? It was impossible. He must have missed his entrance. He had been deep in thought, after all. Even the guards at the door looked startled. *How had they—*

"You didn't miss me," Hora said, and sat down at the council table without the customary invitation. Ortzi frowned again, but if Hora had judged him correctly, his curiosity was piqued. "I have good news," the magician continued. "All the hours I've spent looking for spells, conjurings, summonings—they have paid off. Paid off, I tell you!" He slapped his hand on the table, and Ortzi jumped.

Hora wondered if he'd gone too far. Ortzi's already sullen face grew even darker and his head turned toward his guards. He raised his hand as if to beckon them over, but then he paused, slowly lowering his hand.

Hora's mouth twitched. It was clear now. Ortzi burned to know why the sudden change from obsequious court sorcerer to this confident and brash man sitting in front of him.

Ortzi's mouth was a thin line. He stared at Hora with a look—a look that one gets from a dog before it bites.

"Last night," Hora continued, as if he'd missed Ortzi's outraged mood, "I met with a powerful demon from Iochodran—"

This was too much for Ortzi. "Demon! Iochodran?" He hocked and spat. The gob landed with a wet smack on the floor. He waved away a servant who stood by with a mop and bucket. "What were you thinking? I don't consort with demons, and neither should you. I'm looking for six healers, not demons! They're nothing but trouble."

"Yes, I understand that," said Hora.

Ortzi stared, then blinked. There was not even a flicker of fear in the sorcerer's eyes. Something was not right. Hora was known for his cowardice.

"But," Hora continued, "this one is one of the most powerful of all. Its name is—"

"Don't tell me," Ortzi interrupted. "I don't want to know. But go on."

Hora smiled. "I summoned it. It worked. We have a foolproof plan." For a few heartbeats, he stared at a spot on the far wall, his gaze unfocused. Ortzi waited, trying not to show his impatience. Hora's eyes focused again, and he licked his lips.

"I told the demon about your desire to find the six healers. Glah—" He stopped. "I mean *it*—the demon—it's familiar with these six healers. Can you believe that? It, too, searches for them, but in the five or six years since it last came into contact with them, it has not been able to find them again."

"Why would the demon search for them?" Ortzi asked.

"I gathered they share a past history. The demon wasn't specific, but the way it spoke about them, I understood that it desired to make use of the healer's skill in programming crystals, and also revenge."

"Cut to the chase. Where are they?"

"It said they are on the island of Mu'A."

"Mu'A? Where is that?"

"It took me to this island, in my physical body no less. We soared through the air—like birds! I don't know myself where this island is exactly, but it's south of here. We flew much too fast for me to judge distances. One moment I was in my body in my workshop in the tower, the next flying over the island." Hora's eyes became unfocused again, but he rubbed his face and continued. "We hovered above the island, and I said to—to the demon, whose voice I could hear speaking to me in my head—that I didn't see any sign that the island was inhabited."

He remembered how much, the first time he'd heard the demon's voice in his head, it had surprised him: its tone had been that of a woman, and an educated woman at that. Hora wondered to himself why he always thought demons would sound, well, like demons. He had no time to dwell on wondering, though. He continued with his tale.

"The demon said it only appeared that way, that it was protected—shielded—from everyone, including the demons of Iochodran. They could not access entry, and neither would we. I would need special codes embedded in my hands to get in, and I don't have them."

"So they're there then?"

"The demon believes so, my liege." Ortzi had a one-track mind, thought Hora. He had been obsessed for years with these healers, ever since he'd lost them at the crystal caves after an earthquake. He'd thought them dead, at first, but then a spy of Ortzi's had reported seeing them as captives of King Brenin at the Battle of Mannanon. The spy was almost certain the six had escaped.

Hora remained silent. Ortzi chewed on his lower lip as the battle between fear and greed waged, the outcome predictable. "The crystals are rightfully mine. They always were, but I was unable to understand how to use them so I could rule Ialana with their powerful magic. They are still there, and only the six healers can help me understand how to make use of their power," Ortzi finally said. "Uncovering them has been costly and time consuming, but we've succeeded. Do you think your demon can do what I want it to do? Or do I still need the six healers?"

"If my demon, as you put it, could reprogram massive crystals, why would it be looking for the six healers? You need them still." Hora thought a bit. "Wait, there is more. There's a daughter who is even more powerful."

A spark in Ortzi's dead eyes. "More powerful?"

Is there an echo in here? Hora wondered, but he said, "Yes, my liege. She could easily do whatever you want her to do. It would be easier to watch her—her alone. The demon believes she often leaves Mu'A, and while she's not vulnerable, it would be a simple matter to wait for an unguarded moment—"

"And pounce!" Ortzi's eyes glittered, and he hocked and spat again.

Hora continued. "Luck was with us. As we watched the island, a small light appeared. It shot north at a tremendous speed, and we followed. It led us to a small farm in Aelfar."

Ortzi gave a small growl. He was permanently at war with Aelfar, the fertile farming land to the north of Galon.

Hora continued. "The demon was delighted. It knew this farm, and it recognized the girl—the daughter—who had emerged from Mu'A entirely unprotected."

"So you've got her, then?" Ortzi grinned.

"Oh no, my liege."

Ortzi's smile vanished.

"We waited. This demon wanted to see what business this girl had at that place. We watched and listened, but could not get a sense of why she was there. She spoke to no one."

Ortzi's eyes lit up again. "Tell me more," he said as he rubbed his hands together, but then he shuddered as his body spasmed in a coughing fit. His face turned blue. Hora expected to see lung matter expelled as Ortzi hacked and coughed then spat again. Finally, the coughing lessened, and he breathed heavily, his expression daring Hora to say something. Hora remained silent, but he turned his head away. The spittle gobs on the floor were stained red. He didn't want Ortzi to see the elation that spread over his face. The old man didn't have long. His time would come, there would be a power vacuum, and Hora, with the help of the demon, was ready to fill the vacancy.

Ready to ease Ortzi into the next world.

"We waited—"

His words cut off as Ortzi doubled over with another spasm. The court healer hurried over holding a goblet of foul-smelling potion.

"You must go," he said to Hora. "Lord Ortzi needs to rest."

"We can continue our discussion when you're feeling better, m'lord," Hora agreed, ignoring the upstart healer. Once he was ensconced as Lord Hora of Galon, he'd need no healer. Only the girl. He climbed the tower keep stairs to his quarters, unable to suppress a toothy grin that spread over his face. Guards parted as he approached, pressing themselves tightly against the wall, fear and terror in their eyes.

Good. He'd waited a long time for this. One day, he thought, they'd fear him even more.

He settled in his comfortable chair, his scrying bowl still covered with the cloth. He lifted a corner and peeked cautiously into the bowl. Just water. But he still had the memory of the night's events clear in his mind. He wanted to relive it, every moment of the most thrilling thing that had ever happened in his dull life. He wanted to experience again the sense of power, the possibilities for his future, that it had stirred up in him. As he had told Ortzi, they had waited. But that was not all. His thoughts returned to the previous night.

He recalled how uncomfortable, how frightened, he'd been as his feet dangled precariously over the farm roof far below them. Flight, except for birds and insects, was unnatural, but he'd thought he would do exactly as the demon instructed.

After a short time, the tiny spark of the blue orb had emerged again, exiting via a window of the farmhouse. As they'd followed at a distance, it had flown on a southwesterly course, over the Osgoi Range, and sped across a barren and empty desert, then more mountains.

Like lightning, they'd flashed across the night sky, the demon's voice emerging from his mouth in his own voice, singing out commands and syllables—a hideous incantation that sent shivers down Hora's spine. They had been joined by dark shapes that flitted and fluttered around them as they followed, the orb ahead still oblivious to their presence.

The demon muttered, "I need my hag-wraiths to do the job. I can't keep you aloft and deal with the girl at the same time." He hoped that she would not decide to vacate his body while they were in mid-flight to help her hag-wraiths.

The orb ahead slowed as they approached a moonlit valley. Dense forest, as far as the eye could see stretched to the south and west, a wide, silver channel winding lazily between the foothills of the mountains toward the distant coast. The trees of these forests were gigantic. They dwarfed anything he'd ever seen, either in his sunny, southern homeland of Galon or Mannanon to the northwest of Galon. He'd had no idea this land existed. It was beautiful, even at night. Perhaps after he'd grown tired of ruling Galon, he would settle here. Find a peaceful valley, just like this—

The demon interrupted his thoughts. *If you obey me to the letter, I will reward you as you wish, but first we must get the girl. Astrabal will be so pleased with me. He has been on the lookout for this one for years.*

The murky shapes and glowing eyes of the hag-wraiths closed in around the orb. He and the demon watched from a nearby peak as the battle raged in the valley. Shrieks that made his neck hairs rise drifted toward their position of safety, while fireballs hurtled far below, blazing back and forth over the forest. The orb faltered, a flickering spark of blue as it plummeted, disappearing with a flash moments before it reached the forest. A small shape dropped into the trees.

"She's dead, no doubt!" the demon snarled. "The fools. I should have released you and done it myself. I'll flay them alive when we get back to Iochodran. A dead girl is no use to me although her parents won't know that she's dead, but I was hoping to get some information out of her first. She's worth ten of her healer friends."

Hora shivered. "I will do exactly as you ask. Together, we'll both get what we want."

"Mmm, yes, we will. Now let's go and see what we've got there."

They descended to where they'd seen the girl fall. It wasn't an easy spot to find since the hag-wraiths had disappeared into the deep forest, too, but they set up a search pattern, and soon they saw the huddle of dark shapes in a small glade. As they drew nearer they heard a sound that did not fit this lonely valley, an odd sound, one that sent tremors through them both. Was it a flute, Hora wondered, and if it was, why did it affect the demon—and him—so?

Light, sound, and color radiated from the glade. A hag-wraith howled, a screech of pure terror that cut off abruptly as the writhing shade imploded into nothingness. One moment it was there, and then it was gone. Hora felt his body quiver, and he plunged toward the forest floor. A hiss escaped his mouth, and he rose again with a jerk as the demon within regained its grip on his consciousness. Again the flute. The demon shook in his body. His head jerked until he thought it would disconnect from his neck, his arms and legs flailing as foam bubbled out of his open mouth.

"We must go!" the demon screamed. "Get out of here! Leave the girl! We'll come back and find her later." Hora, and what was left of the hag-wraiths, rose into the night sky. Hora felt as if all the air had been sucked from his lungs as they flashed away. He wiped the drool from his mouth. *That was a close one*, he thought.

"Take me home, please," he begged the demon. "I can't take any more of this." She said nothing, though, and he squeezed his eyes closed as the creature vacated his body with a jerk. He screamed, dropping again, but felt himself tightly gripped by something hard and cold. They hurtled with a loud pop through a barrier. His body crackled and small shocks ran through him, but then, in an instant, they were on the other side.

He opened his eyes, but he was not home. Instead, he was in a place that made him want to close his eyes again. A cratered landscape of shadow and mist, towering cliffs that rose into a lavender sky. What was even more frightening to him was the sight of the demon that had vacated his body. She had him gripped in a large claw on the end of one of her spider-like legs.

"Where are we?" Hora asked, his voice trembling.

"Raghat Rise."

"The Shadowlands?"

"If that's what you want to call it, but remember, it's Iochodran here. Now shut your mouth. Don't speak unless you're spoken to."

Not for the first time this evening Hora wondered why he had ever summoned a demon. He had made a mistake. No one ever returned from the Shadowlands, or Iochodran, the abode of demons. No one.

"I would take you to Astrabal, but I don't think he'd be pleased with us," said the demon. Her voice betrayed her fear. "We must make another plan. Fortunately, I need someone like you, someone with skills. Someone I can put on the outside to do my work. It's difficult for me to exist in the manifest world in my current form, that is why I had to take your body." She sighed. "Once it was easy, but I lost some of my own skills, thanks to the girl and her parents." The demon clacked her mandibles together, making the hairs on Hora's neck stand up. "Revenge will be sweet."

"Where are you taking me?" Hora asked, forgetting the demon's admonition to keep quiet. "Will I ever see my home again?"

The demon did not answer. They flew on and on, over a landscape filled with crawling things and scurrying shapes. At last they reached a tower that looked like the spire of a ruined castle and entered via a dim, gaping hole halfway up. They emerged into a dungeon-like cavern that was lit by a dim, reddish light.

His body collapsed to the floor as the demon released him.

"You want magic?" she muttered. "Well, we've got it. All you desire, but first your body template needs work." She led him to a stone table. Embedded chains clattered as she grasped them with enormous claws. He turned, her form more clearly visible now, and he went limp. A monstrous spider, with claws on the end of each leg, eight eyes glittering red in the light lifted him like a sack of potatoes onto the stone table, bracelets clamping with a metallic *snap* around each of his legs and wrists. He could not move. He could not even speak. His voice had fled, and his muscles went limp.

"My name is Glahivar," she said, "Astrabal's second in command. My job is to find the best human vessels on the planet to do Iochodran's bidding, and that is why I found you." She shook a claw at him. "While you're not the most outstanding specimen, you were available." She opened her mandibles, hissing, as green slime dripped from her jaws onto his face. "Don't worry, our little procedure won't hurt, at least not too much."

6.

Askoroth

As Glahivar clamped the chains and bracelets around his ankles and wrists, a goblin-like imp darted forward, its pale-yellow eyes eagerly sizing up the man on the table. "Mistress, is this the body you desire? I am surprised—"

Glahivar snorted. "Don't be silly. Of course not, but it was available at the time." *Shadow Goblins,* she thought. *I hate them. Iochodran is full of them.*

"You dragged it through the portal, and it *survived*!" the goblin-imp cackled. "A sorcerer, no doubt. They're easy pickings!"

"You're testing my patience, Stinker. I don't need your help on this one. Get back to your lair, but first find my assistant. He should have been waiting here with the crystal."

Stinker flew out of the opening still cackling.

Poor man, Glahivar laughed to herself—a hissing gurgle—*he had been so frightened!* Well, she'd only use his body for a while. He was not her ultimate target anyway. She had found her prime choice, and she was perfect.

A slither on the stone floor behind her.

"Askoroth. So you showed up at last," she said. "I thought I asked you to be waiting here?"

Hora's eyes widened again as he caught sight of what had just entered the room. He whimpered, and Glahivar waved her claw impatiently over his face. She didn't need him wriggling and whimpering, perhaps even screaming while they worked on him. His eyes closed, and his body relaxed. She turned to face the thing behind her.

"Give me that," she said. The dragon-plated body slithered toward her, venom dripping from snakehead jaws. It held a dark crystal that she snatched from its talons, and turning back to the unconscious man on the table, she waved one of her appendages at the scaly creature. "Stand over there," she gurgle-hissed again. "Oh, sorry, of course, you can't stand, so *place* yourself there and assist with the activation as you're supposed to be doing."

The creature snarled, but its long body snaked to the other side of Hora, its scaly saw-tooth tail whipping in annoyance.

"I realize you don't like being my assistant any more than I like having you as one, but Astrabal's orders—"

"We'll work together as long as it suits both of us." Askoroth's voice was deep and resonant. "After that, I'll have your job."

"Of course, you will. I fully expect it, and that was my goal, too, when I arrived here. I find your ambitions admirable, but you'll only get my job once I get a better one: that of Astrabal's, or alternately, a better and more powerful human body. Now pay attention."

"What are you changing this man into?" Askoroth asked. "He looks like a puny specimen to me."

"I'm not changing him into anything. I'm making it easier for me to use his body. First, though, I will give him all the powers necessary to accomplish my aims, powers such as shape-shifting, telepathy, merkaba flight—to name just a few."

The dragon laughed, its jaws stretching over jagged fangs. "Oh my, how the mighty have fallen! I remember your beautiful appearance as the Raven—Branwyn, was it? This man is, well, not the best example of humanity." Askoroth poked Hora's protruding belly with a scaly talon. "Well fed, too."

Glahivar pinned him with an indignant gaze. "Be careful, or you'll be food for my hag-wraiths. They're probably quite hungry by now. And just for your information, he's only a temporary solution. I haven't told him that naturally. He thinks I'm helping him to power just because I'm such a nice demon." She tittered as she held the crystal over his body. "These humans never learn that help from Iochodran is worse than no help at all. He'll pay with his life."

The dragon-like Askoroth opened his jaws and chuffed, a hiss-hiss that may have been a laugh. "I like your style, Glahivar. So tell me then, what's the point of this little exercise?"

"You're correct. I wouldn't dream of inhabiting this ghastly body for eternity, but it's useful for now." The dark crystal glowed with a reddish-orange light as they passed it back and forth over the man's body, pausing over certain areas briefly before moving on. Askoroth waited. His patience was rewarded. Glahivar continued.

"I have another one in mind. One far more suited to my goals and much more like the body I lost in Rhiannon. This body is that of an enchantress—although she wouldn't call herself that—who possesses skills beyond even my own."

Askoroth's slit pupils widened, and he quickly looked down, as if immersed in the job at hand. "Enchantress? Tell me more."

Glahivar snorted. "I thought you'd be interested, but I don't trust you to know too much. Just do as I tell you, and you can have my job once we've succeeded. That's all you need to know."

They continued their work in silence. Glahivar thought it just as well she'd rendered Hora unconscious. This was a painful process, the forcing open of the chakras. It was unnatural for humans, and even if she didn't plan on disposing of him in the future, he would not have the ability to remain in the body very long after she'd finished with him. But his demise didn't matter, she thought, by then she'd have the girl's body.

7.

The Tree

As darkness fell, Grayfell returned. He strode into the bedroom, a scowl on his face as he removed his cloak and sat heavily in a chair. He looked tired, the girl noted, and irritable. Bean had joined her for dinner, their plates piled high with aromatic fungi, but he continued to eat as if he hadn't even noticed Grayfell's demeanor. She had barely touched her food, and she was already tired of it. Did they eat nothing else but this mushroom stuff?

Grayfell, his voice stony, came straight to the point. "I'm going to take you back to the spot where Bean found you." Bean looked up from his plate and frowned.

"Why?" she asked. "Do you think—"

"You don't know what I think!" he snapped. "We can't know what will happen until we get there. Perhaps nothing at all, but it's worth a try. Maybe you'll remember something." He looked at Bean. "Yes, tonight. She's well enough. You told me she is, so don't cover for her, Bean. I'll take her out of here so fast your head will spin if you can't remain objective. Our survival depends upon getting this right."

31

Bean's face crumpled. He looked dejected, the girl decided. He had been so kind to her today, and she felt ashamed she had ever thought he was strange. In her heart, she knew he was different, but not strange. There was something about him that nagged at her, but she couldn't place it. She wished she could think clearly, her head felt as though it was stuffed with rocks. She felt heavy, *earth-bound*. *Why did I just use that word*?

Something must have shown on her face, because Grayfell's eyes locked onto hers expectantly.

"I-I," she began, and stopped.

"Yes? Please, think. You remembered something, didn't you?"

"Oh, it was nothing. The word *earth-bound* came to me. I don't know why. I feel heavy."

Grayfell's silver eyes searched her face as if looking for a clue there. After a long pause he asked, "Well, you can walk, right?"

"Yes, I walked to the window today." She had briefly stood up this afternoon and opened the slats. A mist-shrouded forest, surrounded by gigantic tree trunks, enormous ferns, and mossy, lichen-covered rocks met her awestruck gaze. The tree's thick roots spread out below her, and the rough bark of the trunk disappeared into the dense mist that hid the tops of the trees from her sight. Her eyes widened, and she took an involuntary step back. She was inside a tree!

She felt the sleek texture of the sill in the open window, then hurried over to the other window. It was as she had thought: no blade marks. She ran her fingers along the walls. They too felt smooth to the touch: This room had not been carved out of the tree by a human. She knelt and inspected the bed, and then, crawling over to the chair, she pushed on it. It did not move; it, along with the bed, was one with the sleek floor.

She wanted to ask Grayfell how this room, with windows and furniture, had formed inside a tree, but just as her mouth opened, he spoke. "I'll wait until you've both finished eating." His head turned toward Bean almost, she thought, as if Bean had spoken. "No, I'm not hungry. Did you drink your potion today? Do I need to keep reminding you?" He looked back at the girl. "Eat your litch. You must build up your strength."

32

So that was what the fungus was called—*litch*, and, she wondered, how did he always seem to know what Bean was thinking? She had tried, unsuccessfully, to communicate with Bean today. "How did you find a tree like this to live in?" she'd asked him. Even to her ears, the question was a crazy thing to ask someone, but he'd only looked at her intently for a while, shrugged as if she was stupid, then turned and walked to the door. Maybe *he* is the one who is stupid and crazy, she had thought as she'd folded her arms, directing a glare at his departing back. He'd hesitated in the doorway, turned his head, his silvery eyes regarding her with what seemed like amusement, then he'd left. She hadn't seen him again until he'd brought their dinner. They sat, eating silently, until Grayfell's return.

Now to demonstrate to Grayfell that she did feel much better, she swung her legs out over the side of the bed and stood up. Her legs, although still a little shaky, could hold her.

"You don't have shoes," he remarked. "They must have fallen off your feet. But the forest floor is not sharp, so you'll be all right. Perhaps it will be a bit muddy."

She looked at Grayfell's and Bean's feet, wishing she had their boots. Bean sat down and began to remove his boots.

"Keep them," she said to him. "I don't want your boots." Why did he annoy her so? "I think we should wait until morning anyway. It's getting dark out there."

"Yes, it is," Grayfell agreed, "but we can see just fine in the dark."

She gave a small sigh. They could see in the dark—silver eyes—she should have guessed.

She shook off Grayfell's helping arm as she walked to the door. She didn't need his help. Together, they walked down a flight of stairs that spiraled around the interior of the tree and entered a living space below: a round room with more chairs and brightly colored silk cushions. It all looked quite comfortable. A table covered with a linen cloth stood in the center of the room. Recessed shelves in the interior wall held wooden plates, cups, and earthenware items. A wood burning metal stove sat in a rock-lined alcove, and a metal pot, still warm to the touch, sat on it. Curious, she found herself drawn toward a familiar aroma. She sniffed. *So he makes his own jam. He's just full of surprises!*

As the thought left her head, Bean turned to look at her, giving an imperceptible nod of his head. A small smile played around his lips.

Oh, for the love of—he can read my thoughts!

Still reeling from that embarrassing discovery, she stepped outside into the forest. The moss-covered floor of the forest felt soft and spongy underfoot. This time she did not reject the help as Grayfell grasped her by an elbow and Bean, her other arm. They led her gently through the giant ferns that rose over her head. Vines and roots fought for space among rocky outcrops, and the going was tricky, but even with the twilit dimness they knew where each obstacle was, easing her over the worst of the forest floor detritus. Looming firs of a size that astounded her competed with the huge trees that Grayfell pointed out as the uakus tree.

"That is what Bean lives in," he explained as they walked. "They are not the only large trees here. The tanna fir is impressive, but the uakus is the monarch of the forest."

"Perhaps you can tell me then, how does Bean hollow out a tree to live in?"

"I can't tell you that." His tone was abrupt. He remained silent for a while, but then, "How do you know he did it? Did he tell you?"

"Bean tell me? Of course not. He doesn't speak. I only know he did it somehow."

Grayfell gripped her elbow tighter, and she cried out in pain, but he did not relax his grasp. "If I hear you mention this to *anyone*," he said, each word clipped and precise, "I will kill you. That is a promise."

She did not say anything for a while, but then she spoke. "I won't talk, and not because I'm afraid of you. I don't know why I'm not afraid, since I know you meant what you said. I feel you are Bean's protector, and for the short time I've known him, I can understand that. Your secret is safe with me, and I won't ask about it again."

"Good. Then we understand each other." He fell silent again as he released his forceful grip on her arm. She rubbed it, wondering if it would leave a bruise.

While she had been curious about Bean before, it was nothing compared to what she now felt. She wanted to know even more about him: how he did what he did, and what his considerable abilities must be. *Why did he need to take potions? Was he sick?*

She glanced at Grayfell. *He only wanted to keep Bean safe*, she thought. She couldn't fault him for that. Danger had always seemed to follow her, too—but that did not arise from her memory. It was one of those facts about herself that even her memory loss could not erase. Details were not there, but this was not her first brush with death and it wouldn't be her last. From the treetops above tendrils of mist snaked down toward the ground, covering the forest floor in a chilly, damp blanket. She shivered.

They crossed several shallow streams, their path taking them over a few small rises before Bean stopped and pointed to a small clearing near the river. She could hear the gurgle of the water nearby. Something nagged at her memory again, but it wouldn't take hold.

They walked to the place Bean pointed out, a spot of flattened grass, a small crushed bush, and footprints in the soft earth.

"*Aha*. My sandal!" She reached down into the grass and moss, picking up a sandal. "I wonder where the other one is?" They searched around, and Bean found the other one nearby. She gratefully placed them on her feet. While sitting on the grassy earth, she looked around, patting the ground around her, slowly at first, then increasingly faster, desperation in her moves.

Grayfell watched, saying nothing as she crawled around the area, pushing at debris, digging, moving leaves and rocks out of the way while she searched. She stopped, lowering her eyes, and placing her head in her hands.

"I lost it." There was a wretched crack in her voice that could only arise from genuine despair.

"What did you lose?" Grayfell asked in a low voice.

She shook her head. "I don't know. *I don't know*."

He sighed. "We'll help you look, then. Maybe we can find it."

They searched the whole area as much as they could in the dark before they gave up. There was nothing there that didn't naturally belong to the forest.

"I think that's all we're—" Grayfell stopped. Bean had frozen in mid-step, looking up at the sky through the lacy branches overhead. "What is it, Bean?"

Bean put his finger to his lips and then pointed upwards.

"Hide!" Grayfell grabbed the girl's arm, and they scurried under a large fern.

The girl felt a cold chill go up her spine. Bean was right. Something was there. Every hair on her arms rose.

They had found her.

8.

The Problem in Mu'A

Irusan, the shape-shifter, had arrived.

The Council Chambers, filled to capacity, were in an uproar. People overflowed into the halls, straining to hear what was occurring inside. The once peaceful island, protected by a shield of invisibility from the outside world, was a cacophony of confusion.

Tegan, along with the other six healers, sat at a large, round table in the center of the chambers. She dabbed at her wet eyes as Jarah, his arm around her shoulders, comforted her. No one could be heard above the commotion. Irusan strode to the speaker's podium, his tall, cat-like figure cutting a swathe through the tightly packed citizens of Mu'A. He held up his hand for silence since he was unable to vocalize in human speech with his cat's mouth, and the chatter slowly died down so they could all hear his thoughts.

I have been over the area myself, but it was only a quick look on my way here. Since the healers are the only ones, besides Anwyn and myself, with merkaba capability, one of you must accompany me on a search of the area.

Irusan paused. He wasn't certain that everyone present knew what "merkaba" might mean.

As he looked around the room, he did not see any blank looks. They all were familiar with the spirit vehicle that could also convey the physical body at the speed of thought, and it looked to him as if everyone understood his telepathic way of communicating. He continued. *Tegan, have you heard anything at all from your daughter?*

Tegan shook her head. Her voice, although breaking with grief, was strong. "I would not sit here crying while my daughter is in danger. I will go with you."

Jarah gripped her shoulder. "I will, too."

There were nods all around, and Tristan, Djana, Adain, and Kex raised their hands. "We too," said Tristan, but Irusan shook his head.

Anwyn is not easily harmed. She may well be somewhere we've not yet checked, unaware of our worry. But it won't hurt to set up a search for her in the area. I did say only one of you will accompany me. Mu'A needs the rest of you here. We have a situation that is critical, and we are already losing ground. The Council of Twenty-Four, my advisory group in my dimension, has informed me that parts of the island—small, uninhabited areas—have disappeared. You all have your jobs to do, and I hesitate in even taking one of you away, but two of us searching will be faster than one. He looked at Tegan. *You are too emotional to be of much use. Jarah, you're coming with me.*

Jarah jumped up from his seat at the table. He walked through the crowd to stand next to Irusan.

Tegan's voice was tremulous. "We should have known she'd go there by herself. She must have slipped out while we slept. If only I'd offered to go with her instead of telling her to wait until daylight!"

"She's a grown woman, Tegan. We can't watch her all the time. She'll be all right, I promise." A quiver in Jarah's voice belied his confidently spoken words.

Irusan continued to share his thoughts. *Finn told me he'd seen Anwyn the day she went missing. She entered the portal to Ardvale, and they vis-*

ited for awhile. Nothing seemed amiss, other than a few personal concerns she had regarding a friendship. All was going according to plan, it seemed.

Irusan did not have to explain who Finn was: the liaison between humans and the elemental kingdom, Ardvale. It was where Anwyn had been born, and where she and the six had trained for years in healing and elemental command.

He continued to speak. *Finn's elementals are on the lookout, too. They sensed the presence of Astrabal's hag-wraiths in the area, but they had no way to tell if they were aware of Anwyn.*

A shudder ran through the crowd, and Tegan cried out in horror. She could not forget how Astrabal and his demons from the underworld, Iochodran, had almost destroyed Mu'A five years ago—not just Mu'A, but the whole planet. Thanks to Anwyn, Blaidd, and the Sentinel—the enormous bat-like creature who had saved them—the deadly crystal skull-weapon had been destroyed. Astrabal had not been pleased. He would be out for revenge, and even though Anwyn was more than capable of taking care of herself, Astrabal was not a demon-lord to be trifled with. He was patient, and he would bide his time. Tegan tightened her white-knuckled grip on her chair.

Blaidd stepped forward. Tegan noted again how quickly he had grown into a strong and capable man. He was no longer the monster he used to be; the beast, Yagmak, had been healed back into his human form by their crystals.

"Irusan, if there's anything Isa or I can do to help find Anwyn, we will do it."

A tall, dark skinned man stood next to him. He grasped Blaidd's hand. "That goes for me, too." Blaidd smiled at his partner, his eyes shining with an emotion he had never dared show to any living human in his dark past. Isa smiled back, but again Irusan shook his head.

Your task with the crystals, the containers of the knowledge, is what's important right now. It will take too long for the Sentinel to fly into that area, so we should not ask for his help. Thank you, Blaidd and Isa, it is appreciated, but you both are an important part of what is occurring in Mu'A right now. You are needed exactly where you are.

Isa nodded. "Our work with crystals is at a critical stage. We still have a lot to do, and transferring the energy from the large generator into smaller receptacles is not easy."

Tegan managed to eke out a smile. She remembered how Blaidd had done his best to atone for the misdeeds of his past. He was a respected teacher of Mu'A once more, even teaching her's and Jarah's son how to use and program crystals. There was no one else on Mu'A, besides Blaidd and Anwyn, who were as skilled in crystal technology.

What Blaidd had always longed for, she thought, *he had finally found in Mu'A, and he hadn't needed to lie, cheat, or steal as he had in the past to get his heart's desire.* Tegan was happy that Blaidd now possessed the love and respect he'd always craved. He wanted for nothing else. He was content. She brought her attention back to the matter at hand as Irusan stepped down from the podium.

I am not going to waste any more time, Irusan said. *Jarah, let's go.*

With that, they left. They were there one moment and gone the next. No one thought that strange. They were all just so used to it.

They began their search in the area near the river, close to the mountains where Finn's elementals had reported seeing the hag-wraiths.

We'll stay in contact all the time, Irusan insisted. *Never let your guard down for an instant. We must always be aware of what is around us.*

As they began a grid search pattern in their merkabas, they telepathed back and forth constantly.

Still not seeing anything.

All looks quiet here—I'm moving along, said Jarah.

No sign of dark ones—I'm going to check inside that cave.

Those trees! They're enormous! It's so thick down there, how would we ever find a person in that?

Jarah, keep your eyes and senses peeled. I'm going down for a quick look.

By evening, they had not seen anything of note. They both wondered if Anwyn been captured by Astrabal and taken to the underworld of Io-chodran. If so, they'd never see her again. At least, not as Anwyn. They each hid their thoughts from the other.

There's too much cloud cover, and the mist is getting thicker down in the valley, but we haven't really looked hard at the water itself, Irusan said. *Check carefully along the riverbanks, Jarah. Sometimes things wash up—*

Yes, I know, Jarah added hastily. He didn't need Irusan to complete the thought. The river was still free of the encroaching mist that had begun to roll down the valley slopes and would be visible for a while yet.

They began their search of the banks, Irusan on one side, Jarah taking the other. They worked their way downstream from where the river spilled through the gorges of the high peaks on either side, and down into the valley where it gathered up all the down flowing streams and tributaries on its way to the ocean. There were plenty of logs, vegetation, a few dead fish—but no sign of a body.

They both saw it at the same time.

Jarah! There's a suspension bridge across the river!

I see it. I thought this land was uninhabited.

This is not good. It puts another complication into the mix, one we did not consider.

They debated on whether they should continue their search. Night fell quickly in the valleys, and with the cloud cover still rolling down the slopes and peaks, visibility would soon be limited.

I don't want to give up just yet, Irusan. Let's take one more look at the river. I keep getting the feeling she may be nearby. I can feel an energy. It's faint, but it's worth checking on.

Irusan had learned to trust Jarah's sixth sense, especially since this time it involved his daughter, so they continued to move slowly down the river. They reached the first large bend where it flowed briefly north, swinging abruptly to the south again.

Jarah hesitated and slowed down even more. The hair on his arms stood up. The temperature seemed to drop, and there was a sense of foreboding in the air.

Irusan! Something is here!

41

I feel it. Here I am, next to you. Stay alert.

The spark of Irusan's merkaba flickered briefly. To any observer, they'd be invisible, but an alert dark one might notice a small spark of their merkabas, flickering like fireflies. They pulled up their protective shields so that not even their sparks would be visible. Rising higher, they had a better view of the river, even though the forest had long since slipped into darkness and mist.

Irusan pointed down to an area of the forest near the river. *There. Can you see them?*

Jarah could: dark forms that descended through the swirling mist, a small clearing, and then more shadows below in the clearing itself. He thought there were three. The mist had closed in fast and it was difficult to see anything at all, but they drifted downward, as low as they dared, until they hovered just above the clearing.

A sharp scream cut through the swirling fog like a blade, and then, a shout.

This is not going to be easy, Jarah thought, but it could be his daughter down there. They had to investigate.

9.

Hag-wraiths

The girl screamed. One of the shadows had her in a vice-like grip. It had pulled her out roughly from under the fern as Grayfell bellowed to Bean, "Your flute!" But Bean, his arm pinned to his side by a smoky tentacle, was also in the clutches of one of the shadows. Grayfell rolled away just in time as a limb snaked toward him. *It happened so fast*, he thought. They had been completely unprepared.

Just before the tentacle wrapped around his neck, he swept his cloak over his head. The wraith snarled and lunged in the direction where it had last seen him, but he was no longer there.

Invisible under his cloak, he bolted toward the spot where Bean and the shadow beast had been, but he was too late. Bean was gone. He roared in frustration, brandishing his fist at the wraiths as they rose into the fog, Bean and Anwyn each gripped in a tentacle. The one that had the girl shook her like a terrier shaking a rat before they, too, disappeared. Their triumphant cackles, each one a punch to the gut, ripped through the thick fog bank toward him. Grayfell dropped to his knees. "No, no," he gasped, tears flowing down his cheeks, his fists pounding the ground.

If I could catch a glimpse of them through the fog, he thought, *I could follow.* At that moment there was a flash of light so bright that he saw spots in front of his eyes. He lifted his arms up to shield his eyes. There was a cry and a thud as a shape sprawled at his feet.

Bean!

Bean rose quickly to his feet. Another light flash, and then the shadows, along with the girl, vanished.

"Are you hurt?" Grayfell asked, pulling back his hood. "Why did they let you go?"

I'm fine. I don't know why they let go of me. There was a flash of light and—what happened to the girl?

"I don't know. Those things got her. We won't see her again." He was sick at heart. He would never discover her secrets.

In silence, they left the clearing. He would have to decide what to do now that things had gone so badly. The king would not be pleased if he found out about this.

10.

Who Am I?

One moment she had been in a teeth-rattling grip of a dark shadow, and the next moment there was a brilliant and blinding light, a brief fall, and she felt herself embraced and held tightly by a strange creature, a creature that did not look like a dark shadow. Another flash and a completely different sight appeared in front of her astonished eyes: they were in a brightly lit room filled with people.

The white, fur-covered creature with a face like a blue-eyed cat placed her gently in front of an open-mouthed group of men and women, and she sank to the floor, weak with fear. *Was this Iochodran*? It was not what she would have expected. One of the women, a pretty lady with dark blond hair and hazel eyes, screamed and ran toward her. She shrank back, holding her hands out protectively as first the woman, then a red-headed man, and then even more people rushed toward her. The first woman hugged her tightly.

"Anwyn! Oh Jarah, Irusan, you found her! Thank you, thank you!" The woman was overcome with emotion, unaware of the girl's confusion.

Who are these people? Why are they so happy to see me?

The odd creature observed her carefully. Oh no, not another Grayfell, she thought. *They don't seem to be demons, though. Perhaps I died . . .*

The creature strode into the happy group, and one by one, he pulled them away from her. Slowly each person stepped back, until finally the blond woman let her go reluctantly. They stared at her and then back toward the creature, bewilderment and anxiety on their faces.

"She doesn't know me," whispered the woman. "Is she something pretending to be Anwyn?"

The red-headed man Jarah spoke, too, while he looked harder at her. "No, it's Anwyn, but not all of her is here. Something—something has gone away."

The girl cringed as the creature stretched out a fur-covered hand toward her. It didn't look human, she thought. Its appearance wasn't like any of those who looked human just like her. It was huge, like a large cat, but stood upright on two legs just like humans. It pressed a large finger on a spot in the middle of her forehead and she heard a loud click in her head. It felt as if something had shifted inside her brain.

We must take her to the healing chambers. She may have done this deliberately to protect her conscious mind and the knowledge it contains. We will have to let that part of herself know it is safe to return.

The creature had not moved its lips, yet it had spoken! It looked at her, its blue eyes gentle. *Yes, you can hear me. My name is Irusan. I stimulated your pineal gland so that we can communicate since human speech is not possible for me. We brought you here to help you. Oh,* he added as an afterthought, *your name is Anwyn.*

It—Irusan—picked her up again. His arms felt comforting, and she was no longer afraid. Apparently her name was Anwyn. The name wasn't familiar, though. If she was not in the Shadowlands or Iochodran she would allow them to help her.

"Bean!" She had suddenly remembered. "Where is Bean? Is he safe?"

Strange looks passed between them, uncomprehending frowns, and shakes of the head.

"Who is Bean?" asked one of the women.

What she didn't add was, "since Angus died." She had felt a deep sadness over Alroy's adoptive father's passing, but was thankful their old friend Genove had Alroy to help her on the farm.

"Too busy? The farm will still be here after you leave. I've done most of my work for the day. Let's go inside and talk. I have so much to tell you."

Genove stood outside the farmhouse feeding chickens, and she dropped her grain basket as Anwyn and Alroy appeared. "Oh, Anwyn! I had hoped you'd come and visit us soon." She beamed, her sun-reddened cheeks flushing an even deeper scarlet. "We have some wonderful news, but let us first go inside and get us something to eat."

They entered the homey little farmhouse that was so familiar to Anwyn. It felt like a third home to her, after Ardvale and Mu'A, of course. She couldn't stay long, though. She needed to go to Ardvale next. Finn, her godfather, had sent a message with an air elemental that he had something important for her. But first, she must hear from Genove and Alroy what the wonderful news was.

They no longer asked her how she arrived so suddenly or where in the world she had come from. Anwyn would just smile and say she had been nearby and thought she'd stop in. They would look at each other as if to say, *We always knew she was a strange one—maybe we don't really want to know how she gets here.*

As Genove and Alroy talked, mostly about livestock, crops, and the weather, Anwyn's thoughts began to drift. She faced a dilemma, one that had preoccupied her thoughts for many years now. Alroy had long suspected that she was a "sorcerer." She knew that. It didn't seem to frighten him, though, and she had been reassured. She'd corrected him once, asking him to use the word *adept* rather than *sorcerer,* but he had never been able to remember that word.

"I am an *Adept*, Alroy. We don't use magic or sorcery. It's all perfectly understandable if you'd just let me explain." But he'd shake his head, saying, "It's all the same to me. Maybe you can explain it later. I need to go milk the cows," or "Isn't that a calf trying to get out of the gate? I must check. Genove will have my hide if it escapes."

As she set the table for Genove, placing the familiar stoneware plates onto its rough-hewn surface, she wondered how she could broach the subject to him again. If their relationship had any chance of going where she wanted it to, she would have to tell him everything about herself. She hoped it wouldn't permanently frighten him off. One never knew with men what they expected from a wife. She'd had no experience at all with these strange creatures. There had been no opportunity in Mu'A to foster a relationship with anyone else.

She had to admit to herself, though, that Alroy had never discussed marriage with her, but their relationship had always been so easy, so comforting. It had always suggested to her that marriage was the next logical step for them.

He is slow on the uptake, though, she thought, as they sat down to eat. Hadn't she dropped enough hints over the years? She smiled to herself as she poured herself a mug of creamy milk. Well, she wasn't going to wait too much longer. It would have to be today. She would just have to wait for the right moment. *I do understand the importance of my duties as an ambassador between Ardvale and the material world, and that of a farmer's wife, but I know I can handle it.*

The three talked for a while over a luncheon of cold ham, fresh baked bread, and plump red strawberries. The conversation remained light, focusing on Anwyn's family and the six healers. Anwyn had told them they all lived somewhere "south" of the farm. She wondered to herself as they talked and ate why Alroy had never asked if he could visit. She had already prepared her response, but he never did ask, so the lie remained unspoken. After they'd finished eating, Anwyn and Alroy told Genove to put her feet up while they cleared the table and washed up.

After they had placed the dishes back on the shelves, Anwyn sat down on the kitchen bench next to Genove and Alroy lit his pipe. She wondered when he'd taken up smoking a pipe. Perhaps it had been too long between visits.

"So what's the news?" she asked, barely able to contain the excitement in her voice.

Genove looked at Alroy, who kept looking out the window.

"Actually, the news is arriving. I see her coming down the path." He smiled mysteriously. "I thought at first you were she, but she's a little late."

Anwyn frowned. *She?*

After a cursory knock, the door opened and a young girl entered. She was pretty, like a much younger version of Genove, with rosy cheeks and a bright smile. She carried a basket of vegetables.

"Good day, Genove—Alroy! Mum sent me with these today. They're fresh from the garden. Oh, Alroy! This must be the Anwyn you keep talking about. The girl—the sister you never had!" She placed her basket on the table and clasped her hands together in delight. "I am so happy to finally meet you."

"Yes, Rowena, it is she," said Alroy, his face pink with pride as he turned to face Anwyn. "This is my fiancée, Rowena!"

For a heartbeat, the world stopped spinning on its axis, and it took every bit of self-possession Anwyn could muster up not to clutch at Genove. Somehow, though, she managed to stay upright. She pasted a toothy grin on her face, her lips stretching wide. She felt certain that she must have appeared quite insincere.

"Alroy!" she exclaimed, her voice cracking with effort. "I would never have guessed." This was the truth, indeed, but what gushed out of her mouth next was not believable even to her ears. "I am delighted! I wish you both so much happiness." She blinked back tears, and Genove smiled.

"My dear, I can see how happy you are for our Alroy. Don't cry! I cried myself when they told me the news!" She laughed, and hugged Anwyn.

They engaged in lighthearted chit-chat for what felt like hours, and when she thought she couldn't bear another moment of pretense, she looked outside. "I must be getting along. The sun will not stop for me, and I still have another visit to make." That, at least, she told herself, was true.

It seemed to take even longer to get away from the happy threesome, but at last she found herself alone in the nearby woods, where, she said, she had left her horse. Rowena had looked at her strangely. She'd opened her mouth as if to ask something, but Genove had interrupted with a story about their neighbor's horse that was about to foal.

Sinking down to the ground, she rocked back and forth on her heels. Putting her face in her hands, she sobbed—naked, howling sobs. Finally, her face wet with tears and saliva, she just sat, unable to move for a while, but the sun had begun its journey into the west. She needed to leave. She must make the portal to Ardvale, the elemental kingdom, before dusk fell. The portal she used was difficult to find in the dark, but she had no problem during daylight hours. Taking a deep breath, she dabbed at her face with her cloak and willed her merkaba to pop up around her.

Nothing happened.

She took another breath, closed her eyes tightly, and tried again. Still nothing. She sat down and wondered if it was time to panic. She could always ask to spend the night at the farm and leave in the morning, but then she would have to put on a happy face again, one she didn't feel. Come what may, she must bring up her merkaba, and immediately.

Ah, there it is! Her emotional upset had blocked her. She sped off into the setting sun and soon arrived at the portal. She found Finn waiting, as he always did, by the door.

12.

The Stone of Creation

"How do you always know I'm here?" Anwyn asked. "Can't I ever surprise you?"

Finn looked at her closely, but didn't say anything. Instead they walked in silence to their favorite spot. Her friends, the elementals bobbing along in their colorful orb forms so they could be seen, followed, but they, too, sensed she didn't want their joyful prattle today, so they drew back, following at a distance instead.

They sat on a stone bench overlooking a small lake, and Finn finally asked, "Well? Why the long face?"

Anwyn's face crumpled, and Finn pulled her toward him as she sobbed into his chest. All she could get out was, "He's getting married! To a Rowena!"

"There, there," said Finn, who was beginning to get the picture. He pulled out an embroidered handkerchief from his pocket and handed it to her, patting her arm comfortingly. "He wasn't right for you, but I'm aware that bit of advice doesn't help."

"No, it doesn't," she said in between sobs. "Deep down, I know you're right, but I always had hope, but now, I have nothing. No hope. Just Rowena."

"You know that she's right for him."

"Of course, she is. That's what makes it so painful. She's perfect!"

"And you aren't. You understood all the problems right from the beginning, but your heart had other plans and wouldn't listen to your head. Anwyn, emotionally you're a normal eighteen-year-old girl. Allow yourself to grieve. I've never understood human affairs of the heart, I can only see the practicalities involved, and there were few to be found between you and Alroy. I wish I could heal your heart, but it is something you must experience so you'll be more like other humans. You will get over it."

"I hate it when people say, 'you'll get over it.' I can't! At least not right away."

"No, of course not. I didn't mean it like that, but there is something I need to tell you, and I need you to be fully present. I hate to be so harsh, but life continues, and right now I need your full attention."

Anwyn sat up, patting her swollen eyes dry with the handkerchief. "Alright."

"You must return to Mu'A straight away. Irusan will be there, and he will fill you in. Something is happening, and while it's a good thing, it is also something that needs much planning and attention to detail."

"Finn, you've succeeded in making me curious. Can you give me a hint?"

"No, because Irusan asked me to leave the details to him. He doesn't want me to concern you unnecessarily with sketchy details. But I do have a few items based on what little I already know to give to you."

He reached into his pocket and pulled out a finely crafted silver chain with a pendant on the end. The pendant was silver, in a teardrop shape, and in the center, surrounded by symbols, was a blue stone the size of a cherry.

"That is so beautiful! Is it my birthday?"

Finn smiled. "It's more than just a pretty bauble. It was designed to look like one, though, but nothing that others would covet and want for themselves. I'm giving it to you now, along with the knowledge of how to use it, because the time is right for you, and the Mu'Ans, to have it."

Turning to face her, Finn placed the pendant around her neck, and he rose from the stone bench.

"This pendant was left with me a long time ago by beings who used to live on your planet. They asked me to pass it along when conditions were right, to someone of my choosing whom I thought possessed the wisdom to use it correctly. That someone is you."

Anwyn looked up at him in surprise. "I hope I can do justice to it, you, and them."

"Lie down," he commanded, and Anwyn picked her feet up, stretching out on the bench. "Close your eyes."

She did so, and at first she felt nothing, but she sensed Finn's hands passing over the pendant as he began to intone words that she did not understand. His voice rose in pitch and tone, and she felt herself drifting to a place where there was no time, no space—a place of abstraction and expansive knowledge that did not come in words, but that arrived as a package of immense proportions that she could not see, hear or feel, but that she sensed was there in its entirety. As she tried to reach out, to grasp the meaning it contained, it slipped away from her, its elusiveness always out of reach as it slowly dropped into a murky void, a place where she could not follow.

Finally, her everyday senses returning, she opened her eyes. "Is it over?"

"Yes," Finn replied. "You will not remember anything just yet. It takes a while for the knowledge about how to use the pendant to surface. If it had been placed into your conscious mind all at once, you would likely experience severe negative effects. This way you can retrieve it little by little, in a way that is safe."

"What if I need to know something quickly? Will I be able to access urgent information?"

He tapped his cheek with his fingertips, thinking deeply before he spoke. "The beings who designed the pendant may have allowed for that possibility, but that is something I can only guess at. Your mind must be allowed to grasp everything in its own time. I would not recommend forcing it, though." He smiled, and taking her hand he raised her upright on the bench. "I would like you to return here for more training on its proper use in the upcoming months. While you will be able to understand most of what arises, you will need more guidance on just exactly how to use this information in a positive way. Remember, too, that all information is neutral. It depends upon the user or co-creator, how conscious they are, to put it to either good or evil use." His voice trailed off. He did not need to go on. Anwyn knew what he meant.

"I am fully aware of how others might misuse it," she said. "I'm already finding the knowledge, the abilities of this stone, resurfacing. It is indeed a powerful object, Finn. I am humbled that you allowed me to have it. I understand that it is my responsibility to be a good steward of the knowledge it contains. I only hope I can." She felt a quiver in her stomach as the full impact of what it all meant hit her.

Finn's normally merry eyes turned kindly.

"I didn't want to burden you with it at first," he said, "because it's an enormous responsibility for a person as young as you are. After you return to Mu'A, though, you will understand why it must be done now and not later. The Mu'Ans will need you, they will need your skills, wisdom, and protection as they've never needed it before. Irusan is not able to interfere in the affairs of humans to that extent. He can, as you know, offer guidance, but that is all. Anything else will upset a balance in the universe that could be disastrous for all.

"I did not choose your parents—or any of the six—for this responsibility, either. It has not been their mission to be the stewards of this level of knowledge. They will still play an important role in the future of this planet and its evolving life, but you were birthed in here precisely for this purpose. You chose to become human, to be able to assist in ways that the non-human cannot."

Anwyn nodded. She understood that her birth had not been accidental.

"You need to get back to Mu'A," Finn continued. "You have an urgent assignment, and once you understand more I'll be able to train you on the use of the Stone of Creation. I did not name it. In fact, I know very little about its capabilities, so I can't tell you any more than that. Just wear it around your neck, and never allow anyone else to touch it. It must not fall into the wrong hands."

Anwyn put it around her neck. "Is it keyed only for me or can others…"

"They can. Especially if they divine what the symbols mean and decipher the sound tones. Astrabal might be able to. He began his apprenticeship here in Ardvale, eons ago, but he chose the path of destruction instead."

"Oh, yes. I understand. One's quantum slowly diminishes and is trapped in ever lower frequency cycles until they're reduced to the smallest particles with no memory of previous experiences. That could be merciful." Anwyn sighed.

"But all do return to the Source, one way or another."

"You mentioned sound tones? I don't hear anything."

"You will once we start our first lesson. It lies in the names of the symbols." He reached again into his pocket. "I said I had a 'few' things for you." His hand emerged holding a crystal that looked to her like a small, green grape. He placed it into her hand where it fit neatly into her palm. "I told you there is nothing I could do to help you forget your young man, but that is not entirely true. This stone is called a locator stone. I wanted to give it to you once the time was right. That seems to be about now." His lips twitched, and he gripped her gently on the shoulder.

"When I said Alroy was not right for you, I meant it. The only person in the world who is exactly right for you is *you*."

Anwyn pressed her lips together, shaking her head.

"I don't mean you're doomed to be alone your whole life. Before you birthed into manifest creation you split yourself in two. One part of you birthed here as the female. The other part birthed as a male . . ." He stopped. There was a spark of understanding in Anwyn's eyes.

"Is he in Mu'A?"

"I don't know. I don't know who he is or where he is. All I know is that this stone will tell you when you find him. It will glow when he is close by. I am not sure how big the radius is, but if you see it glowing pay attention! It's keyed to the frequency of your male counterpart—your twin flame. Go, and try not to think about Alroy. He will be fine, and so will you."

Anwyn nodded, but she asked herself how she would make it through this endless day.

13.

Evacuation

I rusan telepathed Anwyn as she exited the portal to tell her where she could find him and the six. Anwyn flashed at the speed of thought directly from the portal into the Council Chambers of Mu'A, the enormous room that overlooked the terraces and the ocean.

"Hello, Mother, Father—all." Their faces were uncharacteristically somber as they nodded a greeting, and she took her place at the table. The Council of Twelve, Mu'Ans, had assembled, along with Irusan, Blaidd, his partner Isa, and the six.

Irusan began. *I've already told everyone here what is occurring. I will fill you in.*

Anwyn looked around the table. What could possibly make everyone this funereal? No one had been told about Alroy yet, so it couldn't be that, but then why would anyone here even care about him? She didn't have long to wait as Irusan continued.

As you know, Mu'A was created generations ago to serve as a sanctuary for those Basajaun fleeing the reptilian invasion. It became a part of this reality for that purpose, but it was never meant to remain here indefinitely.

Anwyn's foot tapped the air impatiently. These were all things she'd learned in her childhood.

Its time here is determined by many factors, not the least of which is its own frequency holding capacity.

Her foot tapped faster. *Come on, Irusan! Out with it!*

He gave a slight grin. *I know you're impatient, Anwyn, but stay with me. Once the consciousness of the inhabitants of the island expands, so does the consciousness of the energy fields that surrounds and permeates the island itself. This has happened here in Mu'A, at an unprecedented rate, far quicker than anyone had anticipated.*

He stopped for a moment and gave Anwyn a penetrating look.

I see you are beginning to understand where I'm going with this.

Anwyn had lifted her hand to her mouth, with a small intake of breath. She spoke softly. "Yes, I think I understand, Irusan, but please continue."

This process we thought would take an eon or so to occur, but in fact, the island and many of those who live here have already reached a critical mass. He looked around the room. A few faces stared back at him blankly. *It means our universe is not static. It continuously grows—expands—and that goes for its spiritual evolution, too.*

He stopped, looking up and thoughtfully rubbing his chin. *Do you remember how you learned in your early school days that in order for humans to birth here, they had to step themselves down through the dimensions?*

A young woman raised her hand. "Yes, Irusan, I remember. It was because if our higher dimensional selves came in here with a full load of quantum, with all their twelve DNA strands firing and running frequency into the planet, it might blow the planet up!" A chuckle went around the room, and Irusan smiled.

So instead, you split yourselves off into little pieces, coming into this dimension with less quantum—much less—and began the process of accretion, the process that allows you to regain your quantum.

There were nods of understanding around the room, so Irusan continued. *But once that happens, and your quantum reaches a "critical mass," you must return to the dimension you left your higher quantum in, the dimension that can contain that level of accretion.*

"Oh, I see now," the young woman said, understanding dawning in her eyes. "The island is like a person. It, too, is accreting and evolving!"

Exactly! Irusan smiled. *It is the people on this island who have evolved faster than we anticipated, thus helping the island itself—the land—to accrete as much frequency as it could in this dimensional level. Its particles are moving into another frequency range, changing its angle of particle spin, and…*

The woman put her hands over her eyes. "We will either be able to go with it, or not!"

There's no need for alarm, Irusan said, over the buzz that arose in the room.

The chairman rapped his gavel on the table. "Silence!"

The buzz died down as Irusan continued. *It is true that not all of us are able to go with the island, back to its place of origin. I wish we'd noticed it sooner, but it was only during a routine scan of the fields of consciousness that surrounds the island that almost by accident we discovered this. We were not looking for it, but there it was. It surprised even us.*

The island, along with its inhabitants, will simply disappear—go to another reality that matches its own frequency. Its particles will revert to align with the place it originated, a fraction of spin from this one, and many of its inhabitants will match the spin and go with the island to its original home.

"So what's the problem, then?" Anwyn asked.

I said "many" of the people. Not everyone is ready or able to make this shift. Some have suffered template damage from ancient karmic imprints and have not been able to clear that. It's not about who is good or who is bad, it is more about whose particles and templates are able to withstand a sudden shift into another dimension.

Anwyn blinked as the full impact of the situation hit her like a blow. "How many?"

Too many. The majority can make the shift, hence the "critical mass" aspect, but there are several hundred people on the island whose templates just would not be able to make it, and the consequences for them could be dire.

"People such as me," Blaidd said. "You all have been told what was done to my template some years back with dark crystals. It was changed, and I became the monster Yagmak. Thanks to our healers here," he looked at the six who sat around the table, "I was restored to my human form, but the damage has been done. Isa can make it." He glanced down at his hands, at the sparse, but coarse hairs that still grew there. "My template is still too damaged for a shift."

"So Isa is going without you?" Anwyn asked. It was a horrifying prospect.

"No, he is not. He insisted on remaining with me."

There are many more like this. Families where some can make it, while others can't, said Irusan.

"How long?"

Too soon, I'm afraid. Since we only just deduced the island was rapidly approaching a critical mass, we estimate a matter of weeks, not years or months, before it would simply disappear from this reality. We need to evacuate everyone off this island, everyone who is unable to make the shift, along with those who choose to accompany them. And, yes, we need to find a place to relocate them all.

Anwyn recalled what Finn had said: He had asked her to return over the next few months for training. That must mean…

Jarah spoke up. "I, along with the six, will not be going with Mu'A. We—the six—have all volunteered to remain behind to help relocate everyone. You, Anwyn, can make the shift, but we ask you now to make a choice. Do you wish to stay and help, or do you want to go with the island?"

You do understand what this means? Irusan asked. *That everyone you've ever known on this island who goes along with it you will never again see in this lifetime. And if you go with the island, you will not see your parents or those who remain behind until…well, we don't know how long it will be until the next window of opportunity for a shift opens.*

Anwyn's heart sank to the soles of her sandaled feet. How could she possibly make such a choice? It wasn't fair! How could anyone make such a choice? And all in the space of a few moments? People were looking at her expectantly. But they had all made just such a choice, and no one was whining that it wasn't fair.

She took a deep breath and slowly released it.

"You, as well as I, know what my choice will be," she finally said, but thinking to herself, *Finn knew.* "I'm staying. Finn has given me a task, one that will help us once we relocate." Her hand went to the pendant around her neck, and Irusan looked at it with interest in his blue, cat eyes. "Just tell me what I need to do."

Tegan gave a sigh of relief. Anwyn knew she'd been afraid she might never see her daughter again. Everyone seemed to breathe easier.

First, Irusan continued, *we need to find a location for a new settlement. I have something in mind. The western coastline of Ialana has long been uninhabited by humans and remains uncharted territory. Boats have been discouraged from sailing there by tales of sea monsters. While these stories are greatly exaggerated, they have kept ocean explorers away.*

The mountains and forested areas to the south of Unala are guarded by aggressive, mutant species who are an effective barrier for humans from Ak-Gala province. The land is considered by them to be cursed, and no one will venture north. The same applies to the Cloud Mountains; they are crawling with unpleasant creatures. The Dalnoor Desert to the east is nearly impossible to cross.

We are aware of some other non-human races, such as the Elluin, who settled the northern ranges, the New Mountains, eons ago inside a mountain named the Golden Tip. We've not seen any signs of them in Unala lately, and feel they may have left to return to their other dimensional home.

He looked thoughtful, tapping his fingers on the table.

I hope I'm right about that. I have not made an extensive search. So far, it's only been only a cursory look.

"Why are we not resettling our people in the more hospitable areas of Ialana, such as Aelfar?" Anwyn asked.

They would be considered a threat to those in power, Irusan responded. Anwyn opened her mouth to object, but Irusan anticipated her question. *Yes, even to King Deryn, and his mother, Queen Catrin. I know she's your friend, but she's handed power over to her son, and unfortunately he is a little too much like his father. We've kept an eye on him, and while he's not reached his father's capacity for cruelty and greed yet, he soon will.*

The six and Anwyn shook their heads sadly.

"I remember him as such a sweet boy," said Djana.

"We healed his legs," said Tegan. "Could he really turn on us?"

"He could," said Blaidd. "Don't you remember how I turned on you more than once? I understand the way he thinks, and Irusan is right. We must not settle in Aelfar. The Mu'Ans are not submissive like the citizens of Aelfar. King Deryn rules his kingdom with a sword and a clenched fist, and his people accept it because they think it brings them peace and stability. It's a common mistake, and they'll end up paying the price."

Your system of governing is not compatible with the rest of Ialana, Irusan agreed. *Your freedoms would end, and you would not be free to live as you choose. It would not be a happy life for anyone from here. It would be the same situation on other continents. This planet is settled by many different races and forms of governing that are not compatible with the Mu'Ans'. Unala is our best and only choice. It is a few weeks journey by boat, and it's lush, with fertile soil, a navigable river, a large lake, and a lot of rainfall.*

Jarah spoke up. "We are working on establishing three settlements, one on the coast in a natural bay called Morodon, one on the coastal side of the Cloud Mountain Range, and one just across the mountains closer to the Dalnoor plains."

"Why three?" Anwyn asked.

This, we also discussed while you were gone. Irusan looked at Blaidd. *Blaidd and Isa will work on storing all the knowledge of Mu'A on crystalline discs. It's a formidable task and will take working day and night for them, the scribes, and our crystal experts, to get everything we know onto the discs and scrolls. This is the way that your knowledge will be preserved.*

Blaidd dipped his head in agreement. "It will be too risky to have all this knowledge contained in one place, so that is why we must split up into three groups. Each group will possess artifacts that contain the knowledge, so if one settlement is..." he hesitated and took a deep breath, "...destroyed, then we will still have it in two other places."

Anwyn nodded. "I see. It's a good plan."

She did not mention her pendant. The time was not right yet. She carefully shielded her thoughts from Irusan and the others. *I will tell them all about it, later, once I know more myself. Irusan suspects, but that can wait. I am still too upset about Alroy to be coherent, but it seems my pendant is yet another backup.*

She looked up. "Can we go to Unala now?" She had never been there before, and didn't even know this part of Ialana existed. There had been no need for her to fly over the western coast, but now her curiosity burned hot.

"It's dark out there," Tegan said, her brows knitting together in a small frown. "We were going to investigate the area in the morning."

Also, added Irusan, *it's far too dangerous at night, even in our merkabas. Finn's elementals reported some strange activity in the area. We think that the denizens of Iochodran use the cover of darkness to spy. They no doubt got wind of our interest and want to find out why we are so curious about this area. I will take you there tomorrow, Anwyn*, he said as he looked at her, and then back to the six. *I think we're done here. I'll return in the morning.*

With that, he disappeared, and everyone else decided to turn in and get a good night's sleep.

"We'll be busy tomorrow," Jarah said.

They walked to their quarters, excitedly discussing ideas, plans, and activities. All except Anwyn. She was lost in thought.

14.

The Locator Stone

Anwyn couldn't sleep. She tossed and turned, shedding silent tears, stifling her sobs so that she would not awaken her parents in the next room. The pendant felt like an anvil around her neck. *For such a small stone*, she thought, *it has considerable weight*. She lightly rubbed the symbols on the filigree. What did they mean? She closed her swollen eyes as she held the pendant near her heart. *Just feel*. Where did that come from? It was not her thought. She gripped the pendant tighter. Colors began to spiral behind her eyelids, colors that turned into a tunnel of light and sound tones. Frightened, she let go of the pendant and opened her eyes. The room was quiet.

She sat up and quietly opened the drawer next to her bed to again look at the green stone that Finn had given her.

She picked it up, caressing its smooth surface. *Where is he, stone?* she asked, but its green surface remained as stubbornly ambiguous and inert as before. She moved on her bare feet around the room, holding the stone high, then low, up against the walls, by the door, but still it refused to glow. *Finn didn't know the radius,* she thought, *but perhaps—if I move outside, over the island, I'll have a better chance of finding my twin, if he's here in Mu'A.*

She slipped on her sandals and activated her merkaba. In only a moment she hovered over the island, the stone glittering in the light of the blazing full moon. She would be aware of even the faintest glow that it might produce. She flew back and forth over Mu'A, but the stone remained just that—a stone. She sighed, but then her eyes lit up with a thought. Perhaps—perhaps it *was* Alroy? *Even Finn doesn't know who...I must go.*

She had to make up her mind, and quickly. She ignored the small voice—the voice in her head that was appalled that she'd even considered doing this. Spying on someone using her abilities? Finn and Irusan would be disappointed in her. She squelched this voice by telling herself that Finn gave her the stone for that purpose and that she was not really spying. "I only want to know the truth," she muttered to herself.

She slipped the stone into a small pocket in her night robe, and before she could change her mind, she was suspended directly over the Aelfar farmhouse.

She descended, still stifling her misgivings, and moved closer to the window that she knew was Alroy's bedroom. Her merkaba entered easily, and she stood at his bedside next to his sleeping form. She felt the tears welling up again, but she blinked them back. She pulled the green stone out of her pocket, and held it closer to Alroy.

Nothing. Not even a glow. She tried again and again, almost touching him with the stone, but there was no spark at all. He stirred in his sleep, murmuring unintelligibly. She froze. He murmured again, and this time she heard him clearly: "Rowena."

Her face sagged, and still holding the crystal, she darted out the window, her heart as heavy as a boulder. She must leave before she allowed her emotions to get the better of her. It wouldn't do to be caught here in the morning. Rising into the night sky she was about to set her destination back to Mu'A, but then, she hesitated.

She didn't want to return to Mu'A. Not just yet. She would have even more trouble sleeping now that she knew Alroy was not her life's partner.

What harm could it do just to swing by the new lands and look? A quick look. The moon was full. It was a perfect night for exploration.

I'm not afraid of demons from Iochodran. I can protect myself. I'm not a child anymore, she told herself. Absent-mindedly holding the stone in her hand, she flew as quickly as she dared in a southwesterly direction, over the Ozgoi Mountain Range, over the Dalnoor desert, and then again over another snow-capped mountain range. These must be the Cloud Mountains Irusan had mentioned. Slowing down she flew up and down the western flank of the mountains until she caught the glimmer of a river that wound lazily to the west through thick forest.

Taking her time, feeling the comforting coolness of the stone in her palm, she cruised slowly back and forth above the valley. She was thankful the moon was out and there was no cloud cover. She dipped down for a closer look.

It was then that something flashed in her peripheral vision. She glanced down. The stone—it glowed! But in an instant, the glow was gone. Her mouth dropped open. No one, according to Irusan, was down there. No human, that was. The stone must be malfunctioning. She moved back to the area where she had just been, and the faint glow reappeared. She gazed at it, incredulously.

This can't be happening!

It was then, her attention still focused on the stone, that her world turned upside down. She screamed as a deafening thunderclap sounded close to her. Her merkaba ground to a sudden halt, throwing her forward. She placed the palms of her hands on its shell to brace herself as it wobbled and gyrated. The stone slipped out of her grasp and fell, rolling around her feet. Ignoring it, she twisted her head around trying to see what had attacked her, but she couldn't see anything. Another bolt hit her broadside, and the impact flung her again like a rag doll toward the outer shell. She looked down in dismay as the bottom of her merkaba split open. The stone slipped out through the large crack, tumbling down to the forest far below.

I can't worry about that now, she thought, as she braced her hands and feet against the sides. *I must protect myself.* She tried to set a course back to Mu'A, but now it was evident that her merkaba had been badly damaged. It refused to obey her commands. Another bolt slammed into it, and the crack became a large hole. Dark shapes with red eyes, holes for mouths, surrounded her. They grinned as they closed in for their next assault. *Hag-wraiths!*

"*Anwyn!*" One of them screeched. "What a reward we'll get from Astrabal when we bring you to him. He has long been searching for you..." The creature lifted his arm again, and a red fireball flew from a tentacle. It couldn't miss. Flames roared into her merkaba through the opening, and it rolled, top over bottom. She spun dizzily around inside it, the forest over her head one moment, then beneath her feet the next, while flames scorched her.

Fear gripped her heart. *Astrabal! If he can capture me, he will extract every bit of knowledge I possess. Why, oh why, did I not listen to Irusan?*

"Irusan can't help you now," the creature crowed as it released another fireball. This one shattered against her merkaba with an unimaginable force. She made more futile attempts to move her merkaba out of the way, to set a course for anywhere as long as it was away from here, but she was firmly pinned in place by the shapes. Her merkaba was moving in one direction only: down. She saw the tree tops drawing closer, but the fireballs and energy bolts would not stop.

The hag-wraiths danced, shrieking with delight, as each bolt smashed against her shielding. The pain was unbearable, and she could smell burning hair. She cried out as tears ran down her face. She was finished. But she knew what she had to do.

Removing her pendant, her feet and elbows bracing against the sides of her merkaba—now all that kept her from plummeting out, she did it quickly. The knowledge seemed to push up from the depths as if the pendant spoke to her. The tunnel opened up. *Ah, so that's what had tried to show itself to me earlier!* It took only a few moments to do what she must do. Her merkaba split wide open, and her vehicle disintegrated with a flash and a *pop!* The last thing she saw before she lost consciousness was the faint, blue glow of the pendant as it fell from her hands.

15.

The Eldred

Irusan and the six healers were puzzled. They had used a healing crystal on her that should have worked, yet Anwyn still stared at them as if they were all strangers to her. Irusan left for a while to consult with Finn in Ardvale, and using the time portal, he returned a short time later with another crystal.

This should do it, he told the anxious group waiting for him in Mu'A.

After several intense hours, it became obvious to all that none of their crystals had worked. By dawn, they had tried every trick they knew with the same result: Anwyn's expression remained submissive and agreeable but vacant.

This is not the girl we know, Irusan said as they withdrew to another room to discuss the situation.

Everyone agreed.

"We are just healing her body," said Jarah. "It should have worked if her memory loss was caused by a blow to her head, but it hasn't, so that leads me to believe something else has gone awry."

Irusan rubbed a hand thoughtfully over his chin. *I've heard of this type of thing before*, he finally said. *Is it possible? I don't know, but...*

"But what, Irusan?" Tegan asked.

I didn't think she had the capability, but perhaps she isolated all her memories and put them somewhere. Everything that makes Anwyn who she is, is gone. Her personality, her memories—all have been removed. We can heal her brain and her body until it's in perfect condition, as it is presently, but there's a part of her self that is no longer there.

One of the healers, the dark-skinned one they called Djana, spoke. "You said that Astrabal's hag-wraiths had attacked Anwyn and brought her down. Who's to say that before bringing her down they did not remove that part of her and put it somewhere to take back to Astrabal?"

"All her memories would be very valuable to him," said another healer, a woman named Kex. "Maybe he had no use for her physical body."

"Then why would he send his minions back to retrieve her physical body?" Tristan asked. "As a former soldier, I can't see any strategic sense in that."

"And what about the two people on the ground who were with her?" said Jarah. "I couldn't see them clearly, but they looked human, except that their eyes glowed silver."

"They could have taken her memories!" Tegan exclaimed. "They may not be human."

Their eyes were silver? Irusan's nose twitched, and his large, blue eyes blinked in consternation. *When we took her from the hag-wraiths, we were vaguely aware of another person, perhaps two, but we did not pay attention since we thought they might be in league with the wraiths.*

Jarah and I noticed a bridge across the river. I thought it may have been from a human settlement that no longer existed, but now it seems the Eldred, a non-human race, still occupy those lands. We cannot relocate your people there. It would be considered an invasion.

The six stared at him, aghast.

"Then, where will we go?" asked Tristan. "That area was, by your description, the safest and the least inhabited."

Give me a moment. Irusan closed his eyes. *I will consult with the Light Beings of the Council of Twenty-Four.*

They waited in silence, the only sound their anxious breathing, as

Irusan shielded his conversation with his advisors. Their long-time association with Irusan had made them familiar with the Guardians of Agra-Tan, his advisors on a level beyond the material world. They also knew that although he would tell them what had transpired he liked to keep his conversations with his mentors' private. Finally, he looked up.

The Council was not privy to what happened to Anwyn, he said. *They do not follow us around and only get involved with the drama here when it is necessary or for the greater good.*

The six nodded in agreement. They were aware of that, too.

They do agree, though, that Anwyn could isolate her consciousness and place that quantum in a receptacle. However, the receptacle would need to be created especially for that purpose, or the knowledge and memories stored would soon dissipate and be lost forever. Crystals, as we know, can hold these memories, but can they hold even more than that? Our conscious self? Theoretically, yes, but to my knowledge we don't have any here in the manifest world, that could do that.

"We must find out what she used," said Tristan. "It can only be at the place you found her."

The Council recommended we return to the area. We will find the Eldred who were with her, and we will discover if they had anything to do with her memory loss, and at the same time we'll assess the situation regarding the settlement location. Are there more? Or are these the only two surviving members of an ancient race? We won't know until we get there.

"Let's go then," said Jarah. "What are we waiting for?"

I'll return with Anwyn to Unala. Irusan's tone was firm. *I will personally ensure that nothing happens to her. We must find out what the situation is there before we can evacuate Mu'A, and we must get Anwyn's greater consciousness back before it is lost or dissipated—discover what receptacle it is currently housed in. I say again, you must not go to Unala with me. If Astrabal is searching for Anwyn, it means he is also looking for you. Putting all of you in danger is the last thing we need. Trust me enough to know that I can do this myself.*

"If you find the receptacle you'll need to transfer the quantum back immediately," said Tegan.

"Do you know how to do that?" Djana asked.

Irusan shrugged. *I'll find out.*

They returned to the healing room where Anwyn waited.

She isn't going to like this, thought Irusan. Finn had told him about the Stone of Creation, explaining that Anwyn was not yet trained in its use. *It couldn't be that*, he thought to himself. *Or could it?* He shielded his thoughts again. Anwyn had great abilities, and maybe they all had underestimated just exactly what it was she was ready to do. But she wasn't wearing the pendant, which meant she had hidden it away either before or during the attack. He didn't want to think of it as being lost or as having fallen into the wrong hands.

He must find it before Astrabal did. Before Anwyn's consciousness was permanently lost.

16.

Bean

"But I don't want to go back," Anwyn looked back and forth at the group gathered in front of her. "Can't I just stay here? Grayfell doesn't trust me. I don't know what he'll do with me if I go back."

This…Grayfell, Irusan asked. *Did he happen to mention if there were more of them—Eldred—in Unala?*

"Oh yes, he's not the only one. There's Bean, too, and Grayfell asked me not to say anything about Bean and his flute to anyone there, so I had the impression there's a lot more of them."

Flute? Irusan wondered.

"I promised not to say anything about that," Anwyn explained. "Not even to you."

We have little choice then, said Irusan. *We must go to Unala*. With that, he scooped up Anwyn and set his merkaba.

In a flash, they arrived at the riverbank where he and Jarah had found Anwyn. He lifted his eyes to the shrouded mountain peaks. *The Eldred like to dwell in high places*, he thought to himself. *It gives them protection, and they are first-class tunnelers. They will not live out in the open like humans. Unfortunately, today is not a good day. I won't see anything up there with this mist.*

Anwyn pointed down.

"There! That's where Bean lives."

The forest was still visible below. The cloud cover had not yet rolled down the slopes and over the forest, but they would have little time; a fog bank approached, the impenetrable mist rolling down toward them.

Irusan descended in the direction Anwyn had pointed.

"Go there." She directed him to a section of forest where tall trees clustered thickly. "I think that's where Bean lives inside an uakus tree!"

Well, that's a new one, Irusan thought. *I've never heard of anyone living in trees before. I can't wait to meet this Bean character.*

"He is a little different," Anwyn acknowledged, "and that's all I can say about it."

They slowly drifted over the forest, away from the mountain slopes. Anwyn would point to certain trees—it was a big one, she said—and they'd descend so she could get a closer look, and then she'd shake her head and they'd rise again. They continued in this fashion for a while, but as they moved toward a tree that stood well above its neighbors, she looked down, pointed, and grinned.

"That's it. I remember that big root!"

Irusan descended, and he stared open-mouthed at the tree.

"Let me go inside first," said Anwyn. "He knows me."

Irusan nodded, although reluctantly.

Anwyn ran to the tree and pounded on the door. "Bean!" she cried, "It's me, Anwyn. I'm the girl you saved!" But the door remained shut. She pounded again. The crack widened, grew slowly larger, and there in the doorway stood a strange figure: a tall, dark-haired man with silver-gray eyes.

"Bean! I've brought a friend who wants to talk to you."

Bean regarded her for a while, then his silver-eyed gaze scanned the forest behind her. "Where?" he asked.

Irusan did not miss the jaw-dropping, eye-popping look of surprise that came over Anwyn's face.

"You speak?"

"Of course," said Bean, as if astonished she would even ask. "Who is this 'friend'?"

"Oh, yes, I forgot. You can't see him. But first promise me you won't be afraid."

"I have my flute," Bean stated, pulling his carved, wooden flute from his robe. "If I don't like him, I'll send him away."

"I'm still surprised—angry—that you *can* speak. All this time, I thought you were mute! You lied to me!"

"I did not lie. I just never said anything about it," he smiled.

"Well, you led me to believe—"

We don't have time for this, said Irusan as he suddenly lowered his merkaba. *Who are you?* Bean's thoughts hit Irusan loudly and clearly.

Irusan stopped. *You hear me?*

Naturally. Do you think I'm stupid, too?

No, not at all.

"Come inside," Bean said. He stood to one side as he opened the door wider. He couldn't take his eyes off Irusan. *What are you?* he asked, as Irusan stepped inside.

I'm Irusan, a shape-shifting cat-man, and that's all you need to know for now.

"So your name is Anwyn? Did you remember that?" Bean asked Anwyn.

"No, but when Irusan saved me from those hag-wraiths, he told me who I was. I still remember nothing about what happened before. He put his finger on my forehead so I could hear his thoughts, too." She directed a withering glance at Bean. "And yours."

Bean gestured toward the chairs. "Sit."

I'll stand, said Irusan. *We have a lot to talk about. I want you to know, first, that you have nothing to fear from us.*

Bean shook his head. "I already know that, but the others will not."

There was an uncomfortable silence as they looked at each other. Irusan did not know where to begin.

17.

King Sinhail, Ulovia

The girl was back.

Grayfell was in the middle of a consultation with the king. He had just responded to King Sinhail's advisor, Goren, who had stated that he had put the weapon makers on alert so they could step up production. "I asked you to wait . . ." He stopped. Much to the surprise of Goren, Yuki, and the king, he arose from the table where they all sat. "I've just remembered," he said, "that I had another appointment." They gaped at each other, speechless, as he hurried out of the war room.

He sped down the corridors and tunnels, and as fast as he could move he headed back down the mountain and over the river. As he half walked, half ran, he tried connecting with Bean, but something interfered with his transmissions. There was another energy there. He hoped that it wasn't the hag-wraiths of Iochodran, but then, there had been no fear in Bean's warning to him, only surprise and anticipation.

He wondered how the girl had escaped the wraiths. She was obviously far more powerful than even he had first thought, or it could be a trap set by Iochodran. He must be cautious.

As he neared the uakus tree where Bean lived, he threw his cloak over his head and disappeared. The door to the tree was open. Bean had deliberately left it open. He approached carefully, his footfalls soft on the mossy ground, and stopped at the threshold.

The thoughts hit him like a hammer blow to the head.

. . . *And the healing crystals we had did not work. She doesn't remember anything. We decided to come here and see if you can help us. We think she put her memory into something, but what we don't know, and she doesn't remember. If you will help us find it, we will leave.*

"You *will* leave." Grayfell threw off his cloak and stepped across the threshold into the tree home. "In fact, you may feel free to leave immediately. I'll escort you to our kingdom's borders."

You must be Grayfell. I wondered when you'd show up. I heard the call go out. I am Irusan.

Grayfell stopped, staring at Irusan in astonishment as his eyes adjusted to the indoor light. "The girl. You saved her from the hag-wraiths, I assume, and then brought her back here so you could find her memory?"

The thing she placed her memory in, Irusan corrected. *Her name is Anwyn. She is a special kind of person. She was raised in Ardvale by the elementals, and while she is fully human, her abilities are extraordinary.*

Grayfell nodded. "I thought there was something different about her. I suppose that's how she got here. She flew?"

Yes, she has learned how to use the merkaba, the vehicle of the spirit body that is also able to transport the physical body, the atomic matter, from place to place as I do with mine, but she has forgotten who she is. We tried healing her with our crystals, but it has not brought her memory back. We feel that she has placed a large part of her own quantum somewhere outside of her physical form for safekeeping. That is why we returned, to see if we could find the receptacle, and restore her knowledge. The person you see here is not all of her.

Grayfell looked hard at Irusan. "You're hiding something, Irusan. I can't help you until you tell me everything."

It is true, I have not told you everything, Grayfell. I am not yet sure if I can trust you.

Grayfell sniffed. "I'm not an evil man, Irusan. I do what's best for my people, and if you and your friends truly have no ill intent toward the Eldred, I'll do my best to help you and the girl. But I would hope that you will make it worth our while."

Oh, those sticky strings. Irusan's cat-mouth stretched into what might have been a grin, and he shook his head. *Do you not do things just because it's the right thing to do?*

"I will decide what the right thing to do is, Irusan. I do what's best for me and my people. It's as simple as that."

Bean lifted his silver gaze to Irusan. "I will help Anwyn. I don't need anything in return."

Grayfell shrugged. "Do what you like, Bean, but be careful. As much as they don't trust me, I don't trust them, either." He turned to Irusan. "You do know that I will be obligated to report your presence and agenda to Sinhail. Sinhail is our king. He's easy enough to deal with but his advisors are not, and his daughter, Yuki, is the one you really should not trust. I am giving you that information for free. Also, watch out for Goren, the king's top advisor. He's not as friendly as I am."

I expected as much and thanks for the advice. When do you wish to take me to your king?

"I don't think we should take the girl. Only you, Irusan. Bean and Anwyn will stay here. There's no time like the present, but first—" he turned to Bean and an unspoken communication that he blocked from Irusan passed between them. Bean disappeared up the crooked stairs. There was an uncomfortable silence as they waited, and soon Bean reappeared holding what looked like a rag in his hand. "I am sorry," said Grayfell, sounding anything but sorry, "I must blindfold you. I cannot allow you to discover the entrance to Ulovia, our city."

Irusan sighed. *Fine, but does it need to be done in the forest? It will be difficult walking.*

"No. I'll do it after we cross the river."

Irusan walked out of the forest to the river with Grayfell. It was only after they'd crossed the rickety suspension bridge that Grayfell blindfolded Irusan. Taking him by the elbow, Grayfell began their climb up the mountain. He cautioned Irusan when they came to steep or tricky areas in the path. They soon left the path, and Irusan felt pine needles and small twigs crunching under his feet. Proceeding more slowly, they clambered over rocky areas, down into muddy, trickling creek beds, up grassy banks and over fallen logs—all the while moving sharply uphill.

You do this every day? Irusan asked.

"No, only when I visit with Bean. That is not often. Mostly we communicate nonverbally."

They continued in silence, each one blocking his thoughts from the other. They sensed the reluctance of the other to open up, not even to engage in mundane conversation. Irusan sensed the strong resentment and distrust that emanated from Grayfell. He tried not to think of what he'd say to King Sinhail, since he did not want to telegraph his strategy, and he sensed, neither did Grayfell. They continued in this way until his feet felt the smooth, cold stone of the interior of the mountain.

Grayfell commanded the guards to allow him to bring his prisoner in, and they entered an even darker place, but still his blindfold was not removed. They moved in what seemed like a maze of smoky tunnels and echoing halls until they reached an area that was more brightly lit than the others. Grayfell removed the blindfold.

Irusan blinked. Torches, resting in sconces embedded in the marble walls, blazed in an enormous hall. Glittering granite pillars, inlaid with gold and gems, formed an avenue down the center. A group of Eldred, their silver-eyed gazes locked onto the strange sight in front of them, stood in front of a golden throne where a portly man sat, his jaws moving as he chewed on what looked like a roasted, rodent-like creature. As they drew nearer, Irusan contrasted the image of the king with the woman who stood nearby. She was coldly beautiful, he thought, but he felt an immediate repulsion from her, a prickly energy that clearly stated, *You are not welcome here.*

She must be Yuki, the daughter, he thought.

Next to her stood an Eldred with a thin, gray face. *Goren, I presume.* Irusan discreetly observed how the man's jagged and muddy aura radiated outward, causing the fur on his nape to rise. A group of Eldred who stood nearby appeared to be council members or advisors, but their energy and stance deferred to that of Yuki and Goren, and they stepped back as Grayfell and Irusan approached.

"What is *this*?" Sinhail asked, his jaws still working, as he stared at Irusan. Bits of meat adhered to his beard, and he wiped his mouth with the back of a greasy hand as he gave a final swallow. He threw the bones onto the floor. A flunky appeared, shadow-like, to remove them.

Yuki stared, too, as did everyone in the hall. Irusan knew he cut an imposing figure, and he was certain that they'd never seen a life-form quite like him before.

"This is Irusan," said Grayfell. "He's a non-human ambassador from…well, let's just say from a place far away. He represents…some humans, and their interests. He does not speak, but I can translate his thoughts for you."

"Well, well, Grayfell, you never cease to surprise me. You can read thoughts, too?" Sinhail's eyes narrowed as did Yuki's and Goren's.

Grayfell gave a small sigh.

This admission has cost him, thought Irusan. He felt Grayfell had not shared many of his abilities with the Eldred court.

"I am able to read only Irusan's thoughts, not those of anyone here," Grayfell said. "Irusan is a telepath, and unless one is able to telepath, I cannot read their thoughts."

Sinhail and Goren seemed to relax, but Yuki asked, her voice heavy with suspicion, "What does he want with the Eldred? And how did he find us?"

"He was here searching for a young girl who had wandered into our territory. She was attacked by unknown creatures and lost her memory. He found the girl, but he believes that she placed her memory into a receptacle, and he wishes to search for whatever it was she used to place her memories in. It could be anything."

"A receptacle?" Goren asked. "What object is powerful enough to contain a person's memories? Is the girl a witch?" His eyes glittered.

Please speak for me, Irusan turned to Grayfell who nodded.

"Irusan is telling me that the object, whatever it is—he does not know, but thinks it may be a crystal of some kind, would not benefit anyone else except the girl. It could be considered a journaling of some kind. It would have no value to anyone except her."

Grayfell's eyes narrowed as he glanced again at Irusan, who sensed he did not believe his assertion that the receptacle had no value. Apparently, neither did Goren. He had not taken his silver wolf gaze off Irusan once.

Tell your king, said Irusan, *that the receptacle is not the main reason I am here.* Grayfell's eyebrows rose. *The reason I am here is that I represent, as you put it, humans who are looking for a peaceful land to settle. We had thought to settle here in the Cloud Mountain valley and the Morodon bay at the mouth of the river, but we had not realized it was already inhabited—by you, the Eldred.*

Grayfell gave a start then recovered. So, *these* were the invaders he'd seen? He repeated Irusan's words.

"I knew it!" Goren exclaimed, his face a mask of hate. "These are the colonizers you saw, Grayfell. We cannot allow—"

"I am still the king," Sinhail thundered. "You do not speak for me, Goren. You do not speak for me. Grayfell, is this—thing—the forerunner of the colonizers? A scout?"

Grayfell looked uncertain.

Tell him this, Grayfell, Irusan directed. *Tell your king that I am not a scout, but an ambassador. We have no intention of forcibly taking your land. The so-called colonizers are fleeing a land where circumstances have forced them to leave. They are a peaceful people with much knowledge. They will be able to live in harmony with the land, and they'll share their knowledge with the Eldred. They are healers and farmers.*

Irusan glanced at Sinhail, then back at Grayfell. *They can show you how to grow food that is palatable. I saw the creature your king gnawed on as we entered. It was a rodent of some kind. I know that your ancestors, the*

Elluin, were more like me once. They did not eat food, but inhaled the energy of our sun. I see things have changed, and if that is your choice, then we—the colonizers—will show you how to grow your own food and raise livestock.

Grayfell dutifully translated Irusan's words to the king.

"Food, eh? While I don't object to rat—they overrun our city and hunting them and mountain stags bring joy to my people—I would enjoy something new occasionally, and we don't have much in the way of vegetables. I'm getting tired of litch. No, Irusan, I wouldn't object." He licked his lips. "Goren," he looked at his advisor who still glowered at Irusan. Yuki's face was inscrutable. "We should consider this offer. If they are indeed peaceable, then—"

"But my liege," Goren interrupted, "it was Grayfell himself who said that these colonizers were aligned with dark forces. Are we going to allow humans, humans we don't know, on the word of this—*thing*—to enter our kingdom, to know our whereabouts? It's insane!"

"Are you calling me insane?" Sinhail spluttered, his face turning red. He stood up. "Did you just say I was *insane*?"

"Father!" Yuki's voice, thought Irusan, was brittle. "Goren is right. What do we know of these people? I have a suggestion, though." The corners of her mouth turned up in what might have been a smile. "We will agree to your proposal, but on one condition," she said as she turned to face Irusan, ignoring her father's huffing as he sat back down.

Apparently, she was not afraid of her father and did as she pleased. Irusan wondered if it was her he should be talking to, instead of Sinhail.

"The condition is: Give us the girl with no memory. Let us speak with her. She will have no lies in her since she does not remember her past, and we can get to know her. If her family, whom I assume will be part of the intruders, wish to get her back in one piece, they will not break your promise to settle here peaceably, and more importantly, there will be an exchange of knowledge."

Sinhail blinked. "You're very clever, Yuki. Yes, that sounds like a plan."

Goren still looked uncertain and started to shake his head. Yuki looked at him, hissing, "Fool! We can't turn down this opportunity.

There's more to this than meets the eye. We will find out the truth from the girl, and if she is aligned with dark forces, then you will know. So will he." She inclined her head toward Grayfell. "That's your job after all, isn't it?"

Grayfell nodded. "I will know."

They all looked at Irusan. He had closed his eyes as they spoke, and after a few moments he opened them, and Grayfell translated for him.

"He will agree, up to a point, and only on a condition of his own. You may talk with the girl in his presence. If you try to harm a hair on her head, hold her as a hostage, or even think about it—and he will know— you will answer to him. He says he cannot state enough how badly that might turn out for you. He is not without abilities of his own."

With that Irusan disappeared, and Grayfell and Yuki gasped. Sinhail gave a small "Humph!"

Goren shook his head. "He'll get lost. You blindfolded him, didn't you?"

"I did," said Grayfell, "and I brought him here on a circuitous route. But I think you underestimate him."

There was a startled yelp from Yuki as Irusan suddenly appeared again in front of them, but this time he held the girl in his arms. Standing her gently on the floor, he looked at Grayfell.

"He says make it quick. He doesn't have time to waste.

King Sinhail's mouth opened and closed as if he couldn't think of a thing to say. Goren still stared, incredulous. Only Yuki had the presence of mind to speak.

"H-how did you find your way back?"

"You think a mere blindfold can stop a cat-man?" Grayfell translated Irusan's thoughts, smiling despite himself. Irusan had known where he was all the time apparently, but he kept translating. "He says, don't try to fool him. He can read your thoughts, and his enhanced senses are not his only assets."

Yuki walked toward Anwyn. Her mouth stretched into a smile that did not reach her wintry eyes. "I am Princess Yuki, the daughter of King Sinhail," she said. "We are the Eldred. When did you get here and how?"

Anwyn looked at Irusan, who nodded.

"I can't remember. I woke up in a strange place. Irusan found me, and then we came back here. That's all I remember."

"Bean found her," said Grayfell. "He took care of her until she recovered, but unfortunately, her memory did not."

Yuki snorted at the mention of Bean.

"What did you place your memory in?" Goren asked, having finally found his tongue.

"I don't know…"

Grayfell spoke. "She felt around her neck for something after she awoke. It was probably a pendant of some kind. It might have been a crystal, as Irusan says. That would be the only object that might be able to hold someone's memories."

"Where did she get it?" asked Goren, looking sharply at Irusan.

"Her people have many crystals," said Grayfell for Irusan. "If it is indeed a type of crystal that can contain a small amount of information, what they call a memory crystal, it could have been made into a pendant."

"Again, I'll ask," said Yuki to Anwyn. "How did you get here? The Cloud Mountains are far from human habitation, and guarded by fearsome beasts. A young girl on her own? That seems unlikely to me. Who came with you? Him?" She jerked her thumb in Irusan's direction.

Anwyn looked at Irusan. "Probably," she said, but doubt was on her face. "I don't really know."

"She's not lying," said Grayfell. "I doubt she can be of much use to us."

"Are you sure?" asked Yuki.

"Of course I'm sure."

"Did you speak to Bean?" Goren asked almost as an afterthought.

"Bean does not speak!" Grayfell retorted, a sharpness to his tone. "I found out about the girl only after he'd rescued her, and I was there most of the time. They did not speak."

"Bean is a mute and a simpleton," said Yuki. "I am surprised he was able to care for her. He is not even able to care for himself."

"He's feral," said Goren.

A shadow fell over Grayfell's face.

Anwyn's lips parted as if to contradict them, but Grayfell, throwing a hot glare in her direction, spoke quickly.

"We searched the area we found her in, and we found nothing. What-ever it was, it must have been lost somewhere in the forest or perhaps even the river. We have no idea where she had been before she was found."

Tell your king that Anwyn has no more information to give, said Iru-san. *I have kept my side of the bargain, now you keep yours. Allow Anwyn's people to settle in this valley so that they can share their knowledge with the Eldred people and live together peacefully. I can bring representatives to meet with you, and we can work out the areas that will not infringe upon your own land and communities. We are not here to take, but to give.*

Grayfell again translated Irusan's words. King Sinhail rubbed his chin, his beard still greasy from his feast. His face wore a doubtful look.

Irusan sensed the energy that radiated out from the group—a con-flicted energy—but also there was an excitement mingled with the doubt. They were not stupid. They knew, or felt, that Anwyn had once possessed great powers. If they accepted a people with ancient knowledge as their new neighbors, perhaps it would benefit them. But there was a grasping energy from Goren and Yuki. *They would not hesitate to take by force what they desired,* Irusan thought.

"Alright," Sinhail finally said. "Alright. You are free to bring your representatives here to meet with us. Mind you, that does not mean we agree to their settling here. We need to discuss this first and ensure our interests are protected."

The Mu'A and I will have to tread carefully here, thought Irusan, but his responsibility was to find areas for the three groups to settle, and the first hurdle had been crossed: the Eldred had at least allowed the matter to enter the negotiation stage. His duty now would be to ensure the Mu'A and their knowledge were well protected.

"You may take the girl," Sinhail continued, "as you will anyway. We obviously cannot prevent you from doing that, but I hope that once she regains her memory we'll be able to talk with her again."

"We'll see. No promises, but we'll do our best to share information with you at all levels," said Grayfell for Irusan.

With that, Irusan folded his arms around Anwyn, and they both disappeared.

18.

Peatatoo

Almost instantly they appeared again in Bean's home. He didn't seem surprised. He had been practicing on his flute, and Irusan could still see the colors pulsating and undulating inside the tree home.

Anwyn didn't tell me about your flute, Bean, thought Irusan. *It's apparently quite powerful, according to the mathematical formulas I see emerging from it. Who taught it to you?*

My mother, Bean replied. He looked at Anwyn. "It was my mother who taught me. I used it to heal you." He looked at Irusan. "My mother was a healer. She was killed by Shadow Goblins. We were at war with them at the time."

I am sorry. Irusan shook his head.

"What are Shadow Goblins?" Anwyn asked.

"We've shared this land with them forever," Bean said, "but they are ugly and nasty and they compete with us to mine gold, silver, and gems." He glanced back at Irusan. "How did you find your way back to the Eldred city?"

I have a merkaba, said Irusan. *It's a spirit body vehicle that allows instantaneous travel between places. I also could program locations into it without anyone else knowing that is what I am doing. I did that when we found your tree, and I did it again when we reached the king's throne in your city. My merkaba brought me here and back in an instant.*

Bean nodded, as if Irusan had just explained to him why grass was green. "The Elluin could do that, too."

We must find the receptacle, Irusan continued. *I feel that the Eldred will be looking for it, too, and I want to find it before they do. Yes, I know you're one of the Eldred, Bean, but I feel you're different. I trust your instincts, and I feel your protectiveness toward Anwyn. You are running no personal agendas of your own. Please help us. I am putting Anwyn's life in your hands.*

Bean didn't hesitate. "I wouldn't do anything else, Irusan. Let's take her back to the place where we found her again. Perhaps we missed something the last time when the hag-wraiths interrupted our search."

Led by Bean, Irusan and Anwyn following, they approached the glade where she had been found.

"It looks a lot different in the daylight," Anwyn said. "Not so scary."

"You can do a more thorough search." Bean's eyes blinked in the strong sunlight that filtered down through the trees. "I feel sure though that if it had been here, I would have found it, even in the dark."

I have no doubt, Irusan agreed, *but it doesn't hurt to take another look.*

"I feel safer now with Irusan here," said Anwyn. "He will protect us."

Bean's hand went to his flute. "I am ready, too."

Before they moved into the clearing, Irusan put his hand out in caution. *I don't expect any hag-wraiths will be waiting here,* he said, *but let me check first.* He disappeared, and Bean and Anwyn waited in silence.

Anwyn clenched her sweaty hands. She wanted to look at Bean, to ask him about himself, about his flute, but the awkward silence between them seemed to stretch into infinity. She sensed that he glanced at her once or twice, but she did not—could not—meet his eyes. She wasn't sure that she could even shield her thoughts from him. She did not want to offend him more than she'd already had.

87

"We did get off to a bad start..." Bean began, but just then Irusan reappeared in front of them, and to Anwyn's relief Bean never did finish his sentence.

It wasn't important what Bean was going to say to her, anyway, she thought. She'd probably never see him again once things got sorted out with her memory.

All clear, Irusan said.

Bean kept to the shady areas, exploring under grassy tussocks, running his fingers over the mossy ground, and pushing his hands through dried leaves and pine needles, while Irusan inspected the lower branches of trees and the lacy tops of the ferns.

Anwyn had a strange feeling that she couldn't quite explain. What they were looking for wasn't there, not in this glade. How she knew that she didn't understand. She wandered into a dark thicket of ferns on the opposite side of the glade where Bean and Irusan searched. *Everything here is so big,* she thought. Ferns towered over her head, and sunlight filtered through the fronds making dappled shadows on the ground. She sat down on the forest floor, and like Bean, began to sift with her fingers through the dried leaves and pine needles under the ferns. Her thoughts were far away, back in Mu'A. She wondered about her parents. It felt odd to her that she didn't even know her parents. They felt like strangers to her. Irusan seemed more of a parent than they, and she had known Bean longer than any of them.

Get out!

A voice chittered in her ear. Startled, she turned. Was it Bean? No, he and Irusan were still searching the other side of the clearing.

Gitgitgitgit!

What? She looked up. Beady, pink eyes regarded her from a nearby tree, and a white fluffy tail swished angrily back and forth.

"Oh!" She laughed. It was a squirrel, and a white one, too. She didn't think they were white, though, were they? Squirrels were usually red or gray, and for a moment there, she had thought it had spoken to her. She waved her hand at it. "I'm not going to hurt you, nitwit!"

You'se goin' to take it! You'se lookin' for it! The tail swished back and forth, and it chittered again loudly.

88

Anwyn's eyes widened. The squirrel had spoken to her. It was not merely chittering. She had heard actual words in her head!

"Looking for what?" she asked aloud.

It chittered again, and Bean turned his head. "Did you say something?" he called.

"Uh, no. Just a squirrel." She decided she had been hallucinating. It must be the forest. There were a lot of strange things about this forest, and this had affected her. A white, talking squirrel, indeed. But then, there was Irusan...

Just a squirrel? And what are you?

Are you speaking to me? She stood up, her eyes wide. She had heard words. It wasn't only Irusan or Bean's thoughts she could hear!

Ya see anyone else I be speaking to? Go 'way. It's mine!

What's yours? Anwyn felt as if her world had suddenly become dreamlike. Perhaps she was asleep and...but she had heard the squirrel's words. It must be in her head, though. Maybe she had been damaged more than anyone thought. It was called hallucinations, she told herself.

The squirrel jumped from branch to branch, still chittering, then scampered down the tree trunk, eye level to Anwyn.

The pretty stone. It's mine.

Where's the pretty stone? Please tell me. It may be important to me.

No! Peatatoo will not tell. Never!

With that, Peatatoo—this must be the squirrel's name—ran back up the tree trunk, disappearing from her view.

"Irusan! Bean!" She ran back into the clearing. "I think I know where it may be!"

"Huh? You sure?" asked Bean.

"I was sitting under those ferns, and I thought I heard a voice. It was Peatatoo, the squirrel. He spoke to me! He says he has the pretty stone. He doesn't want me to take it away from him!"

Irusan looked at her, hope dawning like a sun on his cat-face.

"Well, that's promising," said Bean. "Where do you think this squirrel might be stashing the stone?"

Anwyn pointed up. "That tree, maybe?"

Irusan disappeared. They heard leaves rustling in the upper branches, more squirrel chattering, and Irusan reappeared, holding a stone in his hand that he handed to Anwyn. She took it and held it in her hand. It glowed.

"Do you think this is the stone, Irusan? It's glowing!"

Irusan shook his head, but he stared hard at Bean as if seeing him for the first time, then turned to Anwyn. *This is the stone Finn gave you to find something unrelated. It's not important. There's another crystal, a pendant, that you used.*

"Let me speak to Peatatoo again," said Anwyn. She walked back to the tree. *Peatatoo!* she called.

Silence.

Peatatoo. It's me. I need to talk to you. Here, I will give you the pretty stone back. She held the stone up, and a pair of bright eyes peered at her through a mass of leaves. *Here! Come get it!*

Peatatoo cautiously crept, head down, down the tree trunk, until he was just above Anwyn's reach.

You nasty. You take pretty stone. Give back!

Yes, here it is. But before I give it to you, I want to ask you something. Did you find another stone, perhaps?

Peatatoo darted downward and snatched the still-glowing stone out of Anwyn's hand. He scampered back up the tree, chit-chitting happily. *Yes, she has the other pretty one,* was his parting shot as he disappeared into the foliage.

Their expressions reflected their confusion.

"Well, do you think it's another squirrel that has it?" Anwyn asked.

Who knows, Irusan replied. *It could be anyone or anything. Let's hope it wasn't something from Iochodran. That's an unusual squirrel. He's an albino.*

"What's an albino?" Bean asked.

It's a condition in humans and animals, although rare, where they have no pigmentation in their skin so they are white with pink or reddish eyes. I am surprised he's survived this long in the wild.

"We need to talk to this squirrel some more," said Bean. He lifted his flute to his lips, and began to play a soft tune. He played for some time, and soon the trees around them became alive with movement. Small gray shadows darted from limb to limb, and the rustling of foliage could be heard above them. But still Peatatoo did not appear. Bean stopped. "It looks like his brothers and sisters heard my call, but they're not the squirrel we want."

He's a clever one, said Irusan, *but I still have some tricks myself.* He disappeared, and a few moments later, reappeared in front of them. Bean no longer seemed surprised by Irusan's appearances and reappearances, and even Anwyn felt as if she was getting used to them. *I had to take the time portal to the elemental kingdom. I was there quite a while, and met with Finn. We talked to the elemental family of consciousness, the Deva, that manifests here as "squirrel." It—the Deva—will cooperate and bring the little imp to us.*

As the rustling in the treetops quieted, all they could hear now was the twittering of birds and the distant screech of cicadas. They did not have long to wait. An angry chattering in the distance grew louder, and soon a pale shape darted into view.

Peatatoo! Anwyn exclaimed in relief. *We need to talk. Please don't go away yet.*

Tch-tch-tch-tch! The squirrel hopped down on a limb just out of their reach. *I have important business, what you want? I tell you all!* He glared down at them, his tail twitching back and forth furiously. *Who men with you? Not like. Not like at all!* Peatatoo shivered as he looked at Irusan. *What that? No see that here, ever!*

Don't worry, I won't eat you. Irusan's small mouth stretched open. *See—no teeth!* He held out his hands. *No claws. You are quite safe with us, Peatatoo.*

Peatatoo *tch-tch'ed* some more, his snowy tail flicking as he considered Irusan's words. *You take stone. Why trust you?*

It was returned, wasn't it?

By girl, yes. She take it from you. Bad...thing.

I am Irusan, not "thing." The girl is Anwyn, and this man is Bean. Will you speak with us?

Peatatoo leaped off the limb. He crawled, head first, a little further down the tree trunk, stopping every few moments to look around until he was eye-level with Irusan. *I hide stone, not in nest anymore,* he said, and gave a small *cha-cha-cha* that may have been a chuckle. *You not find.*

We don't want your stone, Peatatoo, said Anwyn. *We want to know about the other one. The one on the silver chain. The one the…lady…took?*

Chah! No lady. I no tell you.

Irusan spoke. *Shall I call your Deva again?*

Peatatoo's body trembled from head to tail. *Deva make Peatatoo come here. Peatatoo frightened. Deva never show to squirrel unless squirrel die. Tch-tch! If Deva come again, Peatatoo die! Come to take Peatatoo to… other place where squirrel mama go.*

Mama? Anwyn asked. *Is that who took the other stone? Your mother?*

Silly girl. Silly, silly! Squirrel mama go when Peatatoo still baby squirrel. Long ago. Mama leave nest. Peatatoo almost die. Deva come to take, but— He stopped. His head drooped as he turned and hopped onto a higher branch.

But what, Peatatoo? Bean spoke now. He looked at the others as he spoke, and said in a quiet whisper, "It's like trying to pull grimworms from their hole, you have to do it a little at a time." There was a blank look on Anwyn's face. "They burrow under plant roots and gnaw at them, digging in with their hooks until the plant dies." He turned back to Peatatoo. *Tell us about your mama.*

For a moment, Peatatoo looked as if he wanted to leave. He hopped higher up the tree, chattering to himself as the three waited below. Anwyn felt as if her heart would stop beating. *Please don't go, Peatatoo,* she thought. *We need you. Help us!*

With a quick movement, he turned himself around again, facing them. *Mama have other stone,* was all he said, surveying them from his perch as if he'd just imparted some deep wisdom that would solve all. Perhaps, too, he thought that now they would leave him alone. He turned back as if to leave again, but Bean wasn't having it.

Your mama, Peatatoo. Tell us.

Nah. No remember mama. Remember hunger. Cold. Brothers and sis-

ters cold. Not move. Only Peatatoo alive. Deva come to get them all. Peatatoo so hungry he fall out of nest. See big snaky thing. Crawl. Hiss. Come to eat Peatatoo. Maybe snaky thing get Mama too. Peatatoo so frightened. Close eyes. Peatatoo rise up. Warm. Feel…move through forest. Peatatoo open eyes again, see new Mama. Mama give Peatatoo water, food, make nice, soft nest. Mama take care of Peatatoo until Peatatoo big. Now Peatatoo must find mate. Peatatoo need pretty stone to find mate.

Your mama, Peatatoo. Can you take us to her? Irusan asked, because Anwyn's eyes had teared up, and even Bean looked away as if he didn't want anyone to see his face.

The little squirrel thought for a while as his tail twitched back and forth, but this time it was not an angry swishing. Anwyn noticed for the first time that he was a young squirrel. She wiped her eyes. How frightened he must have been.

Irusan squeezed her shoulder with a large hand. *Everybody has a story. If we stop to listen, we will understand more about them.* He turned to Bean. *Good work, Bean.*

Finally, Peatatoo spoke. *I take you to Mama. But first, I go tell her. You come here tonight. Tonight, when moon up here…*He jumped to a branch high above them and looked directly up. *I take you.*

With that, he gave a leap onto the large trunk and like a white streak he disappeared.

They looked up at the branch. "I think he meant that the moon must be up there," said Bean as he pointed to a bare patch of sky above.

We'll be here early then, just in case, said Irusan. They turned and headed back for Bean's tree.

At Irusan's suggestion, Anwyn and Bean slept for the rest of the day. *We don't know how long this night will be,* Irusan had said. *While you are sleeping, I have some errands to run. I don't need sleep, so I will see you tonight.*

19.

Yorli

That night, Irusan returned, and Bean and Anwyn were awake and ready to go.

Bean had supplied Anwyn with warmer clothing—a hooded cloak and boots. Along with his flute, he had concealed an Eldred dagger inside his own cloak. He carried a sack that emitted the aroma of litch.

"We may need food before the night is over," he explained.

"And maybe we can bribe Peatatoo with it if necessary," Anwyn said with a smile. "I am getting used to this litch. Can I have a small piece now?"

Bean obligingly allowed Anwyn a chunk to nibble on as they traipsed with Irusan through the forest.

"Where did you go today, Irusan?" Anwyn asked.

To Mu'A. I talked to your parents and assured them you were safe. That was all Irusan seemed to want to say about it, so she did not press him for more details. They reached the glade where they had left Peatatoo. Even though they were early, he was already there, a lighter shape that materialized from a tree trunk as they approached.

Tch! Heard you, like a herd of snapping boar. Let's go. He jumped into the next tree, and then the next. A blur of movement and then he was gone.

Peatatoo! Come back! Anwyn cried out in her head. As if by magic, the impatient squirrel reappeared.

So slow. C'mon! But he moved slower now, looking back, his pink eyes glinting bright in the moonlight. They walked east, following the river in the direction of the mountains through thick clusters of uakus, cedar, pine, and tanoak. In some spots, the heavy underbrush slowed them down and Irusan picked them both up, one under each arm. They soared up and over the towering columns of sweet flowering honeysuckle and creeping ivy. Large ferns posed little problem for them as long as they could still see Peatatoo, who would often jump down from a tree and lope along the ground in front of them, casting impatient looks at them as they plodded along.

The moon was now high in the sky, and it felt to Anwyn as if they'd walked forever. *Where was this Mama?* she wondered. *Was the squirrel lost?*

The trees gradually thinned out, as did the undergrowth, and they clambered up a rocky slope, picking their way carefully through massive boulders. Peatatoo scrambled over the boulders, waiting for them on the other side, and once they rounded the boulder, he'd scamper away as if he'd just enjoyed a nice, long rest.

Not far now, not far now, he said as they approached a large cliff face. *Wait here*, he ordered as he scampered alongside the cliff, disappearing into a hole in the cliff face.

Must be a cave in there, said Irusan. *I do not like this. Wait here. I want to see what is in there before it comes out.*

Bean and Anwyn nodded, and Irusan disappeared. Anwyn didn't think humans or other squirrels lived in caves. She didn't know, of course, but the hair prickled on her arms. Bean had taken out his dagger. It glinted in the moonlight, as silver as his eyes.

"Shadow Goblins live in caves!" he whispered. "Get behind me."

"Why would Peatatoo take us to a Shadow Goblin den?" Anwyn whispered back. "I didn't feel as if he was taking us into danger."

Bean did not reply. They waited, jumping at each small sound: a pebble tumbling down the cliff face, a squeak from a bat that fluttered too close. Without warning, Irusan appeared next to them, Anwyn's small scream cut short by a large hand over her mouth.

Shhh! Irusan said. *We don't want to startle her.* He leaned over and took Bean's dagger from his limp grasp.

Startle her? Startle what? Bean asked, his eyes as round as moons.

But before Irusan could say, something emerged from the opening, and they both gasped. Anwyn sagged against Irusan as Bean whipped out his flute, which also disappeared as Irusan's other hand wrapped around it.

A monstrous shape, eclipsing the mouth of the cave, towered over them as a smaller shape hopped excitedly onto the ground.

Mama! Peatatoo chittered. *Mama!*

Anwyn and Bean couldn't speak. They hardly dared breathe as they stared up at the giant. It gazed back at them with eyes as big as plums in a pinkish face that seemed only vaguely human. Its arms hung down nearly to its knees, large muscles rippling under its light fur. Its thighs were as thick as Anwyn's body, the top of their heads no higher than its waist. It was taller than Irusan, who was the tallest being Anwyn could ever remember seeing.

This is Yorli, or "Mama," said Irusan. *She is one of the oldest races on this planet, and you have nothing to fear from her. She won't eat you. I have been in contact with her species before.*

Anwyn finally found her voice. "Does she speak, or is she like you, Irusan?"

I speak, said Yorli. They heard her voice in their heads clearly. *I also speak with my mouth, but you would not understand my language. We shall communicate this way. I don't meet humans—*and she looked at Bean—*or Eldred, who understand me. They would try to kill me, but Peatatoo has told me about you.*

Peatatoo chittered again and scampered back up Yorli's body as if it were a tree trunk. He sat on her shoulder with a self-important look on his face. *Mama not angry with Peatatoo. Peatatoo did good!*

Yorli's massive hand came up and stroked the little squirrel. It seemed as if she smiled. *Come inside,* she said, and inclined her head toward the cliff. *My home is not much, but it keeps me dry and warm.*

They followed her as she ducked down and disappeared under a low hanging ledge that they could now see was the entrance to a cave. It was dark inside, but Irusan produced a crystal in his hand that emitted a warm light. They followed a winding passageway for a short distance. The light from the crystal blazed even brighter as they entered a small cavern. Anwyn thought she would ask Irusan later how he got the crystal. He had no pockets or clothing, and it had appeared in his hand as if by magic. Right now, she wanted to know more about Yorli and Peatatoo. She looked at Bean, and his eyes shone curiously as he regarded the crystal.

The cavern had been swept clean of scat, and they detected a tang of fresh pine that masked a slight animal odor. Thick straw and pine needles were spread in the rear. *That must be Yorli's bed*, she thought.

They sat on the hard, rocky floor. Even seated, Yorli still made them look puny, but her bulkiness aside, her reddish doe eyes were gentle, her pink nose small and flat, and her soft mouth wide. She looked more carefully at the three who sat in front of her, taking in every detail of their clothing as she slowly reached over to finger Anwyn's cloak. *Pretty!* She smiled, showing human-like teeth more suited for chewing fruit than raw meat. She reached for Bean's small sack, and he handed it to her without protest. She opened it and pulled out the litch. She sniffed and looked uncomprehendingly at Bean.

Mushroom?

Eat. He made eating motions with his hand, but he took the sack back and from it pulled out a small, metal flask. "It's my daily potion," he told Anwyn and Irusan, as he took a swig from it. He recorked the flask and placed it back in the sack. "Grayfell will be angry if I don't take it."

What is it? Irusan asked, but Bean just shrugged.

"He says I will get very sick without it. That's all I know."

Yorli had divided the litch into five sections, giving Anwyn, Bean, Irusan, and Peatatoo a chunk. Irusan shook his head and handed his portion back to Yorli. To show Yorli it was safe, Bean ate first and so did

Anwyn. Peatatoo did not wait for anyone, but dove in right away, stuffing his cheeks until they bulged. Yorli slowly lifted the litch to her mouth and nibbled. She took another bite, and then another, and the litch was gone.

Tasty, she said as she swallowed. *Now, why are you here? Peatatoo said you were looking for a stone?*

Yes, said Irusan. *He told us you had found a stone—a pendant. It's a metal chain with a silver setting that contains a small crystal. Did you find it? It is very important to us, and we must retrieve it.*

Peatatoo found the pendant, she said. *He brought it to me today. He also gave me another stone for safekeeping.*

They looked at Peatatoo who paid no attention to their glances, glances that clearly said, *You lied to us, you little imp. You had the pendant all the time!* But no one said it or even thought it. Anwyn knew they needed to maintain trust with both Peatatoo and Yorli, and giving in to their anger or annoyance would undermine the delicate relationship they needed to maintain with both the squirrel and Yorli.

Still chewing, Peatatoo finally spoke. *Peatatoo not trust.* He threw a small pebble toward them. *Peatatoo ask Mama to decide. Mama like pendant. Pretty! Mama keep. Not let you take.*

Yes, it's pretty, Peatatoo. But that's not why we need it back, said Irusan, kindly. *We need it back because it has something in it that will help Anwyn to retrieve a part of herself she placed into the stone. If she does not get that part back, whoever does end up with the pendant could retrieve it and use it for evil purposes.*

Peatatoo not understand. The squirrel picked up a chunk of litch that Yorli had not yet eaten, and turned his back on them, chewing furiously. *Mama decide.*

Yorli rose and walked to the back of the cavern. They heard a scraping noise like a rock being moved, and then she walked back holding something that glittered in the light of Irusan's crystal. It seemed small in her hand, but it was a pendant. She placed it down on the rocky floor in front of them.

Is this what you seek?

Irusan reached for it. *I think so. Do you recognize it, Anwyn?*

Anwyn shook her head, her mouth turning down. "No. I don't know."

It fits the description Finn gave me, he said. He looked at Yorli. *Do you mind if I borrow this for a while? I will bring it back, but I need to return to the elemental kingdom where this came from to see if it's the Stone of Creation. If it's not, I promise you may keep it. If it is, though, I ask your permission to keep it so we may help our friend here get her memories back.* He looked at Anwyn.

Yorli nodded. *It seems like a reasonable request to me. What would I do with a pendant, anyway?*

Peatatoo spun around, baring his prominent front incisors. *Pretty stone gift—gift! For Mama! Not them.*

Thank you, Peatatoo, Yorli said. *It was your gift to me, but now I will gift it to someone else. We Dwellers own nothing. Squirrels own nothing. It is the natural order of things, and you must learn that. Mama has a lot to be thankful for, and so do you. We have each other, Peatatoo.* She turned back to Irusan. *Please take it. Peatatoo will get over it.*

We are very grateful for your generosity, Yorli—and yours too, Peatatoo. He stood up, then looked at Bean and Anwyn. *Wait here, I will be back soon, and yes, I will tell you how I manifested the light crystal—although I am sure, Anwyn, you will be able to tell me very shortly how I did it!*

He disappeared, and there was an awkward silence at first as they continued to stare at Yorli, who stared back, but then Bean spoke.

Tell us about Peatatoo.

Anwyn looked at him in admiration. He always seemed to know the right thing to say. She had been wondering what to say that would not offend this incredible creature. Her own question would have been more direct: "What are you?"

20.

Peatatoo's Tale

Peatatoo was about to become a meal for a snake when I rescued him, Yorli began. She paused. *You may wonder why a Dweller would bother saving a small creature from another creature. He looked like me, that is why. Suddenly, I did not feel so alone.*

I would do it, too, said Anwyn. *Is that what you are, a "Dweller?" What is that?*

Well, most Dwellers look like me, only with darker fur, skin, and eyes. We were created by the Sky Gods as the stewards of this land, but our species split into different factions. The people of my clan still consider themselves the first people with the original intention: we do not kill unnecessarily; we do not interfere with the natural order of things; and we learn what the natural order is from a young age.

But I... she stopped, her eyes dropped, then she looked up, a firmness in her thought-speak that they did not miss. *I am different. I am different even to those of my own species. I often disturb the natural order. I look different. I behave differently. It is why I was banished from my family. It is why I do not have young of my own. Who would mate with a female with my coloring? That trait is not conducive to survival, and I was considered unlucky to our clan.*

The dominant female of my family made the decision when I was but a young Dweller. She consulted with the other females in the clan, and they all decided I would not benefit our family's survival. They told me to leave, and I came up out of the forest to live here alone. I don't know how long I had been alone, but after I found Peatatoo, I felt myself come alive, and instead of eating him, I raised him.

Her lips stretched wide and she hissed through her teeth. *I ate the snake that ate his mother instead!*

Bean and Anwyn laughed.

I have never seen your species before in my forest, said Bean, *but I have heard that there are some like you farther south, deep in the forests of Unala. We call them Screamers because of the sound they make. My people fear them and stay away from that part of the forest.*

And they are wise to do so, said Yorli. *They are not my people. While we are the same species, my people diverged from them many eons ago. If we ever met up with what you call the Screamers, we'd be at war with them, but we'd also lose. That is why we moved to a different area, far away from the abode of Screamers. The Screamers will eat anything that moves. We prefer fish, frogs, roots, berries, and small rodents. I would never eat Peatatoo, though. I hunt mainly at night, because strong sunlight hurts my eyes. That is why Peatatoo brought you here tonight instead of daytime when I sleep.*

Your teeth don't look like fangs, said Bean. *I heard Screamers possess huge fangs and claws, and they rip their prey to bits.*

They do, Yorli agreed. *They are the most frightening things in the forest, worse even than Shadow Goblins.*

You've told me a little about Shadow Goblins, Bean, Anwyn said. *Tell me more.*

They are the most frightening things I've ever encountered, other than the hag-wraiths that tried to kill you, Anwyn. They killed my mother. They live underground, dig tunnels, and will hunt humans and animals for food. We Eldred have managed to keep them at bay for a while with our superior battle skills, and I believe we have a peace treaty now, but I know they are just waiting for their chance to overrun the city and drive us out of our territory. There is a lot more that I can tell you about them, but I want to hear more about Yorli and her people.

Yorli nodded. *While Shadow Goblins are indeed terrifying, remember that one Screamer is worth a hundred Shadow Goblins in battle, perhaps two Dwellers—and they'd make short work of any of you!*

Anwyn shivered. It must be the wee hours of the morning, she thought. *I wish Irusan was back.* Her eyes drooped, and before she knew it, she was fast asleep.

21.

The Pendant

Anwyn awoke with a start to find her head resting on Bean's lap. He was asleep, too, leaning against the cave wall. She sat up, rubbing the sleep from her eyes. Bean stirred and opened his eyes. The cave was lighter, but the sun was not yet up.

"How long have we been asleep?" Anwyn asked.

"I don't know," said Bean. He stood up, stretching his arms over his head, and rubbing his posterior. "I feel so stiff." He looked around. "Where are Peatatoo and Yorli?"

Looking for food, I would guess, Irusan said as he entered the cave.

"You shouldn't scare us like that!" said Anwyn, her voice petulant. Her stomach rumbled, and her tongue stuck to the roof of her mouth. Her eyes prickled from lack of sleep. She wanted some water, then some food, and a long, long nap in a comfortable bed.

Irusan ignored her irritation. Without a word, he picked them up, one under each arm, and in moments they were standing next to Bean's tree home.

I have some news. Let's go inside, but I see you must eat first, then I'll tell you what I've learned. I left some food here for you before picking you up.

"Where did you get the food?" asked Anwyn, her heart lifting.

Ardvale, said Irusan. *I made a quick stop there first. I needed to speak to Finn. But first eat, then I'll tell you everything.*

Bean and Anwyn tucked in to the spread as if they'd never seen food before.

"I'll never eat litch again," Anwyn said, her mouth full. There were ripe figs, a loaf of bread with fragrant cheese, honey, and a dessert that was creamy and satisfying. They cleaned their plates and sat back, looking at Irusan expectantly.

"Well?" Bean asked.

Irusan laid the pendant on the table. *It's what we were searching for. Finn confirmed it. Unfortunately, though, he doesn't know how to use it. He says that it was left with him eons ago by an advanced race.* Irusan paused as he thought back to what Finn had revealed. *What surprised me, though, is that he said this race was the "Elluin." He said that one day they would return a representative of theirs to this world, a representative who possessed the right coding for the pendant.*

Bean's brows rose as he regarded Anwyn. "Her? An Elluin?" He shook his head, smiling.

Anwyn's eyes flashed and her face grew hot. "Why not?"

"You look nothing like an Elluin," Bean responded, his face turning a shade of pink.

"So you know what they look like then. Congratulations." Anwyn's lips tightened.

Enough of your squabbling. Irusan's tone was as close to irritation as Anwyn had heard, but he allowed the matter to drop as he continued to speak: *He said, too, that the stone is not big enough to contain anything as complex as Anwyn's quantum or memory. He says it is more of a gateway stone.*

"What is that?" Anwyn asked.

It means that the information it contains is located elsewhere, and that the stone will take the wearer to it.

"So does that mean—"

Yes. Anyone who wears this could potentially access the information—or your quantum. But that doesn't mean they will be able to. He said that they would need the codes to open it first, and so far, only you have them, Anwyn. But now you've lost your memory and can't remember them.

"It's quite the conundrum, isn't it?" Bean stated.

"*Conun*—what?" Anwyn looked annoyed. "What does that mean?"

"Just that it's a perplexing problem," said Bean.

You will have to try, said Irusan, and he rose and placed the pendant around Anwyn's neck.

"We have our people on the ground." Glahivar genuflected before the monstrosity that sat on the maggoty carcass, the throne of Iochodran.

Next to her, Askoroth lowered his head in respect to Astrabal's seniority. "I have not been idle either, my lord. Luck has been on our side, for once, and my prospective host is doing all the right things so that—"

"What do you mean?" Astrabal asked. "We don't rely on luck here."

He seldom spoke under a roar, but the deceptively soft tone he adopted now sent a ripple of fear through Glahivar. She knew this would be her last chance. She had somehow survived the punishment of her last mistake—the loss of the girl and the weapon—but it was only her skill at manipulation that kept her in one piece. Her mentor, Shegami, had not been so lucky. Astrabal had reduced her to dust, her consciousness scattered at the quantum level over the desolate landscape of Iochodran. It had been after their last operation failed, and it would take eons for Shegami to reassemble her self—if she managed it at all.

She'll get no help from me, though, Glahivar thought to herself. She enjoyed the new status she held, even if tenuous. She enjoyed lording it over Askoroth, her erstwhile competitor once known as the Dragon King Amrafalus, for the throne of Rhiannon, and who was now her lowly assistant.

"My lord," she explained, "Askoroth only meant that we've both been successful in locating host bodies. I was recently summoned by a sorcerer whose existence I was not previously aware of. He has the same goals as we do: to locate the girl and the six healers. His master, the Galonese warlord Ortzi, wants to use them for his own ends, but ultimately it is we who would use them and not Ortzi."

"Go on. Who is this sorcerer?"

"His name is Hora, and he possesses a few natural esoteric skills, my lord. I ensured that they were enhanced to match those of the child—who is no longer a child, but now a young woman. I have been able to use his body to operate in the manifest world, and the enhancements will help my template to completely replace his own. We will always be able to use him as one of our operatives, for our own ends."

"Ah, a full-body possession. Well done." Astrabal nodded thoughtfully, his long, split chin resting on a bony, taloned hand.

Glahivar took this as an indication for her to continue. "He is not our only asset on the ground, my lord. I have learned to always have a back-up plan, and there is another one in place—perhaps even two more. We will provide one of those bodies to my assistant, Askoroth." She looked around, and furtively approached the throne. "My lord, I will whisper that name to you. I don't trust the loyalty of every imp, hag-wraith, shadow, and goblin in here. I have learned the hard way that information is power."

"Good thinking, Glahivar." He nodded as Glahivar viper-hissed softly into his ear. His face split into a fanged grin. "Clever. Yes, the other operative must not be revealed. Not yet."

Glahivar felt a warmth course through her bloated spider body, a feeling she'd not had for a very long time. At last, she was getting the recognition she deserved. She'd not fail this time.

"My assistant here," she waved her claw toward Askoroth, "will now return to Ulovia, the underground lair of the Eldred, and claim his human vessel. This vessel is about to do something quite stupid. And I will return there, too, and continue to do what I do best: the game of deception."

Astrabal grinned, his fangs shining redly. "Excellent, excellent."

22.

Shadow Goblins

"I may need your help." Goren's voice shook. Dealing with Shadow Goblins was never easy, and despite their long relationship, he still feared their leader Eng. His orange, bulbous eyes glinting with skepticism sat like gooseberries in his sallow face.

Eng ran a clawed hand through his white, scant hair. "So, what you are really saying is that our original agreement is no longer valid? Is that what I'm hearing?"

The underground lair was not Goren's favorite place to meet. It reeked of unmentionable things, and he wrinkled his nose, his eyes stinging. It could also be a trap, and he preferred the dark shadows of the forest where escape was still possible. The blade of Eng's scimitar gleamed in the dim light of his torch. He hated how Eng seemed able to read his thoughts. He was right, though, their original agreement must now be reworked.

"Well, not exactly. Our original agreement was power sharing once I became king. You could have the whole forest—Eldred do not need forests—we are quite happy in our mountain. But now—"

"Now you are telling me we will have to share the forest with these… these humans? Why not just let us wipe them out once they arrive?"

"Because they have great magic. There is a girl—"

"A girl?" Eng spat and his courtiers growled.

"Not an ordinary girl. She has a pendant, a magic pendant, that gives her great power and knowledge."

Eng opened his mouth to speak, but Goren anticipated his next question. "Why has she not used it already? That is because she has lost it."

"And you know this—how?"

"I have my sources, my lord." He paused for effect. "Direct from Iochodran." Goren smirked at Eng's discomfort. Now, perhaps, he would be given the respect he deserved. He drew nearer, seating himself without an invitation on a rough-hewn stool, and in a hushed whisper, told Eng what little he knew.

"I will send my goblins out to scour the forest. We'll find it, and use it for ourselves."

"Not so simple, my lord. She has a protector. One with even more abilities than Grayfell. Also, Iochodran needs this pendant, and they will find it much faster than we can. They will take the girl and force her to reveal its secrets."

"How will we benefit from this if we have neither the girl nor the pendant?"

"Here's how. I have a plan that I will set into motion soon." Goren leaned in closer still, and as he spoke, Eng's bulbous eyes popped out so much that Goren wondered how they ever remained in his skull-like head. He had to admit to himself, though, it was a good plan.

Something was not right. Yuki shook with cold as she gazed into her scrying bowl. She must continue, though. Grayfell was not to be trusted. She thought it true, too, that Goren was not trustworthy as well. He was supposed to be her friend, but she harbored no illusions about his character. He would throw her to the Shadow Goblins as surely as he would her father, just as he had done with Kiya Faervel.

She didn't want to think about Kiya, though. Anyway, it had not been her fault. Goren had forced her hand. She'd cried for days after Kiya's death, but Goren had not shed a tear. Had her tears been for Kiya, though, she wondered, or for herself? She pushed her thoughts away. They were unproductive.

The water in the bowl stirred as if something lurked at its bottom, but how could it? All it was, she told herself, was just a bowl of ordinary water. This kind of thing worked for Grayfell, but would it work for her? She shook her head. She'd tried the herbs. Rumor had it that they allowed one to commune with the spirits. They had tasted bitter, and perhaps she had not taken enough.

She tried once again and pulled the scroll toward her. The symbols made no sense, and the incantations were almost unpronounceable, but it had cost her much in bribes to find a burglar to pick the lock to Grayfell's workshop and then to locate the right scroll. She began the intonations again, the black candles flickering as she spat each syllable out.

This is stupid, talking to the empty room! Who does that? Only the insane—or sorcerers. She sighed and looked back into the bowl. Was the air colder in here? She shivered again. Something was not right. For the first time in her life, she felt fear.

23.

Deception

Anwyn's hand slowly rose as she touched the pendant with the tips of her fingers, feeling the strange symbols etched into the silver. "I don't know what I'm supposed to do with it," she said. Despair threaded through her voice.

I didn't think you would, but perhaps by wearing it, it may trigger something...I am not sure, either, what to expect, said Irusan. *Let's just—* He broke off, blinking, and glanced at the window. *I thought—*

Bean interrupted. "I have a message from Grayfell," he said, alarm on his face. "He wants Irusan to meet him in the king's chamber in Ulovia. He says it's urgent."

Irusan's head turned away from the window, and he looked at Bean. *Urgent? Did he say what it's about?*

Bean shook his head. "He just says to go right now."

Why didn't he contact me directly?

"I don't know," said Bean. "He seemed a little strange, as if he was not quite himself. I'm worried that something bad has happened."

I'll go and check, said Irusan. *Both of you wait here. I'll be back as quickly as I can.* With that, he disappeared, and Bean and Anwyn looked at each other.

"Do you want me to play my flute?" Bean asked. "It may help you remember something." His hand moved toward his flute that lay on the tabletop, but to his and Anwyn's astonishment, it rose into the air by itself.

"Oh no you don't!" a whispery, raspy voice said as a man materialized in front of them. His eyes were obsidian black with red flecks. "I'll have it, thank you very much. I've heard what you can do with this little thing." He held the flute in both hands and snapped it in half, then wrapping his hand around the pieces, he squeezed. Shards of what had once been Bean's flute fell to the floor.

Bean cried out in horror. "My mother gave me that!" He sank down into his chair, his face white as he gazed down on the tiny pieces of flute the man had thrown to the floor. He bent over to pick them up and held them in his hands, disbelief on his face.

Anwyn rose as if to run, but at that moment a claw shot out from the man's body. It pinned her to her chair. Another claw emerged, grasping Bean around his body. They both screamed, struggling, as the man drew them closer to him, but their efforts were futile. They could not escape the grasp of those monstrous claws.

In a heartbeat, they felt themselves moving through the air, enclosed in a giant bubble just like Irusan's but bigger.

Irusan's entrance in the king's chamber was sudden and unannounced. The king looked startled, as did Goren and Yuki. Grayfell was not there, though.

"What do you want this time?" Yuki asked, the pupils of her eyes enormous and black.

Something does not feel right here, Irusan thought, but there was no time for him to ponder over what did not feel right. Since he could not speak, he shape-shifted into his mountain man persona.

Goren shook his head and Yuki blinked. The king's mouth dropped open.

111

Now I can speak, Irusan thought, but to no one in particular. "I can't hold this shape too long," he said aloud. "Where's Grayfell?"

"I'm not privy to Grayfell's whereabouts," said Goren with a smirk. "What do you want with him?"

"I don't want him. He sent for me. He asked me to come here."

Goren, King Sinhail, and Yuki looked at each other, shaking their heads. Goren also shrugged. "Well, he didn't say anything to us. Perhaps you're mistaken."

"Perhaps I am," said Irusan, and he quickly shifted back to his cat-man form, pulled up his merkaba, and in the blink of an eye he was back at the tree home.

Bean, Anwyn! he called. The home was empty. Irusan ran up the stairs to the bedroom area. No one was there. He felt a sense of rising panic. *I've been deceived. Grayfell!* For the first time in many years he felt a wave of anger move through him. He stopped and took several deep breaths. *I must think. I must not give in to anger—that would cloud my judgment, and I can't allow that.*

Just to be sure, though, he left the tree home in his merkaba and took a quick look around the nearby forest. No, they had not gone outside for a breath of fresh air. They were gone.

Returning to the tree home, he felt something under his foot as he stepped on it, something next to the table. He removed his foot, bent down, and picked up a shard of wood. It was the remains of Bean's flute. He was now convinced: something was terribly wrong. Bean's flute was precious to him—it could not possibly have been accidental. He laid the pieces gently on the table and setting his merkaba, he shot off at the speed of thought to Ardvale, popping through the portal in front of Finn with a loud *snap*.

"Irusan, what a flashy entrance! Is something wrong?" Finn asked.

It is, Irusan responded. *They're gone—just gone, and I don't know where to find them. I need your help.*

"Calm down," Finn ordered as he led Irusan over to the bench in the glade, overlooking the lake. "I find this spot quite calming for the emotions. Now start from the beginning. What's happened? Who's gone?"

Irusan told Finn everything, how he had been fooled—*me, Irusan! I felt the presence of something just outside the tree, but before I could investigate it, Bean relayed the message from Grayfell. It took my attention, my focus, away and now I'm paying the price. Anwyn and Bean are paying for my mistake. I can't locate them. I tried to put out energetic feelers for Anwyn, but something is blocking me. Whatever it is, Finn, it's powerful. It has all the hallmarks of Iochodran. My biggest fear is that they've been taken there. If so, it will be impossible to get them back.* Irusan shook his head slowly. *Finn, I'm an idiot. For the first time in a long time, I have no idea what to do.*

"Have you checked with the Council of Light Beings, the Council of Twenty-Four, yet?"

No, that was my next step. But I doubt they would have any idea where Anwyn and Bean are. They do not monitor things on the manifest plane unless they have a good reason to, or they've been asked, and they would not have been there at the moment of the abduction.

Finn caught the utter despair that emanated from the cat-man. "I've never seen you in such a state before, Irusan."

How am I going to tell her parents?

"Don't worry about that, now. There's nothing they can do, and they need to focus on evacuating Mu'A." Finn thought for a while, scratching his beard, then he snapped his fingers. "I'll put my earth elementals on it. If they're not in Iochodran—and we'll hold that hope—then they will find them. They must go to ground somewhere with their hostages."

If your elementals can't locate them, then we're sunk. Irusan put his head in his hands and closed his eyes. *I can't go into Iochodran. My skills do not work there. It is a reversed energy to mine, and I'd be as helpless as a kitten.*

Finn rose and spoke to an elemental orb that hovered nearby. It chirped, bird-like, and sped off across the landscape. They did not have long to wait.

"I am Eirnin," a soft voice spoke, seemingly from under their feet. "How may I be of service?"

Finn and Irusan took turns telling the earth elemental what had transpired. "So we need you to put out feelers across Ialana for Anwyn and the Eldred boy. We want their location and any information you can tell us."

"Wait here," said Eirnin. "I'll be back shortly."

24.

The Halls of the Elluin

They were in a vast, empty space, one that was dark and cold. Anwyn shivered as the man placed her none too gently onto the stone floor, while Bean was dropped awkwardly next to her. They both blinked as a flame flickered nearby, and then another, and another—torches, lining the walls of a cavernous hall.

They could now see the enormous spider shape that overlaid the man-form, and Anwyn felt a familiar fear rising in the pit of her belly, but why it felt familiar to her she could not say. Her hands trembled and her body shook. Bean took off his cloak and placed it around her shoulders. His hands were shaking, too.

"*Anwynnnn!*" the spider said, her voice sending shivers down Anwyn's spine. The man looked at them with empty eyes, his body moving jerkily like a marionette on strings, as the spider form held it upright. She rubbed her claws together, her eyes glittering. "Long have I searched for you, my dear, but now I have you, and you will not escape this time. You have a lot to answer for."

"First things first," said the man in a whispery, raspy voice, "she's mine. I must learn her secrets."

"Oh, you will. We will both benefit from this alliance, Hora, and then she and her little friend here will be my slaves—for eternity."

Anwyn shuddered. What was this monster? And why had she been looking for her? What had she ever done to it?

The man came closer. He reached for the pendant around Anwyn's neck, but the spider knocked his hand away. "Uh-uh, no, no, no! Not until I've had a look," she screeched, and Anwyn and Bean put their hands over their ears. The sound of her voice was painful. The spider claw yanked the pendant over Anwyn's head and brought it up to one of her eight eyes. "Hmm. Yes. Yes. Hmm…" She nodded, mandibles clacking, as she gazed at the pendant. "I see what this is. Clever. But it's not beyond my skills to learn how to use it. You have the codes in your hands." She pulled Anwyn's hands toward her. "Let's go."

"What about me, Glahivar. I need to go, too. You promised!" The man, like a child, pursed his mouth into a petulant mouè.

"You must remain here and make sure he does not escape." The spider waved a claw at Bean. "Don't worry, I'll be back for you. I must go first with this one." She pulled Anwyn toward her.

25.

Anwyn: The Hall of Records

P ain shot through her body. She must do it, and she must do it fast. Anwyn still held the pendant in her hand as she plummeted from her merkaba. In a few heartbeats, she'd be dead. She cupped her hands around the pendant, croaking each word out in a wheezing exhale. A final explosive gasp that she directed into her palms, and with every bit of strength she still possessed, she hurled the pendant away from her falling body. As her consciousness faded, she looked up.

Her last sight in this world would be of the stars glittering in a cold sky above. Blackness…a rushing, like many rivers tumbling over rocks, a roar in her ears, and a white flash.

Where was she? She sat up, her eyes opening wide. She ran her hands over her body—no pain. No burns. It was as if she had awoken from a long sleep. She sat on a flagstone floor. A table, with a single chair and a flickering candle, stood in the center of this shadowy room; a dim light filtered through an arched window high above the floor, and a warm fire crackled in the fireplace. Positioned in front of the fireplace, as if waiting for its owner who would return any moment, was an over-stuffed armchair.

There must be someone here, she thought, someone who had lit the candle and the fire.

An arched doorway led into another room. Slowly and carefully, she stood. She walked on effervescent feet, feet that wanted to fly. As if she was a gossamer dandelion, she allowed them to rise as she floated toward the door.

"Hello!" Her voice echoed emptily through the space. She peered around the doorway. Another room, almost the same as the one she had just left, with yet more doorways and an intricately carved wooden staircase that spiraled into darkness in one corner. She floated to it and ran her hands over the carved railings. *Interesting.* The symbols—yes, she knew them. Just like the other rooms, a table sat in its center. Recessed shelves lined the wood-paneled walls, shelves with neatly stacked scrolls, parchments, and thick, dusty tomes that looked as if they'd lain there for centuries.

She floated from room to room. Each room, all the same size, looked almost the same as the one before, but none of these had a spiral staircase. Some had blazing fireplaces with comfortable chairs next to them, while others held only a desk or a table. Each were filled with scrolls, books, and papyrus sheaves on the shelves. A few scrolls were unfurled on the table, as if left there by a previous occupant.

"Halloo!" she called again. "Is anyone here?" No one came to greet her. All she heard was the snap and sizzle from the fireplace. How big was this place? She could find no end to it, and she had no idea now where she was. It was a maze. She fought a rising sense of panic, a desire to run—to fly—from room to room, screaming for someone, *anyone.* She took a deep breath. She must stay centered. She must use her inner resources to discover exactly what this place was, and why she had ended up here.

What did she remember?

She drifted into another room. It was the one with the staircase. I'll go up the stairs, she thought. Perhaps there will be someone up there who can help me, a way out. The stairs curved three times around itself as she floated up only to encounter a blank wall.

So much for that. She descended back into the room. *What am I going to do?* She drifted aimlessly again into another room. She had to think. Lowering herself into an overstuffed chair next to the fireplace, she took some more deep breaths and closed her eyes.

She remembered going to the farm. She had gone there to see Alroy. The sense of loss, the sadness, it was all there, but strangely, this was not important to her now. She must focus on getting back. She tried to remember the information she had received in Ardvale after Finn had placed the pendant around her neck. It was hazy, but it had something to do with the symbols on the staircase. It was how she had arrived here.

She gasped. *Mu'A. Oh my, yes, what about Mu'A?* She was needed there! The whole island! *It's about to pop out of the manifest earth and go somewhere else!* They needed her help to evacuate those who would not be able to go. Why had she gone to Unala, the unexplored land to the north? They—her parents—had forbidden her to go there, and yet she'd disobeyed them. They had been right. Irusan had been right. She remembered the attack now, how she had transferred her consciousness into this place using the crystal in the center of the pendant as her portal key. She had hoped that either Finn or Irusan would be able to retrieve the pendant later and release her from her prison.

Instead, she had only made things worse. Her dead body and the pendant, she thought in despair, may never be recovered, and she would remain here, in this barren place for eternity. The tears began to flow, and she wiped her wet eyes with a corner of her robe. She still wore the same clothes, for goodness sake. Her nightclothes!

She giggled and rose into the air, hovering above the chair. Oh, so laughter lightened her body, did it? That was good to know. *I wonder how much I'll have to laugh about here, though?* Her body, weighed down with sadness, sank back into the chair. Now she wanted to cry. Resisting the sad thoughts, she pictured herself rising into the air again. It worked. She drifted into an adjoining room. It was the one that had the arched window, the one she had woken up in.

Rising higher, she peered over the stone sill. The sun had just begun to set over pink tinged, snow covered mountain peaks that stretched into the distance. Snow blew as if propelled by a strong wind horizontally past the window. She did not recognize this place at all. Was she even in Unala? She moved her hand toward the opening. Perhaps she could pull herself through the window and escape this place, but her hand bounced back as if repelled by an invisible barrier. She had seen glass before, in Mu'A, but this was no glass pane. This was an energetic barrier of some kind.

She sank back down to the floor and went to one of the shelves. Reaching for a random scroll, she walked back to the table and unfurled the scroll.

She stared. It was a map, a plan of the rooms that surrounded this one, and each room was labeled. The label for the room she sat in now was YOU ARE HERE. *Well, isn't that just too funny*, she snorted. *Of course, I know that already. It would help to know where exactly "here" is.*

The room to her right was labeled HERE NEXT, and the room she had just left with the staircase was labeled JOURNEY'S END. How could it be the end, she wondered, if there was no exit? But just in case, she returned to the JOURNEY'S END room and picked up a scroll. The room she was in was no longer labeled JOURNEY'S END, but YOU ARE NOT READY. It was otherwise blank.

Alright. Ready for what?

She walked into the HERE NEXT room, picked up another scroll, and now she was in YOU ARE HERE. This was nonsensical. She needed to find someone *now*! She needed help.

"Hello," she said again, but without much hope, as she walked into yet another random room. Still nothing. She picked up a scroll. YOU DON'T NEED ME YET was all it read. She unrolled it furiously, but that was the only thing it had written on it. She picked up another scroll close by. YOU REALLY DON'T NEED ME NOW, it read. She ran from room to room, picking up scrolls, books, and papyrus parchments, and each one contained information of some kind, but nothing that would tell her where she was or how to return.

She sat down again, put her head in her hands, and sobbed. What was she to do? She thought about what she had done. She had done this deliberately. She had done this to avoid her greater consciousness being hijacked by Iochodran. She had left the hag-wraiths with a dead body that would be of no use to them, but now she was trapped. Trapped in a place that had no beginning and no end, a place that made no sense.

Crying about it won't help me, she thought, as she wiped her tears away with a corner of her robe. There had to be some information here that would tell her where to start. She looked at the shelf. Should she try again? She picked up another scroll, again at random.

BEGIN HERE, it read. She began to giggle, a little hysterically at first, but then with great relief. Of course! This place was attuned to her unconscious mind! It was the Hall of Records. Everything that she had brought in via the pendant was here. It was accessible to her, and she could direct her learning. If she paid attention, she would figure out the sequence, for that was what it was: a sequence of rooms with a clear beginning and an end. She must begin.

She had very little time to waste..

26.

The Djinn Stone

He left Ardvale with despair still raging in his mind. Eirnin, Finn's earth elemental, had not been successful.

"I cannot find them," the elemental had sorrowfully told him. "There are areas on our planet that are blocked from my consciousness by Iochodran. I can only assume they might be in one of them."

Give me the locations, Irusan insisted. *I will search each one of them.*

"They'll be difficult to search," said Eirnin. "There are many."

Finn had nodded. "Their shielding technology is almost as good as ours. It will take you some time. That is, if they have not been removed to Iochodran itself." He scratched his cheek and then nodded. "Eirnin, show him what you have."

A map formed in the soil by their feet as if drawn by an invisible hand. "The arrows point to the most likely sites—the areas where strong shields have been erected," Eirnin said. "The lands in many of those places are under the control of Iochodran. Beware, though, they're dangerous areas."

He was right, Irusan thought. *There were many.*

Eirnin did offer a tiny thread of hope, though. He drew another arrow that pointed to a mountain in the north. Irusan recognized the mountain, and his nose twitched. Was it possible? He thanked Finn and Eirnin, and in a flash returned to Ulovia. He must find Grayfell first. After all, it had been Grayfell who'd lured him away from Bean and Anwyn. But would Grayfell sacrifice his precious Bean to serve Iochodran? It didn't make sense.

As he entered Ulovia again, invisible in his merkaba, he began searching every tunnel, hall, and underground room he could find. All he found were the citizens of Ulovia going about their normal business.

Yuki passed him by. Hadn't he just seen her in the hall? He couldn't wonder about that now, though. As he turned a corner, he would have almost knocked over a man hurrying in the opposite direction if he had not been in his merkaba.

Grayfell!

Hurriedly, he deactivated his merkaba vehicle, appearing suddenly next to the wizard, who didn't seem at all surprised to see him.

"Ah, there you are!" There was relief in Grayfell's voice. "I've been looking everywhere for you."

As I have for you. Do you know Bean and Anwyn are missing, and did you—

"Have anything to do with it?" Grayfell grinned, then said cheerfully, "Of course not! What do you think I am? I've been searching for them, and I've found them."

Irusan sagged against the tunnel wall and silently exhaled.

"Come with me," Grayfell said. "I'll take you to them. They're in a safe place."

They hurried through the tunnels, deep into the bowels of the mountain. Grayfell talked as they walked.

"I rescued them from the demon, put my cloak of invisibility around us, and brought them back here. I've been searching for you so that you may help me take them to an even safer place."

Why then, was I unable to connect with them telepathically, he asked. *And how did you rescue them?*

Grayfell put his finger to his lips and whispered, "Shh! Anwyn will tell you all in a moment." He looked around conspiratorially. "Someone may be listening. We need to remain silent."

Something nagged at Irusan—a small itch that wouldn't go away, but he shook it off because they had arrived at a room with a heavy door, several huge bolts, and a padlock.

Grayfell fumbled in his robe, pulling out a metal box and a key. He unlocked the padlock and drew back the bolts.

"Go in," he said, pointing. "They're in there."

And what is in that box? Irusan asked, puzzled, as he stepped inside.

"Glad you asked," said Grayfell. A glowing object flew out as he hurled it inside the room with Irusan. In a flash, he stepped back and simultaneously, slammed the heavy door shut in Irusan's face.

Irusan threw his body against the door, but it was too late. He heard the bolts drive home and the padlock snap into place. He kicked at the door, but it was solid. He shook and rattled the handle, but it, too, held. He banged his large fists against it to no avail. Of course, there was no Bean or Anwyn inside the small room with him. He'd registered that fact as soon as he'd stepped inside. Once again, he had messed up, and this time, badly. If only he'd had his wits about him, it never would have happened. He'd allowed his fear to block his higher senses. He breathed a sigh of frustration: he still had his merkaba, though. He would just pull it up. He'd be out of here in the bat of an eye.

His merkaba did not appear. A shock of fear pulsed through him.

He tried again. His commands rang hollow, and he remained as corporeal as before. *What...?* He turned. *The box.* It was not in the room with him, but what was inside it had fallen onto the floor, a sickly glow emanating from a dark violet crystal the size of a pigeon egg.

A Djinn stone! He froze. He'd only heard about them. He'd never actually seen one before. The Djinn stone, what little he knew of it, was a death stone for any being of the light to encounter. Not only did it reverse the frequencies of that being, but it also began the death process. He shook his head as he cursed to himself—using words that he didn't even know he remembered—and kicked the stone furiously into a corner. He hunched himself into the far corner, as far away from it as he could get.

He tried to cover his head with his arms and hands, but a relentless and murky violet glow, one that ran blighted currents directly from Io-chodran, permeated the room. As small as it was, he could not escape it: its power incalculable, its range unknown. The only thing that could contain it was a lead box, and Grayfell had that. His heart sank. He was now just an ordinary life form, one with no special abilities. He could not even telepath anymore, let alone go into orb and fly through walls, doors, and mountains. He was helpless.

Grayfell! I was right not to trust him. Why, oh why, he thought, *did I not pay heed to my instincts?*

But despite the Djinn stone that smoldered relentlessly in the corner, he continued to attempt to pull up his merkaba. All his efforts were futile. He focused on sending telepathic messages to Anwyn, Bean, Finn, or the six in Mu'A—anyone. He got nothing back. It felt as if he was encased in a stone wall, and now—now his muscles were weakening. It was only a matter of time. How long he had, he did not know. It didn't matter what he did now, though. It was over.

His vision blurred as his gaze desperately swept the room, trying to find something he had missed before, an exit of some kind, no matter how small. How did air get into the room? Or was it airless, too, and he'd die of asphyxiation before the stone killed him?

The walls were carved from the rock, windowless, and devoid of furniture. He glanced up. Solid limestone—but wait! What was that? There was a small, dark area in the corner of the ceiling. He pulled himself up, and on shaking legs, stumbled toward it. Holding his hand up he reached as high as his arms could stretch. Air. *Yes!*

He sank back down onto the floor just under the vent. He had an idea. It was unlikely that it would work, but he had to try.

As the door slammed shut, Irusan's body and fists slamming against it from the inside, Askoroth chuckled, and quickly shifted back into his dragon-snake form. The lead box dropped to the tunnel floor, and he batted it aside with a swipe of his tail. He didn't need it anymore. He must get back to where Glahivar held the prisoners and the pendant.

He must take his chosen vessel with him, though, he thought. He'd need the body once he had control of the pendant. He enjoyed his shape-shifting ability: it was a skill he'd never possessed in his old, reptilian form as Amrafalus, the once living and all-powerful ruler of Rhiannon, but now he could be anyone he desired. Even an Eldred Wizard.

But he had another task ahead. His tongue flicked in and out, and his eyes glittered in anticipation. There was someone else he must get rid of first—the old-fashioned way.

27.

Thief!

Peatatoo clutched the stone in his tiny paws, the stone that the girl had returned to him, and chittered with delight.

He had found her—his future mate. She sat on the tapered end of the branch, her gaze fixed on a bird's nest that dangled pendulously from a thin twig below. To Peatatoo's amazement, it was as if she hadn't seen him at all. She seemed more interested in the single, speckled egg that lay inside the pear-shaped nest. As she placed one cautious foot forward, the nest bounced up and down, threatening to break loose or spill its contents to the forest floor. She stepped back onto the firmer part of the limb and regarded the situation once again.

Peatatoo capered behind her, *chik-chikking* as he ruffled his fur and twitched his tail. His offering, his beautiful stone, was not appreciated. And now...and now a bother on the edges of his awareness: a faint crackle, accompanied by bright flashes of light. He brushed aside the unintelligible noise. He had better things to do with his time, such as—*yes-yes-yes!* He would retrieve the egg for the lady squirrel. That would be impressive indeed. Then, maybe then, she would appreciate his generosity.

Placing the stone inside his pouch-like cheek, he leaped high into the air, somersaulted over the squirrel, and plunged downward, a small, white arrow. As he plummeted past the nest, he reached out and with a smooth motion, snatched the egg. With the other paw, he simultaneously gripped a nearby twig. Dangling high above the ground, he swung himself back and forth and launched his body toward a nearby branch.

You take my egg! Thief!

Peatatoo stared at her in amazement.

You distract me with stupid rock. Give me back egg!

Outraged, Peatatoo *chuk-chukked* and held out the egg. She darted toward him, snatched it from his paws, and scrambled up the tree trunk to the safety of her tree-lair.

Not even a thank you. Peatatoo looked around. There must be other females here. Surely—

Another interruption.

More noise in his head, only louder now. The crackling and rustling of dry leaves, and then, an incandescent flash inside his head that made him chitter in pain. The vision was clear, but it lasted only long enough for him to clearly see another pretty stone! It was the color of a succulent berry in late summer, and it lay in a dark, dark place.

He sat contemplating on the branch for a while. He must have that stone. But where was it? Another flash. More pain. He leaped up in the air and clutched his head. *What happen to me? What? What?*

He grabbed onto the branch just in time to prevent himself from falling to the forest floor far below. He shook with fear, but in that flash, he had seen something. Something that told him where to look. But he must first go see Mama. He must tell her about the stone. It would make her happy, and perhaps the lady squirrel would like it better, too. He took the other stone out of his mouth and tossed it to the forest floor. It was no good to him anymore.

28.

Spherical Coins

She had no idea how much time had passed, if it had been days, or weeks. Scrolls and parchments littered the table and the floor around her. She felt no fatigue, hunger, or discomfort. She was like a sea sponge, soaking up an endless ocean of information. To her surprise, she enjoyed perfect recall as well, only scanning a scroll or parchment once before everything on it became etched permanently into her memory.

I feel like I've done all of this before. It's all so familiar. I know this information; I only had to make it retrievable.

She'd gone from room to room, emptying the shelves and poring over each scroll until she understood every bit of information it contained.

But still, the answer to her escape from this place eluded her. There was no scroll or parchment that told her how to return to the manifest world, to her body. She wondered if her body was still alive. *Probably not, but I would like to return in my spirit form and let my family know I am alright. They must be terribly worried.*

She couldn't help but wonder if Alroy would be worried. He wouldn't know she was dead, of course, unless her family informed him. *Time may be different here*, she thought. *Maybe years have gone by on earth, while here it may have felt like days.* The sunlight coming through the windows moved, waxing and waning from strong daylight into darkness. She kept track of the cycles by scratching marks with a blackened piece of wood from the fireplace onto the table she used the most.

She wondered, too, how many more rooms there were, rooms that she had not even been into yet, with scrolls and documents she had not yet perused. It seemed endless. She also felt a twinge of concern that she would not be able to locate the room with the spiral staircase again, with the scroll labeled JOURNEY'S END, but it had promised her she would find it. She must trust the process, she thought.

She pulled up a scroll in her head labeled INSTANT MANIFESTATION. She'd like to practice this one more. Here, in this world it might be easier to do, she thought, than if she were still in the manifest density in her physical form.

She tried to manifest small objects, such as a metal coin, but it came out spherical instead of flat. She had more success in manifesting a slice of bread and a warm blanket. It was not cold in the rooms, but she enjoyed the softness of the blanket against her skin. It helped her to feel less alone. The bread tasted strange, as if she'd left out an essential ingredient.

I'd better not manifest a kitten or a puppy just yet. She had thought about it, but decided it would be irresponsible and cruel if it didn't turn out right. She spent the rest of that day practicing, researching scrolls that listed ingredients for recipes, chemical compositions of metals, and periodic tables of atomic elements for all matter, listing elements she didn't know even existed. To her relief, they all remained in her memory, and all she had to do now to create or manifest an object was to pull the various tables up and create whatever she wanted, out of nothing but air.

By the end of that day, she had almost filled a room with a variety of objects. More spherical "coins"—she seemed unable to master the technique. They tumbled off the table in the thousands and rolled noisily onto the floor. She sighed, but then she laughed. What would she even do with coins anyway? She manifested colorful silk robes and tunics, and threw the dirty, charred nightgown she'd arrived in into the fireplace. She'd manifested food, which she'd carefully taste. Some dishes met with her approval, while others were demanifested in disgust.

Still not ready to manifest a kitten or a puppy, but at least I'm making progress—except for those wretched coins.

Working through the night, she began to learn languages, languages of the manifest world and those of other dimensions. Not only human language, but those of animals and various other creatures, natural and unnatural, were all contained in these halls. Some were easy, but others required tongue twisting, glottal stopping maneuvers that tested her abilities. She worked what felt like another day on the languages until she felt comfortable with most of them.

One day, she found a room with scrolls labeled PAST AND FUTURE and PROBABILITIES. Debating with herself, she wondered if she should even open any of them. She remembered how Irusan had once told her that for every choice she made, she'd move into a different timeline, a different probability. She'd never given it much thought before, but now she had a better understanding how important her past choices had been. They'd brought her here. They'd been the death of her.

She picked up the scroll PAST AND FUTURE and began to read. As she took it all in, her eyes widened. Could it be true? If so, she wasn't who she always thought she was. Some of it she had known, she thought, but the truth of her past had been deliberately hidden from her. If it had not, she would not be capable of doing what she had come here to do. Nothing was coincidental. She shook her head in astonishment. *Nothing.*

It hadn't been as easy as Glahivar had first thought. The codes in Anwyn's hands refused to work for her, and they remained in the vast, underground hall as Glahivar insistently pressed Anwyn's palms onto the crystal.

"What's happening, Glahivar?" Hora asked. "Why—"

She hissed. "Shut up. I need to focus." She continued to hiss as she waved a claw slowly back and forth over Anwyn's hands. "Hmm…yes…I see now." She flung Anwyn's hands away from her. "They are no longer here. This girl is not Anwyn—or, should I say, she's only a remnant of that girl. She is not *amnesiac*. She is a wraith, a shadow of her former self. No wonder she didn't recognize me!" Glahivar chuckled, a wet, slobbering sound that made Hora pull back in disgust. "I wondered why she was so easy to capture."

Anwyn's face turned pale. "I'm sorry, Bean. I wish I hadn't got you involved in this. I had no idea."

"It's not your fault, Anwyn. I only wish I had my flute. This…thing… could never withstand it."

"Well, you don't have it," Glahivar crowed, "and don't look to this girl to save you. She has no more power now than a mouse."

"So how are we going to use this pendant, then?" Hora asked. He reached down as if to take it, oblivious to the direction the conversation had taken. He wished he had more knowledge of these things, but that was what Glahivar was for.

Glahivar yanked it out of his reach. "Don't even think about taking it. I still have some tricks left. Wait here, and make sure these two are here when I get back. I might still need them." She disappeared with a small flash, and they settled down to wait.

Hora took out a knife. "Don't get any ideas," he said as he began to clean his blackened nails with a rusty tip. "I am not without my own tricks, and unlike Glahivar, I don't think that we'll need either of you."

Do you think he's telepathic? Anwyn directed this thought toward Bean.

Bean shrugged. They looked at Hora, who continued to clean his nails. Anwyn was just about to suggest something to Bean when Hora, who did not even look up, said, *Yes, I am. Don't try it.*

But before Bean could respond, Glahivar had reappeared. "I had to use the time portal," she told Hora, her voice peevish. "I hate using the time portal. It discombobulates me, and it's hard on my template."

Her voice crackled, and her spider body had a threadbare look. It rippled, fading in and out, and sparked with a strange light. Anwyn hoped she would just fade out altogether, but this was not to be. The surges finally stopped, and Glahivar carefully flexed each of her limbs.

"I think I'm better now," she said, her voice stronger. "It took us a while in Iochodran to crack the code, but with Astrabal's help, we did it! Unfortunately, I can't be the one to go. It was not only that I suffered damage from the time portal, my template has no human coding and transit through this portal will finish me off—shatter my template. Astrabal was clear about that. It must be you, Hora."

Hora stood up, a grin on his colorless face.

"Astrabal understood the meanings of the symbols on the pendant and how to use them. We don't need this one," she said as she glanced at Bean. "We only need the pass codes. They're embedded in the symbols. Your template, Hora, is the only one that can withstand the portal since it's human."

"I'll go then," Hora said.

"You must still take this one with you," Glahivar said, waving toward Anwyn. "She can be used on the other side to persuade her spirit form to cooperate with us."

Bean grabbed Anwyn by the arm. "If she must go then take me, too. I'm not leaving her."

Anwyn stared at him, bewildered. "You have to stay here, Bean. Neither of us know what it's like on the other side of the portal. It could kill us both."

"Well, I hope it kills *him*," said Bean, inclining his head toward Hora, "but I am going."

Glahivar chortled and shrugged. "It makes no difference to me. Can you handle both, Hora?"

"Of course. What do you think I am, an incompetent fool?"

"He seems harmless enough without his flute. Alright, take them both, but keep your eye on them. They may look like they're no threat to us, but also take your knife, and remember the powers I've bestowed on you. Use them."

"I'm not your child, Glahivar. I know what to do."

Glahivar placed a claw on Hora's head as she handed him the pendant. "I am giving you the codes of portal command to get back. You will need the pendant, though. Don't lose it."

"Don't come with us, Bean," Anwyn said, her face set in an expression of resignation. "I can handle this. You need to be here to tell everyone what has happened."

"That's exactly what we don't want, dear," said the spider. "He may as well go. It will save me killing him. I really don't enjoy that, you know. I only do it when I must."

"I'm going," said Bean. His expression and tone reflected stubbornness. Anwyn sighed.

"Now, you must—" But Glahivar didn't complete her sentence.

A flash of light. Someone had appeared next to them.

"Askoroth, so, you picked that one," Glahivar said. "What took you so long?"

"I had another task that delayed me." The words emerged in the voice—through the mouth of—the body the reptilian now inhabited, and Bean blinked. It was real enough, though. He shook his head sorrowfully.

29.

Despair

Each breath he took was labored, and Irusan's eyes stung as beads of sweat rolled down his face. Better just to close them, he thought. He stretched his panting body out along a wall, as far from the glowing stone as he could get. It was an effort for him even to think, but he knew he must not allow the blackness to overtake him. He fought the rolling waves of darkness that encroached his consciousness like a rising ocean.

His effort to contact the squirrel had obviously not been successful. Squirrels, he thought, as are all animals, are much more receptive to energy signals than humans, but this one may have been the wrong choice. A squirrel's brain was the size of a walnut. Although brain size often didn't matter when it came to telepathy, it was possible that Peatatoo's obsession with finding a mate would prevent him from receiving even a faint signal. Now, he had nothing more left to give. After one more futile effort to contact the outside world, he sank back and resigned himself to his fate.

Irusan slowly opened his eyes. How much time had passed, he had no idea, or even if he'd been asleep or unconscious. The room appeared darker to him. His sight had faded, too. *How long would it be before—*

Scratch-scratch.

He lifted his head. Had he only imagined it? Silence. His head fell back onto the floor. No, there it was again: *scratch-scratch-scratch*, and then a *bump-bump.* Louder now. Particles of dirt fell onto his face from above, his heart nearly stopping as an object tumbled heavily onto his chest. Claws dug painfully into his fur as they scrabbled for traction.

Peatatoo!

He couldn't hear Peatatoo's response, but the squirrel leaped off Irusan's body and made a beeline for the stone in the corner, chittering softly as he prattled away to himself.

If only I could send a message with him, thought Irusan, but he knew that would be impossible. The squirrel had one thing on his mind, and that was to retrieve the Djinn stone and take it back to his nest or to Yorli.

Well, at least I may yet survive if the stone is removed. He was weak, but given enough time, he could regenerate enough of his strength to stand up. Peatatoo nuzzled the stone, picked it up, and stuffed it into his cheek. Without a farewell glance—although he may have thanked Irusan who had no way of knowing that for sure—he launched himself back onto Irusan's prone form, and with a final leap, shot back up into the air vent.

The stone will not hurt him, Irusan thought. *It is only people like myself, Anwyn, and the six healers who it may hurt, those with their higher abilities turned on. Peatatoo's abilities are too low in frequency to be picked up by the stone and neutralized. That is why Grayfell kept it in the lead box. It most likely would have hurt his abilities, too.*

He closed his eyes. Perhaps if he slept his body would regenerate faster. But it wasn't for himself that he wanted to sleep. He wanted to forget what had happened to Anwyn and Bean, what terrible things they might still be facing, and his own dereliction of duty. A tear rolled down his furry cheek, and he didn't have the strength to wipe it away.

Would he die here? It was likely. Without the sun's energy, he could not replenish himself. He hoped that death, when it came, would be quick, but for his kind, dying from a lack of energetic sustenance would be a slow death. No one would think to look for him in this forgotten room, and Grayfell had known that. Even if someone found him and his body regenerated, his higher abilities would not.

For that, he needed another crystal, one from his own dimension.

Something startled him awake. He blinked. *Where am I?* He remembered and despair flooded back into his consciousness. And then he heard it again. It had come from the other side of the door. Someone—or something—was out there. A bolt drew back and he heard the rattle of a padlock and chain. He sat up in a defensive crouch, his fists balled. Whatever was on the other side of the door, it was no squirrel.

The door creaked open, a sliver of light falling onto the stone floor, and Irusan blinked. There was no one there. The door closed again. A spark flashed in the inky blackness, and a lit candle hovered unsupported in the air. He rubbed his eyes, and his heart sank as a cloak appeared. Under it was the now-recognizable figure of Grayfell.

An interminable silence passed between them, and then, in a low voice, Grayfell finally spoke. "I see you have either lost your telepathic abilities, or you're ignoring my questions. Why are you looking at me in that way, as if you would like to kill me?"

Irusan pointed to his head and shook it angrily. He felt too weak to rush Grayfell, but he made the only sound he could with his non-human mouth, a mewling that didn't come close to expressing how he really felt. *Why was Grayfell here again? Had he reconsidered his past actions? Where was the lead box? Wasn't he afraid the stone would—*

Irusan gasped. Of course! Before Grayfell locked him in here the stone was in a lead box. There wasn't any way he could have known the stone was no longer there. It wasn't Grayfell who'd locked him in here with the Djinn stone, it had been a shape-shifter. Irusan shook his head and tried to stand up, but he stumbled back onto his knees again.

Grayfell held out his hand. "What on earth has happened to you?"

Irusan shook his head again.

"Come with me," said Grayfell as he tried his best to help Irusan rise. It wasn't easy, but at last Irusan shakily got up. Grayfell carefully wrapped his cloak around them both. Assisted by Grayfell, he wobbled out of the room.

At least I can still walk. He only wished he could communicate with Grayfell, too. He had never felt as helpless in his long life as he did now.

Grayfell led him noiselessly up the tunnel, into another one, and then another, past unsuspecting soldiers and other Eldred, until they reached another room that was on a higher level than the dungeon they'd just left. Grayfell swung the door open, and they entered the wizard's quarters.

"We can't stay here too long, but they've already searched this room, and I can only hope they won't be back too soon."

Irusan wondered who had searched Grayfell's room and why, but he was unable to ask.

A stone table, covered in flasks of various shapes, colors, and sizes, dominated the center of the room. A small window high up in the wall allowed some light to filter in. It was only enough light for Irusan to note that Grayfell lived modestly. A single chair beside a wooden bed with a straw mattress and thin blanket sat in one corner. One part of the room held a wood burning stove, a small table with plates and cups, and some shelves with foodstuffs. The Eldred seemed to subsist mostly on litch, berries, and wild fruits.

Grayfell pulled the chair toward the stone table. "Take the chair." It was not a request. Irusan, still trembling from weakness, sat, and Grayfell picked up a blank parchment from a nearby pile. Placing it in front of Irusan, he pushed a bottle of ink and a feather pen closer. "Write. Quickly."

Irusan began to write. It took up both sides of the parchment, but he wrote everything that had happened since he had last seen Grayfell. In the meantime, Grayfell busied himself on the other side of the table grinding herbs with a mortar and pestle, which he then placed into a pot of water on a nearby wood stove. Soon the water bubbled to a boil, and he dipped a cup into the pot and handed it to Irusan, who regarded it with suspicion.

"It won't kill you," said Grayfell. "The herbs will break through the blocks to the area in your head that is responsible for your telepathic abilities. It only lasts for a while, and then you'll return to your present state."

Irusan nodded. It was better than nothing. He choked down the potion in small gulps. He was not used to taking nutrients in through his mouth. He had a rudimentary digestive system, but it had not been used in a long time. He hoped he would not suffer any ill effects.

Grayfell read through the parchment as Irusan drank, before looking up. "Djinn stone, eh? So, that's why you looked as if you wanted to kill me when I came through the door!"

Yes—yes—can you hear me?

"I certainly can." His voice was still low. "I will communicate with you vocally, though. It's easier for me."

Irusan nodded and sank back into the chair in relief. *Did you know Anwyn and Bean are missing?*

"I couldn't contact Bean, and I realized that something bad had happened. I was getting ready to look for Bean when Yuki found me." Grayfell's face grew dark with anger. "She said the king wanted to see me, that it was important, something to do with Bean and Anwyn. She said they were missing, but she knew of their whereabouts."

Sounds familiar, said Irusan.

"Instead, she took me to the king's chamber, and then, with Goren present and backing her up, proceeded to accuse me of treason. I, Grayfell!" He shook his head in disbelief. "When King Sinhail asked how this could be, Goren said that you and I had conspired to overthrow the king using your special powers. Yuki said that she'd done some scrying herself and that Eblenor had appeared to her and told her what we were supposedly up to." Grayfell's jaw tightened, and he shook his head. "I know one thing: it was not Eblenor. He did not trust Yuki—or Goren—in the least. He would never appear to her. But the king trusts his daughter above anyone else in the kingdom. I stood no chance, and as they smiled in triumph, Sinhail ordered his guards to take me to the dungeons. Before leaving, though, he pronounced immediate sentence on me."

Let me guess, said Irusan. *Death.*

"The very next day!"

And, Irusan continued, *you escaped—obviously—by using your cloak of invisibility.*

"You got it right. They sometimes forget about that. It took me a while though to get out of those chains, open the jail door, and to make the guards less alert. I used every trick in the book."

How did you know where to find me? Irusan asked.

"I had no idea you were missing, too. I was looking for Bean—and Anwyn, too, of course," he added hastily. "I thought if they'd been kidnapped by Goren or Yuki, they'd hide them here. They don't know I had had spare keys to the dungeons made some time ago. I prepare for many eventualities."

It seems quite evident now that Iochodran has been using Yuki and Goren—perhaps even the king, but I doubt it. He's merely a tool.

"Exactly my opinion. Who do you think it was that was pretending to be me?"

No idea. Iochodran has many demonic servants, and any one of them could be responsible. Most of them can shape-shift. I should have known. It didn't feel like you. I take full responsibility for my negligence and complacency. If I'd been more on my guard, less distracted by fear, it would never have happened. Irusan placed his head in his hands. *Give me a moment.. I must contact my people so that I can get the crystal that will provide the full antidote to my condition.*

Grayfell nodded, and Irusan closed his eyes. After a short while, he opened them again. *I'm not able to reach them. It seems that my telepathic abilities are no longer where they used to be. For now, at least, I am grounded and out of communication with those who can best help.*

"I'm not surprised. The potion does not work long-range, and only in one dimension," Grayfell admitted. "So, what can we do to find Bean and Anwyn?"

I have a plan.

Grayfell's jaw sagged as Irusan laid it all out for him in detail. All he could do was shake his head as Irusan spoke.

30.

The Battle Begins

Anwyn and Bean both gasped as Bean exclaimed, "Yuki!"
She stood in front of them, still recognizable as the princess, but now overlaid with Askoroth's form. Reptilian, slit-pupiled eyes surveyed the scene. "You all seem ready to begin without me." A forked tongue flicked out from between scaly lips.

"So, you picked that one." Glahivar looked pleased. "Good choice. But there wasn't any need to wait for you. You're not going anywhere. I'm sending this one," she nodded toward Hora, "and the two humans." She paused, then asked, "Did you get rid of the cat-man?"

"Oh yes. He won't bother us any more, nor will Grayfell. In fact, the cat-man should be dead by now—or at least mostly dead—and Grayfell will be dead by morning." Yuki's smile sent chills into Anwyn. Bean tightened his grip on her arm, but Anwyn felt his hand shaking.

"Good. We can continue then."

"Oh, wait." Yuki-Askoroth looked at the pendant Hora held. "On second thought, I will take that. My Eldred vessel should go. She's definitely the better choice."

Glahivar growled and Hora drew back, teeth bared in a snarl, but Yuki, as fast as a striking cobra, lunged toward the pendant and yanked at it. The chain broke with a snap, silver links spilling to the rocky floor, but Glahivar had moved quickly as well. Her claw shot out and grasped the pendant before Yuki could get a solid grasp on it.

Yuki pulled on one end of the chain, while Glahivar clutched the silver filigree with the stone set into it. With her other, clawed arm, she slashed at Yuki's neck. A spurt of blood erupted, but the gaping wound healed over magically.

"You are my assistant!" shrieked Glahivar. "You will do as I tell you!"

"Not anymore," Yuki screeched back. "Your time is up, Glahivar. I am your equal, if not your better, in every sense, and once I have the knowledge in this stone, you will not even be a memory. I'll wipe out every thought of you everywhere."

Instead of the beautiful woman she had once been, Yuki now appeared mostly reptilian. Her fangs dripped venom, her flawless skin turned scaly, her limbs rippled with serpentine muscles. She moved like a sidewinder, her body whipping back and forth, as she and Glahivar fought over the pendant. A liquid stream shot out from a large gland under her tongue, hitting Glahivar in one of her eight eyes. She howled, her eye sizzling and clouding over as if eaten by an acid.

Glahivar was not without her own assets, though. She raised a clawed hand and a bolt of lightning shot out, hitting Yuki squarely in the chest, but the gaping, black hole in the center of Yuki's chest did nothing to stop her. Instead, she laughed. "My heart is no longer there, you fool."

"My mistake," Glahivar snarled back. She raised her claw again, but Yuki dodged the next one easily. Hora had now let go of Anwyn. His only thought was to save himself. He pulled up his merkaba and disappeared.

"Come on, Anwyn," whispered Bean. "Let's go."

"Where's the entrance to this place?" Anwyn whispered back.

"I don't know, but we need to go—anywhere." They fled, down the long hall lined with granite pillars into the darkness beyond.

As they ran down the dark hall, their footsteps echoing far too loudly, they looked back but no one followed. The chamber's end appeared, dark and unbroken, in front of them. "Where's the door?" Anwyn's whisper echoed in the empty space much too loudly.

Bean's silver eyes swept the darkness. He pulled on Anwyn, and pointed to their right. "There's a door down there. We are inside the Golden Tip, the old home of the Elluin. I recognize it from Grayfell's description. If it's designed in the same way as Unala, then there should be a door. It will lead to the kitchen, and there is a back door—" He broke off as Anwyn gave a tiny squeal. She pointed in the direction they had just come.

Hag-wraiths! The dark shadows flitted down the long hall, cackling and screeching as they caught sight of the two escapees. They ran in the direction that Bean had pointed out. Yes, there it was: a dark opening that could have been a door, but before they came even close to it, the hag-wraiths overtook them. They gripped each of them around the waist in a tentacle and soared into the sooty blackness of the upper reaches of the cavernous hall

They swooped, weaving in and out of the pillars like children playing a game. Only, thought Anwyn, this game wasn't much fun. The hag-wraith holding her threw her in the direction of another hag-wraith, who then let go of Bean to snatch Anwyn. Bean dropped, arms and legs flailing, but just before hitting the hard, stone floor, he was snatched up by yet another hag-wraith. It went on and on, a hellish game of catch, until they reached the central area surrounded by pillars where Glahivar, in her spider form, waited.

She had not fared well in the battle. Her body was covered in oozing acid burns, and one eye now a gaping hole. There was no sign of Yuki, only a black slick of ichor on the stone floor that oozed toward a gaping pit a short distance away. She snorted in triumph and held up the remains of the pendant. It was missing more links in its fine chain, but she snapped her claw and they watched, wide-eyed, as the chain become whole again.

"Do you really think you can escape me so easily?" She waved the other claw over her eye. The hole disappeared, and in its place another multifaceted insect eye appeared. She waved the claw again over each of her wounds, and Anwyn and Bean watched as they, too, healed in an instant.

Once she was done, Glahivar snarled. "Askoroth is dead. I threw him down there." She pointed to the hole in the floor. And if either of you make another attempt at an escape, you'll end up down there, too. It's a very deep hole. You'll never climb out of it."

She looked around. "What happened to Hora?" she asked her hag-wraiths.

"He's most likely back in Galon, mistress."

"Go get him. We'll wait here."

"Can we take these two? We were having such fun—"

"No! Now go!"

With disappointed whines, they disappeared.

"Only a small delay, but as soon as they get back with Hora, we'll continue where we left off." Glahivar opened her mandibles wide as she pulled Bean toward her. "I'll keep him very close, my dear," she said to Anwyn, "to ensure you don't try to escape again."

31.

The Six Healers, Mu'A

"It's been too long," Tegan said.

The six healers had gathered in Jarah and Tegan's quarters in Mu'A.

"You are correct," Tristan agreed. "Wasn't the last update we received from Irusan over a day ago?"

"He'd said he had located the pendant—the stone that might contain Anwyn's consciousness," Jarah said, his posture uncharacteristically hunched, tapping his fingers on a tabletop.

"One would think that by now there would have been results, one way or another," Adain's tilted head and narrowed eyes betrayed his own confusion. "Do you want me to go check? I can fly there in a moment, just to see."

Djana shook her head. "Adain, you're needed here. You're the metal working expert, and we're in a critical stage of boat frame construction. If you go and something happened to you, it would take too much time to recover."

Adain shrugged, but nodded. His experience as the blacksmith's son in Meadowfield had come in handy here in Mu'A.

"Well, that settles it," said Jarah. "I must go. She's my daughter."

"She's my daughter, too, in case you forgot." Tegan's mouth was set into a familiar, tight line.

Jarah nodded. His wife was intractable when it came to their children. "My apologies. I did not intend to leave you out." He reached for her hand, lacing his fingers through hers.

Jarah continued. "Djana, you take over my duties here. Tegan and I probably won't be gone long."

Djana rose. "I'm agreeable, but let us know what's happening."

"We are all in the midst of important operations here," Jarah said. "We don't know how much time we have before the island disappears completely."

"We've already lost portions of the island," said Kex in a small voice, almost to herself.

"I'm sure we'll be back very soon," Jarah said. "They are probably in the thick of negotiations with the Eldred, and Irusan simply forgot to keep us informed."

"I have my doubts about that," Tegan answered. "I've not been able to reach Irusan at all. That is unusual. I wish Anwyn…"

Her voice trailed off, and Djana spoke quickly, before the tears began. "He may have returned briefly to his other-dimensional home. That makes it impossible for us to communicate with him."

"Yes, but why not tell us?" Tegan persisted. "I have a bad feeling about this."

They all just looked at each other. They trusted Tegan's instincts, but Jarah's lips tightened. "You worry too much. Anwyn's fine. She's in good hands now with Irusan. You will see that for yourself."

Tegan sighed. She still had a lot of work to do: goats, dogs, cats—they didn't take easily to transportation, but her daughter was more important. She wrapped her arms around her body and shivered. Why did she have such a bad feeling?

32.

The Dwellers

They made their way down the mountain as the evening sun sank to the west, moving as fast as Irusan's still shaky legs would allow. He felt better now, but he wished he had a functioning merkaba. The first part of their plan was to go to Yorli's cave and enlist her help. Grayfell carried a flask filled with the herbal tea.

"The effects will last a day or so, but we'll be needing more," he had said to Irusan before leaving his quarters in the mountain. "I use it regularly, too."

Irusan shook his head in sorrow. Grayfell had been correct: his telepathy was still rather limited, confined to nearby areas. He had tried to reach the six in Mu'A and Yorli, but there had been no response. Grayfell tried as well, but he, too, was limited in range.

"It's the tea," he explained. "It only allows one to telepath a short distance. It was always enough for me to reach Bean in his tree home, so I've never felt the need to explore stronger remedies."

I wouldn't advise it as a long-term solution, anyway, said Irusan. *Potions that force open the chakras are dangerous. If the chakras do not open on their own, forcing the seals will create more problems than we have solutions for. The Djinn stone did the opposite. It forced my seals closed, amongst other things. Once we have found Bean and Anwyn and life is back to normal, you can be taught how to expand your abilities in a more natural and healthy way.*

Grayfell looked thoughtful. "That is always what Eblenor told me, but as a young Eldred, I wanted the quick solutions, so I became dependent upon the potions for results. We Eldreds used to have the same abilities as you. It's in our history scrolls, but over the ages, we always preferred the shortcuts, and finally we lost our abilities completely."

That's the story of the human and non-human races, said Irusan, making a face. *I am aware of the history of the Elluin. We worked together many times on creating a better society here on Ialana, but over time the Eldred forgot about us and were no longer able to communicate with us. But guess who was always still able to communicate with you?* He looked searchingly at Grayfell, hoping he would see some understanding in his eyes. He was not disappointed.

"Iochodran, of course. It too was what Eblenor warned me about. The scrying, the opening of spirit portals, the communication with the so-called dead—all pathways to Iochodran—they have influenced us all at some time or another. I still suspect Yuki and Goren of using these methods from time to time. They want not only my job, but King Sinhail's as well."

They also want an advantage over you. Both are in a race to the bottom, to a fast devolution. Iochodran doesn't give away anything for nothing—there's always a price to pay, and they don't tell you up front what it is.

Grayfell grunted. "I was a hair's breadth myself away from that. I am just lucky it was someone else's body they chose."

They walked through the forest for some time, each with their own thoughts.

It's getting foggy, Irusan finally noted. *I hope we can find the pathway.*

As they rounded a bend, a dark shape emerged from the shadows, and startled, they both jumped. Grayfell pulled his cloak up and disappeared.

Yorli! Irusan puffed his breath out. *How did you—*

147

Peatatoo told me he saw you in Ulovia, she said. *I became frightened when I was not able to reach you. I told him to watch the entrance to see if you came out. He thought you were asleep, and that it was nice of you to leave a gift for him. He is very pleased with the gift.*

What did he do with it? Irusan asked.

He is here, with it— Yorli began to say, but Irusan jumped back.

Don't let him near me with that crystal!

Yorli commanded Peatatoo, who chittered down at them from the trees, to stay at a safe distance. He still carried the crystal, Yorli said, and he refused to part with it.

Will it hurt us, too? she asked.

No, only me, said Irusan. He thought a bit. *Perhaps Grayfell, too.*

Grayfell reappeared next to them, and this time it was Yorli who jumped. *What kind of Eldred are you that you can disappear and reappear? Are you a devil?*

Grayfell looked at her skeptically, but did not answer her, turning instead to Irusan. "So this is the Dweller you told me about? Are you quite sure she's harmless?"

Both of you, stop being so over-dramatic, Irusan said, his cat-mouth smiling. *Yorli, Grayfell has some abilities, but he's not a devil. I'll tell you what has been going on, and yes, Grayfell, she is quite harmless to us.* He paused. *But not so much if you were a frog, so don't shape-shift.*

"As I told you before, I'm no shape-shifter." Grayfell's tone was not amused. "But why does the stone not affect her telepathic abilities?"

She and the squirrel are immune to it. It was only designed for larger threats, such as myself, you, and any human with abilities. We are lucky that Iochodran did not deem it important to code it for animals or animal-like species. Even though I am a cat-man, they probably made it specifically for me. He looked at Grayfell with a smile. *It is important we keep it with us, but at a safe distance.*

"Why," Grayfell asked, "if it's so dangerous?"

Because it will be dangerous to them, too. That's why they kept it in a lead box.

"Oh." Grayfell nodded as understanding dawned.

Irusan explained to Yorli as they walked what the Djinn stone was and what it did, then told her where they were going and what had transpired since their last meeting.

We must first visit my people, she said. *As I already told you, Irusan, I am not in good standing with my tribe. They banished me, but while we walked, I contacted them again for the first time in many years. They were not pleased to speak with me, but perhaps if you go with me to see the matriarch of my clan, they will allow us to speak.*

Then we must go, said Irusan, *but Yorli, are you able to telepath over extremely long distances? My friends in Mu'A—I must reach them.*

Yorli shook her head. *I don't think so, but I'll try. What are their names?*

Irusan told her, and gave her the approximate direction she needed to send her thoughts in. She sat down and closed her eyes, frowning in concentration. They waited, but after a while she shook her head and stood up. *I don't think I was able to get through. My range is probably confined to Unala. I've never had the need to extend it.*

If you received no answer, then I suppose you're right, said Irusan. *At least we tried.*

They set off through the hills on a path that only Yorli and Peatatoo seemed to know. Peatatoo flew from limb to limb, staying way ahead of them as he *tch-tch'd* in impatience. Sometimes he took off on a tangent when a tasty morsel caught his eye: a scarlet glimpse of a wild strawberry; a just-ripened blackberry hanging temptingly from a bush; or the tender, furled frond of a fiddlehead fern.

Night fell quickly, but along with the darkness, a dense fog closed in around them. Yorli stopped, sniffed, and turned off the small path. They scrambled awkwardly behind her, up a steep hillside, through scratchy underbrush, brushing away invisible spider webs and climbing over fallen logs. Yorli's enormous bulk appeared as a dim, smoky shape ahead, her soft snorts answered by quick chits from Peatatoo far to their rear. The night only seemed to get colder, darker, and wetter as a relentless drizzle moved in, but still she clambered effortlessly up the forested hillside as if following an invisible trail.

After what felt like hours, she stopped. *I hear them.* She pointed to their left, and they could just make out a narrow, rocky track. The stones were slippery, and Irusan and Grayfell struggled to keep their footing, but Yorli seemed as sure-footed as a mountain goat, her large bulk leading the way.

She put her hand out. *Stop!* she commanded. She crouched down, and they did the same. To Irusan's surprise, she picked up a nearby large, dead tree limb, and hefting it in her massive arms, she reared up and whacked a nearby tree trunk. The earsplitting crack echoed through the forest and over the hills. They waited, and soon an answering crack came from their far right. Her head lifted, and she howled—a spine-tingling howl that seemed to go on and on. Another howl in response, and then another.

Yorli nodded. *They will allow us into their territory. Follow me.* She looked back. *Peatatoo, not you. They will eat you. You stay here. Wait for us.*

Peatatoo chittered softly from a faraway tree. He didn't like it, but he always obeyed Yorli.

They followed Yorli again, the path upward becoming steeper now and even more slippery. Irusan clambered carefully behind her in his cat-like way, but not for the first time he wished he could have made this trip using his merkaba.

An enormous, dark shape loomed out of the fog in front of them, eyes glowing like fiery embers, then another, and yet another. They were surrounded.

You will not be harmed, said Yorli. *These are my people, and they now give you permission to speak with them in our thought-tongue.*

One of them stepped forward. *I am Negu. I am the matriarch of this clan.* She turned to Yorli. *Why are you back, oh daughter, and why do you bring this...creature and this Eldred, here?*

Her thoughts implied puzzlement regarding his species, Irusan thought to himself, and he couldn't blame her.

Yorli knelt in supplication. *My mother, Negu. I honor you. I respect you. I will never bring anyone here who will harm our clan. But as you have noted, the white furred one is different. He is indeed an unusual being, not from here, but from another place he calls Agra-Tan. It is a long story, my beloved mother, and he has a problem that I feel we may assist him with.*

Irusan stepped forward. *My name is Irusan—*

Negu gave a low growl and glared at Yorli. Her eyes looked redder than before. *You have placed our clan in jeopardy, Yorli. Not only are you an abomination to us, you continually disobey our laws. In other clans, like those to the south, you would be killed. But we are not a murderous clan, we only kill when it is necessary—or for food.*

Negu glared again, but this time at Irusan, before she continued. *You think you know where our clan home is, but this is not our home. It is merely an agreed upon meeting place. So tell me, why should we help you?*

Irusan felt wet, tired, and cold. He hadn't thought this would be easy, but he was not used to physical discomfort. He looked at Negu. *As your daughter said, you are in no danger from us. It is a cold night. Is there a sheltered spot nearby where we may discuss our request over a warm fire?*

We have seen the fires of the Eldred before. We do not make them ourselves, though, said Negu, uncertain.

We will take care of it, Irusan promised.

Negu turned, pointed to a high outcropping above them, barely visible in the misty rain, and the other dark shapes turned with her. *Come, it will be dryer inside the cave.*

They followed, Yorli first, then Irusan, with Grayfell bringing up the rear, his cloak at the ready.

33.

Negu

The Dwellers led them to a dark entrance, much like the one in Yorli's cave, only bigger. They quickly gathered dry twigs, leaves, and a few small branches that were strewn on the cave floor just inside the entrance. It was as dark as a soot barrel inside the cave, but Irusan could see well enough with his cat's eyes and Grayfell's silvery night vision allowed them to make good progress into the depths of the cave. The Dwellers stopped, and they found themselves standing in a large cavern on a flat rock, deep in the interior. After they'd arranged their sticks and leaves into a combustible pile, Grayfell produced a flint from his pants pocket. There was a spark, then another, and after some blowing, a flame licked greedily at the pyre.

Negu and Yorli sat close to the fire with Irusan and Grayfell, but the other clan members gathered in the rear of the cave, as far away from the flames as they could get.

Negu did not waste any time with niceties.

What do you want from us? What could Dwellers possibly do to help

Eldred or humans? She punctuated each of her sentences with a small growl. Her intent was clear: do not attempt to deceive us, tread carefully.

Irusan told her what he knew about Mu'A and the events of the past five days. Grayfell's eyes opened wide as Irusan's story unfolded in far more detail than he'd told anyone in Ulovia, including himself. Irusan only stopped once, to ask Grayfell for his flask. He took a few swigs of the potion, handed the flask back, then continued.

Negu or one of the other Dwellers interrupted a few times to ask questions if they didn't understand something. Why would an island disappear? Or a flying human girl? That one produced some disbelieving grunts and head shakes, but Irusan forged ahead and, with Yorli's occasional interjections explained as best as he could.

Grayfell remained silent, a thoughtful look on his face. Irusan wondered, in the back of his mind, if he'd lost Grayfell's trust. But then he told himself that Grayfell had never trusted him in the first place.

There was a long pause as the Dwellers digested the information.

Where is this squirrel, Peatatoo? Negu finally asked, licking her lips. *Does he still have this Djinn stone?*

Yes, said Yorli. *He is far away from here, though. The Djinn stone is not good for Irusan and Grayfell.*

Negu spoke for a while with her clan in grunts and squeals, whistles and soft calls. Yorli remained quiet, but she listened carefully, translating in her thought-speak whenever necessary.

*Nara says that yesterday she and Enath saw—when the sun was over there—*Yorli pointed to the east—*a strange darkness in the sky.* She made a motion with her hands over her head like bird's wings.

Taro says it was not good energy, but it did not stop here. It flew, instead, to the big mountain. She pointed to the north.

Grayfell's head lifted sharply. Irusan looked at him, and he nodded. *Could be the Golden Tip, a large mountain and the old home of the Eldred that is north of here.*

Negu then remained silent. She closed her eyes, and the clan kept silent, too. Irusan, to show respect, did not attempt to intercept her communication with whoever or whatever she was talking to. He hoped Grayfell would do the same.

After a while, Negu lifted her head, opening her eyes. Her guttural grunts to her clan produced a startled reaction, and even Yorli gave a slight gasp.

Mother—Negu—says she has consulted with the White Dwellers. Noticing Irusan and Grayfell's puzzlement, she explained. *The clan is not happy. The White Dwellers are bad. Very bad. We name them "White Dwellers" because they are white, like me, but large. Very large.*

Where exactly are the White Dwellers? Irusan wanted to be certain he and Grayfell had the correct mountain.

Negu answered. *The White Dwellers live in the big mountain*—she gestured northward—*where the sun god lives. It is a good omen when the sun god covers its peak with gold.*

Grayfell nodded. "It sounds like the Golden Tip to me. I've heard stories—legends—that it is made of pure gold and has magical powers. It's the largest mountain in the New Mountain Range. It was once the home of the Eldred, many generations ago."

You must explain that to me someday, Irusan said. *I have seen it from afar, but when I saw it abandoned, I thought you had all left and gone to your dimension of origin. Instead, here you are.*

Negu continued. *The White Dwellers do not know if the devil birds, what you call "hag-wraiths," went into the mountain or if they flew over. The big mountain is sacred. Our ancestors worshipped the sun-mountain, as do we. It is the home of the sky-sun gods. We do not go there—the mountain is taboo. But the White Dwellers are not afraid of spirits or of sun gods. The White Dwellers are the guardians of the mountain. They will kill all who go there.*

Irusan felt the hair on his arms stand up, and he glanced at Grayfell.

You stay here, said Negu. *We go, come back in morning. We'll talk again to White Dwellers, with proper ceremonial respect, and ask for safe passage for you to go.*

Irusan had only one request as Negu stood up to leave. *Ask the White Dwellers if they would look for a human woman and an Eldred male anywhere near the mountain. Their safety and wellbeing is of great importance to us.*

Without a further word, one way or another, Negu and the clan filed out of the cave, leaving the three sitting by the fire. Yorli stood up, too.

I must check on Peatatoo. I do not trust my clan not to eat him, and Peatatoo is reckless. He will be looking for me.

We may as well try to get some sleep, Irusan said. *I have a feeling it will be a long day tomorrow.*

As they stretched out on the hard rock, Grayfell began to talk.

"Although it's visible on a good day from Ulovia, the Golden Tip is several days' journey on foot through dense forest. Lurking in that forest are Shadow Goblins, and most likely other, less friendly clans of Dwellers, such as the Screamers. Our chances of reaching the mountain alive seem unlikely, but we must try."

So why did the Eldred leave?

"It was long before my time. I've heard that the mines became depleted, but I think it was more than that." He paused. "That is the story we've been fed. Eblenor was perhaps the only one who knew the real story."

And what was that?

"You guessed earlier today, Irusan, after I told you that I used the potion to regain my telepathic abilities. The fact is, I never possessed any abilities. Eblenor did, though. He was one of the last real wizards. He knew the secrets of the Golden Tip, the secrets of the Elluin, the old Eldred. He told me some of it, but it was only after Bean was born that I fully understood."

What about Bean, Grayfell?

Grayfell sighed. "There's much more to him than meets the eye," he said in a soft voice. "I've never told anyone who he really is, and I'm not about to start. Sorry, Irusan. It must be that way. I can't risk it."

Irusan did not press. He lay back on the hard rock as Grayfell's snores reverberated around the cavern. His eyes remained wide open, his thoughts racing. Sleeping would be difficult.

34.

Lost

Hora was lost. He'd fled so fast from the mountain interior that he'd not had time to find his bearings. Glahivar had brought him here, and his conscious mind had known nothing of directions or even their destination. As he hovered over the shrouded mountain peaks in his merkaba, he could not locate the sun. All he knew was that it was growing darker, and if he did not get his bearings before the sun set, he would spend the night wandering aimlessly through thick fog.

Where are these mountains? Glahivar said they're in Unala, but where is Unala? Am I still in Ialana? All she told me was that it was located on the west coast of Ialana.

Why had he not asked more questions? These thoughts sped through his brain at lightning speed, but then he snapped his fingers. He could rise above the clouds. It scared him to do it on his own, but he must. Slowly, as the thought entered his mind, he began to rise. The fog around him grew even thicker until it became so dense he had no idea if he was going up, down, or sideways. His heart pounded faster. He hugged himself, closing his eyes tightly, and his lips trembled. *Heights!* He'd always hated them, he thought. There was nothing solid underfoot, only the thin shell of his merkaba. *And what in the name of Idris was a merkaba anyway?* It seemed to be an imaginary construct, something that could fail as soon as he lost focus.

Glahivar—oh why didn't she show me how to use this thing in more detail? Tentatively, he formed the thought again. *Rise above the cloud cover!* He carefully opened his eyes and parted his lips. He had broken out of the cloudbank just as the tip of the sun's disc dropped over the horizon. *Alright*, he thought, *I think I must go east*. He remembered Glahivar saying Unala was to the west. He hoped he was right.

He didn't look down. He willed his merkaba to move east. With a jerk, it took off like a shooting star, and he squinched his eyes tightly shut again. When he opened them, it was dark. He looked down into a vast black space with no end.

Now I'm in trouble, he thought. He looked up. Stars! He was getting somewhere. Unfortunately, though, he didn't know how to navigate by the stars. *I'm not a sailor, for Idris' sake!* A sliver of moon low on the western horizon did nothing to shed light on his location. He thought he saw something glinting below, so slowly and carefully, he lowered his merkaba. He did not wish to run into a tree. His heart seemed to stop beating as he imagined himself impaled on top of a tall pine, but he wondered if his merkaba would protect him from that. He wasn't sure. It felt as if he must be almost as high as the stars, as if he could reach out and touch them. *How high were stars, anyway?* His thoughts were interrupted as a shimmering shape rose above him, towering over his head. With a small yelp, he fled upward, just in time to see that his feet brushed the top of a large, cresting wave.

By the gods! He was over the ocean. How did he get here? Where was land? He couldn't see which way to go next. Everywhere he looked, he saw only darkness. Judging by the size of the waves, he must be far away from land in any direction. He let out his breath in a long, quavering sigh.

Glahivar tapped her claw impatiently. She had waited long enough in this dank hall, guarding Anwyn and Bean. There was no sign of Hora or her hag-wraiths. She was tired of holding her mandibles open, and her other claw, the one that still gripped Bean, felt stiff. With a heavy exhale, she dropped Bean, closed her aching mandibles, and shook her claw.

"Don't think you're free to run just because I've let you go," she said. "I can move faster than either of you."

She didn't think they would try another escape. Anwyn had hunched herself into a small space between the rock wall and a pillar. Bean fell onto the floor, rubbing his body where her claw had squeezed him. He had a look on his face that she was familiar with, one that indicated complete submission. He would not give her any more trouble, and the girl appeared catatonic.

Now where were her hag-wraiths? She tried to contact them, and they responded immediately.

Ladyship, we are at your mercy. We are unable to locate the sorcerer.

What! What do you mean? He's obviously in Galon—

She stopped. *Of course.* The fool had gotten himself lost. She had never bothered to show him how to get his bearings in his merkaba, and his knowledge of geography was as bad as that of most people in Ialana. He probably thought the earth was flat, for mercy's sake. She heaved a sigh of annoyance.

You get yourselves over here. I will go look for him.

In an instant, the hag-wraiths appeared, swooping joyously around the prone forms of Anwyn and Bean.

And don't play with them. They're not your toys. You can have the boy later, but I need the girl.

She turned to leave, then hesitated as she glanced at Anwyn then Bean. *I almost forgot. These humans will need food and water. Go get some, I want them alive for now.*

Pulling up her merkaba, she disappeared.

35.

The Screamers

*W*ake up, Grayfell!

Grayfell's snore turned into a snort and he sat up. The fire had died sometime during the night. Irusan poked at it with a stick, placing more small branches and twigs onto the coals, and it flared once more into life.

We need to move quickly. Negu called me out before sunrise. They are sleeping now, but Yorli is finding breakfast for you.

Grayfell was just about to ask Irusan why he was not eating, when he remembered the cat-man's food was sunlight. A warm ray slanted into the cave, and Irusan walked over to the entrance and lifted his face.

"Thank the Elluin," Grayfell observed. "It has stopped raining."

Yorli soon appeared with his breakfast of mountain berries, and the remains, the hindquarters, of a large, pheasant-like bird which she handed to him. Taking it, he retrieved an unburned stick from the fire and threaded the thigh and drumstick through it. He propped it at an angle over the hot coals.

159

He finished eating and they put out the fire, covering it with sand before leaving the cave.

"What did Negu say?" Grayfell asked. "Any luck in talking to the White Dwellers?"

Yes. They are expecting us, and they promise safe passage. They have not seen anything of Glahivar, hag-wraiths, or other creatures from Iochodran, but that does not mean that they aren't in the vicinity. They've been alerted now and said they'd contact Yorli if they have any news.

"Well, I suppose that's all we can hope for." Grayfell looked around. "Where is that squirrel?" He didn't care whether Peatatoo followed or not, he just knew that they must keep themselves at a distance from him. A *chik-chik* came from somewhere behind them. "Stay back, pea-brain, you've come much too close." Another angry *chik-chik-chik*, but Peatatoo dropped back.

Yorli moved fast, and it was all they could do to keep up, but they did not object. They had so little time, and the Golden Tip—he didn't want to think about it. It was too overwhelming. One step at a time…

As they walked, sometimes climbing on all fours and mostly in silence, Grayfell had a lot of time to think. Carefully shielding his thoughts, he wondered if he had done the right thing in not revealing Bean's secret to Irusan. Of course, Irusan had most likely guessed some of it, but not all. *Definitely not all.* He wondered how much the girl knew. They had been together a lot since Bean had found her, but he didn't think she was that intuitive or curious. She hadn't seemed too interested in finding out more.

They walked all day, only stopping to drink water from babbling mountain streams or to quickly eat handfuls of berries or mushrooms they gathered along the way. Irusan soaked up the sun without stopping, lifting his face to the yellow disc when the trees parted enough for its light to penetrate to the forest floor. He only needed a little, and he told them he very rarely drank water and did not sleep much. He wasn't sure, however, if this would change, since the Djinn stone had interfered with his metabolism. He grew physically tired more quickly, and he rested while they ate.

That evening they gathered wood for a fire while Yorli searched the forested hillside for food. She was a skilled gatherer, and she soon returned with more handfuls of mushrooms, berries, and wild fruits.

Grayfell looked relieved. Yorli's preferences for eating frogs, snakes, and small birds whole did nothing to whet his appetite.

Irusan only sat, staring into the fire with a distracted scowl on his face.

"How long do you think Mu'A has before it...goes?" Grayfell asked. He knew there was nothing he or Irusan could do, but he felt the need to make polite conversation.

I don't know, Irusan replied. *It may be gone already. Perhaps that's why I can't reach my friends there.*

"There's an old legend of the Elluin—the ancient Eldred gods," Grayfell said. "When you told us about Mu'A, it reminded me of it. The Elluin were our ancestors. They were wise and had great knowledge."

I know of them. They fell to earth many millennia ago.

"What do you mean—fell?" Grayfell was irritated. The word had such a sad and judgmental connotation to it, he thought.

It means that when a being of a certain dimension digresses from the natural order of things—Yorli's head lifted at these words, a spark of interest in her pink eyes, as Irusan continued, *their template is no longer able to sustain them in the higher dimension. Their frequency holding capacity falls, and they must come into a dimension where their template is able to—*

"But they returned," Grayfell interrupted. "They went back to their original dimension. Isn't that the same thing that is happening with Mu'A?"

Not at all. Mu'A did not "fall" due to incorrect choices that resulted in template distortion. It was part of an agreement to separate itself from its location in another dimension, one that vibrated at a different frequency to this one. The agreement to remain here would only be temporary until the refugees from Rhiannon could raise their own frequencies enough to match it, and then they would return, along with the island, to its original home. Since their evolution was interrupted by the invasion of the reptilians, this was the next best thing so that they could continue with their process.

"Alright," said Grayfell. "I see the difference. The Elluin dropped in frequency due to divergent free will choices that harmed their templates, but then built it back up again—"

To resonate with their original home. Yes. Irusan nodded. *But since free will involves choices, not all Elluin, and certainly not all Mu'Ans, will return to eternal life.*

Yorli looked thoughtful. *I think it's what happened to my people, except that we did not go anywhere. We just dropped in frequency over time. I can clearly see the difference between you, Irusan, and my people.*

Grayfell noted that she did not mention the Eldred. He didn't think it fair that she would put them on the same level as the animal-like Dwellers, but he bit his tongue. It wouldn't do to start an argument with their guide.

You have not yet evolved back to your original source, Yorli, Irusan agreed. *But that doesn't mean you can't. Your people were once the stewards, the guardians, of this planet. Something happened, and you began to diverge from the original intention, the worst example of that being the Screamers.*

It happened to the Elluin, who are now the Eldred. It happens to most races that enjoy free will. At some point, some will return to their original source, while others will devolve and must fight their way back or continue to devolve until there's nothing left of them—yet all return eventually to their Source, since there's nothing outside of Source.

"We had the schools of the Magi," Grayfell said. "They taught the old ways, the—" He stopped. A scream came from the forest, a chilling, high-pitched scream that went on and on, and a terrified chittering from the trees.

Yorli jumped up, fear on her face. *We must hide. Screamers!*

36.

Ardvale

Finn met Jarah and Tegan at the portal to Ardvale. "I'm not surprised to see you here. Has this something to do with Anwyn?"

"What do you know that we don't?" Jarah's voice betrayed his worry.

Finn led him to their meeting place, the stone bench where he took everyone when something serious was to be discussed. "Irusan was here, perhaps two days ago in your time. He said that Anwyn and her Eldred friend, Bean, were missing."

Jarah gasped. His worst fears had been realized. "What about Irusan? Is he—"

"I can't tell you. I did not hear from him again after that."

Jarah's face turned ashy and Tegan gave a small gasp. She gripped Finn's shoulder. "Why didn't you let us know?" she asked, a catch in her voice.

"Irusan did not think it necessary to worry you. He wanted to deal with it in his own way first. We both felt he could handle the situation. I did send my elementals out, though, to see what they could find. They were unable to locate your daughter and her friend, but Irusan is fine. He is, right now, in the New Mountains, just north of the Eldred City of Ulovia."

"What does that mean?" Jarah asked.

"I am not sure. I do not interfere in human affairs unless I'm asked."

"Well, now I am asking you." Jarah's voice was acerbic. "We will need your help. Those of us in Mu'A find ourselves unable to focus on the task at hand. We're becoming more and more distraught, more disorganized, thinking that something dreadful has happened to Anwyn, not to mention Irusan."

"It is unusual that you have not been able to reach Irusan, or he you," Finn responded. "He would know how worried you'd be if he didn't report in occasionally. How long has it been now?"

"More than a day and night, and all attempts to contact him have failed."

"I have not heard back from him, either. Have you been to Unala yet?"

"I first wanted to contact you. Tegan and I will go there now."

"I will send my air elementals with you. They will know exactly where he is, and they will guide you there."

Relieved, Jarah stood up. "We have no time to dilly-dally. Tegan, let's go."

Irusan's fur rose on his arms as the scream was answered by another scream, then another—all from different parts of the forest.

Yorli's jerky movements betrayed her panic, and her eyes darted around, trying to find the best direction for them to go, but there was no place to run.

We're surrounded! Irusan shouted his thoughts. He looked up. *Large trees, yes.*

Peatatoo chittered again. *Come up, sillies! Come up!*

Yorli, can the Screamers climb? Irusan asked.

I climb, perhaps they climb, too. They will smell us, though.

Grayfell said, "If we climb trees, we'll be trapped."

Another scream, this one even closer. Irusan did the only thing he could think of. He ripped a solid branch down from a nearby tree. *You run,* he pointed to Yorli and Grayfell. *I will keep them at bay.*

Grayfell shook his head, and Yorli stood her ground.

Irusan felt the anger rising in him. *If you don't go now, we'll all die, and then Anwyn and Bean will never be found. Go, now!*

After a moment's hesitation, Grayfell threw his cloak over his head, disappearing instantly, and Yorli, calling to Peatatoo to follow, moved into the forest. Irusan thought she headed back in the direction they had traveled that day. It seemed the best choice, since she would be more familiar with it than what was up ahead or to the left or right.

Irusan waited. The screams grew closer. The sun had set some time ago, and a sliver of moon above glinted silver through the trees. At least he'd be able to see what was coming for him, he thought, hefting the branch in readiness. He felt the cool, evening breeze on his face and wondered if he'd ever feel it again.

Were those eyes he saw? Reddish glints in the forest moved first one way, then another. The breeze grew stiffer, and leaves and pine needles rustled around him. He couldn't tell if the rustling was the Screamers who approached or if it was just the wind. The branches above him swayed as the wind picked up. The red glints paused. He counted ten pairs—a pack. The eye glints were as high off the ground as he was, so one on one, they'd be evenly matched. But ten? He didn't stand a chance. They continued to move in his direction.

His fur stirred in the strong gusts, and the trees thrashed and swayed. *How had this sudden tempest occurred?* he wondered. The sky was still clear. They were in the mountain foothills, though, where the weather could be unpredictable. His fear turned to hope, but would a mere storm drive away these beasts? Surely, they'd not fear even a strong gale.

They didn't. The first Screamer emerged from the thick brush, then another, and another. They did not remind him of Yorli at all. These creatures were bigger, with dark fur and eyes that glowed red or deep orange. Their fangs jutted whitely from heavy jaws that looked just big enough to crush his pelvis. They regarded him for a moment or two, as if calculating how much of a threat he'd be, before the first one charged, head down, toward him.

Irusan jumped as a white-hot phosphorescence flashed next to him, shooting directly at the onrushing beast. It screamed, and an odor of burning fur and flesh assailed his nostrils. The wind roared and howled now, and Irusan dropped his branch. He fell onto the ground and covered his head with his arms as dust and debris stung his exposed body. Thick tree limbs snapped like twigs around him, and a beast shrieked and gurgled nearby. He peeked out between his fingers. A flying limb had impaled one of the creatures through its enormous torso. There was another flash of lightning and a simultaneous crack of thunder that almost deafened him. Irusan closed his eyes.

Finn! Thank the universe! Finn's elementals had found him. At least, he hoped it was Finn's and not those from Iochodran. He smelled more burning, heard more screams, shrieks, and howls, then a welcome silence. The wind died down to a small whisper of a breeze, and carefully Irusan opened his eyes and stood up.

In front of him stood Jarah and Tegan.

How did you—?

"Know where you were?" Jarah finished. "Thanks to our old friends, the air elementals who love to roar, we found you with no problem."

Air elementals. A soft flurry of air eddied playfully around him. *I thank you, your arrival was timely*, he said with gratitude.

"But what happened to you, Irusan?" Tegan asked. She and Jarah were both puzzled. "Couldn't you pull up your merkaba and do exactly what we did? And why did you not contact us in Mu'A?"

I can communicate with you now only because you're close, Irusan responded. *But first, I must find my companions. They may still be in danger.*

Jarah seemed to listen. "The elementals say they're nearby. In fact, they're right here."

I cannot speak to the elementals anymore, Irusan said sadly. *Ardvale elementals vibrate at a different frequency to this reality. But what did you mean, "they're" still here?*

At that moment, Grayfell appeared from where he had been all along—behind a nearby tree.

I thought I told you to run, Irusan said.

"I don't follow orders well," Grayfell shook his head. "Always been a problem."

And neither does Yorli, apparently, Irusan commented as Yorli emerged, not too far behind Grayfell. Jarah's mouth fell open, and there was an intake of breath from Tegan as they caught sight of the enormous, white creature suddenly walking into their space.

Yorli said, *I can be stubborn, too.*

A *chik-chik* came from the trees, and Grayfell smiled. "I suppose the peanut brain is as stupid as we are." The squirrel responded with an angry *chik-chik-chik*, and all except for Jarah and Tegan laughed in relief. At least Peatatoo was still alive.

I never thought I'd be rescued by you, Jarah, Irusan said.

"It's usually the other way around but you have Tegan to thank for our timely arrival. She is the one who persuaded us to check on things. Now perhaps you'll bring us up to date on what has occurred, and who— or what—this is." He still gaped at Yorli.

They sat on the ground, and Irusan and Grayfell took turns sharing all that had happened so far with Jarah and Tegan.

Jarah shook his head in disbelief. "A Djinn stone? It must be the same as the stone Glahivar used on us once. It knocked out our merkabas, and we couldn't telepath, either!"

It's similar, only much stronger than the one used on you. Ardvale had the remedy for that one, but I would need a healing crystal from my own dimension to restore my template. If I'm not able to contact the Council of Twenty-Four soon, I could be permanently impaired, and I'd have to remain here until my unnatural death occurred before I could return in spirit to my home.

"I know we're not able to telepath on that high a frequency range," said Tegan.

"Not even Finn," Jarah interrupted.

"But is there anyone here who can?" Tegan finished.

Anwyn. Irusan shrugged. He looked at Jarah. *Have you tried to reach her?*

"Yes, while we were still in Mu'A, again while we were in Ardvale, and just as we arrived here, all with no success."

She is out of our range right now, too. Irusan almost added, *and we may never be able to contact her again if she's in Iochodran.* He decided against it, though. They were worried enough as it was. They all looked at each other.

"We must come up with another plan," said Grayfell.

Jarah looked at Irusan. "I'm sure he already has one."

Irusan stood up. He picked up a small stick nearby. *Yorli, show us where the White Dwellers live.* As Yorli spoke, he drew a map in the ground, much as the elemental in Ardvale had done. *Here is what we'll do. Jarah, ask the elementals to stand by. We'll need them again.*

37.

The Dragon

"Anwyn," Bean whispered, "I don't have my flask with me."

Anwyn looked up briefly, a flicker of annoyance in her eyes. "What flask?" She, too, was thirsty.

Bean's voice was tremulous. "The flask with my potion. If I don't take it every day, I'll die."

"You're sick?"

"Grayfell told me I was born with a condition, one that needs his potion to keep me well. I've taken it every day for as long as I can remember. I already feel weak, because I haven't taken it. It's still at home."

"Oh," was all Anwyn said, but she thought to herself, *What can I possibly do about that*? If Bean died, she would be all alone. She preferred not to think about it. Anyway, he appeared perfectly healthy. "We're both hungry and thirsty, Bean, that's why you feel weak."

Bean scowled at her, but thanks to Glahivar's order, the hag-wraiths sent out one of their company to find food. It reappeared some time later with a water skin filled with fresh water, a loaf of bread, and a pot of meaty stew. Bean wondered who out there had lost their meal to a hag-wraith, but they were grateful for the sustenance.

After they'd finished, Anwyn looked a little more alive, and she sat with Bean. They cast wary, sidelong glances at the hag-wraiths, who flitted around the pillars, keening and wailing.

"Perhaps all that wailing is how they communicate," Anwyn said.

"What are they?" Bean asked in a whisper.

"I don't know," Anwyn admitted. "I've never seen them before. At least, I don't remember ever seeing them before, but they seem to know me."

Bean sensed her fears, and he shared them. Where were Grayfell, and Irusan? He and Anwyn had both tried reaching them, but no one had responded. "Don't worry, Anwyn," he said. "It's not your fault. You did not cause this, and you are not responsible for me."

"I feel it is, Bean. I feel that somehow, something I did, started this whole thing. I can't remember what it is or what I did—Irusan never did tell me—but I feel it in my heart."

A hag-wraith flew over and chuckled. "Oh Anwyn, you are so right. It *is* all your fault. What happened to you? Wouldn't you like to know!" It shrieked with delight and did a somersault, but Anwyn wasn't looking at it. Instead, she and Bean's eyes widened as something, its scaly body nearly as tall as a pillar, rose behind the hag-wraith. It had emerged from the pit in the floor where Glahivar said she'd thrown Askoroth. Enormous wings flapped on its back, and slit-pupiled, orange eyes glared at them with a hideous light.

"A dragon!" Bean yelled.

"A dragon?" Anwyn asked. "What is that?"

"Grayfell has told me about them," Bean responded. "I'll tell you later."

The hag-wraiths at first did not seem to know what to do. Friend or foe? The dragon used this hesitation to direct a stream of fire at the wraith that had cavorted in front of Anwyn and Bean. It screamed, its tail on fire, and flew toward its companions who had gathered their wits and formed themselves into an attack formation.

Anwyn and Bean took shelter behind a pillar a short distance from the searing flames. The wraiths were preoccupied with the dragon, but one of them had noticed their absence and headed straight for the pillar where they hid. But the dragon reared up again, and with a large, clawed hand, swatted at the wraith. It screeched angrily, but it retreated. Another wraith attacked the dragon from the rear. Fireballs from its talons smacked into the dragon's armor-plated body and bounced off harmlessly. Wraiths flitted around the enormous hall, their screams and shrill cries echoing off the distant walls, shooting useless fireballs toward the dragon as it roared and spewed flame at them.

They watched as the wraiths scattered, their original cohesiveness in pieces, their howls confused and terrified.

"I think it's safe to run now," Bean said as he tugged her arm.

Anwyn shook her head and pulled back her arm. Bean gaped.

"I can't, Bean," she whispered. "Glahivar still has the pendant. If she has it, I must remain with it. If we allow her to take it back to Iochodran, it's only a matter of time before she finds a way to use it herself, or finds another human who can unlock the portal."

"So you would rather she use you to go through the portal with Hora when she finds him?"

"Please try to understand. I need to find out what is on the other side, but you don't. Run and don't stop, Bean, but I must stay."

"I don't think *you* understand," Bean hissed back at her. "I am not leaving you alone. Not in a million years."

Anwyn reached out and grasped his hand. "Well then, we'd better make a plan."

It *never fails*, Glahivar thought, as she adjusted her sensors to Hora's frequency. *Every single time I give them a job to do, I am the one who ends up completing it. Incompetents!* She sped out into the dark night and took her bearings. The mountains were cloud-covered but she rose easily above them and looked around, expanding her energy field as far as it would go. Nothing.

If Hora was anywhere within the range of her fields, she would sense him. She'd try Abena first, just as her hag-wraiths had done. She didn't trust those hag-wraiths at all. They probably missed him because he had another hideaway, one they didn't know about, but she would find him. Oh yes, she would.

She took her time flying over the continent to the southeast. She didn't want to overshoot him if he was still on his way. *The idiot had probably gotten himself lost.* She hadn't shown him how to navigate his merkaba properly. She hadn't felt it to be necessary since he wouldn't have been going anywhere without her guidance.

She soared over the New Mountains towards the Dalnoor Desert between Unala and the eastern half of Ialana. Sparsely inhabited and hostile to most life, it kept the humans of Ialana out of Unala. She sped over the arid plain, its vastness stretching from horizon to horizon, toward the Osgoi Range, the spine of Ialana that ran down its center. She was reminded of the days when she still had her beautiful raven body, when she'd fly these skies just for fun.

There was still no sign of Hora though as she soared over the mountains, cutting over the forested western land of Mannanon, then southwards into Galon itself, and down to the southern coast. *He must be in Abena. It's the only place he's familiar with.*

At last the lights of Abena, the capitol city of Galon, appeared as a warm glow on the horizon. Descending into the city, she started her search in the most obvious place, the keep on the cliffside where Ortzi, the Warlord of Galon, still held sway. *Someone ought to get rid of him*, she thought, *but it won't be Hora. If only I had a human body!* She chuckled to herself. But of course, she'd have a body, and soon—that of the real Anwyn, and with her knowledge and abilities she wouldn't be ruling only Galon but the whole continent, all the way to Mu'A.

Her fields still sensed nothing of Hora. She began a search pattern, expanding out in a grid all around the city, not forgetting to check every alehouse and tavern she found. His fondness for these places had become a part of her own memory. Still nothing. Her wraiths were correct, he was not in Abena. She ground her mandibles together in frustration.

This could take all night! It was anyone's guess where he was. She rested for a moment, thinking. If she had no idea how to navigate her merkaba from Unala, where could she possibly end up?

Her eight eyes gleamed and she clicked her mandibles. She would use either the sun or the stars to give her a sense of direction. Hora had probably left just as the sun was setting. He would know not to go west, so… he would go east! If he couldn't control his merkaba speed, it was possible that he'd overshoot Ialana by vast distances and end up over the ocean. With nothing to guide him, he could be wandering aimlessly, perhaps even in the wrong direction.

She sped northeast and in the blink of an eye, she was over the ocean. As she set up another grid pattern search, she pulled the pendant off one of her spines where she'd hung it for safekeeping. She gazed at it, her expression tender.

"Ah, my love. Soon all your secrets will be mine!" She allowed it to reflect the starlight, its small facets scintillating in the darkness. She hung it back tenderly onto a spine on one of her legs and hummed a tune as she searched. It took all night, and there was a red glow on the eastern horizon before finally she found him. He was almost to Afarre. His fire-fly merkaba spark bobbed hopefully in the direction of the thin sliver of land on the horizon. *Idiot!*

She descended upon him furiously. He squawked in terror as she gripped him by the throat and pushed herself into his body. There was no gentleness or subtlety in her maneuver, and he gasped in pain and shock as her enormous spider form squeezed into his smaller, human frame, using the unguarded fourth chakra rear opening. His eyes bulged and his face turned purple. She knew it could kill him, but at this point she was angry enough to take the chance. She would not give him another chance to escape her.

Wordlessly, Glahivar, in the choking, frothing body of Hora, headed back toward the still-dark western horizon.

She thrust one of Hora's fists up to the sky. She had the pendant, the human body she needed to access the portal, and the girl. With Hora's body, she could go into the portal and they would return, not only with the knowledge she so desired but also the beautiful body of the girl that would finally be hers. *Now*, she thought, *nothing can stand in my way.*

38.

Elemental Command

We must do it, Irusan said. *It's the only way.*

"But it could kill you," Jarah protested.

"So could the supper I ate this evening," Grayfell noted. "Irusan is right. We must do it."

"If only we could carry you," Tegan moaned. "And what about the squirrel? Are you going to take him, too?"

Of course. Yorli's voice was determined. *He wants to go, and I will protect him.*

"Let me talk to the air elementals first," Jarah said. "I must be sure."

"They seem confident enough," said Tegan.

I can do it, one of the elementals said in a whisper, but Jarah still felt the power of the words that whirled around his head, blowing his unruly red hair this way and that. *They may die, yes, but it is possible for me sometimes to keep them aloft for long distances. The other elementals will assist.*

It is words like that that cause my concern. Jarah used the elemental language they had learned in Ardvale, while Irusan and Grayfell waited patiently.

Look! I'll show you, the elemental insisted.

174

As it moved away from Jarah, a small funnel formed in midair. Tiny at first, it grew, until it was a long, gray finger that stretched upward to the sky. The bottom of the finger moved across the grass, and like a plow, made a small furrow in the earth. It reached the body of the dead Screamer who still had a bough emerging from its chest. The end of the finger lifted and widened, and like a mouth, it gently picked up the body then rose, moving with it over the trees.

Fine, Jarah said, *but can you do this over long distances?*

The elemental dropped the body, and they heard its thud as it hit the forest floor. *I can only try.*

Jarah and Tegan relayed the information to the others. They all looked at each other. Yorli shrugged. *I can only try, too. I will take Peatatoo. I'll keep him safe.*

Unfortunately, Irusan said, *we may still need him. Otherwise, I'd strongly suggest he go back to where it's safe.*

"Well then," said Jarah, "let's get on with it."

Jarah and Tegan intoned the mathematical formulas of elemental command once more. They needed—the air elemental needed—the cooperation of the earth, fire, and water elements to change the air temperature below and to bring cooling air from above. This would create the vortex.

As the tornado formed, its funnel glistened in the light of the moon. Irusan and Grayfell stood closely together while Yorli, cupping Peatatoo gently in her large hands, crouched on the ground near them, but far enough away so that the Djinn stone would not affect them. Irusan had already guessed at its radius of destruction. He felt weak when it came too close.

I suggest we embrace and don't let go, Irusan told Grayfell. *Remember, that doesn't mean we are now best friends.* He winked, but Grayfell's face had paled and beads of sweat appeared on his forehead. He stepped closer and they wrapped their arms around each other. The vortex gradually widened until it spanned the width of the large, open area of the hilltop. Jarah and Tegan were only fireflies now as they hovered far away from the forces of the elementals.

Irusan looked up. The mouth of the tornado directly above them began to descend. Grayfell, eyes closed, gripped him tighter. Irusan lowered his head and closed his eyes so that the flying dirt, grass, and debris would not damage them. He couldn't afford to lose any more of his senses, he thought, even the everyday ones.

It happened quickly. Before he could take a deep breath, his feet flew up, and the blood rushed to his head. Although they still embraced each other tightly, the force of the wind ripped at them and in an instant his grasp on Grayfell broke. With a cry, Grayfell fell away. *I can't worry about that now*, Irusan thought, as he wrapped his arms around his head. It was every man—or every shape-shifter, wizard, Dweller, and squirrel—for himself. He couldn't breathe. He tried to remember the mathematical equations of wind force and air temperatures so he could calculate how long it would be before the elemental was forced to drop them, but his brain would not function. His only thought now was to stay alive and aloft.

His ears roared and popped. He tumbled, head over heels, as he spun around the inner vortex. He wanted to open his eyes, but he dared not, so he kept them tightly shut.

This is not like flying in my merkaba, he thought. *I will never take that for granted again.* He wondered if he would even remain conscious during this horrific journey, and how would Yorli and Peatatoo fare if it was this rough for him? He couldn't imagine how it might affect the others. He'd hoped they'd all survive it, but he wasn't so sure that they would.

His body dipped, spun, twisted, and rose like a feather in a hurricane, and he felt the crackle of lightning around him. This was worse than anything he'd ever experienced before, except maybe for the Djinn stone. He hoped that the stone would not be lost on the way, and the squirrel along with it. If only he still had his functioning merkaba—but then, if he had, it would all be over by now and he wouldn't need the squirrel, Yorli, or Grayfell. Anwyn and Bean would be found, and perhaps they would have even figured out the secret of the pendant. But could-have-beens didn't help anyone. He had to deal with the reality of the situation, and it wasn't optimistic.

He felt a familiar weakness. Yorli and Peatatoo must be close. Something that had all the impact of a boulder smacked into him, and he cracked open his eyes for a moment to see Yorli spinning, tumbling away, but still cupping her hands.

Good. The squirrel and Yorli are still with us, and conscious.

It was too dark to see Grayfell, and he closed his eyes again. He wondered how long they'd been aloft. He wished he could see the ground, but that would mean risking his eyes. As with all tornadoes, there would be too much debris in the funnel to see anything below.

It felt like hours, but at last the roaring diminished and his body began to drop. He clenched his jaw so hard it hurt. He opened his eyes and the ground below, all too fast, rose to meet him. Another suck of air, his ears popped, and he lifted slightly, just clearing a sharp crag. Then—an open space below. He couldn't see what it was exactly, it was still too dark, but again the falling sensation, and before he could catch his breath, he plummeted, plunging with a heavy splash into icy, black water.

I hate cold water! he screamed to himself as he sank like a stone into the depths. *I must get out of here!*

Flailing with his strong arms and legs, he bobbed to the surface and gasped for air. He looked around, his body numb with cold and fear. It was still much too dark to see anything, but he could hear the roar of the tornado as it moved over the water. There was an enormous splash next to him, and Yorli surfaced.

Where is Peatatoo? he asked.

A frightened chitter and small splashes came out of the darkness.

I must go get him, Yorli said, as she swam smoothly toward the splashing.

Irusan could now wonder about Grayfell as he paddled in the direction of where he thought the shore might be. Did he make it? *Grayfell!* There was no response. He kept calling, but Grayfell did not respond. They seemed to be in a lake, probably a mountain lake judging by its bone-chilling temperature. He felt his feet touch a sandy bottom, and he stood up and waded onto the shore. The moon broke out of the clouds. He could still see the remnants of the tornado, but it was now dissipating. The elemental had discharged its load in the water.

"Irusan! Grayfell!" The voice of Jarah came from somewhere above. Jarah and then Tegan appeared, demanifesting their merkabas on the ground in front of him.

I can't find Grayfell, Irusan said, *but Yorli and Peatatoo are all right.*

"Thank heaven," said Tegan. "I can't believe how worried I was about that little rodent!"

Me, too, Irusan agreed, shaking the water out of his trembling arms and legs. *I've grown quite fond of him in the short time I've known him. We must find Grayfell.*

"I'll go look," said Jarah. "I think Peatatoo is not the only one you've grown fond of." He didn't wait for Irusan's response. He disappeared, reappearing in a trice. "He was out of your range, in the middle of the lake, and swimming to the far shore. I pointed him in the right direction, and he'll be here shortly."

I hope he's a good swimmer, Irusan said.

"He seems to be," Jarah responded. "Tegan and I found this mountain lake and thought it might be a better landing spot to dump you in rather than on the hard ground. Since we're in the mountains, there isn't much in the way of soft landings. It's all rock and ice."

Thanks a lot, he said, trying to keep the sarcasm out of his tone. *We need a fire. Do you think you could take care of that?*

"Of course," said Tegan. "I should have thought of it already." She flew off and returned with dry kindling and sticks she'd picked up on the lower slopes. With a snap, a flame emerged from her fingertips, and they soon had a blazing fire going on the lake shore.

Yorli and Peatatoo had also emerged from the lake, but they kept their distance while Yorli held the little squirrel in her arms, trying to warm him up.

Does he still have the Djinn stone? Irusan asked.

Yes, said Yorli. *He's a determined creature when it comes to pretty stones. Not even the big wind could make him lose it. It's still in his cheek.*

"Well, I see we're all alive," a wheezing voice panted out of the darkness. It was Grayfell. His teeth chattered as he removed his dripping cloak, hanging it over a rock to dry. "That was quite a ride." He hugged his shivering body tightly with his arms. "Irusan, as soon as you're back to yourself again, you must teach me this merkaba thing."

178

They talked as they sat around the fire, Jarah and Tegan bringing them up to date on the situation in Mu'A.

"So things are moving quickly," said Jarah. "We almost have the boats finished, and will load the animals, people, and supplies in a few days. Those who are remaining with the island have been quite generous with supplies. They feel that where they're going they won't need as much anymore."

They're right, said Irusan. *They, too, will adapt their bodies to pure sun energy, as I have with mine. It will still take some time, perhaps generations of genetic adaptation, but eventually they'll be successful. Their world is more advanced than this one, and food is not in short supply whether it be the sun's food or vegetable matter. They do not consume animals in that world.*

"I half wish I was going," said Tegan, "but that would mean leaving my mother and father, those I care for, here. Jarah is not willing to do that, either, and neither is Anwyn…" Her voice broke and she looked away.

Has anyone gone yet on the parts of the island that have already disappeared? Irusan asked.

Jarah shook his head. "They're all waiting to leave together. They all want to ensure those of us who are staying behind get off safely. But now we must return." He rose and stretched his limbs, yawning. "We'll be back in the morning. You need your sleep—even you, Irusan. It will be easier for us to search in the daylight, and we'll also bring some food for you."

"I'm curious to try food from Mu'A," said Grayfell. "It will be a change from litch, berries, and whatever Yorli can find."

"We'll bring food for her, too—and Peatatoo," said Tegan. "We looked over this area while you traveled in the not-so-tender arms of the air elemental. It seems safe enough. No Screamers or other creatures in sight, but don't wander far afield until we return. We'll guide you to the Golden Tip. It's not far from here."

Irusan and Grayfell nodded as Jarah and Tegan in their merkabas shot off into the distance. They stretched themselves out around the embers of the fire. *It will be a long, cold night*, thought Irusan. If the White Dwellers did not allow them into the Golden Tip, if they could not find Anwyn and Bean…his thoughts drifted off into the blackness of sleep.

39.

The Golden Tip

No one slept much, and long before dawn they'd all awoken. Jarah arrived before sunup, but this time with Tristan.

"We're taking turns," Jarah told them. "We're all needed in Mu'A, but some of us can be gone for short periods. I seem to be the least essential person on Mu'A right now. I am mainly a job coordinator, and sometimes I overestimate my importance." He smiled and winked. "Tristan's more suited for the search of the Golden Tip. He's an ex-soldier, and we may need his tracking skills."

True to their word, they'd brought food with them. Tristan handed a large bag to Yorli and one to Irusan and Grayfell. They hungrily attacked the boiled eggs, huge loaves of bread, cheese, and honey.

"There's little food in these mountains," said Grayfell, chewing noisily as he spoke. "It's one of the reasons the Eldred abandoned this place. The climate changed, bringing colder, drier weather, and we no longer had access to our normal food supplies."

Irusan filled the water skins brought by Tristan and Jarah with water from a burbling mountain stream that rushed through a boulder-strewn gap into the lake. As they ate, the sky grew lighter in the east. They could not yet see the sun's disc that remained hidden behind the towering peaks surrounding them on every side.

Awestruck, Yorli gazed up at them. *These are much bigger than our mountains to the south.*

According to the instructions your mother Negu gave me, said Irusan, *we must attempt contact with the White Dwellers, let them know we're here.*

They already know. Yorli, the whites of her eyes showing, gestured toward a cloud-covered mountain to their north. *I feel their presence.*

Yorli, frightened? Irusan hoped the White Dwellers weren't anything like the Screamers.

At that moment, the heavy cloudbank over the large mountain parted, and a ray of sun struck the peak on its eastern flank. They all stopped, mouths agape, as they stared at the sight in front of them. A golden pyramid gleamed atop a mountain so lofty that it seemed to reach to the heavens. Its sides hinted at a smooth and reflective surface, and to their eyes, it comprised a full third of the visible part of the mountain. Grayfell stood staring at it for a while. No one said anything, then Grayfell spoke, his voice soft and reverential.

"I've been told it's real gold, but I can't say for sure. No one was ever able to access it. When the Elluin left, they took their secrets with them."

Yorli sank to the ground. *Sun Gods come. They'll kill us! This is taboo. We should not be here.*

Calm down, Yorli, Irusan said. *Please feel free to remain here while we search. You are not obligated to come with us, but we'd like Peatatoo to stay at a distance in case we need him and the stone.*

Yorli shook her head and rose on her hind legs. *I am not a coward. I promised to go with you and to take care of Peatatoo.*

Peatatoo leapt down from a nearby rock and onto Yorli's shoulder. *I go, too! I take care of Mama.*

"We're all going," said Tristan. "Jarah and I will start looking at the base of the mountain, something like a cave or tunnel—anything that looks like an entrance. Do you remember, Grayfell, where the entrance is located?"

"I've never actually been here," Grayfell admitted. "My elders left many centuries before I was even born." Jarah and Tristan's glances were curious. "We Eldred are long-lived. I, for one, am three hundred years old, and I'm still a young Eldred."

Jarah gasped. "You don't look it," he said. "I thought you were perhaps thirty-something. Tristan and I will make a quick reconnaissance. We'll be back soon. Wait here."

They disappeared in their merkabas, and the group sat down to wait. It felt warmer with the sun on their backs. The dampness from the morning dew gradually evaporated from Irusan's fur and Grayfell's clothing. Yorli's fur seemed almost waterproof, Irusan thought. She was the only one who'd not experienced an uncomfortable night. He didn't know how Peatatoo fared, but he'd probably kept warm, snuggled with Yorli.

I do remember flying over that peak when I scouted this area some time ago, Irusan said. *I sensed something strange about it then and remembered the Elluin had constructed the pyramid and hollowed out the interior of the mountain. Unfortunately, I did not explore the interior. I now wish I had.*

"Eblenor said the interior was magnificent—much more impressive than Ulovia. Our city is but a shadow of this one, and of course, we don't have the golden pyramid."

How did the White Dwellers come to be the current guards of the mountain? Irusan asked.

"Eblenor told me that the Elluin returned after we abandoned the mountain and had appointed guardians to keep intruders out. I didn't know the guardians of the mountain were White Dwellers, though, and neither did he."

Hmm. It seems odd that they didn't ask their own descendants to guard it, Irusan commented, his face thoughtful.

"You were right before, Irusan." Grayfell's silver-blue eyes betrayed a recognition of a truth that could no longer be denied. "Our race had degenerated so much that whatever it was the Elluin had built here, whatever secrets may be hidden in that pyramid, had to be protected." His arms swept out. "You've seen our current state. We've descended into ignorance and greed, and we're not what we used to be. Eblenor remembered a time when we were still a great race, an advanced people who knew and understood universal laws—much like you."

I do remember being told that my people in my other-dimensional world had worked with the Elluin for a while.

They sat in silence, each with their own thoughts, and then Irusan lifted his gaze to Grayfell. *What really happened to Bean's mother?*

"She was murdered by Shadow Goblins," Grayfell said, "but I blamed Yuki. It would never have happened unless—"

Yorli interrupted him as she leapt to her feet, her eyes rolling wildly. *They're here!*

Who, Yorli? But Irusan already knew. He sensed them, too, as did Grayfell. Irusan was comforted by that. *I may yet have a few senses left.*

They appeared through the stony gap where the rushing stream spilled through on its way to the lake. The first one to appear was a colossal creature. It looked much like Yorli, its fur-covered body only a few shades darker than hers. It wore a wide, silver-studded belt around its waist, and it carried a broad-bladed knife as long as its arm. Those that followed in single file were not as large as the giant in front, but there seemed to be little difference between them and Yorli. Some wore leather belts or rawhide loincloths, and all carried weapons of some kind: knives, long sticks, or pointed javelins.

They rose, Grayfell reaching for his cloak, and Irusan motioned to him and Yorli to remain at the lakeshore while he began to walk slowly forward. As he approached the creatures, they stopped. He stopped, too, and the larger creature in front stepped forward again. They continued in this fashion, until Irusan and the creature were now only a pebble's throw from each other.

Greetings, Irusan began. He held up his hands and sat on the ground. He had no idea how these creatures would react. He hoped he was playing it right.

The large creature sat, too. Irusan breathed again. Its eyes regarded him curiously.

What are you, it asked, *and why are you here?*

Excellent, they were telepathic. *I am Irusan. I am an ambassador from another land. I seek two missing humans—young people—who have most likely been brought to this mountain. We are not here to harm you or the mountain.*

The creature stared at Yorli. *Why is one of our kind with you?*

She is not of your kind. She belongs to another clan, but was rejected because of her coloring.

The large Dweller regarded her thoughtfully for a while longer, then he turned his eyes back to Irusan. *I am Jangon. I am the chieftain of my clan. The penalty for entering this sacred ground is death. Do you still wish to proceed?*

We do, but we will do it only with your permission. We do not wish to disturb anything here. You may already have intruders within the mountain. They are demons from Iochodran, and they have two of our people.

The Dweller growled as Irusan mentioned Iochodran, as did the others behind him. *How did they get inside, unseen by us?*

They have great powers—shielding technology—and have probably put a shield around their location or presence that makes it difficult, if not impossible, to track them.

The Dweller nodded. *We've not had this problem before. It cannot continue, though. We will help you find your people, get rid of the intruders, and then we ask you to leave and never return.*

That is exactly what we wish for, too, Irusan agreed. *First, though, I must inform you we have two more of our own people scouting the area. You will meet them later.*

The Dweller Chieftain, Jangon, growled again. *They must leave.*

They have no plans to remain, Irusan said as they rose to their feet. *They are better equipped than we are to locate our children.* He turned and beckoned to the others. They had gathered what remained of the food, picked up the full water skins, and Grayfell—Yorli and Peatatoo falling behind as much as they dared—approached.

Anwyn and Bean, sheltered by a pillar, could only watch as the dragon made quick work of the hag-wraiths. It swatted each one down, pinning a writhing form under its talons. The dragon inhaled deeply as a stream of energy emerged from each hag-wraith into its open jaws. They continued to watch, horrified, as the dragon became even larger with each inhale, its wing span expanding until the tips stretched to the top of the cavernous hall. It folded them back with a boisterous rustle, its long, scaly tail lashing precariously close to the supporting pillars. When it had dispatched the last of the hag-wraiths—now no more than small piles of ash on the floor—it turned its gaze to Anwyn and Bean, who had by this time emerged from behind their pillar.

"*Ssssooo*, you didn't run, eh? I wonder why? I was fully prepared to chase you down, but you've saved me the trouble." The dragon laughed, its guffaws reverberating around the vast chamber. "Ah, but I see you don't have the pendant on you. Glahivar must have it. Speaking of Glahivar, where is she?"

Anwyn stepped forward. "She left to find Hora, and yes, she does have the pendant."

"Hmm. We are just going to have to wait for her to return."

"We were quite impressed with how she defeated you and threw you into the pit," Bean said.

"Oh, the runt speaks? I—or Yuki—thought you were mute. Never mind. As for her defeating me, do you really think that's what happened?" The dragon snorted and hot sparks flew out of his nostrils. "Allow me to brag a little." The dragon puffed up its chest. Its scales separated, revealing an iridescent membrane that held them together, before the dragon gave a smoky exhale, its chest flattening out once more. "I allowed it."

He stopped, and gazed at them expectantly.

"You allowed what?" Anwyn asked.

"I allowed her to defeat me."

Bean placed his hand over his mouth as if astonished by the revelation as the dragon continued.

"I needed the raw material of Yuki's body, along with the pure energy that supposedly 'destroyed' me, and what remained of my Iochodran form, to recreate this one. And, as you observed, I also incorporated the spirit and physical matter of the hag-wraiths. Glahivar, and her minion, Hora, will make a generous contribution as well, once they return." Again he puffed his chest out proudly and strutted a little closer, bringing his enormous head down to their level. "I present to you, Askoroth, Lord of the Dragons."

"You are a splendid specimen, Askoroth," Bean said. "Eldred wizards have been trying for generations to do exactly what you have just done."

"What would you know about that?" Askoroth asked, suspicion in his serving-platter-sized eyes. "I still have Yuki's memories, and she had no knowledge of you being versed in the ways of wizards."

"No, but my father, Grayfell, does, and he will be here to rescue us soon."

Anwyn jerked her head around, her eyes widening. "Grayfell is your father?" *Of course*, she thought to herself. *They had the same name: Ironweed.*

Bean only nodded.

"Don't you understand?" Askoroth asked. "You've already been told Grayfell is dead, along with the shape-shifter. There won't be any rescue. Do you think the king will send his soldiers? He's only concerned with his next meal." The dragon snickered.

Bean remained enigmatically silent, and Askoroth, as if bored by the direction the conversation was taking, turned the subject back to himself. "There is no one left who can challenge me, not even Glahivar. Their quantum—their spirit matter—will feed me. Nothing can stop me now." He looked around the great hall and nodded. "Yes, this will do. It will make a suitable lair, but my goal is to learn the secrets of the Golden Tip, and for that, I will need the pendant."

"Why?" Anwyn asked. "What does my pendant have to do with the Golden Tip?"

Askoroth thrust his head closer to Anwyn, his breath hot on her face and his eyes narrowing. "Everything. And that's all I'm telling you. Do you think I'm stupid? I know what you two are trying to do. You're trying to get information out of me by flattering me, but it won't work. Once I have the pendant you'll both become a part of me anyway, and you'll know what I know, so you might as well just sit back and wait." Askoroth pulled his head away and settled his gargantuan body onto the floor. "I'm still watching you, so don't think to run."

"What is it that you think I—or Bean—can do for you, besides become part of your quantum?" Anwyn persisted. "I don't have the pendant. I don't even know how to access the portal, and Bean doesn't know anything."

"You don't need to know, Anwyn. That will be accomplished by Glahivar right after I absorb her, and as for Bean," Askoroth lowered his voice to a conspiratorial whisper, "I need Bean alive to ensure your cooperation. Oh yes, I can see how you two stick together. You wouldn't be doing that if you didn't—" he shuddered, "care about each other." He snorted and glowered at Anwyn. "You will go through the portal, and I will enter with you."

Anwyn looked at Bean, then at Askoroth. "You're wrong about that caring thing. Bean's almost a stranger to me, but I will cooperate because I don't like to see people killed." She hesitated, then asked, "Wouldn't going through the portal shatter your template, just like it would for Glahivar?"

"It would."

Anwyn and Bean looked puzzled, and Askoroth gave a hearty chuckle. "That's why I have this!" He reached up toward his head, and pulled at a horn. With a snap, it came off, and he turned it upside down. A bright object fell from inside the horn—which they could now see was hollow—into his talons.

A crystal!

"I came prepared. Astrabal and I conjured up this little item. Oh yes, Astrabal is an old acquaintance of mine from way back."

"So what is the crystal for then?" Bean asked.

"I thought you'd have guessed. It places a protection field around me so my template doesn't shatter when entering the portal. It is a portal key, almost like a skeleton key, and will allow the bearer access almost anywhere, even into these halls. Aren't you curious as to why he didn't give it to Glahivar?"

Anwyn and Bean remained silent, but Askoroth puffed out his chest again.

"He's not pleased with Glahivar. I persuaded him to assist me in return for the knowledge of the pendant. He knew Glahivar would not share the knowledge with him, but will use it instead to usurp his power."

"And you would share the knowledge with him?" Bean asked, disbelief in his voice.

"I know when to make deals, and when to take it all," Askoroth said. "In this case, it was better to promise a share of the pie in return for his help."

"Doesn't mean you'll keep your promise, though," Bean said, and Askoroth gave an impatient sniff.

"This is a game. Things change all the time. Promises are for fools. But enough of that. Once you become part of my mind and body, you will understand—" He broke off as Hora appeared in front of them. "Ah! Here at last, Glahivar. Surprised to see me?"

Hora hesitated, eyes wide in shock, just long enough for Askoroth to direct a surge of flame toward him, but Hora—or rather Glahivar—disappeared before it could reach her. The dragon's immense head pivoted back and forth, as he searched for Glahivar, but she was nowhere to be seen. She appeared again, this time behind the dragon and now in her spider form.

"I've left Hora in a safe place," she said, simultaneously discharging a flurry of flaming balls toward Askoroth. Unsurprisingly to Bean and Anwyn, the flames bounced harmlessly off his armor-plated body.

Askoroth's high-pitched, triumphant *whoop-whoop* echoed around the chamber as he turned and launched another volley at Glahivar, who again disappeared, appearing just over his head as she pelted him with bolts of lightning. They found their mark, but with ear-splitting cracks, they rebounded back in her direction.

Anwyn and Bean retreated from the war zone, placing themselves once more behind a nearby pillar. "We have to keep watch," Bean said.

Anwyn shook her head. "It'll be difficult, if not impossible," she said. "We don't know where it is. It could be with Hora."

"I don't think so," Bean responded. "She won't trust him to have it. It's on her body somewhere. It just has to be."

188

"Let's hope I can get close enough to her before I'm incinerated."

"If we don't succeed, we'll die."

"There's no 'we' here, Bean. You make your escape. Tell Irusan and Grayfell what has happened. Remember, it's our plan. It's the only chance we might have."

Bean pressed his lips together and lowered his eyes.

"You must, Bean. You *must!*"

40.

Goren's Plot

King Sinhail knuckled his bloodshot eyes with the backs of his hands. It had been a long night, and now Yuki was missing, too. *Chaos*, he thought, *just chaos*. His hall bustled with activity. Soldiers and guards ran back and forth on endless missions. His courtiers huddled around his throne and talked in low voices. No one knew what to do. No one seemed to understand what had even happened. *It wouldn't be long before the news spreads throughout Ulovia, and then— then it might be over for me. My subjects will revolt.*

Goren blamed the shape-shifter. "My lord, this is all his doing. Yuki and I discovered that he conspired with Grayfell—"

"Yes, I know," Sinhail interrupted. "He, Yuki, and the shape-shifter— all missing. Grayfell has disappeared from the cells, a trick taught to him by the shape-shifter, no doubt. But they can't all be conspiring with each other, and definitely not with my daughter."

"Where is the girl, Anwyn, though?" a courtier asked. "She was with Bean—"

"We don't know where Bean's forest dwelling is," Goren said. "All we know is that he has a den somewhere, deep in the forest. He lives there like an animal. Grayfell is the only one who knows how to find him."

"Do you think they could have taken Yuki hostage," Sinhail asked, "and they're all hiding out in the forest?"

"It's possible," Goren said, scratching his nose. "But here's another possibility. The shape-shifter could have removed them, taken them to that island as hostages. He has great powers, and we don't know what his true motivations are, but if they are still somewhere in the forest, we have an option. It's an unpalatable one, but it's the only one I can think of."

"At this moment, I'll take anything," Sinhail said with a deep sigh.

"The Shadow Goblins."

The courtiers gasped, and Goren held up his hand as he spoke. Sinhail, despite his previous statement to the contrary, had opened his mouth to object. "No, my lord, members of the court. Hear me out. We've had a peace treaty with them for some time now, as you all know. What you may not know is that I have developed a closer relationship with them over the years."

"What do you mean, 'a closer relationship'?" Sinhail asked, his voice edgy. The courtiers shuffled their feet in confusion. "Why didn't I know about this?"

"Yuki knew. She suggested it," he lied. "She thought that it would help to keep the peace with Eng, the leader of the goblins. We need to know what they're up to."

"Shadow Goblins," said Sinhail, "won't do anything for nothing. What did you promise them?"

"A higher percentage of the ores and gems from our mines." Sinhail opened his mouth again, but Goren spoke quickly. "It's not a lot, my lord. We can easily absorb it, and it also guarantees us freedom from war with the goblins for many years to come. I can have them scouring the forest and the mountains for them today."

"Tell them to eliminate Grayfell and the shape-shifter—Bean, too, and the girl, but Yuki is off limits," Sinhail said. "Do you think she's…" He could not finish, but Goren shook his head.

"Oh no, my lord. I am sure she's well. The shape-shifter only wants to gain the upper hand. She will no doubt be returned to us as soon as we acquiesce to his demands."

King Sinhail sagged back into his throne, placing his head in his hands. "Grayfell," he murmured to himself, "why, oh why, have you betrayed us?"

Goren suppressed a smile. He had no idea what had really happened to Yuki, but the opportunity to further smear Grayfell and the shape-shifter was too good to pass up. "I will speak to the Shadow Goblins today, my lord. If he has truly kidnapped Yuki with the help of the shape-shifter, they will find them. No one knows the mountains and forests like they do."

"Why, Goren? Why did he do it?" Sinhail still looked dazed.

"I presume you speak of Grayfell—his betrayal?"

"Of course. Why him? He was always so loyal to me."

"He hated Yuki, my lord. Since the death of his wife, he has always looked for ways to remove her influence over you. He blamed her, you know."

"He did? I never knew that. Why didn't he tell me? I could have told him Yuki had nothing to do with her death." The king bit his lip, shaking his head in confusion.

Oh, but she did, my king, Goren thought. *She most certainly did, and now that she's missing or dead, there is nothing standing in my way to power.* He just hoped the Shadow Goblins would do their part, and quickly. His lips twitched in a small, sly smile as he thoughtfully rubbed his chin. He had an idea where the missing Grayfell might be.

41.

Glaciers and Gravity Wells

Jarah and Tristan returned just as they were setting off through the gap with the White Dwellers. The Dwellers cried out, "Sky Father Gods!" dropping to their knees and placing their foreheads on the ground.

Not Sky Gods! Irusan insisted, shaking his head. *These are our friends I told you about. Get up.*

Jangon, the Chieftain, frowned. *Not sky gods? Only sky gods can do this!* But he rose and motioned to the other Dwellers to rise.

Our apologies for startling you, Jarah thought-spoke. *We have little time, though, and had to do what we thought best.* He turned to Irusan and Grayfell.

"We've located the entrance. It works on portal mechanics, but we could not enter because we do not have the right coding. Perhaps you or the Dwellers will have better luck. We will show you where it is, but then we must leave."

Jangon growled. *Speak in our language. We do not understand your mouth-words.*

Again, we're sorry, said Jarah, this time using the telepathic communication. *We did not mean to offend. We told our friends that we will guide them to the entrance of the mountain.*

No one can enter the mountain, Jangon said. *Not even us.*

Someone already has, Irusan stated, *and we must find out how they got in, and how we can do it, too.*

They began to walk, Peatatoo and Yorli bringing up a distant rear, while Jangon threw occasional furtive and suspicious glances her way as they proceeded.

Jarah and Tristan, out of respect for the White Dwellers, remained corporeal and allowed them to lead the way, only using their merkabas occasionally to make certain they were headed in the right direction. Although the White Dwellers knew exactly where the entrance was, they could not trust them yet to lead them there. Jarah and Tristan were their insurance that all went as promised.

The sun rose high in the sky as they clambered up rocky slopes of loose scree and over sharp ridges that dizzily fell away near their feet. Irusan, once again, wished he had a working merkaba, but even if he had, Grayfell and Yorli would not. Jarah and Tristan climbed with them, not taking the easy way out unless it was to ascertain their route. The route was difficult, but not impossible.

They arrived at a glacier that Irusan deemed would be the most challenging part of their ascent. *I wish we had ropes*, he said. Jarah, Tristan, and Grayfell agreed. Crevasses gaped on each side, but Jangon deftly maneuvered them around each abyss, jabbing ice bridges with a long stick before anyone stepped on to them.

As they crossed the last ice bridge, Yorli, bringing up the rear, gingerly placed her foot on it—one step, then two—before they heard a crack that reverberated over the icy expanse. The bridge began to crumble under her bulk. Peatatoo launched himself like an arrow over the gap, scampering away from the crumbling crevasse bridge, but Yorli was not as quick. She toppled, head first, into the blackness below.

Two flashes, and her plunge halted, her body dangling in midair over the gap. Held by something unseen, she flailed her arms helplessly. Jarah and Tristan, deactivating their merkabas, materialized at the rim of the abyss lying face down, each one gripping Yorli by a foot, their bodies sliding closer to the edge. Digging their feet into the snow, they tried to stop their momentum, but it wasn't enough.

The Dwellers, Irusan and Grayfell, were already hurrying toward the abyss.

Let go of me, Yorli commanded. *Take care of Peatatoo.*

No, Yorli, we won't do that, Tristan insisted, but their slide forward continued. He felt his upper body approaching the lip of the crevasse. As it slid, closer and closer to the edge, he knew that it was only a matter of moments before he would reach the point of no return, and then they'd have to reactivate their merkabas in the hope they could still hold her. Jarah, too, unable to dig his feet deep enough into the ice and snow to prevent his own drift to the rim, got ready to try floating above the abyss.

He yelped in pain and Tristan grunted as a crushing weight bore down on each of their legs. Jangon knelt on Jarah's lower body, while Irusan sat on top of Tristan. With their long arms, they both reached over the heads of the two men, their massive hands gripping Yorli's legs tightly. They heaved upward, but they, too, were unable to gain enough traction to pull her out of the crevasse.

By now, the remaining Dwellers had reached them. The first to do so wrapped their muscular arms around Irusan and Jangon, while the others formed a chain behind them. Grunting and straining, they heaved, and Yorli popped out of the chasm onto the snow, her body trembling with shock. Everyone sank down on the snow, exhausted, while Peatatoo screamed and chittered from afar. Irusan was grateful the squirrel still had enough sense to keep his distance from the group.

Yorli slowly rose to her feet, dusting the snow from her body. *You saved my life,* she said, looking at them all in turn. She knelt in front of Jangon. *I was afraid of you, but now—now I see you are an honorable Dweller. I am in your debt.*

He grasped her under her arm and lifted her up. *We must keep moving.* He looked at Peatatoo, confused. *Take your—familiar—and let's go.*

Peatatoo is not my familiar, Yorli said, indignant. *He's my friend.*

Jangon raised his hairy brows. *So you're not a witch?*

Of course not. If I was, would I not have been able to get myself out of the crevasse?

Only witches have familiars, Jangon insisted. *I've never heard of Dweller and squirrel friendships before.*

Well, you have now, Yorli replied, her brows furrowing.

Jangon shrugged, but they kept moving. Yorli fell back, allowing Peatatoo to jump back onto her broad shoulder. Soon they stepped gratefully off the glacier and onto firm rock.

Phew, Irusan blew out his cheeks. *I thought we'd never get across that!*

Jarah pointed straight ahead. *The entrance is just over there, under that overhanging cliff and behind that ridge. Now that you're all safe, Tristan and I must go. We'll return here this evening to check on you.*

They disappeared, and Jangon and his Dwellers gaped but didn't otherwise react.

They crossed the ridge. A towering cliff loomed ahead. A series of staggered staircases led up the side of the cliff face to a large opening halfway up.

Doesn't look too difficult to access to me, said Grayfell.

Take a closer look, Irusan responded.

Grayfell caught his breath. "I don't believe it!" he said, completely forgetting the Dwellers request to only use their thought language. "How?"

I've seen this before, said Irusan. *If I still had my other-dimensional abilities, it would be a snap, but now—*

So, Grayfell said as he gazed up in awe, *that's why no one can get in. I've really underestimated my ancestors. What is it? It's making me dizzy to look at it.*

It's a gravity phenomenon, Irusan said. *Only those knowledgeable in other-dimensional technology could achieve something like this.*

Grayfell nodded. He observed how the first flight of steep steps looked perfectly normal, but the next intersecting flight looked as if it were upside down. The third, perpendicular to the second, appeared as if it were a descending flight, but led to a landing above that stopped at the massive doorway.

It doesn't make sense, Irusan. What is happening?

There seem to be at least three gravity wells, maybe more, and perhaps these also lead into different dimensional vortices. If I had my normal abilities, I could navigate the stairs, but they are only the first barrier. I'd still have to gain access to the shielded doorway.

What about Jarah—the six—can they access the stairs or the doorway?

No. They are not coded for this type of inter-dimensional portal travel, or for the door.

How would Iochodran get this coding? If they have access…

Don't underestimate Astrabal, Irusan replied. *He could decode it. So could I, given enough time and my—*

Other-dimensional abilities, Grayfell finished, and Irusan nodded.

You must proceed through each dimension first before you even reach the door. Human bodies—and now those of the Eldred—do not possess this ability without a key to unlock it, but Iochodran does.

How did Bean and Anwyn get through, assuming they're there?

A shielding could protect them from the effects of the dimensional doorways, Irusan said. *Assuming they're there,* he agreed.

It's the perfect place to hide something. I give my ancestors credit. No one could storm this place!

Sky Gods make it so. Jangon had joined them. *I did tell you.*

You did, Irusan said, shaking his head. *You most certainly did.* He sank down onto a rock and wiped his brow. *All this for nothing.*

Grayfell's clenched his hands into fists. "If we can't get in," he said, "we're sunk. We'll never find Bean or Anwyn."

Irusan just looked at him, and gave a long, low sigh.

They were not certain how long the battle raged. Anwyn and Bean retreated farther down the hall, as distant from the fray as they could get but still observe what was happening.

"We can't go too far," Bean said. "If an opportunity arises, we must be able to take it."

"I can't even see it," Anwyn replied. "How am I going to take it?"

"She has it on her, I feel sure. Let's just wait and see."

They waited, but the flashes and flares of the conflagration made it difficult to see anything, and they often had to look away, if only to preserve their eyesight. Screams, shrieks, roars, and thunderous crashes reverberated around them, and they placed their hands over their ears. They hunkered down, sweating and straining to breathe in the scorching air that now filled the cavern. When Askoroth's whipping tail came too close, they retreated to the next pillar and crouched behind it.

"I hope his tail doesn't smash these pillars down," Anwyn said. "The whole thing could collapse down on top of us."

"My ancestors carved this hall out of solid rock," Bean replied. "I don't think one or two broken pillars would bring the whole thing down."

"How would you know?" Anwyn asked. "But I hope you're right," she added as an afterthought.

Bean didn't say anything, and Anwyn wished she hadn't spoken. *Why am I always so disagreeable to Bean?* She didn't understand herself at all. She reached out and took his hand. "I'm sorry, Bean. I'm just frightened."

Bean gave no indication he had taken any offense. Anwyn almost wished that he had, but they didn't have time for apologies and regrets. They must keep watch. Their patience paid off. The smoke and fire cleared. Glahivar was much the worse for wear: Two of her legs had shorn off, and they lay twitching on the floor, ichor oozing from the holes in her body. She had lost a few eyes as well.

Askoroth, his impenetrable scales protecting him well, had suffered no damage at all. Armored plates slid down over his eyes as Glahivar directed another one of her energetic beams toward them. It bounced off the armor-plating and shot off on a tangent to hit the far wall of the cavern.

We better watch out for those ricochets, Anwyn thought. The still-twitching spider leg on the floor fascinated her. It was covered in long, black spikes, and—she almost stopped breathing before gripping Bean's shoulder.

"Look!" She pointed at the leg.

Bean was puzzled. "What? I don't see—"

"No, look!" She shook his shoulder, pointing insistently. "There!"

He looked again and gasped. They had found it. A silver glint under a large spike. The pendant.

"I'll get it," said Bean, and he rose, but Anwyn pulled him down again.

"No. I have to go. It's my responsibility. You stay here."

Bean wanted to argue, but before he could get a word out, Anwyn jumped up, and began a sprint toward the severed leg. Bean gasped, slow to react, but then he sprang up and hurtled after her.

Glahivar and Askoroth paused in their battle long enough to turn their amazed gazes onto the small figures that charged toward them. Glahivar shrieked and lunged, turning her back to Askoroth, who began a slow lumber toward her. With a deep, heaving breath and a roaring exhale, he launched a torrent of boiling incandescence at the spider. Like a hideous tumbleweed, she rolled herself up into a ball, covering her head with her giant claws, but it was too late. Her body exploded as if hit by a solar flare. Flaming chunks rained down in every direction.

Dodging each fiery particle, Anwyn and Bean continued their sprint toward the leg that lay quiescent now on the stone floor. Anwyn reached it first and kicking it over, she bent down, plucking the pendant from the spike where Glahivar had hung it. She stood up, placed it quickly over her head, folded her hands around the stone in the center, and closed her eyes.

"*Noooo!*" Askoroth roared as he rushed toward her. "Not yet!"

Bean launched himself like a projectile at the spot where she stood, stretching his arms out as if to pull her back, but before he could connect, there was a bright flash, and Anwyn—along with the pendant—was gone.

42.

The Fourteenth Magus

The pillar behind Anwyn cut the boy's trajectory short. His head thudded into it with a *smack*, and Askoroth stopped his own onward rush as the boy closed his eyes and slid to the floor, moaning in pain. The dragon wanted to stomp on the prone figure, reduce it to ashes, but instead he stopped, staring at the boy. He wondered how—or if—he could still use him. Hastiness had been an old failing of his, he remembered, but he was learning.

Tears of pain spilled down the boy's face. He flinched as his hand moved over the large bump on his bloodied forehead. Askoroth stepped closer, but paused as the boy's face began to glow with a strange light. What was this? There was no light in here other than the few ever-flaming torches Glahivar had placed around the hall, and of course, his own fiery breath.

The boy blinked several times, squeezing his eyes shut. He gasped, and the glow disappeared. A trick of the light, Askoroth thought, and he snorted. The boy rolled over onto his back and stared at him blankly.

"Stupid boy. You should have stopped her," Askoroth trumpeted into his ear. "Now what am I going to do without her or the pendant?"

The boy's limbs jerked as if he'd been startled awake from a deep sleep, his eyes focusing on the dragon. "I don't give a flaming newt what you do, Askoroth," he said as he shakily rose to his feet. "Why don't you just go back to Iochodran. You do have one thing you wanted: your new form. Take that repugnant lump that you call a body, and go lord it over those who are actually frightened of you instead of wasting your time roaring at me."

Askoroth's reptile eyes widened, and his immense jaw sagged. For a moment he stood speechless, then he threw his head back and bellowed. The hall shook, but the boy, rooted to the spot, only stared back at him. Askoroth roared again. Bean did not even flinch. The dragon glowered at him, spread his wings, and pawed at the ground in fury.

"I'll incinerate you!" he boomed. His fetid breath washed over Bean like a scorching wave. "How dare you speak to me—*me, Askoroth*, like that! You'll…you'll regret it, I'll make sure of that. You're an *idiot*, boy. Now, I have no reason to keep you alive. None at all."

It was then that Bean straightened up, lifted his chin, and fastened his silver gaze firmly on Askoroth's slit-pupiled, orange eyes. "I am not '*boy*.' My name is Lhathron Faervel. I am the fourteenth Magus, the ninth Adept of the Elluin bloodline, and it is you who will show the proper respect to me before I reduce *you* to a pile of ashes."

Askoroth stared, his face a rictus of amazement. He opened his jaws again, but this time with a peal of laughter that echoed around the large chamber before it abruptly ceased. "You must have taken leave of your senses, boy. Don't worry, I like your spunk, but it won't stop me from killing you. Before I do that, though, I will absorb you. I want to look at your face as I pull your quantum in. It's not a painless process, and I will keep you alive for as long as possible, but—"

"Silence!" Lhathron Faervel thundered, and the dragon's open mouth shut with a snap. It opened, snapped shut again, and Askoroth closed his eyes, lowered his head, and drew in a deep breath. With another roar, the incandescent stream of plasma he propelled from his maw toward the boy reached clear to the other side of the hall.

Perplexed, Askoroth looked at the spot where the boy had been and where, according to his calculations, there should only be a small grease spot, but there was nothing. His horned head turned this way and that, swiveling on his long neck, but still he could not see the boy or even any of his remains.

He slowly turned his bulk around and scanned the hall behind him. *Ah! There he was.* A corner of the boy's green cloak stuck out from behind one of the pillars. He knew now what had happened: the boy had darted under him, scooting to his rear between his tree-trunk legs. He wouldn't get away this time, Askoroth thought as he prepared to unleash another torrent of flame. This time, though, he'd keep his eyes wide open.

The flame jetted out once more, wrapping itself around the pillar that momentarily glowed red-hot. Sparks rose as if something on the other side had combusted. He gave a satisfied snort. *Got him!* He turned back, his body shaking in glee. It was too easy.

What? The boy stood in front of him again where he'd been standing only a few moments before, but this time without his green cloak. The fury that rose in Askoroth reached a full boil and he inhaled—eyes open—and delivered another stream of plasma-hot fire, but the boy stood motionless even as the plasma ripped through him, unimpeded in its trajectory, clear to the other side of the hall. Blinking, Askoroth shook his head and directed another blast in his direction, but now the boy was not there!

Were his eyes playing tricks on him? He spun around as quickly as his gargantuan body could move. The boy sat behind him, long legs astride his tail! Again, he directed a flame toward him and winced as the burning plasma penetrated his armor plating. In anguish, he whipped his scorched tail back and forth, but the boy had disappeared. Was he dead?

A noise like a falling pebble came from behind him. He shuffled his body around. He couldn't see anything, but he sent another plasma burst to the place where he'd thought the sound had come from. The pebble plunked again, but now it was to his left. Snaking his head in that direction, he roared, shooting another plasma stream toward it. Still nothing.

He felt a smack, as if that of a hand, on his right flank. He turned his head just in time to see the boy disappear behind another pillar. *Ha! Got him this time!* A white-hot stream emerged from his maw, wrapping itself around the pillar. He waddled over to the pillar and peeked cautiously around it. Nothing, not even a flake of ash. That was impossible. No one could survive his plasma fire. Even he—Askoroth—was not immune. His tail still smarted badly. But he'd seen the boy take a direct hit and stand there, unaffected, as if it were a stream of water.

For the first time Askoroth began to doubt himself. Had he greatly underestimated the boy? Perhaps—perhaps he had told the truth that he was a powerful Eldred wizard. He had not believed him, but maybe he should have. Glahivar had told him about the boy's flute, that she had destroyed it. They had both thought this was the only trick he possessed. They had been wrong.

And now his supply of plasma was almost exhausted. He roared and pawed the ground. *I've been tricked*, he thought. *The wizard has forced me to use up my fire on phantasms.* The boy—the wizard—had somehow caused him to hallucinate. He could use a wizard like that. Perhaps he had been too hasty in deciding to kill him. He would capture the wizard alive, learn his secrets, and then once he was done with him, he'd make a good addition to his quantum.

Something puzzled him, though. Why had the wizard waited before using his spells and tricks on him? He could have chosen any time to demonstrate his abilities. Why wait until the girl had disappeared with the pendant? Thoughtfully, he swung his massive head back and forth. *I must take stock, rethink my position.* He ruffled his wings and lifting his head, bared his fangs. *It must be! The boy-wizard is inextricably linked to what I seek.* He screeched, spreading his wings out as far as he could. *I must find him. If I don't have the girl, and he is linked to the Golden Tip...* Askoroth snorted. *Yes, he may well know where the portal to the knowledge of the Elluin is located. All is not lost. Not yet.*

He wasn't Bean anymore, and he'd never be Bean again. He'd accept-ed that fact at the same moment that his head had exploded into a mil-lion shards of light and sound. As he'd sprawled face down on the floor, wiping away his blood and tears, forgotten memories, knowledge of his identity erupted like a long-dormant volcano into his conscious mind.

He'd scarcely heard the words of the dragon. As he'd stared up into the orange eyes of Askoroth, he'd unleashed his own dragon within: a rising anger—fury—at this creature of Iochodran, resentment for what he now knew Grayfell had done to him, and regret at himself for allow-ing it to happen. For the first time in his life, he understood exactly what Grayfell's potions were for. They had subdued—no, *shut down*—his life force, reducing him to a shadow of his former self. Like Anwyn, he, too, had lost his soul, and he hadn't even been aware of it. He'd only grasped the full extent of his loss once he'd regained it.

As he'd toyed with Askoroth, he'd felt his abilities returning. There was so much to remember he could scarcely keep up. Like a child at play, he disappeared then reappeared as he taunted the dragon, trying out new tricks—the gestures that controlled what the dragon could hear, what he could or could not see, and the phantasm of himself that sat astride the dragon's tail.

He remembered, too, as he pranced unseen around the bulky crea-ture, that he had not always been an ordinary boy. As a young child, he had been fully aware of his full name, his title, and his destiny. His mother, Kiya Faervel, had known who he really was, as had Grayfell. After his mother had been killed by the Shadow Goblins, Grayfell had inexplicably hidden his only son in the forest, telling everyone that he was mute—a half-wit. The potions had begun soon after, and after a few years, no one remembered Lhathron Faervel anymore. There was only Bean Ironweed, the mental defective.

No more! We are one, Lhathron told himself. *I will never be afraid or helpless again. I am the fourteenth Magus, the ninth Adept of the Faervel Elluin bloodline.*

He watched in amusement as the dragon searched the hall for him, directing streams of ever-diminishing plasma at darting shadows—some that he, Lhathron, had created himself—roaring in frustration. *I must stop this playing,* he thought, *and deal with this dragon so I can find Anwyn.* How, he still did not know. The pendant was gone. Something else bothered him though. The answer was here, in the Golden Tip. If only he could remember…

It was that part that eluded him. The secret of the Golden Tip. As a magus, he should have known, but his awareness had been stifled for too long and he had not developed as much as he should have. He'd returned here to find the secret, the knowledge that would save his people from ignorance and the stagnation of their once great civilization.

He had found the steps to the balcony half hidden in the dark recesses of the hall. The winding stairs were crumbly and unsafe, but he'd navigated them without much trouble, and now he sat behind the stone balustrades, watching the dragon below. He was sure it couldn't see him up here, but he must think of a plan before it did.

Something in the air around him had changed. Was it colder? His senses on full alert, he carefully looked around him but didn't see anything. He went back to his thoughts, but in only a few moments the cold returned. He shivered and wished he still had his cloak.

"Too bad it burned up," a whispery voice said in his ear.

He jumped. Hora stood behind him. He sensed the gleeful confidence that emanated from the man's squat body. *No matter,* he thought, *he has no idea who I am.* He smiled.

43.

The Girl

By keeping track of the light and dark cycles in the window with the charcoal marks, Anwyn thought she had been in the hall of records for perhaps one hundred and forty-four days. That was about four—nearly five—months. How much time had passed in the manifest world, though?

Today she had returned to the room with the spiral staircase. Every few days she made the trek up the staircase, hoping to find a door at the top. Was she ready yet? She had no idea. Today it was no different from the past one hundred and forty-four days she'd been here. She slammed her fist against the wall and turned around to go back down.

Five months! She blew her breath out in frustration. Well, almost five months. Perhaps, though, that wouldn't seem as long after an eternity—

At that moment, she cried out, and sinking to the staircase, she grasped her head with both hands. *Pain!* No, it was not possible—there was no pain here— but the knife-like spasm moved through her head again. She whimpered.

She lifted her head, listening, and her mouth sagged open. Someone was downstairs! Footsteps, soft ones, as if someone walked slowly and carefully over the stone floor. The pain subsided, so she dared to rise and float cautiously down the rest of the stairs. As she came to the last curve she warily peered over the bannister and into the room. A girl stood at the door, wearing a cloak with a hood that covered her head, her face in shadow.

Was she from Iochodran? Anwyn sank down on the staircase again, half hidden now behind the bannister. She carefully peered out as the girl took another step into the room. The girl hesitated, as if unsure what to do, but then she walked to the fireplace and with a single movement pulled the hood of the cloak away. She had her back to Anwyn, and long, reddish-blonde hair cascaded down her back.

It couldn't be…but it was. The girl turned around to face the staircase, and this time Anwyn could not stop herself. She cried out. The girl was her—Anwyn.

The girl looked up, startled but unsurprised as Anwyn stood up. "I've found you! What is this place?"

"Who—who are you?" Anwyn asked. *She could be an imposter from Iochodran.*

"No, no, I'm not an imposter."

The girl could read her thoughts!

"Then who are you? Why have you taken on my appearance?"

"I am just who I appear to be. I'm Anwyn. I found the pendant. I have your consciousness, but there's only enough to keep me alive and aware. Irusan says that you left me, your physical body, behind when you used the pendant to escape the hag-wraiths—"

"Wait, you said 'Irusan'?"

The girl nodded. Anwyn walked down the rest of the stairs and stood in front of the girl. "We have work to do."

"Where's the pendant?" Hora asked.

"I don't know," Lhathron replied. "I'd forgotten about you."

Hora smirked. "Askoroth did, too. When he reduced Glahivar to the tiniest particles, her hold over me died, but all her memories are mine now. I am part Hora, part Glahivar. She will live on in me and so will her abilities. She always has a backup plan, and while my body was not her first choice, she did keep it intact. So tell me, where's the girl, and where is the pendant? I'm losing patience."

"I've already told you. I have no idea where she or the pendant is, and that's the truth."

Hora glanced at the dragon who still searched behind each pillar, lighting up all the dark corners with his glowing eyes. He had come to the far end of the hall and was now making his way toward their hiding place.

"I must not let him see me," he said. "I'll take you with me."

"Alright," said Lhathron.

Hora sniffed. "I thought you'd protest more, but never mind. We must go."

"Where to?"

"You'll see," said Hora, and putting his arms around Lhathron, he hefted him up and they both disappeared.

Lhathron breathed a sigh of relief. His main concern was that they'd end up in Iochodran or someplace equally unpleasant, but they hovered over his forest, his tree home below them. Hora, or Glahivar—Lhathron wasn't sure what identity this thing now claimed—lowered them down. His front door was wide open. Was anyone inside? He hoped that no one was there, but it would have been comforting to see Grayfell there or even Irusan. He fought back tears. They were probably both dead by now.

"We're going to check every place where she might be until we find her," Hora said. "I must have that pendant."

"How would she have gotten back here so quickly?" Lhathron asked. "She doesn't have merkaba flight."

"No, but making assumptions has gotten Glahivar into trouble before, so I'm taking no chances. If she has the pendant, who really knows what it's capable of?" They materialized inside the house. "I'm keeping a close eye on you. Don't think you can escape."

Lhathron clenched his jaw, tamping down an impulse to put this creature in its place, but he needed Hora now, at least for a while. He did not have merkaba capability, and his natural born abilities had atrophied to a degree that he must take great care, only using what resources he had available. This was one. He wondered if he could pull it off. It didn't seem likely, but what choice did he have? Sitting in that hall with a dragon searching for him wasn't his best option.

They searched his home quite thoroughly. He showed good faith by searching as hard as Hora. He wanted him to begin to, well, not exactly trust him, but at least relax his guard a little. Hora needed to know he was just as eager to find Anwyn and the pendant as he was.

Hora had allowed him to eat some litch, watching him as he thirstily drank from his water pitcher. Lhathron was careful to shield his thoughts.

He placed the empty water pitcher on the table. If Grayfell was not dead and he did return, he would know that at least his son was still alive. This had always been an old signal of theirs. Full pitcher on the shelf, all's well; empty pitcher on the table, I'm in trouble.

"What about Ulovia?" Lhathron asked. "Are we going to search that, too?"

"Don't worry your little head about it, pretty boy," Hora said. "It was next on my list. I know what I'm doing."

Lhathron again fought his instinct to kick this creature across the room, but instead, he allowed himself a small twitch of the shoulders.

Hora grinned. "You'll learn. Perhaps I'll take you back to Iochodran with me. You can be my imp."

"It beats being dragon food," Lhathron said.

Hora grabbed him under the arms. "I like you, boy. I really do. Maybe there are bigger and better things waiting for you. I can teach you a lot if you're willing to learn."

Lhathron nodded, keeping a vacant smile on his face, and they hurtled toward Ulovia in Hora's merkaba.

They searched the mountain city from top to bottom, staying invisible in the merkaba, but there was no sign of Anwyn. They sped into the king's hall and alit in a quieter area close to the throne. Chaos reigned. The hustle and bustle made it difficult to hear anything, but they moved around, still in the merkaba, overhearing snippets of conversation.

"Someone's head is going to roll for this," one courtier said to another. And from Goren, "We were foolish not to confiscate his cloak."

The king bellowed orders from the throne, adding to the chaos.

Lhathron's heart skipped a beat. Was Grayfell still alive? Hora growled softly to himself, "So he's not dead after all!"

Lhathron took a deep breath, letting it out slowly. He remained silent but inwardly, he rejoiced. What had happened? He knew Yuki's fate, but his concern now was for Grayfell and Irusan.

As if wondering the same thing himself, Hora told him to be still. "Stop that wriggling so I can focus!" he demanded. Lhathron sensed him probing the king's mind. Hora shook his head. "The king has no idea what happened to Irusan. He thinks he kidnapped Yuki and they're in Mu'A with his co-conspirator, Grayfell. They have Shadow Goblins out searching, too." He yuck-yucked, jerking his merkaba upward. "But as for us, we'll go to Mu'A next. Anwyn's from there, and she may have regained her powers of flight. She is the only one I am interested in capturing."

They sped off to the south. The ocean below appeared in a blur of movement, and quicker than a blink they hung over the island from a great height. Lhathron briefly closed his eyes. Despite his revulsion, he held tightly on to Hora, whose body odor and foul breath gagged him.

"It takes some getting used to, this merkaba thing," Hora said, "but if you do as I say and be a good boy, you may have your own one day."

Lhathron grimaced. He thought he'd rather die being stung to death by barb-tailed wasps than "be a good boy" to this thing. He cleared his throat.

"How would you know if she's in there or not?" he asked, as he opened his eyes and looked down at the conical mountain. The deep shadows of the late afternoon sun brought the mountain features into sharp relief, but still he could not perceive an entrance or any sign of habitation.

Hora's face took on a peevish expression. "We'll just have to wait here until someone comes out. I'll be able to see a merkaba as it exits the shielding. It leaves a little spark at the exit point."

"That could take a long time," Lhathron responded. He didn't fancy hanging precariously over the island for an indefinite period.

"I'll go down to the beach. I am sure you won't mind sitting with me on the warm sand."

Lhathron's stomach did a flip as they descended much too fast, but they alit gently enough on the beach to allow his trembling legs to support him. Hora was still not skilled at flight. He didn't even want to think about their journey back.

What if Grayfell and Irusan are really dead? he wondered. He didn't think they, or Anwyn, were on this island. He could not sense Grayfell's presence at all, and something told him that Anwyn was no longer in this reality. *How am I going to find anyone if they are no longer here?* His stomach churned and he felt dizzy. He had no idea how to proceed. All he knew was that he had to keep trying however he could to get Anwyn back.

44.

Journey's End

He lowered his bulk to the floor. He'd almost forgotten how physical bodies had their limits, and he had not counted on wasting so much energy searching for a boy—no, a wizard—who had somehow exited the hall unseen. After a fruitless search through the deserted, crumbling underground structures of the mountain interior in his merkaba, he had to face facts. The boy was no longer inside the Golden Tip.

He must rest, then he'd continue his search, only this time outside the mountain. He needed to replenish his source of energy. He must seek life forms, preferably those with their own enhanced supply, so he could absorb them. He lowered his great head and closed his eyes, and in a few moments he had begun to snore.

"Where, or what, is this place?" the girl asked Anwyn. "And how are we going to get out of here?"

"First, we must bring your physical body and my consciousness, or spirit body, back into co-resonance, or alignment, again." She pointed to herself with her thumb, "I'm vibrating at a different frequency to you."

"It sounds difficult. Could we do it?"

"Either we do it, or one of us must return while the other remains."

"Did you know there's a dragon down there? He was after this." She opened her hand. The pendant gleamed in the firelight glow.

"I know nothing about what is occurring in the material world," said Anwyn, "but I'm really happy to see you still have the pendant. Without it, we'd never get out of here. We only have to learn how to use it to re-unite us so we can both leave."

"Glahivar tried to make me use it. She tried pressing it into my hands and speaking the commands, but it would not work. It only worked when I wanted it to work. I don't know how, but I remembered them when I had to, and I didn't even have to say anything."

Anwyn laughed. "I've learned a lot about the pendant since I've been here. She didn't know that the commands have to come from you, and only you." She shook her head. "I can make it work, too."

"She also thought that by just hanging on she would be able to come through the portal with me."

"That could have been disastrous. No, she can't do that, either. A part of her would end up floating around for eternity in a vast nothingness. It's unthinkable to bring someone with us."

The girl shuddered. "I almost brought Bean with me," she said, her eyes wide with shock. "I decided at the last moment not to take him."

"Who is 'Bean'?"

"He's a very dear friend who saved my life. You'll learn about him later."

"It's just as well you didn't try to bring him, whoever he is. Unless he, too, is connected to the pendant in some way, his body is more than likely not keyed for gate travel." She glanced meaningfully at the girl, then back toward a scroll that still lay open on the table, her face thoughtful. She walked over to it and picked it up, looking at it closely. "Yes!" she exclaimed, while nodding her head vigorously. "The scroll label has changed. It now says JOURNEY'S END. I have to read this."

213

The girl moved over to the fireplace and seated herself in the arm-chair. "I won't disturb you. Please take your time."

"That's the problem," said Anwyn. "It says right here that our time is up." She pointed her finger at a line on the scroll. "There is something I have to do quickly, or we'll never leave this place."

Irusan had not been able to navigate the stairs. He didn't think he could, but he had to try anyway. Grayfell tried, too, but as soon as they were halfway up the first flight, Irusan put a halt to the effort.

If we go any further, he said, putting his hands out, *we'll combust*. He showed Grayfell his hands: blue sparks surged over them, only dissipating as he pulled his hands away. It was an effective barrier that kept them from accessing the next level. Even if they had rope, which they did not, they would not have been able to get past the energy barrier. The sun had sunk closer to the horizon and there was little daylight left.

The Dwellers sat on the ground, regarding their efforts with amusement. *We've tried, too*, said Jangon. *Every few moons someone tries. It's become our test for the younger ones to show what they're made of. No one has ever made it any farther than you have. Some have died trying.*

I didn't think we'd be successful, said Irusan. *It beats just sitting, though, and—* He stopped. He cocked his head slightly as if he was listening to something. A scrabbling noise came from above them. Their heads jerked up.

A dark shape appeared in the cavernous doorway above the last flight of stairs. At first, they could not see what it was, but it was immense, filling the opening with little space to spare. Before they could react, the silhouette squeezed out of the door and spread its wings. It flapped, screeching, and launched its monstrous form into the air.

Run! Irusan shouted. He couldn't believe what his eyes were telling him. *A dragon?* Grayfell hesitated, too astonished to run, and the Dwellers shrieked in their language as they scattered down the slope. Irusan gripped Grayfell by his elbow, and together they ran toward the shelter of a large, nearby boulder. *It will afford little cover for us*, he thought, but it was better than the open slope.

Grayfell pulled his cloak over himself and then Irusan. "It will help us somewhat," he said, as they crouched down behind the boulder.

I think very little can help us now.

The dragon shrieked in delight as it flew circles over them. It dropped like a stone to the slope, snatching up a Dweller as if it were a child's doll in its taloned claw. Irusan and Grayfell could only look on in horror as the dragon lifted the screaming Dweller toward its maw. But it did not open its mouth. Instead, it took a deep breath, and a fluorescent stream of bile-green energy gushed from its nostrils. It flowed into the Dweller. Unable to tear their gaze away, they watched. The Dweller glowed red, its corporeal form reducing in moments to a pile of ashes that dribbled between the dragon's talons. The dragon inhaled, a blissful look on its face, as the Dweller's luminous life force entered through its nose.

The dragon rose into the air again. Swooping, it discovered another Dweller, plucking the wailing creature from where it crouched behind a rock.

"It's going to hunt us down one by one," Grayfell observed.

Where is Yorli? Irusan asked. *I haven't seen her, or Peatatoo, for several hours now.*

"I told her to take the squirrel and keep their distance," Grayfell responded. "It kept coming too close to us, and I was annoyed. I let her know that next time I saw him, I'd kill him." He shook his head sadly. "Of course I would not, but my threat worked. I didn't see either one of them again."

Just as well. I hope at least they will escape the dragon.

"It seems that the dragon has found another one." They watched helplessly as the dragon drained yet another Dweller of its life force. It was taking its time now, picking them off like fat fleas on a monkey's back. The main body of Dwellers had regrouped a short distance away, reluctant to desert their companions and duty-bound to protect the Golden Tip. They flourished their weapons, bellowing, but none dared challenge the dragon, none that is, except Jangon, who approached with raised knife, shaking off his tribe's attempts to pull him back.

*Jangon! He's going to...*Irusan began to say, but then hesitated, as a small shape darted over the ground, moving *toward* the dragon. He blinked. It was Peatatoo, and one of his cheeks had a familiar bulge to it.

Too preoccupied with its feeding, the dragon paid no attention to the tiny white varmint that scurried over the ground. Peatatoo edged around the monster's huge bulk, hopping first under its large belly, then scampering toward its tail. With a quick leap onto the tail, it bounded along the spiny backbone and up onto the dragon's head.

Irusan and Grayfell couldn't move, even though they wanted to spring to their feet and scream at Peatatoo to flee, to go to where it was safe. He would only be a small bite for this horrifying colossus, which would surely sense his presence any moment. But the dragon continued to feed, oblivious to the pocket-sized creature that now sat and surveyed the world like a king between its horns.

The dragon paused, lifted its head and shook it, the half-consumed remains of the Dweller still in its claws. It blinked its enormous, platter-like eyes and slowly turned as it surveyed its environs. It roared, but Peatatoo only held on more tightly, hunkering down on top of the massive head. The dragon roared again, but this time the roar trailed off in a high-pitched screech. A modest but fiery jet of flame spurted from its nostrils as it flapped its huge wings. Its body lifted slightly, then slammed like a collapsing monolith into the stony ground, its feet and wings scrabbling frantically to gain traction. It struggled to raise itself up, but instead lay helpless on the hard earth, its body twitching as dark smoke erupted from its nostrils.

The Dwellers roared as they surged toward the helpless dragon, flourishing their knives, machetes, and heavy sticks. Some hefted big rocks. Peatatoo held his ground, chittering in delight, dancing and capering over the dragon's bulk. The Dwellers ignored him as he chattered and *chuk-chukked* while they stabbed, slashed, and jabbed the dragon. He scuttled away from the head as Jangon raised his broad-bladed knife and with several downward slashes, severed the dragon's head from its thick neck.

It was only then that Peatatoo jumped off the twitching body, scampered around the severed head, and ran back in triumph to Yorli, chattering all the way.

The Dwellers cheered, shaking their knives and sticks at the steaming carcass. Irusan and Grayfell emerged from behind their rock, but Jangon, still carrying his ichor-stained blade, turned to Yorli and Peatatoo. *That is a brave familiar*, he said, pointing to the squirrel with his knife. *I now understand why you keep him.*

Yorli frowned, but she didn't say anything, only nodded and retreated farther back.

Irusan and Grayfell cautiously approached the dragon. *We must be careful*, said Irusan. *This is a creature of Iochodran. It could reanimate itself, although I think that it would be difficult given the condition of the body.*

"I've only heard about these creatures," said Grayfell, nudging the body with the toe of his boot. "They have populated our myths and legends for generations. I didn't think they existed, but I was wrong."

They exist, said Irusan, *but I've not seen them on this world for millennia. They were created by intruder "Gods" who used them to fight proxy battles for them. They caused tremendous destruction, and finally the so-called Gods, who were nothing more than highly advanced other-dimensional beings like myself, found it prudent to destroy them. Their game had proved unsustainable, but Iochodran found a use for them. Astrabal must have unleashed this one into this reality.*

"I hope this is not what kidnapped Bean and Anwyn," said Grayfell. "If so..." He didn't finish his sentence.

We must not think that way, said Irusan. *They're alive. Iochodran kidnapped them not to kill them but to gain control of the pendant. I doubt that can be achieved without Anwyn.*

"Yes, but what about—" Grayfell stopped in mid-sentence, raising his eyes to the sky. Irusan looked up, too, and quickly stepped forward. A plummeting shape dropped into his outstretched arms only moments before it would have hit the ground.

45.

Return to Golden Tip

They waited all day, but no one emerged from the island. Hora paced up and down the empty beach while Lhathron took the opportunity to get some rest. He was exhausted. He thought he'd fallen asleep once, but he jerked awake as Hora's foot nudged him in his ribs.

"Wake up, boy! I want them to know you're here. Perhaps they'll come out if you move around. They won't see you here if you're fast asleep."

Lhathron rose and walked toward the tree line with Hora following closely behind. A small footpath led into a shallow cave with a sandy bottom. "This must be an access point," Hora said. "We don't have the codes for it, but we could wait here until someone comes out, grab them, and make them take us into the mountain."

Lhathron looked thoughtful. "Did you know I could contact Grayfell telepathically?"

Hora raised his brows. "No, I did not. I was informed by Glahivar that you were an idiot, although what I witnessed in the Golden Tip disabused me of that notion." Hora squinted at him suspiciously. "Go ahead, then. Contact him."

Lhathron sat down on the cave floor and closed his eyes. He didn't really need to do that, but it would convince the real idiot that he was in fact trying. After a while, he looked up. "No. Nothing. He's not here."

Hora's eyes narrowed. He seemed to be weighing his options as he shifted restlessly from one foot to another.

"We could wait here," Lhathron said, "or we could go back to the Golden Tip and see what Askoroth is up to. Don't you think Anwyn would return there to find me?"

Hora stood in silence for a while, reluctant to admit Lhathron's words made sense, but his covetousness for the pendant won him over, and he gave a brief nod of the head. Lhathron was grasped again in Hora's thick arms and up they flew, shooting off into the darkening sky to the north. Lhathron found it interesting how as they neared Unala the mid-summer sun hovered farther above the horizon. They still had daylight, although it would not be for long.

He had never seen the Golden Tip in the rays of the sun before, and awestruck, he gazed at the pyramidal shape that loomed ahead. Grayfell had been right, it was real gold! He recalled the tales his parents had told him about the old home of the Elluin. He had thought the tales were exaggerations, bedtime stories, but now, he could clearly see they were no exaggeration.

As they drew closer, the peak gleamed ever brighter, until Lhathron could barely open his eyes in the glare. He had to blink several times, looking at it through half-closed lids as the light bounced off the golden upper third of the peak. Hora circled the peak, as if checking to see what lurked outside the mountain before descending to the entrance.

As they circled once again, Lhathron's breath caught in his throat. Something odd had drawn his attention. At first, he thought it only a trick of the light, a reflection, but he craned his neck to look more closely as they approached the peak. There it was again. A silvery white gleam that looked out of place in the smooth surface. It could be a window, he thought, with someone standing in it, but they had passed by all too quickly.

He hoped Hora had not seen it, but his attention was on the ground.

"I think I see something down there!" he shouted. "I'll go around again for another look!" They made one more circle of the peak, and as they sped past the area that had attracted his attention, Lhathron was prepared, his sharp eyes already scanning the spot. This time he was quite sure, even though the small arched window was hardly noticeable in the glare of the sun. He rubbed his eyes, baffled. *Was that…* He jerked, as something in his head exploded with a crack and a snap. His world went black.

The boy went limp and Hora looked down. Did he just die on him? He looked dead. His eyes were open, but now they stared unseeing, up at him. He shook the boy.

"Wake up!" he shouted, but he flopped around, unresponsive. And now, as they once more approached the entrance side of the mountain, he drifted downward to get a better look. There were figures on the ground—and—what were they? Large, white shapes, milling around in the twilight around a dark and bloodied carcass. As he got closer, it all came into sharper focus. *Askoroth!* He felt the strength draining from his arms and his mouth dropped open. The boy, now a dead weight, slipped from his grasp, plunging down to the slope below.

He tut-tutted to himself. *That was careless, but the boy was dead anyway.* He did not want to stay in this area too long. The abilities of the creatures below were unknown, and he didn't want them sensing his presence. Whoever they were, they would not be able to get into the mountain, but if they could do that to Askoroth, what could they do to him? He must go inside and prepare himself for an attack. Fortunately, Glahivar had supplied him with all he needed to get back in, and after she'd possessed him so cruelly, they'd returned to Iochodran where this time he'd received an intensive upgrade to his template. His abilities were on a par with—no, perhaps better—than Glahivar's had been.

He could take care of himself. He would not allow Askoroth's fate to be his own. He'd find the girl, retrieve the pendant, and the world would be his.

46.

The Portal Key

Irusan laid Bean down gently on the ground, and Grayfell felt for a pulse on the boy's wrist.

"He's alive," Grayfell said, blowing out his cheeks in relief. "But where did he come from? He just dropped out of the sky!"

The Dwellers had reacted with startled cries and grunts as Bean had fallen into the cat-man's arms, but now they stood by, watching curiously as Irusan and Grayfell took command of the situation. Irusan thought that perhaps they were getting used to the sudden appearances and disappearances of these strangers.

Irusan gazed grimly up at the mountain entrance. *Whoever—or whatever—brought him here is up there, I can feel it. Our battle is not yet over. We have to gain entrance to the mountain!*

"I agree," Grayfell responded, "but how?"

Let's first see to Bean, and then we'll cross that hurdle, said Irusan, and they bent over the boy again. Irusan ran his hands over the boy's body, but shook his head in frustration. *My healing abilities are gone, too.* He reached for Grayfell's water bottle, poured a bit into his hand, then wet the boy's face.

"He's breathing. Perhaps we'll just have to wait," Grayfell said, and they both drew deep breaths. Bean's eyes opened wide, staring into Irusan's, and he sat up abruptly, as if shocked by a lightning eel.

"I know it all now," he said. "I remember."

"Know what?" Grayfell asked. "What happened to you, Bean?"

Bean looked at him. "I am not Bean. I am Lhathron. Lhathron Faervel. Don't ever call me Bean again."

Grayfell's face sagged. "Bean? I-I mean Lhathron—tell me what happened to you. Are you alright?"

"Of course," he said as he jumped up. "I've never been better. Irusan, I'm glad you're alive."

Grayfell and Irusan looked at each other, perplexed, but they stood back.

Who is this…Lhathron? Irusan asked Grayfell.

"Lhathron Faervel is Bean's real name," said Grayfell. "I didn't think he remembered it."

"You didn't think about a lot of things," Lhathron responded. "But we don't have time to discuss that now. It can wait until later. I have to find Anwyn."

Hold on, young man, Irusan said. *We must talk first. There are things that we need to know, and you, too, before we go anywhere.*

Lhathron shifted his feet impatiently, lifting his head to look at the peak that was now cloaked in thick cloud cover. As he looked away, his gaze fell on the hideous carcass nearby. Without a word, he walked over to it, the Dwellers parting as he approached, apprehension in their eyes. He peered at the severed head on the ground, then looked back at them.

"You killed Askoroth?" he asked.

"Not us," said Grayfell. He pointed to the Dwellers. "Them, and Peatatoo."

"Peatatoo? The squirrel?" Lhathron's mouth formed an O of surprise. "What's he doing here?"

"That's why we need to talk first," said Grayfell. "Sit down. We aren't going anywhere until you listen."

The dusk had given way to nightfall and the chill mountain air made them shiver, but they agreed that lighting a fire, even if they could find wood, was not a good idea.

There may be more creatures of Iochodran lurking nearby, Irusan said, *and we don't want to draw attention to ourselves.*

The Dwellers consulted among themselves while Irusan and Grayfell spoke with Lhathron, and then they melted away into the night. Yorli and Peatatoo withdrew to a spot not too far away from where they sat, Yorli keeping a close watch on them as Peatatoo perched on her head like a fur hat.

Grayfell and Irusan took turns relating all that had happened since Irusan had left them at the tree home, and after they had finished, Lhathron filled them in with all that had occurred to him and Anwyn up until the moment when he and Hora had flown past the peak.

"She's up there." Lhathron pointed up toward the peak. "I didn't see her clearly, but she contacted me. She told me everything. I know what we have to do. We have to return to the hall where she disappeared with the pendant."

Irusan had been observing Lhathron closely as he'd talked, while Grayfell sat hunched as if defeated, wrapped tightly in his cloak. He still shivered, and since he no longer seemed capable of speech, Irusan spoke instead.

It is fortunate for us that Glahivar has been defeated, but this Hora, he is obviously quite capable of being a problem, and that doesn't answer the question: how are we going to gain access to the doorway?

Lhathron rose and walked over to the dragon's head that gazed at them with opaque eyes. He stooped, and with a quick twist of his wrist, a large horn snapped open as if on a hinge. A bright object fell out. Returning to the stunned duo he held out his hand. In it lay a small crystal.

"This is a portal key," he said. "The dragon showed it to us. He was bragging about it, that it will allow anyone to use it for any portal entry. I do believe it will allow us into the mountain."

Irusan recoiled, eyeing it as if it were a poisonous snake. *It's a creation of Iochodran!* They heard the dismay behind the words from the cat-man. *Do you expect me to use it? Who knows what effect it may have on my template?*

223

Grayfell finally spoke. "I will use it, then," he said. "Bean—I mean Lhathron—you tell me what to do. You and Irusan wait here." He reached out to take it, but Lhathron pulled his hand away.

"I'll test it out first," he said. "If it has any bad effects, let it be on me first."

"That makes no sense," Grayfell said. He folded his arms across his chest. "You are the only one who knows what is going on. We need you, and I…I am expendable. I insist on going first. You can tell me what to do once I'm in there." He inclined his head toward the mountain.

Irusan nodded, narrowing his eyes. *If you're willing to take the chance, Grayfell, I agree. My template is already damaged. We'll both go.*

Grayfell reached again for Lhathron's hand, and Lhathron reluctantly opened it, the crystal in his palm, but before Grayfell could touch it, a white streak appeared out of nowhere. It snatched the crystal out of Lhathron's hand, Yorli's large bulk hurtling close behind.

"Peatatoo!" Lhathron exclaimed.

The squirrel jumped up onto Yorli's shoulder. They did not stop in their headlong rush. Irusan and Lhathron didn't even have time to feel weak before they had already reached the stairs. With Peatatoo holding the crystal in one small paw, Yorli leapt onto the stairs and they promptly disappeared.

For a moment, no one could speak. It had all happened way too fast. They gazed up at the entrance, holding their breath. A large white shape appeared in the doorway with a smaller one perched on her shoulder.

We will go in, said Yorli, from the entrance. *Peatatoo still has the other stone, the one that will destroy whoever dropped Bean.*

So you were listening to us, Irusan said, shaking his head, but they got no response. Yorli and Peatatoo had dissolved into the darkness.

Hora wished he still had the boy, though. He wiped the beads of sweat away from his face with his hand and gazed around the hall, his eyes dark pools of fear. He wondered if Glahivar had really been destroyed. He had some of her memories—inevitable due to the overlay of their templates. Some coding had been exchanged, but she was a product of Iochodran and they did not destroy easily. If she returned, though, she might destroy him instead.

It was small comfort, but he had seen the body of Askoroth. It had appeared dead enough to his eyes, but again, these creatures could always reanimate. He needed to be on his guard.

He hoped the boy had been right, that the girl would return here. It was his only chance to get the pendant and make his escape back to Galon where he would find a way to protect it from the denizens of Astrabal. If Astrabal knew, he would be as charred as the remains of Glahivar that still littered the floor around him.

He hummed to himself as he waited, a little tune he'd learned in the tavern back home. He wished he was back there, in front of a warm fire with a tankard of beer in his hand. He remembered the young serving girl, buxom and friendly too—no one ever showed friendship toward Ortzi's warlock, he thought. Perhaps he'd return to the tavern once this was over and…

His head whipped around. The torches that Glahivar had lit still burned on the wall sconces, and there were no shadows that did not belong. He had heard something, though. Just in case, he would pull up his merkaba. He did not want to be surprised by intruders. He rose into the air and began a sweep of the hall. As he arrived at the far end, the scurry of tiny feet came from the tunnel that led to the entrance. He moved toward it.

A large white shape emerged silently from the murk. It was one of those creatures he'd seen below. How did it get in here? With an exasperated cluck of his tongue he raised his hand and launched a fireball in its direction. It dodged the fireball easily, roaring in fury, and rushed headlong into the hall. Didn't it know it was courting death? Hora chuckled. This would be fun. He would play with it first, perhaps just singe it a little…

He raised his hand again and lobbed another ball of fire toward the fleeing creature. With a quick twist of its body, it again evaded the missile and it now began to weave in and out of the pillars. What was it doing? Did it think it could play with him? Angry now, he used both hands, this time discharging two flares at once. One caromed off a pillar with a *boom!* while the other flew wide, bouncing off the far wall before it fizzled. He needed more practice at this, he thought, but no matter; he would consider this his opportunity for practice. He took a deep breath and got ready to launch another salvo.

He held up his hands, but then something strange happened. A small white creature struck his arm, its claws scrabbling for a foothold. He screamed and shook his arm, but it had dug in, glaring balefully at him as it chittered and squeaked. A squirrel? What was a squirrel doing here? He hated them. With a shudder, he tried again to shake it off while he swatted at it with his other arm. And why were its cheeks so oddly distorted?

As he began to lose his focus, his merkaba spluttered, and then like an extinguished candle, it was gone. He rolled onto the hard floor below, the snap of his ankle making him cry out in pain, but still the creature held on to him like a sticky burr. He raised his other hand to discharge yet another fireball, but now it was only a splutter, one that singed his arm. He growled. This was not as easy as he'd thought, but he would roll on top of it. Yes! That would squash the little rodent, and his problems would be over.

He moved to tuck his arm in closer to his body, but an enormous hand seized him by the neck in a choking grasp. He rose off the floor, his feet kicking the air. The squirrel still hung on, though, its glittering eyes and bared teeth a mere finger's-width from his face. And now his body had been overcome by a debilitating weakness, a paralysis; he could barely move.

Hora's last thought before darkness descended on him was that he'd probably never see the girl or her pendant again.

47.

The Tree Wizard

*N*ow *what do we do?* Irusan asked as Grayfell shook his head.

"I don't need it," Lhathron said.

"What? What don't you need?" Grayfell asked.

He seemed irritated, Lhathron thought. "I don't need the portal crystal." The shape-shifter and the wizard looked at him oddly.

"Why didn't you tell us?" Grayfell asked.

"I just did."

Alright, Irusan intervened. *Now, someone must go in and make sure those two fur balls don't get into trouble, and find Anwyn. I wish it was me, but we have no choice. It has to be you, Lhathron.*

"That's easy enough for you to say," Grayfell said. "He's not your son. For years and years, I've tried to keep him from wizardry and dangerous situations, and now my worst nightmare has come true."

"Father," Lhathron interrupted, "Irusan is right. It has to be me. I am no longer a boy, and you've done me no favors by trying to protect me. For years, our people have considered me a simpleton, and while that may have kept me safe, it did not allow me to develop as I should have. You crippled me instead. Do you think Iochodran will stop with me? After they get what they want, you, the Eldred, and everything we know and care about will be expendable."

Grayfell stared at him for a long time, then blinked and took a deep breath. "I may have had my reasons, but I didn't realize...I wish I could go for you, but I can't. Irusan is correct. It must be you."

Lhathron turned, and holding out his hand he touched the stairs, disappearing from Irusan and Grayfell's sight. A moment later he reappeared in the entrance, looked down at them briefly, then turned and walked into the darkness.

After Lhathron vanished, they stood silently at the foot of the stairs. Even though there was nothing they could do, they both sensed each other's reluctance to move away from the entrance.

After a while, Grayfell looked at Irusan, his silver-sheened eyes glinting in the scant starlight. Irusan wondered if those were tears that he saw. "You may judge me for what I did to Bean," Grayfell said, "but until you've had a son, you will never understand."

Try me, Irusan replied. *I've had children, sons and daughters whom I've lost. I lived here at one time you know, having experienced many lives in the worlds of manifest reality. I am not a novice when it comes to the problems of existing in places of extreme polarity.*

Grayfell mulled over this for a moment, then walked over to a small boulder. He sat and began to speak, as if he needed to unburden himself of something he'd borne alone for much too long. "Bean's...I am going to have to get used to calling him Lhathron...his mother, Kiya Faervel, was my wife. She was an extraordinary woman." He glanced up at Irusan, who stood like a stone statue at the foot of the stairs.

Irusan nodded. *I'm sure she was. You told me she'd been killed by Shadow Goblins. I'm very sorry.*

"I don't believe she was," Grayfell said, and Irusan looked down at him in surprise. "It was only made to look that way. In truth, Kiya was a throwback to the old Elluin. Eblenor knew it, and he warned me. He told me her genetic code was something he'd never seen before, and her powers were almost unlimited. He thought she'd be a threat to Yuki and Goren. He warned me that I needed to remove her from Ulovia, but I never did. Yuki was her friend. Why would she be a threat?" He sat, his forehead puckered as he massaged his temples. "I thought since she was such a skilled sorceress, she could protect herself better than I could. She was also an independent woman with her own mind. She would not allow me to remove her from her home."

His voice broke, and he took a deep breath before he continued. "Kiya, however, had two fatal flaws: one, she trusted too much, and two, she saw no need to conceal her considerable abilities. In King Sinhail's court, that was as suicidal then as it is now."

I am aware of his ineptness, said Irusan, *and that his kingdom's business is carried out by his daughter and his court advisor. I can see, too, that what you perceive as magic—which is only knowledge of the laws of the universe—can be regarded as a dangerous advantage by those who do not possess it.*

"Yes. It has always been that way, but my wife and Yuki were close. She shared many of her secrets with her. It was only once Lhathron was born that she became more circumspect, more 'discerning' if you will. She and I began to discover that our young son possessed as many talents, if not more, than she did. Eblenor told her that she was from an old Elluin bloodline, a line that was genetically gifted in the science and art of magic. The Faervel line. That is where Lhathron received his name: from his mother, not me."

Grayfell picked up a small rock, rose to his feet, and threw it toward the steps where it disappeared in a fiery flash. "That's us—or at least an ordinary person. The Elluin set it up this way, that if we diverged from the path of knowledge and wisdom, we would also lose our heritage. We don't deserve entry to the halls of the Elluin."

When I first saw Lhathron, Irusan said, *it was evident to me that he possessed latent abilities. His command of sound, for example, was exemplary. I was impressed.*

"He got that from Kiya," Grayfell said. "It is part of her genetic heritage. She could bring down a mountain, although she would never have done that, just by using her voice. Do you think Lhathron really needs his flute?" Grayfell shook his head and laughed. "That was just so he would not use his voice. Kiya and I both agreed it was too dangerous to reveal the full extent of his abilities, so we told everyone he was mute and that he had not inherited her voice command. We also allowed them to think that he was a simpleton. We both brought him up that way, although I do know Kiya secretly taught him much of what she knew, only with the flute."

He created that tree home with his skills? Irusan asked.

"Of course. I had nothing to do with it. He'd find small trees, uakus trees that were not yet mature, and play his flute around them. I thought it harmless at the time, but then I saw that one of the trees was growing rather oddly. It seemed hollow, but it did not die. The growth of the tree accelerated, too, and it was then that we couldn't ignore what had happened. Lhathron had created a tree home. He chose to live there, away from the people who bullied him and called him names. We didn't stop him."

So tell me what happened to Kiya. How did she—

"Die? I can only suspect, but I don't know for certain. It was around the end of the Goblin Wars when her bloodied body, bearing hideous wounds of teeth and claws, was found at the entrance to the Shadow Goblin's lair in the mountains. Her death could only have been caused by Shadow Goblins, but my heart told me she would never have allowed this to happen. What was she doing there, anyway? The Kiya I knew would not venture alone into or near their lairs."

He hurled another rock at the staircase where it exploded in a shower of sparks, then another, and another. Irusan held his patience while he waited for Grayfell to continue.

"Yuki told me, with great sorrow and many tears, that Kiya had told her she wanted to broker an agreement with the goblins to end the war." Grayfell imitated Yuki's voice: "'*I dissuaded her from going herself, but she did not listen to me.'* She said, too, that Kiya planned on using her voice to destroy the goblins, but instead, they destroyed her. I knew that would never be Kiya's way. She was a skilled diplomat, yes, but using threats? She didn't operate that way. It was more Yuki's way, and Goren's. My belief is that somehow the two of them gained her trust and lured her into an ambush. They could have rendered her unconscious somehow, drugged her perhaps, so she'd be unable to defend herself, and then allowed the goblins to…" His voice trailed off, and he turned his head away.

Irusan walked over and placed his hand on Grayfell's shoulder. The mental picture he was getting was too much even for him. Grayfell's shoulder twitched, and he jerked away. "No need to feel sorry for me."

I do not, Irusan responded, but he removed his hand. *I understand now why you did what you did. Please continue.*

"Shortly after that, Goren did broker a peace agreement with the goblins. He has been friendly with them ever since, even though he doesn't know that I suspect him of anything untoward. He got the praise and recognition for the peace it brought between deadly enemies, and I feel we ceded far more than my wife in the deal. Goren and Yuki benefited somehow, but how, I do not know."

Irusan sighed. *They became the heroes, while Lhathron had to go into hiding. The time is over now for that, and Lhathron has stepped into his role. It is time for you to take a step back, Grayfell, and support him in every way you are able. It is what Kiya would have wanted.*

"I know that," Grayfell agreed. "I know."

They sat together in a companionable silence. Grayfell wondered how Lhathron was faring, but Irusan's thoughts were on Anwyn. Would he ever see her again? And how, he wondered, could he ever forgive himself if he did not?

48.

The Secret of the Golden Tip

The tunnel stretched ahead into an inky infinity. Lhathron briefly pondered if he should use his newfound skills to light his way. He thought better of it. Hora might be watching the entrance, and announcing his arrival would be reckless.

Were Yorli and Peatatoo all right? He set off into the darkness, his thoughts stampeding ahead. What skills did Hora possess, exactly? He wondered, too, if Glahivar and Askoroth were truly destroyed. While their bodies, which had temporarily manifested here in the physical, could have been destroyed, their energy could never be eradicated. Their spirit forms were now most likely back in Iochodran, furious and vengeful, but he hoped that it would take more time for them to reconstitute themselves.

It's useless to speculate. I need to focus, to be in the now moment, he told himself. He reined in his thoughts and carefully picked his way over fallen rocks and debris as he made his way down the tunnel. Far ahead, a small glow appeared, and he commanded his shield of invisibility to manifest. As he crept forward, he could hear the small, crunching noises his boots made on the gritty bottom of the tunnel. If anything from Io-chodran were here, they would hear his approach. He paused after every step, his senses on high alert for non-human energies.

At long last he emerged into the brighter hall where the torches still burned. Here, the floor was comparatively clean, and his footsteps no longer betrayed his presence. At first, he couldn't see anything, then he saw her: a light blob at the far end of the hall. He hurried over as quickly as he dared, lowering his shield of invisibility. "Yorli!"

She jumped, almost dropping the body she held. *Bean! You startled me. How did you get in here? We had the crystal.*

Never mind about that now. I'm here, and that's all that matters. I see you killed Hora?

No, not killed, Yorli insisted, as she laid the body down on the floor, face up. *He's unconscious. I cannot kill. It is not who I am.*

That is admirable, said Lhathron. *Where is Peatatoo?* He felt his muscles twitching in apprehension. A chitter came from the balcony.

*Here…*said Peatatoo. *I leave when Bean appear.*

Thank the Elluin you are fast, said Lhathron. *You must leave, Yorli. Take Hora, Peatatoo, and the portal crystal. Go back to Grayfell and Iru-san and give them the portal crystal. Tell Irusan it is safe for him to use it. After he and Grayfell get here, they must listen for me. I will tell them what to do.*

Yorli pulled Hora up and placed him over her shoulder. As she walked back to the tunnel, she called to Peatatoo who scampered over and jumped up atop Hora. He waved the Djinn stone triumphantly in a paw.

As they disappeared into the tunnel, Lhathron turned and strode purposefully to the center of the hall to the place where the dragon had emerged from the depths of the pit. It gaped ahead, a malefic hole that drew him unprotestingly to its crumbling edge. As he stopped at its lip, the tips of his boots overhanging the rim, he spread his arms out, and in a smooth movement dropped headfirst into the blackness below.

After reading through the JOURNEY'S END scroll, Anwyn thought-fully rolled it up, placing it back onto the shelf. She did not share her findings with her counterpart; she would not understand. It was not only the other Anwyn she needed to reunite with, there was someone else she had to connect with, someone essential not only to her survival, but that of the Eldred, the Mu'A, and their future. She gave a slow, disbelieving shake of her head. *Who would have thought...* But now she knew exactly what she had to do. The scroll had outlined it all, point by point, step by step. Standing up, she walked to the arched window. She rose, placing her hands on the window and stared at the mountains and the setting sun.

The girl observed her actions with a puzzled look. "What?" she be-gan, but Anwyn, turning her head, shushed her, then returned her gaze to the window.

Yes! There! She closed her eyes and concentrated with all her might on a moving glimmer behind the window. She exhaled with all the force she could muster, and she collapsed to the floor as the girl hurried over, her brow furrowed in concern.

Anwyn pushed her away. "I'm all right," she said, rising onto her feet. "It just took a lot out of me."

"What took a lot out of you?" the girl asked.

"You ask too many questions." Anwyn's tone was impatient. She took the girl by the hand and pulled her toward the spiral staircase. "You must do ex-actly what I tell you to do. Timing is important, and we have to get it just right."

Together they walked up the staircase, and as they rounded the third curve of the spiral, Anwyn was relieved to note that the wall that had always been there before had now vanished. Instead they faced a heavy, wooden door with symbols like those on the bannisters and pendant carved deeply into it. Placing the palms of each of her hands onto a sym-bol, she directed the girl to do the same, her palms overlaying Anwyn's. They did not have long to wait. The door slowly creaked open, and they stepped into a room that was directly above the room they'd just left, only this was no room they were in, but an impossibly vast space that appeared to have no end.

They both caught their breath as they gazed around them. The floor beneath their feet gleamed as if it had been forged from metal and polished to a high sheen. They turned, crying out in astonishment as the door behind them evaporated like a mist on a hot day. Only the endless space remained. They could not return even if they wanted to. "We have to keep walking," Anwyn commanded, pulling the reluctant girl behind her.

"Where to? There's nowhere to go."

"Please, be quiet. You have to trust me, but we also have to be quick." Anwyn tugged harder at the girl, and together they jogged into the emptiness ahead. As their legs moved across the floor, nothing changed. Anwyn thought of the expression "running in place," but the scroll had said this is what they must do, so she'd do it.

"I'm tired," the girl said after a while. "Where are we going?"

Anwyn didn't answer, but only tugged harder. This girl was her? She sighed inwardly. She must have been a whiny little thing. If they ever reunited, she hoped it would not become her main trait. The girl began to lag, and it took a lot of effort to pull her along. Anwyn stopped, placing a supportive hand under the girl's arm. In this way, she could propel her forward and prop her up at the same time.

She didn't know how long they ran, but at last something in the landscape changed, giving new impetus to their resolve. They stumbled toward a large circle of light on the otherwise empty floor. As they approached, they could now sense their forward momentum. An enormous beam of white light spilled onto the floor from above. They looked up to locate its source, but it seemed as if the beam stretched into infinity.

Anwyn pulled the girl into the circle of light with her. "We're here. Give me the pendant."

The girl shook her head and pulled her fist that tightly grasped the pendant away.

"Look, I know you feel responsible for the pendant, and you still can't trust that I am who I say I am, but we have to—"

A high-pitched whine like nothing they'd ever heard before, assaulted them from within the beam. As the beam grew even brighter, they closed their eyes and sank down on their knees to the floor, whimpering. The girl crawled over to the edge of the circle, her face a mask of fear. Mustering together every bit of strength she had left in her, Anwyn reached over and gripped the girl by her foot with both hands moments before she reached the perimeter and dragged her back into the center of the circle. The girl screamed and flailed, but Anwyn did not let go. With her last iota of strength, she fell on top of the girl and pulled her hand up, the one that held the pendant. She cupped both her hands over the girl's hand, and then, in a swirl of sound and light, everything changed.

49.

The Hall of the Elluin

After Lhathron disappeared into the entrance, Yorli and Peatatoo returned along with Hora. Their arrival was heralded by a flash and a pop, and they tumbled from the staircase onto the ground. Yorli rose and dusted herself off, picking up Hora, who appeared to be returning to consciousness. He groaned and rubbed the back of his neck. She gestured to a nearby flat boulder, and Peatatoo headed toward it as Yorli placed Hora's body onto the boulder. Peatatoo leaped onto the boulder still clutching the Djinn stone in his paw.

"Good work, Peatatoo and Yorli," Grayfell said. "Did you see Lhathron?"

I saw Bean, she replied. She held up the portal stone. *I must give this to you. Bean asked me to. He said it is safe for you to use, Irusan. He says that when you get to the hall, you must listen for him. He will tell you what to do.*

Irusan and Grayfell looked at each other mystified, but Irusan took the crystal, albeit with some trepidation. He glanced at it suspiciously, then closed a giant fist around it. *Well, should we go? Peatatoo, stay there. Good squirrel.*

Peatatoo chittered and sprang on top of Hora's ample stomach. Hora slumped back, and Irusan nodded in satisfaction. He and Grayfell headed over to the staircase, but just before reaching it, Jarah materialized next to them.

"Sorry to startle you," he said. "Thought I'd check in. Any new developments?"

"We have a way in," said Grayfell.

Irusan showed him the crystal in his hand. *Let's talk, but I'll make it quick because we need to get in there.* They sat down again and Irusan gave Jarah an abbreviated version on what had occurred since they last saw him.

Jarah listened quietly, only interrupting once to say, "I'm overjoyed you found your son, Grayfell." The unspoken words were felt by all, that Jarah thought there was hope for his daughter, that she would be found next. He rose to his feet.

"I'll go with you," Jarah said, his voice not leaving any room for argument.

Alright, Irusan agreed. *You can scout ahead for us.*

"But will the crystal work for all three of us?" Grayfell wondered as they headed back to the stairs.

I don't know, Irusan said. *We'll hold on to each other.*

As they had done with the tornado, they linked arms and approached the stairs. To their surprise, they instantly found themselves at the top with no memory or recollection of ever navigating each flight. They turned to look down the long, dark tunnel.

"I'll go ahead in my merkaba," Jarah said. He returned shortly. "It's clear. Nothing inside the hall, either." Producing a light crystal in his hand, he led the way down the tunnel.

As they walked, Irusan turned to Grayfell. *Here, you take the portal crystal.*

They reached the great hall and Jarah went in first, then motioned for them to enter. Grayfell paused as he took in the enormous expanse, broken only by massive pillars that stretched into the darkness above.

"So this is the great hall of the Elluin!" he exclaimed, awed. "I have only heard about it in legends. It's even bigger than I imagined."

It is impressive, said Irusan. *It reminds me of the handiwork of the old Basajaun, the "stone builders."* He ran his hands over the surface of a pillar. *This is high technology, not like the comparatively rough-hewn pillars of Ulovia.*

"We've lost a lot of our former skills," Grayfell admitted, sadness in his tone.

As they explored the perimeter, they discovered the balcony. "We can see anything approaching from here," Grayfell said. They tried telepathing Lhathron, but received no response to their silent calls. "He's not here, I would have sensed it if he were."

"Where could he have gone?" Jarah asked.

Grayfell shook his head. "No idea. This place must be enormous. A maze of tunnels, halls, and rooms. They hollowed out the whole mountain."

We have no choice then, said Irusan. *We must wait.*

Jarah shifted uncomfortably around on the hard stone balcony and took a deep breath before speaking. "I haven't told you yet. I can't remain here too long. Things are critical at Mu'A. Half the island has disappeared already, and the ships still aren't finished."

You didn't have much time to begin with, Irusan noted. *Good ships take time to build.*

"I know," said Jarah. "It looks like many of us will be swimming, and we'll have to leave the livestock and pets behind. It's going to be a mad scramble at the last minute to get everyone off the island safely, and to be honest, I'm not sure all of us will make it."

Have you lost anyone yet? Irusan asked Jarah. He wasn't sure he wanted to hear an answer to that.

"Not yet. We take roll call every day. But we're running out of useable space. It won't be long—perhaps even by daylight—before we do begin to lose some of our people."

They sat in silence after that, each with their own thoughts. Irusan contemplated just how catastrophic it was that he'd lost his merkaba and his skills. He could have done so much to help the Mu'Ans. With his strength and speed, they would be ready by now, and he could always remove the most critical evacuees. Now the children would all have to go by boat, if a boat would even be ready by morning. It all looked so hopeless. They'd need a miracle. He gave a deep sigh. Did he even believe in miracles anymore?

Suddenly Grayfell shifted and sat up straighter. "I hear him!" They all listened, but now it seemed that it was only Grayfell who heard Lhathron. Grayfell cocked his head. "I hope it *is* Lhathron I'm hearing, and not some imposter from Iochodran!"

Test him, Irusan commanded. *Ask him a question only he'll know.*

Grayfell nodded, and they waited impatiently. "It is him. I asked him what our danger signal was at the tree home, and he said he already left it there—the empty water pitcher on the table. Only he and I knew that."

What does he want us to do? Irusan asked.

Grayfell told them, and they stared at him in horror.

"You can't be serious," said Jarah. "Without merkabas, it could kill both of you."

As he plummeted into the darkness below, the stone walls of the pit rushing past, Lhathron briefly doubted that he'd understood the instructions correctly. What if he'd been wrong? What if all of this was some trick of Iochodran to kill him? He had to stop thinking like that, he told himself. It would undermine him and paralyze his decision making. This had to be right, but he closed his eyes anyway. If he hit bottom, he didn't want to see it coming up to meet him, even if it was so dark down there.

Abruptly, light and the darkness fled. Was this death? His downward plunge ceased and turned instead into an unanticipated acceleration in the opposite direction, which made the blood rush from his head to his feet. He opened his eyes. A brilliant white light surrounded him and he couldn't see the stone walls anymore. A high-pitched whine stopped as soon as a round door, like an iris, opened above him. He floated gracefully through the portal, his feet alighting gently as the door soundlessly closed beneath him.

Anwyn stood in front of him. She wore the pendant around her neck. He smiled and stretched out his hand toward her. "Anwyn! I can't tell you how happy I am to have found you."

She looked at him strangely, but held out her hand toward him as well. "You must be Bean. I have a memory of you."

"W-what do you mean, you have 'a memory' of me?" His brows knit together. "You know me. You took the pendant and disappeared not so long ago."

"A part of me did that. We have reunited, but her memories are still a little fuzzy. It may take some time for them to integrate properly. The girl you knew as Anwyn was only a smaller part of my quantum. I was elsewhere, and she has rejoined me." Anwyn laughed. "She was frightened at first, but now she's fine, and we are as we're supposed to be."

"Oh." Lhathron scratched his head. He wasn't sure if he was happy about this new development at all. "I will miss the Anwyn I knew. She was rather sweet."

"Childlike, almost," said Anwyn. "But then so were you if I remember correctly."

"You do," Lhathron had to admit, "but I would prefer it if you called me Lhathron. Lhathron Faervel. Long story." He looked around. "Where are we?"

"Let's step out of here, Lhathron, and I'll show you."

They could not see beyond the bright light that surrounded them, so taking him by the hand, Anwyn stepped out first as he followed. "Welcome to the observation deck of the *Dawn Star*. I had a bit of time to look around before you arrived."

He stopped in midstride and stared. He wasn't sure what he'd expected, but it wasn't…this. He couldn't find the words to describe what he saw. They stood on a round, metal floor, and where the floor ended there was no wall, only a smooth, transparent dome that curved high above them. What was outside of the dome made his knees go weak with shock. An enormous blue and green horizon curved away from them, and beyond it a velvety-black, star-studded expanse. He rubbed his eyes. Was he dreaming?

"I know, it's a bit much to take in at first," Anwyn said, "but come over here. This is where it was explained to me." She led him toward a console in the middle of the deck, but Lhathron held out a hand, stopping her.

"I have to first send a message." He stopped, shielding his thoughts from Anwyn, then he nodded and they continued toward the console. Anwyn pushed a single, silver button in the center. In an instant, a woman materialized, hovering in midair. Lhathron reared back, but Anwyn steadied him, holding onto his elbow.

"Welcome aboard," the woman said, a friendly smile on her Eldred face. She wore form-fitting, silver clothing, and her dark hair was pulled back, but her eyes were silver-green, her ears pointed. "My name is Alysa Farwenys." Lhathron wondered why she looked through them, rather than at them. "You are on the observation deck of the *Dawn Star*, one of our division fleet ships of the Aurora Flotilla—"

"Why am I here?" Lhathron interrupted, but Alysa Farwenys continued to speak as if she hadn't heard him.

"She's a hologram," explained Anwyn with a small smile. "She can't hear or see you. I got her, too."

Lhathron's face flushed pink. He didn't know what a "hologram" was, but it was now obvious as Anwyn ran a hand through the hologram that Alysa wasn't solid.

"…here many millennia ago," Alysa continued, "when we, the Elluin, abandoned this planet before our genetic imprint was lost completely. We have purposely left this ship behind for those of our descendants who are able to recover from the forgetfulness virus, the condition that was implanted here by the Dherog, long before we arrived. You or your ancestors, chose to remain to help find a cure. The mere fact that you have made it on to the deck of this ship has demonstrated that there has been some success. You may use the ship as you wish. We hope you choose wisely." She turned and pointed to another console at the far end of the deck. "Another of our crew members will show you how the *Dawn Star* may be operated." The woman disappeared, and they moved to the other console. Two chairs sprung out of the side, unfolding themselves in front of them. This console was larger and more complicated, possessing many buttons, lights, a lot of strange symbols, and blank screens.

"Don't worry," said Anwyn. "I am sure they—" They both flinched as another figure, triggered by their approach, appeared next to the console.

"I hate it when they do that," Lhathron laughed.

"We're going to have to get used to it," Anwyn said, but her eyes twinkled. She looked so much like the other Anwyn. Of course, she *was* the other Anwyn. His whole world view had been turned upside down in the past few days. He wondered if he'd ever get used to all the strange new things in his life.

"Welcome to the training module," said the man, who had waited for them to be seated. He, too, wore the silver, one-piece suit, but his silver eyes looked directly at them as he spoke. "I am an interactive hologram. My programming can 'hear' you and 'see' you, so please feel free to ask questions. Just call me Chief. You've been through the introduction, but what you don't yet know is that the *Dawn Star* is a biological, conscious being. I am part of this entity's conscious mind, as are our crew members."

"How can the *Dawn Star* be biological?" Anwyn asked. "I know what that word means, but I see a lot of metal and glass here." She pointed to the floor and the dome.

Chief inclined his head as if in agreement. "You're right, I am composed primarily of metals, crystals, and other elements, but flesh and blood is not the only elemental form that can be sentient. The ship itself is my body, but there is far more to me than meets the eye. You will learn it all in due course. Now, let us begin…"

The expanse below had progressed from daylight to night. Anwyn, at one point in their training, recognized the western coastline of Ialana directly below them. Chief, an excellent teacher, helped them to master the basics of how the craft operated.

Chief warned them that they wouldn't remember everything. "I will be your pilot. You will instruct me on the bridge where to go and what to do." He pointed to the screen and the expanse below them appeared, only more visible than the darkness below. "If you wish to travel to another spot, all you need to do is place your finger on the screen, move the screen to that area, and I will pilot us there."

Anwyn placed her finger on the screen and the land below them moved along with her finger. She continued to move her hand until the desert appeared below.

"Now, for example," Chief continued, "if you wish to land in any spot, you just press three times on that spot, and the landing sequence will begin. Of course, we are not over this spot right now. This is a training module only. You will find the real commands on the bridge of this vessel. I will always be available if you need assistance. You will find other interactive holograms on other decks. We are the crew of this vessel, and we are all at your disposal."

Chief's head turned toward the iris door. "I do believe you have visitors."

The metallic click of the iris door made their hearts skip a beat, and they heard the high-pitched whine of the transporter. A bright beam shot upward, blocking their view of whoever had just entered. It was no surprise to Lhathron, though, when Irusan, Grayfell, and Jarah stepped out.

"Father!" Anwyn screamed. She ran to Jarah. "Irusan!"

They hugged, crying—even Irusan—as Grayfell and Lhathron looked on. Grayfell turned from them, surveying his surroundings in some astonishment.

"I have to let your mother know you're alright," Jarah said as soon as they'd finished hugging. He stood quietly for a moment, then looked up baffled. "I can't reach her. Something is blocking me."

"Father, it's the *Dawn Star*. Chief explained to us that it's surrounded by an impermeable shielding. It prevents detection by hostile forces."

Lhathron added, "I could only reach Grayfell earlier because he was already inside the Golden Tip."

"Your mother's going to be worried, Anwyn."

"It can't be helped," said Anwyn, shrugging. "We'll remedy the situation as soon as we can. Let's go someplace we can talk. Chief showed us the other decks and how to get there." They walked to the iris door, and as they approached, the beam shot up again.

"Lower deck," said Anwyn, and they felt themselves alighting gently over another iris door. They stepped out of the beam into a large, round room containing shiny metal tables and chairs.

Grayfell took a step back as a hologram appeared. This one was male. His skin was dark, although his eyes and ears identified him as an Eldred. He introduced himself as their deck guide.

"I've never seen an Eldred like you before," Grayfell said.

"He looks like our friend Djana," said Jarah.

"She doesn't have the silver eyes and strange ears, though," Anwyn said.

Their guide seemed to take all this in, processing it before he spoke. "The Elluin are many races, I am only one of them. On our planet of origin, we learned to work together and understand that appearances are only skin deep. You may want to visit our information center. This is where you will find—"

"Never mind about that now," said Lhathron. "We'll call on you later. Right now, we have a lot of things we need to do first."

"I understand," said their guide with a smile. "I look forward to our future interaction." With that, he disappeared as they each took a seat around the table.

50.

The *Dawn Star*

"**N**ow then," Grayfell said after they had made themselves comfortable. "What's all this about? I was scared out of my wizard boots when I jumped into that hole, but I wasn't going to let Irusan do it first. If your dead body was down there, Lhathron, there would be nothing left for me, so I thought I may as well do it."

And I, said Irusan. *If we had been tricked into jumping, then I would have to finally admit defeat by the forces of Iochodran.*

"You're all way too suicidal," said Anwyn. "I do understand, though. Things looked very bad at one time, my other, smaller self keeps reminding me of that." She grasped her father's hand. "I thought I'd never see you again."

"And I thought you'd never recognize me again," he laughed. "But tell me, Anwyn, why could Lhathron telepath us in the Golden Tip, while I cannot reach Mu'A?

"The shielding allows communication with the Golden Tip directly below us," she said, "but not for long distances. It's too risky."

Jarah pursed his lips, nodding. "Makes sense, although I'm sure they didn't anticipate an invasion of the Golden Tip itself by hostile forces. Now can you please explain what happened? Everything."

She began with her visit to Alroy and Genove on the farm. When she reached the part about her reaction to Alroy's impending marriage, Jarah's face revealed his surprise. "I wish you'd told us. I had no idea. I thought you two were merely friends."

"We were, or, at least that's all I was to him. I felt more for him than friendship, though."

Lhathron looked down, his hands twisting in his lap, and Irusan's gaze softened as it fell on him. *Don't worry,* he said, blocking his thoughts from the others. *She doesn't know it yet, but she soon will.* Lhathron looked up, his eyes still sad and perplexed. *You'll understand,* Irusan said. *It won't be long. There's still a lot you don't know.* Quickly, he proceeded to tell Lhathron exactly what it was he did not yet know.

Anwyn continued to speak during this exchange, not realizing that Irusan and Lhathron were enjoying their own private conversation. She told them about her visit with Finn, but strangely, although she discussed the pendant Stone of Creation, she never mentioned the Finder Stone Finn had given her or what it was for. Irusan smiled to himself. Maybe it wasn't so strange.

When she described the attack by the hag-wraiths, Jarah shuddered. "I wish I'd been there with you. I'd have made quick work of them."

"So would I," said Anwyn, "if I hadn't been so distracted. I'm so embarrassed about the way I behaved." She went on to describe her stay in the tree home, her meeting of Lhathron and Grayfell.

Jarah glanced at Lhathron in amazement, but didn't say anything.

Irusan filled in some blank areas and so did Grayfell, and sometimes they all seemed to talk at once, but finally the whole story unfolded, including Jarah's description of the dire situation Mu'A now found itself in.

"Here I am, discussing my problems, and all the time my friends and family in Mu'A are in danger," Anwyn said, her eyes filling with tears. "Father, you should have said something right away. We need to get over there! I've caused enough trouble as it is."

How fast can this thing go? Irusan asked.

Lhathron looked up. "As fast as light speed, whatever that is. Chief told us."

We need to go to Mu'A then, Irusan said. *I do believe this craft is large enough to evacuate everyone.*

"Yes, it is," Anwyn responded as she jumped to her feet. "Lhathron, we will find the bridge. Irusan, Father, and Grayfell, you can go back to the observation deck and ask Chief to prepare for a mass boarding."

What about Yorli and Peatatoo? Irusan asked. *Are we just going to leave them at the Golden Tip with Hora?*

Anwyn stopped in midstride, as did Lhathron. "I forgot about them. We can't leave them there with that creature. He could still have some help from Iochodran for all we know."

"I will go back and help," said Jarah, but Anwyn shook her head.

We need you here for the evacuation, Irusan said, *and besides, Peatatoo still has the Djinn stone. It could disable you.*

"I will go." Grayfell rose from the table, his icy blue gaze accepting no dissent. "I am as useless as a woodlouse in this craft anyway. In fact, I suspect the Djinn stone may have little to no effect on me since my talents and abilities are all garnered from herb potions and artifacts, such as my cloak."

It didn't take long for everyone to decide Grayfell was right. He was the only one they did not need on the *Dawn Star*.

"You will go, then," said Lhathron. "I will take you as far as the hall in the Golden Tip, then I'll return." He looked at the others. "I won't be long. In the meantime, you make arrangements for the evacuation."

Irusan wanted to object, and he could tell Anwyn did, too, but no one could fault Lhathron's logic. Someone had to escort Grayfell out of the craft and into the hall. Anything could go wrong in the process and it needed to be someone who had greater knowledge of the multidimensional mechanics than Grayfell did. He watched, with much misgiving, as they exited at the iris door. He hoped all would go well.

The squirrel sat on Hora's chest pinning him with its beady eyes. Its cheek still bulged with the Djinn stone. Hora closed his eyes. Intense pain radiated from his broken ankle. *I can fix that,* he thought, and he visualized the bone knitting together. After a while the pain vanished. His muscles were a little stronger now, and he chuckled inwardly. The large beast was his main threat, not the Djinn stone.

While Glahivar was no longer part of his consciousness, her template had once unpleasantly overlaid his, causing some of her memories and knowledge to be left behind. One always loses something in a hostile body snatch, he decided. Perhaps she, too, retained some of his own memories. He searched his—no, her—knowledge of Djinn stones, and breathed a small sigh of relief. His vulnerability would only last for a short while. Given enough time, he could recover. The portion of Glahivar that had been left behind told him that the stone was more of a threat to those mages whose energies operated on the other polarity, magicians such as Irusan and the six healers, and of course, the girl. The boy was dead, though, but where was his body? They must have all decided to return to Ulovia with it since it was now only the large creature and the squirrel who stood guard over him. Even the other beasts were nowhere in sight.

The white, hairy-headed beast sat nearby, regarding him stupidly with pink eyes. He had to think of a plan. He needed to get back into the great hall; the secret to the Golden Tip was there. Why else would the Elluin have guarded it so well? Glahivar was sure of it, as was Askoroth, but they had all overlooked something, something that would have been obvious to an insider, but perhaps not that obvious to anyone else. It niggled at him in the back of his mind. Was it his intuition or was it Glahivar's? He squinched his eyelids shut, scowling as he tried to recall what it was that bothered him about the hall. Something had seemed out of place, something with no perceivable purpose.

He sat up, his eyes opening wide. The squirrel chattered an alarm and the creature rose to its feet with an enraged growl. He gasped, sank back, closing his eyes again as if weakness had overcome him, but he didn't need his eyes. His third eye in the center of his head functioned again. From behind his closed eyelids, he turned his gaze to where the large, white creature sat, its teeth bared, eyes locked on him. The squirrel resumed its vigil on his chest.

He had remembered something. He knew now what it was in the great hall that had bothered him—or at least Glahivar—so.

He waited a bit longer, watching the squirrel through his closed lids. His patience was soon rewarded. As the sliver of moon began to sink toward the western horizon, the squirrel's eyes drooped. Hora swiveled his gaze without turning his head in the direction of the white beast. She still stared at him, but her chin had sunk lower on her chest. That was alright, he thought. He could still do it.

He waited a bit longer until he was sure that the squirrel's eyes were closed. His hand shot out like a striking cobra. He seized the squirrel by its neck, and in a single movement, he flung it at the onrushing creature. It slowed down for only a moment, cushioning the squirrel's impact with its massive arms. By this time Hora had leapt to his feet, dashing toward the staircase, the large creature's breath warm on the back of his neck. With every bit of strength he had left in his body, he flung himself at the lower staircase just as a hairy hand swooshed down a fingerbreadth from his neck.

He stood in the entrance as the large creature below roared, alternately beating its chest and lobbing stones at him, stones that came nowhere close to the doorway. The agitated squirrel, its tail fluffy with rage, scolded him from the safety of the large beast's shoulder. He laughed, and shook his fist at them.

"Go pound rocks, stupid hair-heads!" he yelled. Chortling to himself, he began to walk down the tunnel, whistling a tune.

Grayfell and Lhathron popped out of the pit's opening like jackrabbits into the hall. *Interesting how the transport worked both ways*, Grayfell thought. It was all a mystery to him. Interdimensional physics. What the blazes was that even meant to be? None of his training had prepared him for this—even Eblenor would have been stumped.

"Put your cloak up, Father," Lhathron said, and Grayfell obliged, disappearing just as Lhathron activated his own invisibility.

"How do you do that without a cloak?" Grayfell asked as they linked arms and began the trek across the great hall.

"You don't really need the cloak," Lhathron responded. "It's a crutch, just like my flute was to me. I will teach you how to develop your abilities without props." He snapped his fingers as they approached the tunnel exit and a small flame appeared. "This won't boost our invisibility, but it will aid us so we don't break any bones falling over rocks."

They carefully navigated their way around a small rock fall just past the exit, but as they rounded it, Lhathron suddenly stopped, his flame snuffing out.

Grayfell bumped into him from the rear. "What's wrong?"

"Shh," said Lhathron. He had heard something. Was it someone shouting? He listened, but did not hear anything else. "I thought I heard a shout. I have a bad feeling."

"So do I," said Grayfell. "Something is not right."

Lhathron pulled Grayfell up against the tunnel wall. "Let's wait here for a bit and see," he whispered. They waited. All seemed quiet, but the uncomfortable sense that they were no longer alone did not leave them.

"Do you think—" Grayfell began, but Lhathron nudged him with his elbow.

They could both clearly hear it now. The distant crunch of footsteps that drew closer and closer. The dust in the tunnel stirred up by the approaching individual tickled his nose, and for a moment Grayfell thought he was going to sneeze. He slowly lifted his hand, took a deep breath, and pinched his nostrils shut.

The impulse to sneeze passed, and a dark figure loomed out of the murky tunnel only an arm's length away, whistling softly. It swept past them, and they caught a whiff of foul body odor. Lhathron recognized it instantly. He held his tongue, though, guarding his thoughts until the figure vanished into the stygian gloom ahead. Once they could no longer hear footfalls, he whispered, *"Hora!"* in Grayfell's ear, who stared at him in dismay.

"What do we do?" Grayfell whispered back. "What has happened to Yorli and Peatatoo?"

"We must get back to the hall," said Lhathron. "He's returning there for a reason, and we need to find out why."

"If I were he," said Grayfell quietly, "I would have headed back home."

"I think the Djinn stone was only a temporary obstacle for him. He's on a mission, and we can't just let him go."

Grayfell agreed, and they both set off back down the tunnel toward the hall. They stepped into the opening noiselessly, keeping their shielding up. They saw Hora striding into the center of the hall.

"I was afraid of this," Lhathron whispered. "He's making a beeline for the transport pit."

"He must have figured it out," Grayfell said. "How do we stop him?"

They followed as swiftly as their feet could carry them without alerting Hora to their presence. Hora was quicker, though, since he did not need the cover of silence. As he reached the edge of the pit, he paused, spread his arms out just as Lhathron had done, and launched his body into the mouth of the pit.

Grayfell stopped, watching in dismay as Hora disappeared, but Lhathron had already reached the rim. Instead of following Hora down the shaft, though, he knelt and leaned over its lip. His mouth opened, and from it emerged a series of tones, chanting that gave Grayfell goosebumps. The hair on his arms rose as the tones swelled and ebbed, pulsing into a wave of dazzling energy, swirling with flashes of color that filled the mouth of the shaft. Like a living entity, it knifed downward, lighting up the shaft walls as it descended, a brilliant, tornadic vortex.

A howl, a long drawn out "*nooooo!*" and in the midst of the vortex the fleshy form of Hora bobbed up from below. Lhathron stopped toning and stepped back, his arms extended as he pulled the spinning vortex up and out of the shaft. With a fluid movement, he tossed it toward a pillar where it dissipated, releasing its captive. Hora slumped to the floor, gasping for breath.

Grayfell drew his dagger from his belt and moved quickly to Hora's side, placing the blade flat against his neck. "Don't move. Unlike Yorli, I *will* kill you."

Lhathron panted as if he'd just run up a flight of stairs, but he did not seem any the worse for wear as he approached the prone figure on the floor. "Listen to Grayfell," he gasped. "He means it, and if you do move, I'll hit you with another volley that will leave you unconscious."

"Perhaps you need to do that anyway," said Grayfell. "It's better than a rock."

"Or that dagger," said Lhathron. "Too much blood."

Grayfell smiled. "What are we going to do with him? I think he needs to die. Do you have a sound for that?"

Lhathron looked sadly at Grayfell. "I don't kill with my magic," he said, but he didn't miss the spark of interest in Hora's eyes. "That doesn't make me weak, though. I have other options, and I don't think you'll like any of them."

"And I thought you were a simpleton," said Hora. "Shows how wrong Glahivar was."

"Shut up." Grayfell pressed his blade harder against Hora's neck, and he flinched. "Why do you think I wanted everyone to think that?"

Hora raised his eyebrows, disregarding Grayfell's advice to shut up. "Makes sense, I would have done the same. But here's the thing..." He looked at Grayfell. "I can do things for this boy. He can be powerful. He can rule the world. In fact," he said, his voice rising, "he can have any-thing he wants. You just need to let me go."

Grayfell paused, then he laughed, a long, pealing guffaw that rever-berated around the hall, echoing back at them. "Oh, you poor man," he said, finally, wiping tears away from his eyes. "Do you think either one of us will fall for that? As soon as we let you go, you'll be off to Iochodran to restore your powers, and then you'll return, but this time with a force that nothing can withstand. You are making the case for us to kill you, and if Lhathron refuses to do it, I will."

Lhathron stepped forward. "You will do no such thing, Father. I will use my magic on you just as easily as I did on this man. It is the way of the Elluin. We never kill. We disable our enemies, we protect, but kill—never."

Grayfell grimaced. "So how are you going to disable this one? He's already proven himself immune to the Djinn stone."

"If he was completely immune, he would have pulled up his merkaba and vanished. He was quite visible to us, and corporeal."

"That means—"

"Yes. It means that he did suffer some effects, but that it also affected most of his super-human abilities. He cannot activate his merkaba just yet, for example. But it won't be long before he does, and that is what I need to stop him from doing."

Is he telepathic? Grayfell telepathed, but on a broad, unprotected channel, and watched carefully for a reaction from Hora, but his face remained impassive.

I don't know, Lhathron responded, *but it doesn't matter if he is. In fact, I hope he can hear us. I know just the thing that will stop him. He will have as much—or as little—power as he had before Iochodran got involved. Then we can take him up to the* Dawn Star *and release him wherever he wishes. Anyplace except here.*

Grayfell shook his head. "How? How are you going to do it?"

"Watch me," said Lhathron, and he opened his mouth again as Hora shuddered and cringed, but Grayfell kept his knife on his throat, and once again, like a chorus of many voices, a resonant tone emerged from Lhathron's throat. Using his hands, he threaded the wave-like, golden tones with silver, wrapping themselves around Hora.

Hora tried to wriggle away, but the visible sound blanketed him. He closed his eyes, his hands and arms around his head, as his body disappeared, leaving only a silvery-gold, cocoon-like mantle visible. A murky shadow detached itself from Hora's form, and Lhathron's voice rose in intensity. A golden tendril emerged from the cocoon, snaking around the rising shadow, and the shadow instantly vaporized. Slowly, Lhathron lowered the pitch, each tone subsiding until the cocoon faded from their sight, and silence once again settled into the hall. Hora opened his eyes and sat up.

"Where am I?" he asked.

"You took away his memory, too?" Grayfell squinted at Lhathron, his voice tinged with admiration.

"He won't remember a thing before Iochodran got hold of him. Did you see the shadow?"

Grayfell nodded. "That was part of the demon that had possessed him, or, at least, what was left of it. Perhaps now he'll only wish to return to his home." He turned to Hora. "Where are you from?"

"I-I'm from Abena," Hora said, a puzzled pout on his face. "What are you talking about?" And how did I get here?" He gazed around fearfully. "Who are you? Demons?"

"Alright," said Grayfell, as he stood up and removed his knife from Hora's neck. "Let's get him to the *Dawn Star*."

"I will get him to the *Dawn Star*," said Lhathron. "You will go and check on Yorli and Peatatoo. I hope they're alright. I'll be back for the three of you as soon as I can."

Grayfell hesitated. He was not used to taking orders from his son, but Lhathron already had Hora in a strong grip and had pulled him up unprotestingly from the floor. Grayfell shrugged. He turned toward the entrance as Lhathron and a screaming Hora disappeared into the shaft.

51.

Anwyn

Taking Irusan and her father with her, Anwyn stood at the iris door and commanded, "Bridge!" They popped up through another door and stepped out of the beam. The bridge was a smaller room than the others they'd seen, and there were no windows, but they were surrounded by consoles with screens, chairs, and lights that blinked on and off. It was all rather intimidating, and for a moment they just stood there, taking it in.

Chief appeared, standing next to a large console, and Anwyn breathed a small sigh of relief. "This way," he said. "Where do you wish to go?"

"Before we tell you," she responded, "We need to ask some questions."

"Certainly. How may I be of help?"

"How many passengers can the *Dawn Star* hold?"

Chief didn't hesitate. "Three hundred and forty-four manifest life forms. They cannot all be loaded at once, though."

Anwyn looked at her father. "How many need to be evacuated?"

He thought, then said, "Three hundred or so, but we have animals—livestock—too. Can we take them as well?"

"Yes. I will issue an order to our holographic crew to construct suitable pens or holding containers in the cargo bay," Chief said. "What kind of livestock?"

"Fifteen goats, twenty-two chickens, some dogs, I think about seven. Fourteen cats—pets whose owners don't want to leave them—and just in case he would prefer not to fly all the way to Unala—a bat-thing that is larger than the cat-man. His name is the Sentinel," Jarah added, unnecessarily.

Chief only nodded, waited a beat, then said, "All prepared, Commander."

Jarah's expression made Anwyn laugh. He looked so taken aback, she thought. "How long would it take to load them all?" she asked.

Chief consulted a small tablet in his hand. "We can load approximately three humans at one time. The goats, perhaps four at a time, and the others in small groups. It won't take long at all."

Tell him, Irusan said to Anwyn, *that we need to get there in a hurry.*

Chief looked up from his calculations. "I do believe we have an intruder on board," was all he said.

As they leaped into the mouth of the pit, Lhathron kept his grip on Hora, who still screamed deafeningly next to his ear, but soon the whine of the transporter all but drowned the worst of it out. He assisted a whimpering and quaking Hora out of the white light beam, and smiled to himself as Hora stopped dead and stared, his lips quivering in shock.

They were on the observation deck, and the curvature of the earth filled half of the dome, while a black, star-studded backdrop covered the other half. Lhathron understood the man's confusion. The hologram of Alysa Farwenys appeared and she began her spiel, but Lhathron ignored her and walked over to the training console. He pressed the button, and Chief popped up, his face questioning as he observed the trembling Hora.

"I have a prisoner," Lhathron said. "I need to put him somewhere safe until we can drop him off in Abena."

"We'll put him in the cargo hold," Chief responded. "We have a secure area there, and a crew member from the security detail will arrive to assist you."

"Thank you," Lhathron responded.

"We are ready to leave for Mu'A," Chief said.

Lhathron nodded. "We must return here to pick up my father, Grayfell, after we've completed the evacuation."

"Certainly," said Chief, as he vanished.

"I am Kenia Eldor, your security detail." The woman had appeared out of nowhere. She looked like the dark-skinned guide who had introduced himself to them in the room with the tables and chairs. She produced a small, shiny object in her hand and aimed it at Hora's neck. He slumped, but she pressed the object again, and his legs rose as he floated, horizontally, in front of them. Using the object, she steered Hora toward the iris door. Just before she got there, a curious Lhathron had to ask, "What is that object?" He wished he'd had one back in the hall.

"It works using inaudible sound," Kenia said. "At some frequencies, it can put anyone to sleep. He'll have good dreams, though." She grinned. "I'll take him down to the loading bay. We have high frequency pens we've prepared for the livestock. We'll place him in one."

"He won't be able to get out?" Lhathron asked.

"Not at all," she said. She and Hora disappeared into the beam, and once they'd left, Lhathron walked over to the door, wrinkling his forehead.

He wasn't too sure yet about Elluin technology. It all seemed rather strange and magical to him, much like Grayfell's cloak once had. His own abilities, he concluded, were more natural because he had been born with them.

"Bridge," he said, and stepped out onto the bridge where Anwyn, Jarah, and Irusan waited. He told them everything that had occurred. "So we will need to return here," he said, "and pick up Yorli, Grayfell, and Peatatoo."

Chief appeared again. "We're now over Mu'A," he said. "We can begin the evacuation."

52.

Mu'A

It was morning, and Jarah still had not returned from Unala. Tegan had not slept all night, and now she sat in the Council Chamber twisting her damp handkerchief into knots. She had no idea how she would make it through the day. Djana, Tristan, Adain, and Kex looked at her in concern.

"We haven't heard from him since he left last night," Tegan said. "Jarah always checks in. First, Anwyn disappears, then Irusan, and now . . ."

"I'm sure he's fine," Djana said, but her stiff posture told Tegan she was just as concerned.

Even the other healers seemed distracted, thought Tegan, not as focused as they usually were, their mouths twitching and their eyes darting around the Council Chamber. The air of apprehensiveness increased in the chamber as sleepy people drifted in to the emergency meeting the Council leaders had called for in the early morning hours. A white-faced chairman rapped his gavel a few times on the table and called the gathering to order.

"Our ships are gone," he said without preamble.

A clamor arose, and he pounded his gavel again. "Every one of them. The dock we built has vanished, and part of the beach on that side of the island. Sea water has reached the cave entrance, and even that exit will be blocked for those who can't swim."

"What are we going to do?" a woman cried out. "I can't go with the island, and my children—" She broke down, sobbing.

"We have to begin the evacuation, however we can," said the chairman. "We have the submarine, and we'll begin loading it with children first, women second.

"I will stay," said Blaidd. "I can't go with the island, but my last request will be that our child is evacuated." His partner, Isa, shook his head, his grief palpable to all.

"We can evacuate some with our merkabas, if they aren't too heavy," said Tristan, swallowing hard, his voice breaking. "I can probably carry a lightweight woman, or two children. Not all at once, of course."

"And I can take some children, although mine will go first," Djana said.

"Mine, too," said Kex. "We can evacuate many this way, but we certainly won't be able to evacuate over three hundred people."

"The Sentinel can comfortably carry three adults," said Blaidd, "but it will be a long trip that could take several days." All knew he spoke of the bat-like creature who had saved the island five years ago from the deadly weapon of mass destruction created eons ago by Glahivar.

"If he can just get some off the island," said Tristan, "we can pick them up later and transport them to Unala."

"We're assuming that Unala is still our destination," said Kex. "We don't know if the Eldred want us there. According to Irusan, they weren't too welcoming."

"We have no choice," said the chairman. "It was our original destination with the ships. There's a bay at the mouth of the Zeru River that would have been ideal for us to anchor. We must continue with the plan, and hope the Eldred will not regard us as a hostile invasion."

A cry went up as Jarah appeared in the Council Chamber, and Tegan leaped up and ran toward him. "Jarah! Why did you not—?"

"Contact you?" he interrupted her. "I couldn't. The *Dawn Star* has shielding." Everyone gaped at him.

"Listen to me," he said. "We don't have time. Half the island has gone, and the rest will be going any moment now. Get the people who are evacuating up to the crater of this mountain. Have them stand exactly in the center, and bring their possessions—whatever they can carry—and their livestock. Only what is important to them, mind. No unnecessary items. We will begin loading as soon as the first evacuees are in the crater."

He turned to Tegan. "Anwyn is safe," he said, and Tegan slumped against him, flinging her arms around his neck as tears of relief flowed down her cheeks. "I'm sorry I couldn't let you know sooner. I'll explain it all later."

The Council Chamber emptied much faster than it had filled, and the six used their merkabas to bring children to the top of the crater. Tegan was among the first. She stood with her young son, El-Azar, and the other the children, as close to the center of the crater as they could get. The sun had just appeared over the horizon.

Why here, in the crater? It didn't make sense to her. If the island was going, this might be the last part of it to go, but they'd still disappear with the island. She knew she'd make it intact to the other reality, but many—too many—could not. And their animals . . . she couldn't think about it. She only hoped Jarah had pulled a rabbit out of the hat. No one had yet disappeared with the island, though. Even those who could go with it had chosen to retreat until they could retreat no longer—to comfort and be with those who were unable to evacuate in time.

She looked up. The first rays of the sun glinted off something above them. A bird? As she focused on the rapidly approaching silver dot, it grew larger. Was it a merkaba? She didn't think so. It was too big, too visible, and it was shield shaped. What creation of Iochodran was this? She shook her head in disbelief as she was suddenly enveloped in a brilliant light. Her feet left the ground, and she tried to pull up her merkaba, to escape this beam, but it wouldn't work. Something had blocked her. She rose toward the belly of the enormous craft, her son ascending along with her.

53.

Capture

Grayfell could not see Yorli or Peatatoo. The area around the entrance had an abandoned look to it, and although he called and called, they did not appear. He tried to telepath. Perhaps they were not too far away, but still there was no response. How could they have vanished so quickly? Did they go back into the Golden Tip? His logic told him that was impossible. He still had the portal access stone in his pocket.

He mulled over whether he should just sit at the bottom of the stairs and wait, or whether he should begin a search. He thought he'd do both: He'd sit and wait for a while, and then he'd begin a search. He sat on the stone that he and Irusan had sat on only a short while ago and stared at the mountain above. The sun had risen, and its peak glared gold. His thoughts drifted back to what Anwyn had told them in the *Dawn Star*, about her pendant, and how it was connected to the Golden Tip.

"The pendant brought the part of me here that is keyed for the Hall of Records created by the Elluin," she had said as they sat around the table. "I thought I was in the after-life, but in fact I was in another dimension, one that only I or someone with a particular Elluin coding could access. It was only after I'd read the JOURNEY'S END scroll that I sensed a strangely familiar energy moving past the window. It turned out it was Bean, I mean Lhathron," she had corrected herself. "My smaller self is still having trouble remembering his real name."

Grayfell smiled to himself as he recalled her words, since he, too, had had the same problem.

Anwyn had continued. "At that moment, an information exchange occurred between us, and we both grasped exactly where the Hall of Records was located. It, and myself, were inside the Golden Tip. The windows are tiny, impossible to see from the ground. One has to be close to the pyramid, for that is what it is, to see them."

"I remember seeing the window," Lhathron had said, "and then everything went black. I don't remember anything until I woke up outside the entrance."

Anwyn passed along all the information you needed in a neat little package, said Irusan, *to find the dimensional portal in the Golden Tip—*

"Which, in turn, leads to the *Dawn Star*," finished Anwyn. "If I'd been able to access the *Dawn Star* too early, I would not have been able to pass along the knowledge to Lhathron, who just happened to be in the right place at the right time."

There's no such thing as coincidence, said Irusan. *He was exactly where he should have been, and so were you.*

"So your pendant," Jarah said, an understanding dawning in his eyes, "is a portal not only into the Hall of Records in the Golden Tip, but to the *Dawn Star* as well."

"Yes," Anwyn responded, "it is why Lhathron had to remember how to access the *Dawn Star*, and what the purpose of the pit was."

"Why then was Askoroth unable to access the transporter when Glahivar threw him into the pit?" Lhathron had asked, puzzled. "Why would the portal stone in his horn not have gained him access?"

Grayfell's mouth twitched as he had leaned forward. "I think I can answer that one," he had said, but not without some pride in his voice.

"Askoroth has dragon coding. Eons ago, the Elluin were at war with the Dragon Kings who had overrun the planet at that time. With hindsight, I can now see that they would have excluded anyone with that kind of coding from accessing their portals. It was only because of Iochodran's work on cracking the coding for the entrance to the great hall portal that allowed him entry at all."

Irusan had nodded. *So Askoroth's portal crystal would have been useless to him, and since it did not work for him when he was thrown down the pit, he did not realize the pit was the entry portal.* His cat-mouth had stretched into what could have been a smile. *It did help us, though!*

"And the pendant would not have worked for him, either," said Anwyn, "although it might have worked for Hora."

"Well, it didn't stop him from trying," said Lhathron. "I am just lucky Hora thought I was dead."

Dropped you right into our laps, Irusan said and they had all laughed.

Grayfell chuckled silently to himself as he basked in the warmth of the sun's rays outside the mountain entrance. He was cold, hungry, and tired. He couldn't remember the last time he'd slept, or eaten a satisfying meal, but all the discomfort had been worth it, he thought, to have his son back. He blinked back tears as he remembered how angry Lhathron had been with his deception. He reminded himself that even though his motives had been pure, he had a lot of reparation to make in their relationship. Would Lhathron ever fully trust him again?

His eyes began to close and his head sunk onto his chest.

Grayfell!

He jerked awake, and his eyes snapped open. Yorli stood in front of him. *Where are the others?* she asked. *What happened to the bad man? Did he—*

He's in custody, Grayfell responded, and she looked puzzled.

Custody—it means we have him locked up in a safe place. Where have you been?

We looked for food, Yorli said. *There's not much around here, but Jangon showed me where to find some. We had to go farther down into the valley.*

A large shape appeared behind her. Jangon. Peatatoo sunned himself at a safe distance on a nearby rock.

Yorli held out her hands and dropped some berries in his lap. He gratefully began to eat. It was better than nothing. He was thirsty, though, but that would have to wait until he could find a water source close by. He hoped he didn't have too long to wait for the return of the *Dawn Star*.

He finished eating, and he looked up at Yorli and Jangon who patiently waited, seated on the rock next to him.

Yorli, the others will be coming back for me, he said. *You must go with me, and we will take you back to your home in Unala. You and Peatatoo.*

Yorli glanced at Jangon, her expression unreadable, then looked back at Grayfell. *I will go,* she said. *I miss my cave.*

Jangon stood up. He shifted from one large foot to another, scratched his head, and gazed off into the distance. *Yorli,* he finally said, *you may return with Grayfell if it is your wish, but I and my clan would be honored if you and your familiar*—he looked back at Peatatoo—*would be a part of our family.*

Yorli blinked in surprise. *You—you would want me . . . to stay . . . here?*

Jangon moved his massive head slowly up and down. *You are a resourceful Dweller,* he said, *and your familiar is brave. You would both be honored members of our tribe. Also,* he looked away, as if not wishing anyone to see his expression, *I-I think you are beautiful, and I wish you to stay.*

Yorli paused, then out loud, in the tongue of the Dwellers, she said something that only Jangon could understand.

Jangon looked pleased. *We must go, then,* he telepathed for Grayfell's benefit. *Say goodbye to your friend.*

Yorli stood and held out her hands toward Grayfell. He took her hands in his and looked into her pink eyes. *I will miss you,* he said. He was surprised to realize that it was true. *Oh,* he added, almost as an afterthought, *at some point you may want to get rid of that stone.* He pointed to the squirrel's bulging cheek.

Yorli bared her teeth in a smile and nodded. *He will get bored with it, perhaps then I'll bury it somewhere.* Without another word she and Jangon, with Peatatoo following, melted silently into the boulder strewn landscape, and Grayfell was alone.

He yawned. The *Dawn Star* was gone, but should he return to the great hall? He gave an imperceptible shake of his head. The place gave him the creeps. He glanced down, and using his hands, he cleared an area until it was reasonably free of small rocks. He spread his cloak on the ground and stretched himself out on his back, staring up at the sky. They would be able to see him here when they returned, he thought. He'd just have a quick snooze. He closed his eyes, and soon, soft snores escaped his slightly open mouth.

It was only as something poked him hard in his chest that his eyes snapped open. "Wh-what?" he muttered. He rose slightly as if to sit and to focus on the blurry figure that stood above him. The figure, with its foot on his chest, pushed him back down. He rubbed his eyes, and his vision sharpened. His jaw dropped, and his hand flew to the dagger at his waist, but it was no longer there.

"Is this what you seek?" A Shadow Goblin stood over him, brandishing Grayfell's dagger. Behind him, stood more Shadow Goblins, and behind those . . . It seemed as if every goblin in the kingdom was here. The one that stood over him, with his large foot on his chest, grinned. "Eng at your service, and this is my brother, Ekor." Another goblin stepped forward, a wicked looking scythe in his begrimed hands.

He placed the business end of the scythe much too close to Grayfell's throat. "We tracked you and that shape-shifter here. We lost your trail at one point, but the king's advisor seemed to know what your destination would be, and he was right. We'll get a good bounty for you," he snarled. "King Sinhail wants you, badly." He glanced back to where the putrid remains of Askoroth lay. "Who did that?"

"Oh, just some friends of mine," Grayfell said. "They're not far away. I think you should go now while you still can."

The goblin's mouths opened as mirthless laughter, chuckles, and snorts emerged. They shook their heads, pounding their weapons on the ground.

"He's funny," said one.

"He thought we'd fall for that old trick," said Eng. "Its beard is longer than yours, Urag." He held his potbelly as he chortled. "We do have to leave, though." He turned to Ekor. "Bind him."

They bound Grayfell's hands tightly in front of him, and with the same length of rope shackled his feet so that he could only take small steps. One poked him in the ribs with the end of a sharp stave, and he stumbled to his feet. No one offered any help. They began to move back down the hill, and Grayfell wondered how long he'd slept. He looked up. The sun was at its zenith, so it must be noon, he thought. His head jolted as a goblin slapped his face.

"Pay attention to where you're walking, wizard," it yelled at him. "I don't want to have to pick you up."

He now wished he had decided to sleep inside the mountain, but it was too late for regrets. He looked back at his cloak, still on the ground. Had they been warned about his cloak? "Could I have my cloak," he croaked. "I'm cold." It was worth a try.

Eng growled at a foot soldier, who scurried back and picked up the cloak. He fingered its soft silk lining, his eyes lighting up with admiration. "Nice cloak." He looked at Eng. "Can I keep it?"

A chill went up Grayfell's spine. If Shadow Goblins discovered the secret of his cloak, who knew what terrible deeds they could accomplish with its magic. But Eng wasn't having any of it. He gave another snarl, and the soldier hastily threw the cloak over Grayfell, who, raising his bound hands and pulling the cloak over his head, promptly disappeared.

Gasps and growls of astonishment rippled through the throng of goblins. They swung their scythes, axes, staves, swords, and knives frantically through the empty space where Grayfell had just stood. "He can't be far!" Eng shouted. "He's shackled. Find him!"

Grayfell pulled his cloak tighter with his bound hands around him. It wasn't perfect, but it was enough to keep him cloaked. As soon as he'd disappeared, he'd quickly stepped behind Eng, and as Eng turned, he shuffled around with him. If he was correct about their hierarchical system, no other goblin would dare get too close to their leader. He must be careful though not to alert Eng to his proximity. He watched as the goblins scoured the hillside, beating their weapons around and on top of boulders, or slashing them viciously through the air. As he'd hoped, they'd begun their search in a tight cluster, moving outward in an ever-widening circle. Not even a mouse could escape this search, he thought, but for now, he felt safe. Eng remained in the center of the search, barking commands and growling threats as Grayfell spun with him, always remaining well to the goblin's rear.

I am not going to be able to keep it up forever, he thought. *Sooner or later I'm going to have to slip away.* That moment arrived. Eng command-ed his troops to return, still holding their circle and swinging their weap-ons wildly. Although he knew they would not flourish their weapons too close to Eng, sooner or later, he'd be discovered. The goblins drew closer and closer, narrowing the gap between him and Eng with every step. Eng kept turning. He grasped Grayfell's dagger in his hand and viciously stabbed the air around him. It was getting increasingly more difficult for Grayfell to remain behind Eng, out of reach of the dagger's slash. His shackled legs were like heavy weights, and soon enough, a slash from Eng nicked and lifted one corner of his cloak. A glimmer of his legs, and the horde rushed forward with triumphant yells.

Grayfell closed his eyes and bowed his head. "Goodbye, Lhathron," he muttered. "I am so sorry. Please forgive me."

A bright light assaulted his eyelids, and his feet left the ground. Had one of them already killed him? He opened his eyes. He was in the trans-porter beam! His cloak slid off his shoulders, but he clutched it tightly before it could drop to the horde below. He could still faintly hear the cries of the goblins, and then he popped through the portal door, onto the bridge of the. *Dawn Star*

"Well that was a close one," Grayfell said. Anwyn, Lhathron, Irusan, and Chief stood on the bridge. Lhathron moved quickly toward him, and gave him a hug. No one missed the brief smile that flashed across Grayfell's face as he hugged his son back. "How did you see me? I was cloaked."

"Your cloaking only works for eyes," Chief said. "Our sensors picked you up quite easily. I'm glad we were in time."

Only just, said Irusan. *We saw how the Shadow Goblins had you sur-rounded on the monitor.*

He pointed to a screen behind them, and Grayfell nodded and laughed as he caught sight of the goblins still milling around in confusion on the ground. "I wonder how long it will take for them to realize I am no longer there," he said.

"We've picked up the Mu'Ans," said Anwyn. "We have all the evacuees safely on board, even the animals and livestock."

They had enough time to bring their possessions, what little they had, with them. Irusan looked pleased. *And that is not all. Chief has informed me that they are able to contact the Elluin, and that the Elluin are able to contact my people in Agra Tan. I will soon be restored to my former self!*

A woman along with a child, El-Azar—Anwyn's brother—and Jarah, had arrived on the bridge. She introduced herself to Grayfell and Lhathron as Tegan, Anwyn's mother. Grayfell's eyebrows rose as more people crowded in to meet him: Djana and Tristan, and Kex and Adain.

It was while they talked, catching up with what had occurred on the ground and in Mu'A, that Lhathron gave a shout, and pointed to the screen. They'd become bored with watching the Shadow Goblins running around, their mouths working, as kicks flew from Eng and Ekor onto those unfortunate enough to get too close to them. Chief adjusted something on the console, and the scene came into sharper focus.

The goblins were no longer the only ones on the screen. They had been joined by White Dwellers, who, in a sudden onrush, sent the goblins into a panic. They scattered, but the Dwellers had them surrounded. The watchers in the *Dawn Star* could imagine the screams and roars as the silent melèe ensued below. Lhathron pointed out Jangon's imposing form. He swung his broad knife, beheading a goblin in one stroke, while his clan ran roughshod over the screaming horde. There was no escape. Soon the ground was littered with bodies, and not one of them was a Dweller.

"I don't see Yorli," said Grayfell.

"Yorli would not be among these Dwellers," said Lhathron. "She's much too gentle. She'd probably slap them around a little, though."

"But only if they threatened Peatatoo," Anwyn smiled. She had to explain to her mother who Peatatoo was, though, and her young brother's face lit up.

"Can I have him?" El-Azar asked.

"No, he's Yorli's companion," Anwyn explained. "Squirrels don't make good pets, and he certainly has a mind of his own!"

Well, the guardians of the Golden Tip have certainly kept their promise to keep intruders out, said Irusan. He turned to Chief. *I hate to interrupt all of this, but we must proceed to the Bay of Morodon at the mouth of the Zeru River. That is our first planned settlement, and we have much to do.*

"Yes, we do," Jarah agreed, and Chief set a course for the bay. They watched on the monitor as the shift occurred: an imperceptible flash, and then they were there, a large, V-shaped bay below.

Irusan placed a finger on a spot to the northern end of the bay. *That is the place I had in mind,* he said. *It has good shelter, plenty of land, and good soil to grow crops and tend livestock, and it's far enough from Unala that we won't be rubbing shoulders with the Eldred.*

Grayfell stroked his chin, his expression thoughtful, and, thought Anwyn, slightly worried. "I can't return to Ulovia," he said. "There's a bounty on my head, according to the Shadow Goblins. They won't give up looking for me, and now you, too, Lhathron." His eyes narrowed. "I'm sorry for all this. I've not helped you at all."

"Father, I've already told you. You no longer need to protect me. You never did, but you followed your guidance, as wrong as it was. I am a grown man, and I have skills that eclipse all your potions, and lies about me. Let me be now who I was meant to be. I will return to my tree home in the forest. I will be safe there. Where you go, well, that's up to you."

Grayfell hung his head. "I can't leave you, son. I'll join you in your tree home."

Lhathron tossed his head, shuffled his feet, and squinted at Grayfell. "No, you won't," he said, and Grayfell's eyebrows rose. "You must stay with these people." He pointed to the Mu'Ans on the bridge. "Anwyn will ensure you are safe."

Anwyn nodded. "I will, Lhathron, but it's Grayfell's choice if he wants to come with us."

Irusan stepped forward. *Lhathron, I think you and Anwyn need to discuss this matter.* His gaze was intense. *You know what I'm talking about.* He shielded this last thought from everyone else, directing it only toward the young Eldred.

Lhathron's mouth twitched. "You're right, Irusan." He turned to Anwyn, motioning to the portal door. "We need to talk in private." Jarah and Tegan stared at each other, confused, and then at Irusan, who remained cryptically silent.

"So what is it that's so important you can't say it in front of my parents?" Anwyn asked as they stepped out of the beam and onto the observation deck.

54.

Lhathron and Anwyn

His fingers brushed lightly over hers as he motioned toward the glass dome at the end of the deck, but he hastily pulled them back, as if her hand had been a snake. He stopped at the edge of the glass expanse and gestured down at the bay. "It looks like a pleasant place," was all he said.

"You're stalling. That's not what you really wanted to say, was it?" She fiddled with her hair as she gazed at the scene below them.

Lhathron shook his head. "I'm just having difficulty saying it." His ears were bright red. He could feel them burning, along with his face. Anwyn was no help. *Didn't she already know?*

Her eyes narrowed. *Know what?*

He stood straighter, turning away from the dome, and taking a deep breath, he faced her. "That stone," he said, "the one Peatatoo first had. It glowed near me, didn't it?"

"How did you—"

"Know about it?"

Anwyn nodded. "I never told anyone about that."

"Irusan told me," he said.

Anwyn blew her cheeks out. "Of course. He would."

"I know you're in love with that farmer." The words tumbled out, quickly, before he could stop himself. "You told us that yourself. But the stone didn't glow around him, did it?"

Anwyn looked down. Her shoulders quivered, and Lhathron reached out to touch her shoulder. "I'm sorry. I didn't want to make you cry."

She looked up, dry-eyed but smiling, as she met his gaze. "I should be the one who is sorry," she said. "I should have told you—everyone." She turned to gaze again at the vista on the other side of the dome, shaking her head. "I don't know if *that* is meant to be my home." She inclined her head down toward the bay. "Now that I've found out more about myself, I think my future is not in Morodon."

Lhathron felt his heart sinking back down to his boots. His head dropped. "I was wrong to expect you to fall in love with me. We've known each other such a short time. You should return to Aelfar and fight for the man you love."

Anwyn shook her head. "I wasn't finished speaking yet," she said. "You do jump to conclusions a lot, don't you?"

Lhathron's head rose. "What do you mean?"

"I've examined my infatuation with Alroy from every angle. I came to the conclusion our relationship was doomed from the start," Anwyn continued. "I've hardly even thought about him for . . . I don't know how long now. I was in the Hall of Records for several months."

Lhathron frowned. "It's only been—"

"I know. Time is different there, but it was long enough to use my head instead of my heart." She placed her hand on his arm, and he felt a shock ripple through him. "Lhathron, I do know. I've known it ever since I felt you go by the window. You *are* my twin soul. You are a part of me, and I of you. I ask your forgiveness for my past behavior, for my pig-headedness, and my obstinacy in the face of truth. I didn't want to believe it. I so badly wanted it to be Alroy, and even the part of myself

I left down with you . . ." She gripped his arm more tightly. "Even that part, knew on some level, and she resisted it. She was rude and angry toward you."

Lhathron smiled. "I didn't notice."

"Oh yes, you did. But I'm going to make up for that now. I want you to know that you mean more to me than anything in this world. I love you, and I hope we'll always be together."

Lhathron's mouth opened, but he didn't know what to say. His eyes stung so badly that he had to turn his head from her as he brushed the threatening tears away. Her hand lightly touched his back, and he turned to face her, to gaze at her in wonder and joy. He grasped her shoulders with both his hands, pulling her closer. She melted into his embrace, her own arms encircling his neck as they kissed, hungrily and eagerly.

He pulled away suddenly. "What did you mean—Morodon is not your future?" he asked. "What is?"

She laughed. "I was hoping you'd ask me to stay with you in your tree home, instead of Grayfell," she said.

"No problem about that," he said as he pulled her back.

The sun moved over the landscape below, casting late afternoon cloud shadows as they stood on the observation deck, talking, kissing, and laughing. "We should be helping out with the evacuees," Lhathron noted at one point.

"My parents are quite capable of that," Anwyn said. "I think I'll just stay right here, with you. Forever."

THE END

Acknowledgements

My mom, who encouraged me to write, and to always be a truth seeker. My husband, Charles, without whom none of this series would be possible. He has supported me through all the ups and downs and never once complained.

My editors, Lisa R. of Editorial Services of Los Angeles, and Mercy P. of Author Options. They have both provided insightful and valuable feedback that has polished my manuscript into something I can truly be proud of.

My cover artist, Sara Helwe.

My friends Dana B, Pam P. and my sister, Kathy, who are my greatest supporters, along with Brooksie and Stephanie who both have given much of their time and helped steer my books into exciting possibilities.

I appreciate you all.

About The Ialana Series

There are four books in the Ialana Series: *The Six and the Crystals of Ialana*; *The Six and the Gardeners of Ialana*; *The Six and Anwyn of Ialana*; and now, *The Tree Wizard of Ialana*.

As an author, I rely on my readers to help me get the word out about the Ialana Series, and you'll be helping me out in a big way if you take a few minutes to write a review.

Every review helps me understand what's important to my readers, which in turn helps me.

By telling others how you enjoyed the Ialana Series, you'll be helping them make a decision about reading the book.

Just go to the Amazon page where you purchased the book and click on "Review this Book". If you are a member of Goodreads, a review here is also appreciated.

www.katlynnbrooke@yahoo.com

https://www.facebook.com/katlynnbrookeauthor/

About the Author

Growing up in Africa during the '50's and '60's, Katlynn Brooke's childhood was an unusual one, even by African standards. While her city peers were learning how to dance to Chubby Checker's The Twist or preparing for final exams, she was in a camper travelling through the bushveld penning plays and short stories for her family's entertainment.

As an adult her many travels took her to India and Indonesia, where she lived in both countries for several years before settling permanently in the United States. She now resides in Virginia with her husband, and a cat.

Katlynn, always an avid and eclectic reader, is still inspired by authors such as Tolkien, Arthur C. Clarke, and Terry Brooks. Influenced heavily by her past travels, and her quest for spiritual enlightenment, she draws on her sojourns and her intensive study of the metaphysical and spiritual for her plots, intrepid heroes, and the assertive heroines of her epic fantasy adventures.